A Profitable Wife

A Novel
by
KAT CHRISTENSEN

A GRITTY PIONEER TALE OF
ROMANCE, MURDER, AND MANIFEST DESTINY

PAPERBACK ISBN: 978-1-962465-69-4

EBOOK ISBN: 978-1-962465-19-9

HISTORUM PRESS

NEW YORK, NY / MACON, GA

2024

Contents

Foreword

The first time I heard this infamous family lore I was about nine years old, perched on a footstool next to my grandmother's rocking chair. Her coy smile and hushed tone conveyed the secrecy of the tale. It was not shared until you were trusted not to broadcast it—a promise requested and given. My grandmother recited the brutal account, which had been passed down by her own grandmother, who was the ancestor's daughter. As she finished the story, this fair-skinned, red-headed elderly woman of Irish descent tantalized me with the revelation that this ancestor was of mixed Native American heritage.

Although many ancestors are mere placeholders in our family tree, Easter Malinda Hackley has notoriously been remembered by many of her descendants, including my grandmother, leaving us all to wonder about the circumstances. Not only do countless descendants share this story, but James Whitcomb Ellis also immortalized this and other nefarious events in his 1910 Iowan History of Jackson County, thus confirming the family tale.

Regardless of family lore, historical facts show us that Easter Malinda Hackley was a scrappy pioneer, a survivor, and a successful human being. Amidst wild adventures in the Midwest she gave birth to fourteen children and raised thirteen to adulthood. Her offspring went on to produce their own countless progeny, some of which led both adventurous (nefarious) lives of their own. As they say, the branch does not fall far from the tree.

Easter was born in 1812 during the early years of American History. Our country was only thirty-six years old. Her grandparents participated in the Revolutionary War. The nation was new. To say the least, politics was pivotal in shaping our nation. Each president was a greenhorn attempting to lead a form of government that had never before existed. These presidents and congressional actors played significant roles in determining where Easter's family would settle, whether they would prosper, and what they thought of the world. Their actions forged proclamations, presidential vetoes, war declarations, and treaties with indigenous

1

tribes—all of which fed the collective American hunger for Manifest Destiny.

Easter's generation was poised to embark on a grand journey of exploration and expansion. President Thomas Jefferson and his like-minded peers had envisioned a future where this cohort would be self-sufficient agrarian farmers, with the potential for commodity farming. To achieve this, they would populate new lands across the continent, and the gateway to opportunity was the Erie Canal, the most modern mode of transportation ever imagined at that time. This innovative creation allowed travelers to journey west through locks and over hills and valleys at an unprecedented, constant pace.

As New York expanded and developed successful canal routes to link with the massive rivers in this young country, it allowed early pioneers easier access to settle the Northwest Territory (now comprising Ohio, Illinois, Indiana, Wisconsin, and Michigan), as well as to participate in the reverse flow of goods back to the Atlantic economy. This low-cost, low-risk way of transporting goods was unprecedented. Travelers and freight no longer had to brave the Atlantic Ocean or the rugged Appalachian mountain roads. Instead, safe, calm, interior waterways now provided a direct passage from the east to the west and the south, and small, individual farm families could build wealth.

But let us first set the stage leading up to Easter and her generation's dreams of western riches.

Just prior to Easter's birth the nation was led by its third president, Thomas Jefferson (1801–1809), a Democratic-Republican. Facing heavy Federalist opposition, he completed the Louisiana Purchase with the French Emperor, Napoleon Bonaparte, which doubled the size of the country and included much of the central United States. In 1804, President Jefferson sent Lewis and Clark to explore and map this new territory. In 1808, Easter's future husband was born.

Easter herself was born in 1812 under the fourth president, James Madison (1809–1817), a Democratic-Republican and former Secretary of State to Jefferson. Madison continued many of Jefferson's policies, including expansion. He presided over an attack on Canada, which started the War of 1812 with the British and their Native American allies. After witnessing the British retaliation upon Fort McHenry, Francis Scott Key penned the Star-Spangled Banner. General Andrew Jackson was depicted as a key hero in this war for defeating the British at New Orleans, earning him fame that would one day win him the presidency. Despite the British burning down the US Capitol and the White House, the war resulted in a draw, but it sparked a new sense of patriotism on both sides of the border. Easter's mother is rumored to be of Native American descent, most likely Algonquin, a tribe that partially allied with the British during this war.

By the time Easter was five years old, James Monroe (1817–1825), Madison's Secretary of State and War, had been elected as the fifth president as a Democratic-Republican. Despite presiding over the depression known as the Panic of 1819, Monroe acquired Florida from Spain, which included parts of what is now Alabama, as well as British corridors through the Rocky Mountains, west to the Pacific Ocean. His Monroe Doctrine opposed any more land claims and interference by European countries in the Americas. During this time five states were admitted to the union: Mississippi, Illinois, Alabama, Maine, and Missouri.

When Easter was thirteen years old, John Quincy Adams (1825–1829), a Federalist, the former secretary of state for Monroe, and the son of the second president, was elected as the sixth president. This was under a veil of a conspiracy called the "Corrupt Bargain" purportedly in cahoots with Henry Clay, a prominent Democratic-Republican from Kentucky and the House Speaker. Adams's opponent, Andrew Jackson, accused the two men of stealing the election. Jackson won the popular vote count. But no one won a majority in the Electoral College, so the decision was sent to the House of Representatives, where each state got one vote. Jackson believed Adams offered Henry Clay a position in his cabinet to use his influence to sway the votes.

Adams and his new Secretary of State, Henry Clay, were all about infrastructure development, including road and canal expansions. With regard to Native Americans, their unpopular policy was that of assimilation. If Easter's mother was indeed an Algonquin, she was likely assimilated into a colonial family. All alone and still in his teens, one of Easter's future sons-in-law fled Ireland and arrived in Canada.

When Easter was sixteen and during the first year of her

3

marriage, Andrew Jackson (1829–1837), a Democratic-Republican, took office as the seventh president. Amidst the political turmoil, Henry Clay forged the anti-Jackson Democratic-Whig Party, causing a split in the Democratic-Republican Party. As a general in the Army, Jackson won many battles against indigenous tribes and the British. Despite being a self-made man and a popular figure, Jackson was shadowed with scandal, the sordid details of which Americans eagerly consumed via newsprint. During Jackson's presidency, he signed no less than seventy Native American treaties, but his nefarious policy was one of "Indian removal," which ignited a surge of settlers to the western frontier.

The year following Jackson's election, Easter and her new husband embarked on a journey from the Mohawk valley in New York to Monroe County, Ohio, as part of the westward migration to the "First Northwest," aka the Northwest Territory.

Note: This novel is a work of fiction inspired by the historical figure Easter Hackley with pivotal moments in history woven into the timeline. Any resemblance to actual persons, living or dead, businesses, organizations, events, or locales is purely coincidental or used fictitiously. However, readers are encouraged to envision their own ancestors as part of this tale. The imagined Easter and her offspring are based upon family lore, although the Native American aspect of Easter's ancestry has been called into question by other interested parties. Despite this, many of my grandmother's siblings and cousins handed down the same story to their offspring, having learned it from their grandparents, who were Easter's children. Therefore, my fictional tale honors their belief in this heritage.

The author has taken considerable efforts to ensure the accuracy of historical context and background, but reserve all rights to creative license in the service of the narrative. Consequently, certain liberties may have been taken with regard to historical figures, dates, events, and circumstances for the purpose of storytelling.

The views, opinions, and assertions expressed in this book are those of the characters and do not necessarily represent or reflect those of the author or any other person associated with the creation or distribution of this work.

By purchasing or otherwise acquiring this book, the reader acknowledges and accepts that the contents within are purely fictional and created for the purpose of entertainment. Neither the author, publisher, nor anyone else associated with the creation or distribution of this book shall be held liable for any interpretation, inference, or consequential actions taken by the reader based on the material in this book.

The aim of this work is not to present a factual account of the historical events or figures depicted, but rather to entertain and possibly provoke thought and discussion. Any interpretation or understanding drawn from the material is at the sole discretion and responsibility of the reader.

In summary, this is a work of historical fiction, not a historical record, and should be approached and understood as such.

This book is dedicated to the storytellers,
Easter and all her progeny,
One of whom was my grandmother,
Loretta Margaret Wallace

1812 – Of War

Let War's black pinions soar away,
And dove-like Peace resume her sway,
Our King, our country, be Thy care,
Nor ever fail of childhood's prayer.
Calmly, securely, may we rest
As on a tender father's breast.

THE YEAR OF EASTER'S BIRTH…

obert Hackley was fading fast. As he collapsed to the ground, his labored breath puffed miniature clouds into the damp midnight air. Despite trying to stay quiet, he couldn't help but grunt as he felt his innards failing. Sooleawa's skilled hands moved gently over his wounds. Her silky black hair sparkled in the moonlight. The chiseled outline of her perfect features made him recall the day he'd first laid eyes on her. Neither white nor Native, she was an exotic woman of unusual stature. She had been practicing with her brothers at throwing a tomahawk and was much better at it than they. Robert had come to trade furs and had left with a partner for life. To have had this mixed-blood Algonquin as his wife was beyond any dream he'd ever imagined. Now perhaps it was all coming to an abrupt end.

Sooleawa crushed jimsonweed and moss to pad Robert's wound. There was no mistaking the rapid pallor creeping into his face from the musket shot to his gut. She grabbed his hands and examined the nails, the colorlessness foretelling he would soon bleed out. Her heart was breaking but she remained outwardly stoic. Robert gently squeezed her hand and for a moment, she held his gaze. Then he slowly closed his eyes and continued his labored breaths.

Their babe, less-than-a-month-old, was strapped to her back in traditional Native style. Recently fed and snugly wrapped, she would not likely wake any time soon. Sooleawa glanced at Robert's kin, Philo Hackley. He crouched nearby, intently watching the tree line. Their purpose had been to pause here to shore up Robert's wound as they made their way through the timber, attempting to reunite with the scattered troops.

The full moon enabled their travel but also and more deadly, could reveal their position. The northern colonists and their British allies vowed to take no prisoners in this battle. They were well beyond provoked. This whole mess had not gone as anyone had planned or foreseen. True to her Native heritage, Sooleawa had followed her husband's white war-band from skirmish to skirmish and, being well skilled at war-making, had even participated in a few. Robert's fellow soldiers got used to it. Sooleawa's mixed Algonquin and white blood made her beautiful in the eyes of white men, and she had to keep more than a few of them at bay. It was no issue. She could easily rouse a beast within herself when needed. Her own grandmother, Esther Montour, was renowned among whites and Natives for slaughtering those of any race that wronged her or her family. Sooleawa was proud of her ancestors and honored their traditions. But what the white people found beautiful, her Native brethren found odd. They thought her eyes were too big, her forehead too round, her waist too long, the occasional red glint in her hair a defect. Her Grandmother Esther taught her that true beauty and bravery lies within one's spirit. Sooleawa had named her own babe Esther to honor her Grandmother.

Sooleawa caught Philo's gaze, held it intently, and silently shook her head.

Robert grunted again. His eerie breath clouds were coming farther and farther apart. Sooleawa bit her lip, refusing to let her grief surface. A nearby stream sounded gentle notes of a winter run-off while distant coyotes harmonized mournful howls. The hair on the back of Sooleawa's neck stood up. In the stillness of night Robert's breath swirled into mystic, white, moon-lit shadows, as if calling to Gitche Manitou, the Great Spirit. It wouldn't be long now…

Philo watched helplessly as Sooleawa tended his cousin. Robert was not only his blood kin but also the best friend he had ever had. He hoped against hope he was wrong, but the shot Robert had suffered looked to take his life. Robert had always been a dreamer and a wanderer. He was a successful trapper and trader, having crossed up into the Canadian wilderness and back down into New York settlements, showing up at their home or mercantile when least expected. Robert always brought home the most unusual items for trade. More recently, he had shown up with his new Algonquin wife who actually behaved quite civilized and was a beauty to boot. On this campaign her savagery was a sight to behold. She had fought alongside Robert as his equal in more than a few battles. The remote northern lands required savageness from their inhabitants in order to survive, and in this way, Sooleawa was certainly a perfect specimen. She had given birth to her babe along the trail and caught up with the troops the next day with nary a missed step.

It had been Philo's idea to join the Herkimer Militia, although Almira, his wife, had been somewhat less than enthusiastic. When the campaign began, everyone was certain that the colonies in Canada would welcome them with open arms, chase out the British, and happily join the new United States. President Madison and former President Jefferson, as well as their local representatives, had editorials in all the Gazettes and said it was so. Philo had felt it was his duty to join up, as did most of the able-bodied men in the New York townships.

Instead, the Canadian colonists had become completely outraged by the assaults, and the British had thrown several warships into the battle. The last Philo's company had heard, the British were attacking ports not only along the east coast but also from the new southern territories Jefferson had purchased from the French. A new general, Andrew Jackson, had been recruited, promoted, and sent in a desperate attempt to protect and recover lands that had been overrun. It was as if their new country was fighting the Revolutionary War all over again.

Philo's Herkimer Militia had barely won the skirmish at Sackets Harbor, but in chasing down some of the survivors, Robert, Sooleawa, and Philo were now on the run, being chased by the very British and Native troops they had been pursuing. For now, it appeared they had given the Brits the slip. Either that or the Brits had given up and were retreating themselves. Everything was such a mess, and Philo's cousin and best friend was about to die.

The cold night air smelled of wet pine. Philo rubbed moisture from his nose. Moonlight flooded the scene of Robert and Sooleawa, her little sleeping babe attached to her back. Distant coyotes continued their mournful night song. The man he loved as a brother now lay eerily still. Sooleawa knelt before Robert with her arms raised to the moon, rocking back and forth, mouthing her lament in silence, lest her mourning the loss of her mate attract their enemies.

******

Almira kept her thoughts from wandering to where Philo's troop might be as she secured her two-year-old daughter, Harriet, in a sling on her hip. She watched her nine-year-old, Frances, stir the clothes in the large boiling pot. It was laundry day. Frances was quite good at this task, which allowed Almira to tend the family garden. Certainly, the wash was a less dreary task than pulling weeds, which would normally be delegated to children, but with all the menfolk away in the militia a productive crop was critical. Almira did not want to lose a single potato plant, carrot, or cornstalk due to a child's mishap. Varmint barriers must be secured, and pests painstakingly kept at bay. Every potential edible needed to be nurtured. Despite her best efforts, wolves had already robbed them of their breeding sows, leaving only the boar. Almira wiped a tear as she contemplated butchering their plow horse or her prized boar to get them through the winter. She was no good at hunting, and the responsibility of feeding the family rested solely on her shoulders.

Almira shook off her fears and took a deep breath, focusing on what the preacher had told his congregation of women and old men at the monthly service in town: "One task at a time. One problem at a time; God walks beside you during these times of trials." As she knelt down to pull a particularly stubborn weed, for a moment she snorted at the thought that perhaps God could provide a pair of hands and a strong back, rather than a merry walk in her garden.

"Ma, Ma!" She heard Frances suddenly sound an alarm. Almira stood up swiftly to see a very disheveled man emerging from the forest edge with a gun over his shoulder. For a moment, fear bubbled up in her gut. Her musket was not only over forty yards away but also unloaded. There were rumors of hungry British and Canadian soldiers pilfering outlying farms for food. Having fought alongside the local Natives, it was said a number of them had adopted savage ways, taking their ire out on women and children left defenseless by the conflict. A wave of terror spread over Almira as the shaking underbrush behind the man announced he was not alone. Abruptly a very tall Native woman emerged from the forest carrying a baby. Almira froze, unsure of what to do. When the man halted and started enthusiastically waving, she suddenly realized it was Philo.

"Philo!" she shrieked. Almira dropped her hoe and ran past an astonished Frances as fast as her legs could carry her.

Although outwardly stoic, Sooleawa felt a tug in her heart as Philo and Almira melted into each other's arms. Robert's death had left a wretched hole in her spirit. Sooleawa did not begrudge their happiness, but it starkly reminded her of her own loss, never again able to clasp her beloved.

Philo lifted his wife with the babe on her hip off her feet, sweeping her into a circle of love. The older daughter melted into their arms, and the small family laughed and cried as Philo related to them all that they had been through. Sooleawa wondered how quickly the happy reunion would turn sour when Philo announced he only would be there for a few short days. Philo had committed to joining the main battle in the south with General Jackson's Army. This war was not over by a long shot.

******

The Secretary of State and War, James Monroe, stood silently in the Octagon Room, the residence and cabinet of James Madison, the fourth president of the United States. It was a place they had used to run the country since the British had burned the capital. The memory of that horrid day was still fresh in their minds. President Madison was reviewing correspondence summaries from John Quincy Adams, one of his chief peace negotiators. Thomas Jefferson, a dear friend and confidant of the presidential couple, had arrived the previous week and resided there as a guest. His tall form languished comfortably in a chair by the window, with legs crossed and one shoe dangling loosely from his toe. He sat silent and thoughtful as ever.

The three men were gathered in President Madison's drawing room, infamous for the political soirees hosted by Madison's wife, Dolley. She called it the Octagon Room, which was decorated with an odd combination of elegant French and comfortable Colonial décor. Madison sat in an unusual rolling chair that Jefferson had designed and gifted him. He was dressed in his typical attire, a white powdered wig, a white shirt with a lace cravat, a black jacket and trousers buckled at the knee, black silk stockings, and laced shoes. An empty card table sat in one corner, inviting visitors to play. The room was attractive yet comfortable and seemed to foster the creative collective needed for this grim consultation.

A normal meeting would have witnessed Dolley flirting and lording over the group while serving tea and bantering about. This time, however, she had served tea with little conversation and closed the doors behind her to give them complete privacy. Times were grim indeed.

When Jefferson was president, Madison had served in his cabinet. Now Madison held the office of the presidency with Monroe serving in his cabinet. For much of their young lives

Madison and Monroe had been protégé's of Jefferson. During their early years in Congress, they had all stayed at the same boarding house in Washington City and had stayed many a time at each other's farms in Virginia. Trust and loyalty, built over years of friendship, had brought these men together. With such a new country to preserve and hold, it took the greatest minds available to keep it intact before it even had a chance to walk, let alone run. In this war, their country had indeed stumbled.

It was now the winter of 1815 and had been three years since Congress had declared war against the British. Although he was normally a man of peace, the Brits had left them no choice. When his ambassadors protested the conscription of American sailors into the British Navy in their fight with the French, they ignored the protests and had even stirred up the tribes, encouraging heinous attacks on rural U.S. settlements close to the Canadian border. On top of that, the French and the British blockades against each other had made it almost impossible for the United States to trade with anyone.

The young congressional Warhawks, led by Henry Clay and John Calhoun, demanded justice. The original intent was just a few skirmishes resulting in some annexed Canadian territory to remind the British that the United States was not an errant colony but an independent country. That was water under the bridge now. It had all gone badly.

President Madison finished reviewing the summaries and thoughtfully turned to Monroe and Jefferson. As always Madison was a man to think long before speaking. The room was silent.

Jefferson got up and looked out the window at passersby going about their business in the streets below as if all was well. Those involved knew that their young country was in peril, and this new treaty was nothing more than a draw. All their losses would be for naught. Could they walk away from their first significant war with a defeat in their pocket and no wins?

They all had truly believed that the Canadian colonists wanted to join the United States. On a map a successful campaign appeared a thing of beauty, but it had been quite a miscalculation.

When the skirmishes began, the Canadians fought back fiercely with their savage tribal allies alongside the British. Eventually the British forces had started attacking from the south, and General Andrew Jackson had been sent to defend. He'd quashed the Native uprisings and chased the British down to New Orleans, but in this war the United States had thus far too few victories in a sea of losses. Their young country could easily lose this war, and they were dangerously low on funding.

Jefferson cleared his throat. "James, the truth is, the British no longer have any more appetite for this war than we do. Their war with the French has stretched their resources very thin. This new Ghent treaty Adams and Clay negotiated certainly tells us the Brits want an end to it."

A lot of this information was repetitive, things the three of them already knew, but Jefferson was setting a stage. Madison's fingers fidgeted, producing a pyramid as he weighed the decision. Adams wanted to confirm the peace treaty immediately. They had sent Henry Clay as part of the commission to balance Adams' vehemence against this war. Adams and his Federalist cohorts had predicted a disastrous outcome and, unfortunately, they had been correct.

Jefferson continued, "We should counter sue for at least a couple of the Canadian colonies. The efforts and losses we have taken deserve to be rewarded. I…"

Madison held up his hand and looked directly into Jefferson's eyes, "And what of Adams' and Clay's advice?"

For a moment Jefferson frowned. The expansion of the country had always been foremost in Jefferson's mind. Surprisingly, in this treaty, Clay, known as a Warhawk, had sided with Adams.

"I understand Adams suggests we agree, as does Clay. But it's a flat draw with the British; a return of all conquests made on both sides."

Hearing it said out loud, President Madison visibly cringed. The thought of being the first president to forfeit a war was physically painful to him, but funds were slim. An end to this war was needed before the young nation hit bankruptcy. There were more important things at stake than his personal pride. "That's it then... that's it. We will endeavor to make it so." Madison paused for a moment of inretrospection. "Here at home, however, we will not represent this as a draw." Madison acknowledged Jefferson's distasteful frown. "With General Jackson's recent wins in the south, we will declare victory. We will celebrate a re-declaration of independence. Spin up Jackson's name. Make him a hero of the war."

Monroe chimed in, "We can also emphasize that British impressment of our sailors is at an end. It's not part of the treaty per se, but now that their war with the French is ending, they will stop."

President Madison nodded. "That is how we will proceed. Thomas, will you work with our Party's presses on the messaging? And James, you will work with Adams to see that the Federalists cooperate in their presses, while we proceed with our Party and Congress. We must present unified messaging of pride and victory."

Madison tilted his head at Jefferson's obvious disappointment. "It's only a slight setback to our visions, Thomas. There are still vast expansion opportunities westward."

Jefferson closed his eyes and gave a slight nod. Madison returned his gaze to the treaty. John Quincy Adams was as skilled as his former presidential father and namesake at foreign negotiations, and with Henry Clay along, President Madison could be sure of a balanced recommendation. The pair had gotten their young nation past this almost fatal mistake. They would have a few cuts and bruises, but they would remain intact. In any case their country had made a good showing; no soil lost and the last major battle at New Orleans well won by Jackson and his men. It would be a tough lesson learned, but a lesson learned for the better. The resulting patriotism inspired by the press messaging would be priceless... and the soldiers could finally get back to their farms.

******

Philo trudged along with part of the Virginia Militia making their way back north. Exhaustion was etched into every face. All they wanted was to return home to their loved ones. Rumors circulated that General Jackson himself rode among their ranks. It was said that the army would be disbanded in the Florida territories after the war, and they would have to make their way home alone. But General Jackson refused to let that happen. His men had fought bravely and deserved support for the journey north, rather than be left to forage and scrounge for themselves. It was even rumored that Jackson used his own funds to supply the troops.

As they marched along, Philo spotted a commotion up ahead. A group of men had surrounded a wagon filled with fresh supplies brought by a farmer and his family. With no officers in sight, some of the soldiers were ready to commandeer the stuff for themselves, and a scuffle had broken out. Philo's instincts kicked in, and he decided to intervene. The farmer deserved respect, and the supplies would be better used to aid the wounded. Though the troops were all hungry, they were not desperate, as they all had their daily rations.

"Hey, you there!" Philo attempted to appear more authoritative as he approached the group, calling out to them. Although he had previously led men in his Herkimer Militia, he had no real authority over these soldiers, except perhaps their sense of honor— once he reminded them of it. Few of his Herkimer Militia had stayed for the southern battles.

A fight among the soldiers ensued over first pick of the supplies, leaving the farmer and his family visibly frightened. One soldier, much larger than the others, easily dominated the group. Philo recognized him as Pete Flannigan, from Virginia and of Irish descent. A savage fighter on the battlefield, Pete was also known as a bully in camp, frequently pushing others around. Philo had seen him use his tomahawk on countless Native and British enemies. The weapon always hung at his side, and he had an intimidating habit of touching its handle with his fingers, as if ready to pull it out at a moment's notice. This moment was no exception.

At the sound of authority Pete stood up, formidable as a bear.

He turned and appraised Philo. All of them respected the quiet man from the Mohawk Valley for his bravery and leadership in battle, even though he was not an officer.

"What the hell do you want? Wait your turn," Pete barked, his words rough as a jagged rock.

The brute stare of an animal claiming a carcass was what Philo was observing in this man. Philo was having serious second thoughts that he could appeal to this fellow's humanity. Pete was bigger than the rest of them and certainly required more food to quell the rumbling in his belly.

"Pete, we are all hungry, but we have wounded who need this food more than we do," Philo said calmly, his voice steady despite the anger he could see building in Pete's eyes. "Here, I'll give you my rations for today, but let's get that wagon to the rear for the wounded, eh?"

Before Philo knew what was happening, he found himself flying through the air, like a sack of potatoes, tossed aside by Pete's brute strength. The sound of laughter filled the air as Philo hit the ground with a thud, the wind knocked out of him.

Pete chuckled loudly, his eyes scanning over the tempting pile of goods in the wagon. "Sure, I'll give up this fine smoked ham for some of your scraps of hardtack," he said, shaking his head. He felt entitled to the food, having likely killed more enemies than anyone else in the group.

Philo lay there, struggling to breathe and rubbing his sore jaw where Pete had backhanded him. Well, at least Pete hadn't chosen to use his tomahawk. That was something. Abruptly Philo felt a firm hand on his arm pulling him to his feet. He grunted and gratefully looked into the eyes of a very commanding figure who brushed the dirt off of his shoulders and was now turning his attention to the crowd around the new supplies.

"Easy there, soldier. Not a time to rest just yet." The man gave a grateful Philo a wink and then scowled at the errant group. He was accompanied by a tall, thin scout with a coon-skin cap and a long rifle, as well as a sturdy fellow dressed in Native attire who looked nothing like a regular soldier or militiaman.

"You there, all of you back off. Come to attention at once, you sons a bitches!" the new arrival commanded, his voice booming with authority.

Upon hearing the order, Pete turned to see a tall, solid man approaching, his hair well-kept but his clothes soiled and tattered like the rest of them. Angrily, Pete took intimidating steps toward his opponent and demanded, "Who the hell are you? Would you like some of the same I just gave Philo there?"

Although a bit slow, Pete realized everyone was suddenly completely silent. He glanced around quickly to see all of his cohorts standing at attention. The man approaching appeared to be wearing an officer's uniform and was apparently not the slightest bit intimidated by Pete's formidable size. Pete's mouth was watering for that smoked ham, and he made an instant decision he was prepared to beat down this officer for it. "You're in for a shit load now," he heard someone whisper. "That's Old Hickory... General Jackson himself. He'll whip your ass for sure."

Pete gasped, dropped everything and immediately came to attention along with the rest of the misbehaving lot. Jackson stepped into the middle of the bunch. They all took five steps back and stood at attention.

Glowering like a lion, the general circled a now submissive Pete before addressing Philo. "You there, gather up these goods and distribute them among the wounded who are in most need. This man here," he fixed his gaze on Pete, "will assist you. Won't you, soldier?"

"Yes, sir! Whatever you say, sir." Pete replied, his voice full of respect. Nobody crossed Jackson. Although he was well known to have held office as a Judge and Senator from Tennessee, the respect from his men came from the fact that he was also well known to be as savage as any in battle and had seen to it that they won their battles. Jackson was also known for his quick temper. Friends and foe alike held fear and respect for this man.

Jackson then turned to his two escorts and said, "Davy, Sam, you show them where to take it. The rest of you, move along and don't let me catch you brawling again." With that, the general strode off towards the rear of the troops.

The men breathed a collective sigh of relief at getting off so easily. Jackson was notorious for hanging men who disobeyed orders and for publicly whipping those who showed disrespect. As they watched their leader disappear into the distance, one by one the main troop turned and headed up the road. The hunger in their bellies was now forgotten, and squabbles over food had been put aside. General Jackson was loyal to his men and would get them all home. They would proudly repeat this story to any who would listen, so proud they all were to serve under Old Hickory himself.

Philo stood with Pete as they watched Jackson disappear into the marching troops.

"Why the hell isn't he out front on his horse with the other officers?" Pete asked.

David Crockett, the lean sergeant and scout from Tennessee, locked eyes with his comrade, Third Lieutenant Sam Houston, before replying. "General Jackson stays in the back with the stragglers. He doesn't want anyone to get left behind. He gave up his own horses so more of the wounded could ride."

Sam nodded in agreement. Like so many others he and David had become unlikely comrades in this war. Sam had been wounded badly during a battle with the Creek supporting the British efforts and was still nursing an injured shoulder. David, a dead-eye shot with his long rifle, had lost family members to the Creeks. Between fighting the Natives and the British it had seemed to this Tennessee Militia as if their entire world was at war. He and David had made a pact they would see this through with Jackson until they were honorably discharged, and it seemed the end might be close at hand.

As they gathered up supplies for the wounded, David turned to Philo. "Where are you headed, Philo?" he asked. Pete and Sam listened in, curiously.

Philo replied sincerely, "Well, I got my wife and two young daughters waiting for me, running the farm. It's a beautiful place. It has fertile land, a small stream, and plenty of trees. It's not far from our little town of Herkimer. We're a tight-knit community packed full of neighborly people. I just can't wait to just get home and hug my family." Philo's eyes began to water with emotion.

"I got two sons of my own waiting for me back home. You need to get busy on your own sons there soldier." David replied, smirking.

Philo grinned broadly. "Hope to rectify that when I get back home for sure."

David gazed wistfully at the horizon to the east. "It sounds like you have a fine homecoming waiting for you, Philo. I can't wait to get back to my own family in Tennessee. When I left, my wife was expecting. I may have another son waiting for me."

Pete added, "I've been saving up my wages for a nest egg before settling down. I plan on starting a gristmill, like my father used to run back home. Well, that's my dream anyway." David nodded approvingly and patted Pete on the back.

Philo responded with enthusiasm. "Well, we could certainly use a reliable gristmill in our neck of the woods with a strong man like you running it."

Suddenly grateful that the disagreement he'd had with this man from the Mohawk Valley was turning into a budding friendship, Pete shrugged and nodded enthusiastically.

The thought of the reunion with his family made Philo pick up the pace. At this rate he could be back home in a little less than a month. Philo was proud to have served his country, but all he could think about was feeling the warmth of Almira next to him in bed again.

Philo said humbly, "Now that the war is over, I guess we all have our noses pointed towards home to pick up where we left off."

The men nodded in agreement and quickly finished packing, heading towards the rear of the troops. With the brutality of war fresh in their minds and the arbitrary acts of violence they had witnessed during their march, a haunting sense of unease gnawed at each of them, planting a deep sense of foreboding about what they might find when they finally returned home...

1819 – Rural Herkimer Township, Mohawk Valley, New York

On, on she speeds through bush and brake,
O'er log and stone and briar;
On, on, for many a lengthening mile
Might stouter footsteps tire

FOUR YEARS AFTER PHILO'S RETURN FROM THE WAR...

hilo Hackley squinted as he watched the child sprinting from the forest. Something was off. He pulled his stout work horse, Ned, to a halt and watched curiously as the barefoot girl tumbled to the ground, scrambled to her feet, and continued her panicked race towards the farm. "Pa! Pa!" she called.

Sooleawa and Easter had seamlessly blended into the family ever since Philo and Almira had taken them in following Cousin Robert's death during the war. Philo could have easily turned his back on this Native woman and her daughter, but that simply wasn't in his nature. Sooleawa had been a loyal companion to Robert and even fought alongside him in a few battles. She was a skilled hunter and an accomplished cook. When Philo returned from the south, fearing for his family's fate, he discovered Almira and Soolee managing the farm and mercantile better than he could have himself.

Soolee was a sturdy woman, as robust as any man, and her little babe had been no burden. Soolee simply kept her strapped to her back or the plow as needed. Her labor on the farm earned far more

23

than the pair's cost to keep. Besides, Easter was blood kin. Almira had even schooled Soolee to colonial ways, and she learned to cook in Dutch ovens at the hearth, sleep in a bed, and speak English rather well.

As Easter grew, she took to calling Philo, "Pa" and Almira "Ma" just like their own children. Soolee had trouble wrapping her Algonquin tongue around Easter's given name of Esther, so she had always been called Easter.

Now seven years of age, Easter had gone into the woods that morning to forage with her mother. The herbs, wild rice, and Native staples Soolee brought home were invaluable to their farm, as was the wild game she sometimes snared. Easter was well on her way to being every bit as good a forager as her mother.

However, Soolee and Easter had been gone a bit longer than usual this time, and for some reason Easter was now running towards Philo like a scared rabbit, yelling at the top of her lungs. Soolee was nowhere in sight. Philo frowned. He wanted to get this field done before the day ended. A dark sense of foreboding crept over him. He scanned the tree-line. Where was Soolee? What could be the reason for Easter's panic?

Rough stones sliced and stung Easter's feet as they pounded the earth. For a fleeting moment she regretted doffing her shoes at the edge of the field earlier that morning. Ma often scolded her for foraging with Soolee bare foot, like a Native, so she had taken to leaving her shoes hidden so Ma would not know.

At this point her entire body had gone numb. The horrific scene she had left behind pursued her, nipping at her heels and gave her a new found strength. She imagined hot, putrid breath on her neck as if the thing was just a hair's breadth away. Not daring to slow, she begged her exhausted body to move faster. Fearfully, she chanced a glance over her shoulder and then pressed on.

Easter was running for her life, for Soolee's life, in a sprint that numbed her extremities. The warm saltiness trickling down her mouth out of her bloodied nose did not deter her. Hysterical, she raced towards Pa, who stood watching her, leaning his elbow on the plow. "Ya'kwahe, Ya'kwahe!" Easter screeched as she barreled towards him. It took her a moment to realize she had finally reached him and that he had a hold of her by both shoulders, yelling something.

"Easter, Easter, calm down, girl. Christ. Speak English. Since when do you speak Native at me?" Philo was more than a little irritated and truly puzzled by the hysterical girl. At this point, she was panting so heavily she could not utter a word. Her terror was quite alarming. Philo checked the tree line again to see if Soolee was in pursuit…but there was nothing there.

"Pa," At last Easter cried out, her voice thick with tears. "Ya'kwahe got Soolee." She panted heavily. "…in the forest. He jumped me, and Soolee pushed me out of the way. She's fighting him with her knife. Pa, you have to come!" Easter sobbed and backed up, motioning for him to follow.

"Easter, who the hell is Ya'kwahe?" Philo demanded, still unconvinced. Could the girl have been startled by shadows? He glanced back at the house. Almira was not back yet; she had taken the family in the wagon into town the previous day and was not due back until late. There was no one to tie up poor old Ned if he went on this little trek with Easter. He looked down at Easter again. She was trembling like a stray pup.

Philo sighed. It was better to leave Ned behind and see what was going on. If this was just a wild goose chase, he might have Almira administer a whooping when she got back. Philo grabbed his musket, tested the bayonet to ensure it was tightly affixed, and motioned for Easter to lead.

They set off at a trot. Philo glanced back at his horse waiting patiently, harnessed to the plow. He was irked. "Is this Ya'kwahe someone Soolee knows?"

Easter stopped for a moment, listening to the silence. She wiped her sore, blood spattered face and responded, "Ya'kwahe is a horrible beast, a Spirit Bear. He hunts Soolee's people sometimes. Many tell the story. Soolee screamed his name when she jumped between us and told me to run." Easter sniffed and continued at a slower pace. "I think he is an evil spirit of some kind."

"A bear? A bear got Soolee?" Easter had Philo's full attention now. He could feel the hairs on the back of his neck bristle. No, this was not a wild goose chase. It was possibly a matter of life and death. An evil spirit? It sounded like one of Soolee's tales. Perhaps it was just a silly game that had spiraled out of control. Soolee did have an unusual sense of humor at times.

Easter was treading cautiously now, breathing easier, tears still at a trickle. Philo followed close as she peered carefully ahead to find her way, then abruptly halted. "Over there," she whispered, pointing at a small grove of poplar trees. "That's where he jumped us." She looked up at Pa with hope in her eyes. It was time for him to come to the rescue. Easter had done her part.

Philo glanced at the girl then studied the scene. A goddamn bear? Shite. He saw no movement, and there was no noise save the rustling of leaves from the wind. If true, with any luck Soolee had escaped and climbed a tree; she was a scrappy and stout woman. Few men would stand a chance against her in a wrestling match, of that he was certain.

The poplar leaves were just beginning to turn speckled yellow, signaling that fall was nearly upon them. The bears were preparing for hibernation, intent on consuming every last morsel of sustenance they could find. They could be very territorial at this time of year. He checked his musket. Philo had a steady aim, and with his new Springfield .69 flintlock, one well-placed shot could bring a bear down. Nevertheless, bears often had the advantage against a solitary man with a musket. He hoped against hope that Easter was wrong, that she had merely been spooked by shadows. "Stay here," he commanded. Easter nodded, nervously clenching her hands, and stared at the forest with a mixture of hope and dread.

As Philo approached the poplar grove, he noted that bear signs were prevalent, not something Soolee would likely overlook. A few rotting logs had been scraped and scratched for grubs. Raw earth was tossed about from digging up roots and tubers; the same forage Soolee would have been pursuing. Trees displayed more than a few claw marks, some sharply defined, others muted by the passage of time. It appeared as though the two had stumbled upon a bear domain passed down through generations. How could he have missed this so close to home?

Easter stood silent as a statue with her hands clutched tightly. There was nothing but the sound of the poplar leaves rustling…and then Philo heard it—faint grunting and labored, injured breaths, too deep, too heavy to be human. He moved cautiously forward, and then he saw it.

Just inside the grove, a mound of a large, partially furred rump protruded from the tall grass. A hairless pink section of the beast, peppered with black freckles, was visible. The immense creature's ribcage heaved as if in the throes of death. Philo knew that an injured bear could fight fiercely until its last breath. He needed to take one careful, perfect shot to end the creature's life. Somehow it seemed to sense Philo. With a struggle, it lifted its massive head to peer over its shoulder at the approaching man, and then, with a rattling sigh, it slowly lay back on the ground, still and silent.

Philo froze for a few long minutes, musket at the ready. It appeared the beast was dead, no movement, no noise, just the poplar leaves rustling in the gentle breeze. He carefully picked up a rock and tossed it at the mound of hair and flesh, immediately bringing his musket up at the ready. Again, nothing. Cautiously, he approached it. God…what a monster. He prodded the beast with his bayonet one last time to be certain.

For a black bear, the beast was huge. The scarred, partially hairless flesh covering a good third of its body indicated it had been badly burned at some point, perhaps caught in a forest fire as a cub. Upon closer inspection, he noticed bloody wounds around the chest and eyes, as well as a shallow knife wound in the throat, just enough to make breathing difficult and to slowly bleed the creature out.

Suddenly he felt something behind him. He jumped and spun around, musket at the ready.

"Christ, Easter, you scared the shite out of me."

The girl stood wide-eyed staring at the grotesque creature.

"Ya'kwahe ..." she gasped. "Is he... dead?"

"Yep. Dead as dead can be. But it's just a deformed bear, Easter. It appears Soolee must have held her own and slit its throat." Philo looked around; Christ, where was Soolee?

"Soolee called him Ya'kwahe," Easter replied firmly. Soolee had told her many tales by the fire at night, always out of earshot of Almira. Native lore was not tolerated at the house. Soolee had shared many secrets with Easter. She knew that Soolee was her real mother; however, Ma and Pa were the heads of the household, and Easter was one of the children, never treated any differently from the rest. Soolee was just that, Soolee. "You know, you could easily pass as white," Soolee had once told Easter. "You don't really look like the Algonquin. You have our dark eyes and maybe our build, tall and sturdy." Easter had ignored the comment. She was part of this family and did not think of herself as Native at all. Soolee was Native; Easter was not.

But she was certain that this was the Ya'kwahe Soolee had told her about by the fire, an evil spirit bear that preyed upon the Algonquin, feeding on the flesh of the people, which made its hair fall out. Judging by the hairless appearance of this Ya'kwahe, it had devoured many people. Soolee had saved Easter's life. It was Easter who had wandered too far from Soolee and been attacked by the creature. Soolee had come running and leaped in the way. Easter thought about Soolee with her knife drawn, "Ayeeeee, it's Ya'kwahe. Easter, Easter, run! Like the wind, get away, run!" Easter had taken off, the wind seemingly beneath her feet. She could hear the roars of the bear and Soolee's rhythmic, inhuman bellowing in the distance. Those haunting sounds would surely stay with her for the rest of her days. "Hawyeee, Ya'kwahe! Ayeeeee, Ayeeeee!"

Pa squatted down, placing his hand on some gored remains beside the bear. Easter approached to get a better look, thinking it must be the bear's kill.

"No, Easter, get back," Pa commanded.

But for some reason, Easter couldn't obey. With her eyes

fixated on the remains, something drew her closer until she froze, realizing the shredded flesh, bones, and bloodied homespun was indeed a bear-kill. It was all that was left of Soolee…

Numb with grief, Easter watched as Philo fashioned a drag sled and strapped the remains of the brave Algonquin woman to the frame. A little while later, the somber troop exited the forest edge just in time to see a confused Almira stabling the abandoned Ned.

The next day, the family gathered to put Soolee's body to rest. No one from town mourned the death of Sooleawa, the Algonquin woman named for forest rain, who, armed with nothing but a knife, had killed a full-grown black bear to protect her little girl.

Philo looked down at the gently wrapped remains resting in the grave he had dug in the family plot. Until now, only one small grave had inhabited the space, that of his son who had died at birth. Easter stood at his side, arms wrapped around his waist. He gave her a squeeze as she pressed her cheek against him for comfort.

An appropriate Native burial would have involved the wrapping of her remains in skins, knees against the chest, with the body interred and Native ceremonies held. But Soolee had become part of a white Christian family, and so a Christian burial would be her end.

The family expressed genuine sadness; Soolee had been a beloved family member. Philo reflected that his own children were no less grieved at the loss than Easter. Almira held them close, and they cried the tears of loved ones lost, a true testament to how this Native woman and her offspring had blended into his family. His young son, Elihu, barely a year old, was about the same age as Easter when she had come into their home.

Philo would see to it that Easter was cared for. After all, few knew that Easter was anything but his and Almira's own. Those who knew would never remark on the fact. Easter could easily pass for white. More than a few neighbors had taken in orphaned Native children to supplement their families. Besides being the Christian thing to do, strong bodies were needed for survival on the farms that skirted townships. Many Native men had fought side by side with their white counterparts during the colonial wars. A spiritual kinship had been born among the families whose loved ones had been saved by their Native allies, as well as a deep hatred with a long memory for those tribes that had fought with the British-loving Tories.

In Easter, the apple certainly hadn't fallen far from the tree. She had Soolee's height and build, and in sunlight, one could see just a glint of Robert's red hair in her dark chestnut locks.

As he opened his Bible and began the Prayer of Absolution for Robert's dear, deceased Soolee, Philo made a vow. In memory of Robert and Sooleawa, Easter would be cared for and someday as well-wed as any of his daughters.

Philo would see to it.

1825 - Millstreet, Rathcoole, Blackwater, Ireland

And how lest Britain's bull-dog pluck,
Roused by their isolation,
Should make these few, brave, lonely men,
Fight as in desperation

TEN YEARS AFTER PHILO'S RETURN FROM THE WAR...

There was nothing more beautiful than the afternoon sun sparkling on the Blackwater River after a soft, midday rain. As young Thomas Wallace cast his line into the river, he closed his eyes for a moment to savor the sun and moisture on his face. Just moments before, the clouds had parted, allowing brilliant rays to bathe the land below. Opening his eyes, Thomas scanned the horizon, searching for the rainbow that would surely reveal itself. Here in Ireland, although mostly of the Catholic persuasion, folks still held many superstitions close to heart. Tales of fairies and leprechauns dancing beneath a rainbow's arch were endless. As a young man of sixteen, Thomas was no exception to such superstitions and so, as expected, when the rainbow appeared in the field behind him, he instinctively checked for a legendary tiny figure with a cocked black hat, who might be burying his leprechaun gold in just that spot.

The symphony of the brightly colored arch, framed by a misty green field, and the sparkling river filled Thomas with childish delight. It was a glorious day to be about this business. He planned to surprise his Mum with a catch for dinner. She would surely deliver a tongue-lashing for his trespassing on the Blackwater to catch the fish, but the family would relish the feast. He smiled at the thought.

Suddenly he noticed movement at the base of the rainbow. Irish superstition sent shivers down his spine as a whiskered face emerged through the mist. When another face followed and the men strode towards him with purpose, Thomas realized these figures were neither leprechauns nor fairies. Two British Peelers had their sights on him and were rapidly closing in.

The Peelers were ex-soldiers hired by British land owners to prevent Irish townsfolk from poaching. The Brits had passed laws to wit, all game, fish, trees, pretty much everything that wasn't part of a township, belonged to one British overlord or another. With game and fish so plentiful, their abundance clearly a gift from God, everyone knew this was unjust and tended to hunt or fish when the Peelers weren't watching.

Mostly, Peelers spent their time drinking and gambling, flirting with local Irish girls and roughing up the occasional young Irish lad who dared to take exception to their ill manners. They certainly stirred the locals' ire in more ways than one, sauntering around town as if they held more ownership over the place than the Irishmen whose families had lived there for generations.

Thomas's own father taught at a hedge school in a stone house with a thatched roof, educating children from the Drishane Parish in their small village of Millstreet. As a Catholic school teacher, his meager income from the parish provided for some sixty students in two rooms; one for the girls and one for the boys. With their tenant farming the family did a small amount of sharecropping, which provided additional income, making them better off than most. Thomas and his four older brothers had been educated by their father. The Wallace boys were known for their tempers as well as their wit.

At sixteen years of age, Thomas definitely felt his temper on the rise. Assuming the Peelers would be drinking in town, he'd thought a quick fishing trip would be safe, but obviously it was not so. Now the Peelers were close enough for Thomas to smell the whiskey on their breath. He quickly decided that humor just might win these lads over. After all, in this soggy weather, escorting him five miles across the river to the magistrate would be quite a trek, and the drink might have loosened their resolve.

"Bonny day for fishing, eh boys?" Thomas summoned up his most charming dimpled grin and focused on the water, hoping for the best. "You boys bring your fishing poles with ya? If not I have extra line and bait here I can make ya some." 'Act is though nothing is afoot,' Thomas told himself as the Peelers stood silent, sizing him up and down. Both were slightly whiskered, with cropped dark hair and black caps. One was a bit taller than the other. Both had billy clubs hanging off their belts, and one carried a musket with a bayonet affixed. They didn't seem intimidated at all.

"You're poaching, sonny-boy. Ya know that." The tall one folded his arms, jutted his chin in the air confidently and narrowed his eyes. The other one stared sullenly; not a hint of a smile.

"Well now, that depends on your point of view, don't it?" Thomas replied with a stiff smile. "After all, the fish, ya see, they swam all the way in from the ocean, I'm told. So one could say the fish belong to us all. Now the river itself, that surely belongs to Sir Henry; but I'm not taking the water…just a fish or two for dinner, ya see?" Thomas smiled again and tilted his head, trying to coax a grin from the Peelers, but they were having none of it.

"Sir Henry is particularly tired of you Irish trash trespassing and poaching. He'll be happy to make an example of you, sonny-boy," the tall one responded. The short one remained silent, obviously deferring all decisions to his mate.

"But I haven't even caught anything." Thomas was starting to feel a bit desperate. With the obvious enjoyment the tall one was taking in his discomfort, Thomas felt his ire rising again, "Surely you could let me off with a warning. I promise I won't do it again. Here, you can have me pole and all me hooks." Thomas offered, holding them up.

The tall one motioned to his mate to take the gear.

"You're coming with us, sonny-boy," he responded flatly and

motioned toward the river.

Finally the short one spoke up. "I just got me some new shoes. I don't want to get me feet wet," he complained loudly. The tall one looked at his mate's shoes. For a fleeting moment Thomas thought he might be granted a reprieve…

"Well, this sonny-boy here can carry you on his back then," the taller Peeler proclaimed with a vile glint in his eye. "After all, it's his fault we have to cross the river in the first place. And we wouldn't want to get your shiny new shoes wet now, would we?" At this, both Peelers finally broke into grins.

Thomas was far from amused. He forced a smile and retorted, "I'm not sure I'm tall enough me-self to cross. We might all have to swim for it." The tall Peeler leaned on his musket while the shorter one took off his shoes, draping them around his neck, looking at Thomas expectantly.

Despondency gnawed at Thomas as he waded into the water. "Squat down," the tall Peeler commanded, grinning broadly. Thomas's fists clenched in defiance, but the Peeler poked him with his musket. Reluctantly, Thomas squatted down and allowed the shorter Peeler to clamber onto his shoulders. The tall Peeler led the way, musket hoisted over his head, while the shorter one balanced on Thomas's shoulders, gripping his head for stability.

"You know you'll likely get at least a years' time in the workhouse for this, sonny-boy," the tall Peeler taunted as they crossed the river. The shorter Peeler on Thomas's shoulders snickered at the thought.

It was painfully obvious to Thomas that these Peelers were determined to drag him back to town to face the sheriff, one Sir Henry Wallis of Drishane Castle. This man was merciless, notorious for his loathing of poachers and trespassers. With each taunt, Thomas's ire mounted. These damn Brits were always trying to bully the locals, even when there was no cause. It was not fair. Everyone knew there was plenty of game and fish to go around.

As they reached the deepest part of the river, Thomas made a split-second decision. He pretended to stumble, causing the Peeler on his back to lose his balance. Thomas then ducked underwater and burst back up, propelling the shorter Peeler, tossing him onto the taller one. Seizing the opportunity, Thomas turned to flee. He was a strong swimmer, and for a moment, he believed he had a chance. When a hand clamped around his ankle and yanked him back, he knew he was in trouble.

The short Peeler bobbed in the water, not tall enough to keep his head above the surface, while the tall one gripped Thomas by one foot. Thomas, scrappy from growing up wrestling with his kinfolk, was determined to escape. Instead of fighting the tall Peeler, he used the man's grip on his leg to propel himself toward him. Then, in a swift motion, Thomas wrapped his arms around the Peeler's neck in a bear hug, pulling his head to his chest. Simultaneously, he managed to loop his legs around the shorter Peeler's neck, shoving him underwater and using him for leverage. The current had caused the tall Peeler to lose his footing, and now Thomas held both men underwater: the shorter one by the neck with his legs and the taller one by hugging his neck tightly to his chest. Thomas suddenly realized the deadly seriousness of this wrestling match. His limbs transformed into steel traps, holding fast.

A sudden stabbing pain in his leg did not deter Thomas, even when he noticed clouds of his own blood rise to the surface merging with the lazy river flow.

All of a sudden both Peelers stopped struggling. For a goodly time longer Thomas held them in a death grip until at last he realized... He had drowned them both. He made his way to shore towing the lifeless forms. At last he sat on the bank and sobbed, staring at the bodies. Thomas could not believe what had just happened. It was supposed to be a lark. Never in his life would he have ever think of killing these lads. They'd caught him in the act of poaching, pointed a musket at him, and taken him into their custody. He had used as much of his Irish charm as he could muster, joking with them, hoping they would let him go. Instead now there were two British Peelers dead, and Thomas had a bayonet wound in his leg.

He shook his head over what had just transpired and attempted to focus on what to do next. Hiding the bodies seemed the logical thing to do for now. First wrapping his leg to stem the blood, he gathered up rocks and shoved them tightly inside the Peelers clothing. As the last body sank into the slow part of the Blackwater, Thomas shook his head again. What to do now? A trail leading home was not an option. It was not just himself and his family that was in for it. It was his immortal soul. He had committed murder. Thomas began to cry again as he thought of the sheer disappointment on his father and dear Ma's face when they found out. He did not want to involve them in any way. He knew what he had to do…

******

Father Rathmore was tending the garden, his hands immersed in the rich earth. As curate to Father Fitzpatrick, the parish priest, Rathmore was a young man. He had received his training at St Patrick's College in Maynooth, just south of Dublin, was ordained at twenty-four years of age and the church at Millstreet was his first assignment. Animal husbandry and the garden were where he spent his time when not celebrating Mass or at prayer. His mother had been skilled with herbs and tending to ill folk. He had learned much at her knee, as had his brothers and sisters. She was a kind and gentle soul to both man and beast but sadly had not lived to see him ordained. A tragic accident had taken her life. When in town, one sad day, she had been caught in the crossfire between some angry Protestants and Catholics, and her life was snuffed out in a heartbeat.

Why he always thought back to those sad times while tending the garden brought him pause. Rathmore knew that he should try to focus on the warm loving times spent with his mother as a youth, not always upon the moment he lost her.

Movement at the edge of the pasture caught his eye. A young man approached, appearing to be lame. As the man came closer Rathmore recognized him as one of the parish teacher's sons. He closed his eyes to remember the name with the face; ah yes,

Thomas Wallace. Being the youngest, Thomas tended to have too much time on his hands and was oft caught causing some kind of mischief. He must have injured himself and come to see Rathmore to get patched up. The young curate had begun to get a bit of a reputation with his herbs and healing practices. The allure of curatives coupled with the power of the cloth was quite irresistible to both the superstitious parishioners as well as the more edified. Rathmore trotted out to guide Thomas into the root cellar where he kept most of his healing supplies.

"So what have ya gone and done to yourself this time, young Wallace?" Rathmore studied Thomas thoughtfully as he guided him to a bench. Thomas let out a low moan. The leg wound was severe, but it looked like a clean cut. Fear and confusion danced in Thomas's eyes, stirring compassion in Rathmore. Something was amiss, that was clear.

"Father Rathmore. I must say my confession. I must say it now... I..." Thomas's voice cracked as he began to sob.

It was evident that Thomas's soul bore a heavy burden. Rathmore decided he would cleanse the young man's soul first, and then he would tend to the leg wound. Cleansing the soul would not take long. He made the sign of the cross and sat on the other side of the bench from Thomas, their backs now touching.

"All right son, you may proceed."

With faltering words, Thomas recounted his fishing trip, his encounter with the Peelers, the disastrous confrontation in the midst of the river, and his desperate attempt to hide the bodies.

Finally, Thomas concluded, "Father, I am so sorry for me sins. And it's not only that. What's to become of me family once they find out? Me father, me mother, me brothers..." Thomas bowed his head and held his breath. Would Father Rathmore command his penance be to turn himself into the sheriff, who might indeed, besides unleashing his wrath on Thomas, also target his family as an example to the rest?

Rathmore sat frozen in his seat. This was a grave turn of events. This young man was not only part of his parish, but his father was also an active leader. Sheriff Henry Wallis of Drishane

Castle had been a colonel in the British army. What repercussions might he bring down upon the Catholic parish that had inadvertently killed two soldiers who had served with him?

Rathmore cleared his throat. "My son. Your sins are forgiven, in the name of the Father, the Son, and the Holy Ghost. Amen." He cleared his throat again. "Let me think for a moment on your penance."

Thomas put his face in his hands, ran his fingers through his hair and down his neck. He turned his head sideways to see Father Rathmore pacing, deep in thought. Suddenly he came to a halt. "Young Wallace, you wait here. I'll be right back."

Thomas watched as Rathmore walked steadfastly towards the communal church and disappeared inside. After agonizing minutes he re-emerged carrying some kind of paper in his hands, along with a small sack, and it appeared, a heavenly host between thumb and forefinger.

As he approached, he commanded, "On your knees."

Thomas complied.

"This holy wafer is left over from this morning's early mass. Repeat after me.

> *Protect and forgive me, dear lord Jesus, Holy Wafer*
> *most precious,*
> *For I am most heartily sorry and deeply regret my sins,*
> *Free my heart from the darkness of sin,*
> *Fill me with your grace,*
> *Purge my soul from all evil deeds*
> *Now and forever, Amen.*

Thomas repeated the words, terrified at the significance, and then the Priest placed the holy wafer in his mouth.

"All right, young Wallace, I have in my hand here your penance."

Father Rathmore handed Thomas the instructions and began to patch his wounded leg. Thomas read the paper, his eyes widening with each sentence.

"Son, I have a sack of coin to pay for the voyage. You won't be going home to your parents. I'll let them know that you decided to go to America to seek your fortune. There are three other men from the parish going as well. You will all go together, and you will repay me the money for the voyage when you are able. Tell no one what transpired. Make a home for yourself in America, be a good Christian, and raise a proper Catholic family. It's what's best for everyone."

Thomas nodded, silently processing this new turn of events. His family would likely be spared, and no-one might ever know what happened to the Peelers. His family would be sad he'd left without saying goodbye. It would be hard for them to understand. They would think him thoughtless, callous even. But, as Father Rathmore said, it was for the best...

******

It took some seven weeks of sailing to get to the Canadian coast, specifically Prince Edward Island. Through seemingly endless lands, Thomas and his three comrades made their way south on foot and finally reached their destination.

The American flyer had advertised for strong men to come and help build one of the first railroads in the United States, specifically the Schuylkill and Susquehanna branches through the Stony Valley near Auburn, Pennsylvania. The papers had also promised ample work in the coal mines that the railroads were being built to support. Jobs were endless, it said. It was an opportunity to remake oneself in America.

The vastness of the new lands struck the Irishmen first. Having lived out their lives on their beloved island, they had been taught about this country but had never dreamed to experience such vastness. It was humbling. Although a bit homesick, they arrived in

Auburn with a spring in their step and excited at the new opportunities that lay ahead.

Thomas penned a letter to his family to let them know he had arrived safely and to apologize for not having the time to say goodbye. He described it as a once-in-a-lifetime opportunity and a decision that had to be made in an instant, one that might never present itself again.

All in all, it was true. His disastrous encounter with the Peelers had forced him to this time and place. The excitement of making one's fortune in the Americas was contagious. Back home, the average Irishman was stuck in his place, his offspring destined to forever be workers for landowners. Here in America everyone believed that anyone could prosper with a strong back, a vision, and the will to conquer their fear of the unknown. He had never even dreamed of coming to this place. Somehow life had thrust him into this destiny...only to discover a common man's opportunities in America were nothing less than breathtaking.

1828 - Ol' Hickory

Away to the prairie, up, up and away,
Where the bison are roaming, the deer are at play;
From the wrongs that surround us, the home of our rest,
Let us seek on the wide, rolling plains of the West.
Away to the prairie, where the pioneer's lay
Is echoed afar on the breezes; away!

THIRTEEN YEARS AFTER PHILO'S RETURN FROM THE WAR...

Today was far from a typical day in Herkimer. In the midst of a presidential election year, political rallies were in full swing. As the county seat, their rural township would soon host the honorable senator from New York, Martin Van Buren himself, who was coming to promote General Andrew Jackson for president in his race against the incumbent, John Quincy Adams. Everyone eagerly anticipated attending the rally. At sixteen years of age, Easter stood on the wooden sidewalk in front of her family's mercantile, her curiosity piqued. Philo observed her with a smile.

"Your girl's blossoming into quite a beauty, Philo," remarked Pete Flannigan, the local gristmill owner and longtime friend, giving Philo a knowing wink.

Philo tilted his head and examined Easter thoughtfully. She stood taller than most girls her age. The soft curves of a young woman indeed made her attractive. While not a conventional beauty, given her somewhat square features, she was strong, tall, and sturdy with an air of confidence about her that drew a man's gaze. Her wavy tresses of dark chestnut hair caught hints of red

41

from the sunlight, a gift from her red-headed father. Dark eyebrows framed eyes reminiscent of tree bark, giving her a sultry appearance. Her errands about town garnered more than a few men taking a second glance as she walked by. Soon, she would become a prize to be won, sure to provide strong sons and a well-run household for some fortunate man.

"It's too soon to be talking like that about Easter," Philo replied. "It will be a couple years before she'll be a wife." He preferred his daughters to marry no sooner than eighteen, wishing to keep them home for as long as life allowed.

"Well, Philo, you know, some young ladies mature faster than others. My own mother married at fifteen," Pete said. Noticing the sharp look Philo gave him, he averted his gaze and added quickly, "But as you say, of course." Pete smiled to himself as he thought about young Easter. With his gristmill just across the waterway he had observed her flirtatious manner, which had attracted more than a few young men. As a widower he had certainly considered remarrying. Unbeknownst to her father, Easter was a sweet temptation for many, with potential suitors buzzing around the mercantile like bees to honey, and not there for the eldest daughter. Pete could provide a fine home for the young gal and the strong guidance of an older husband. He could father some strong sons with Easter. He was sure of it. But Philo was of a mind for her to wait. It was more than a bit frustrating.

Philo surveyed the men around him, marveling at the journey many had shared. They had begun as humble homesteaders, and when war called, they fought side by side in the militia, mourning the loss of friends and family together. Over time, they had worshipped, debated politics, and navigated presidential decrees. The dreams and challenges they had won and lost together are what forged this community's strength. Although Philo had served under Jackson, a Democratic-Republican, in the war, he was known as a Federalist. People of various political persuasions frequented his store and often engaged in spirited debates out front. As an influential and highly respected man in the county, Philo posted every copy of the Federalist leaning Gazette he could get his hands on in the window of his store for the community to read. The current President, John Quincy Adams, a fellow Federalist, had triumphed over Andrew Jackson in the previous election, and Jackson was taking him on again.

When a child in the Hackley family turned twelve, they began work at the Hackley Mercantile, already well-versed under Almira's guidance. Balancing the management of a farm and the mercantile was no small feat, but during difficult times, the farm supported the mercantile and sustained the family. The Hackley children were refined and well-educated, a legacy Philo intended to uphold, just like his father before him.

His daughters, Harriet and Easter, both toiled in the store. At ten, his son, Elihu, was starting to shoulder responsibilities on the farm and would soon join the mercantile. Philo's youngest, Racilla, merely eight years old, was destined to follow in her brother's footsteps.

Soolee's passing had left not only a void in their hearts but also a huge gap in chores and even provisions. Philo and Almira had taken in another Algonquin widow, Memengwaa, Native name for butterfly, along with her two sons. They had not blended into the family as well as Soolee. Easter had taken to bossing her around and had practically stepped into Soolee's shoes until she was old enough to work at the mercantile. Now, with Easter occupied elsewhere, Almira was spending more time on the farm, while the girls managed the store with their father.

Easter possessed remarkable talents for a young woman. Philo was proud of his own girls, too, but they lacked the survival skills and sheer initiative Easter had inherited from Soolee. He could entrust the store to Easter for hours, but quiet Harriet, two years her senior, would become quite unraveled in such a situation. That same initiative had led Easter into her fair share of mischief over the years, much like her father Robert, which only endeared her to Philo even more.

Now there she was, standing in front of the store, likely scheming a way to wiggle out of work for a couple of hours and attend the political rally.

Easter surveyed the street, her eyes landing on the group of men Pa was chatting with on this gentle early fall afternoon. She had chosen a soft green wool dress with an empire waist adorned with a matching cream ruffle at the neckline. Although the fashion was dated a bit it was quite presentable. The long sleeves puffed slightly at the shoulders, giving her a stylish look. Ensuring not a single stray lock of her wavy hair was out of place, she had brought her matching bonnet, just in case. The outfit was somewhat more formal than her usual mercantile attire, but she secretly hoped to leave Harriet in charge of the store for the day and attend the speeches. It was all so exciting.

As she studied the men around Pa, she spotted that handsome surveyor, Hiram Ayres, whom she'd taken a shine to. He'd been around town on business while performing his job of tracing the lines of the Royal Grant. His father, Jabez Aryres, a surveyor as well, was not looked upon fondly by Pa because of his different political views as a Democratic-Republican. Nevertheless, Jabez owned a substantial farm, which Hiram was set to inherit. Standing at six feet tall, Easter could easily meet Hiram's gaze. When their eyes locked, she offered him a warm smile and a curtsey. He returned the gesture with a smile and a tip of his hat.

"Easter, darlin', how are you this fine afternoon?"

Easter turned to find Jacob Conklin, one of the roguish Conklin brothers, ambling down the tree-lined walk towards her, a bundle of papers under his arm. She stole a glance to see if Pa was watching; he was engrossed in conversation and had not taken notice. The Conklin brothers, Jacob and William, often visited town on various errands, including delivering newspapers from different counties. Her father stocked copies in his store and displayed those he particularly favored in the window for passersby to read. Pa had fought in the militia with William Conklin Sr. and shared his political views, so he enjoyed chatting with the Conklin brothers whenever they came into town. When Pa was not there, Jacob or William always stopped at the store to see

Easter and flatter her to no end. Today it was Jacob, no doubt here for the rally.

"Quite well, Mr. Jacob Conklin," Easter replied playfully, "What brings you to town today, and where is that handsome brother of yours?" Both Jacob and William were quite tall, and unlike most men in town, Easter had to look up a bit to meet their eyes. They both stood at an impressive six feet four inches.

Jacob flashed a grin, captivated by the way Easter looked at him from beneath her thick, dark eyelashes. Her sideways glance and expectant expression suggested she was trying to ruffle his feathers by inquiring about his brother.

"Actually, he is about town somewhere. Come to hear about Ol' Hickory," Jacob replied.

"Ol' Hickory?"

"Yeah, that's what his troops called Jackson when he was a general. They say he was as strong as a hickory stick. He was awarded a gold medal of honor from Congress for kicking British asses out of New Orleans. And..." He paused, arching one eyebrow and leaning in close, as if about to reveal a secret. He glanced around, ensuring no one was eavesdropping.

Easter leaned in closer. He could smell the scent of her hair... lilacs, he was sure of it. She must rinse her hair with the stuff. "Ahem," he said in a softer voice. "His wife was a bigamist." He nodded emphatically as Easter stared at him in disbelief.

"A bigamist? Really?"

"Yes. The lady married Jackson when she thought her divorce was final from her previous husband. It turned out it was not, and so the lady was indeed a bigamist. They had to get the divorce finalized and remarry again. It was all quite scandalous." Satisfied with the juicy gossip he'd imparted, Jacob crossed his arms and smiled.

"Good Lord, that is scandalous."

"And that is not all," he said, rummaging through his papers before folding one and handing it to her. "Don't show this to your Pa. Promise me?"

Easter glanced at the paper. It was titled "Some Account of Some of the Bloody Deeds of General Jackson" and illustrated with a row of coffins.

She nodded and tucked the folded paper into her pocket, refocusing on her father, who was now approaching. He just had to let her go to the rally. She desperately wanted to hear the senator speak about the infamous general.

"Hello young Conklin," Philo greeted, nodding.

"Easter, we are closing up the mercantile for the rally today, go tell your sister." He smiled as she let out a jubilant whoop.

"It's not every day we get to hear our own senator speak in person," Philo told Jacob. "I'm for reelecting John Quincy Adams; I assume your father is as well?"

"I'm with you on that, sir," Jacob replied. "Although my dear brother seems to think that Jackson is the man for the job."

"Really, Will Conklin's firstborn son siding with a Democratic-Republican instead of a Federalist? Well. I'd be delighted to hear why he feels that way. Is your brother here today?"

"Yes sir," Jacob replied respectfully. He looked over Philo's shoulder and noticed Hiram Ayres sauntering towards them. Jacob quickly realized he would have more competition than just his brother for Easter's attention today.

"I'd be wondering, sir, if you'd mind if I escorted Easter to the rally?" Jacob asked hastily.

Philo looked at him thoughtfully. "That would be up to Easter, but you have my permission if she says yes."

Easter reappeared with her sister in tow, affixing her bonnet.

"Easter, your father says I may escort you to the rally if you agree," Jacob announced, observing the disappointment on Hiram's face as he arrived just in time to catch the unfavorable news.

"Yes. Yes, let's go." Easter replied eagerly. She smiled at her father, took Jacobs arm, and off they went.

Hiram's disappointment did not escape Philo's notice, but he feigned indifference. He nodded to Hiram as he and Harriet trailed Jacob and Easter.

******

Martin Van Buren scanned the sea of eager faces in rural New York. They were obviously very receptive to his message. This scene had been repeated over and over again in all the outlying townships, as well as the more populated cities. Jackson's electoral team had crafted a simple message of hope and dreams fulfilled. It proclaimed the destiny of any hardworking man was to be rewarded with the riches of the new western lands, and Jackson was just the man to make it happen.

Nodding faces in the crowd wholeheartedly agreed with the narrative Van Buren painted: the struggle between the few and the many. A greedy minority of wealth and privilege sought to exploit the common man relentlessly. This struggle lay behind the major problems of the day and was supported by the opposition and current president, John Quincy Adams. General Jackson, on the other hand, had proven himself among the common man by fighting alongside them as brothers against both the Natives and the British. Now that foreign threats no longer loomed, economic barriers and the wealthy became the enemy.

Jackson was the hero of the day who would side with the common man against the old Federalist elites. All Americans deserved a right to the rich rewards and freedoms so hard won by their fathers and grandfathers. Jackson would deliver them. He promised to open up rich lands to the west for homesteading to those brave enough to try. Jackson would send his armies to clear out any remaining unconquered populations that resisted their dreams, including any French, Spanish, or British foreign claims, as well as any protesting Native tribes. Lands as far as the eye could see or a wagon could travel would belong to colonial Americans, and no one else, from here on out, if Jackson were in charge.

The message ignited a fire in people's souls, sparking dreams that had never before been realized by the common man. Resounding cheers and excitement spread across the country like a blazing forest fire. The nomadic thirst of their European forefathers now focused on the new lands to the west. It was their Manifest Destiny…

William Conklin numbered among the many in the cheering crowd, absorbing the Jackson campaign promises. Grinning from ear to ear, he heard all his dreams and even some he hadn't considered being articulated in words. As he scanned the crowd, he spotted his brother Jacob with Easter and Harriet Hackley on either side of him, eagerly participating in the rally–clapping their hands and nodding their heads. He quickly made his way towards them, positioning himself next to Easter and leaving Jacob with Harriet. Easter rewarded him with that sweet flirty smile of hers. Jacob glanced at him with irritation. William was certain Easter preferred him over his brother and probably most men in Herkimer. On this spirited occasion, given the friendship between their fathers, there would likely be an invitation from Philo for dinner to discuss the rally. This would certainly suit William's plans. He had layers of plans, made even more exciting by Jackson's promises, and was determined that Easter was the perfect choice to play a part in them.

The small kitchen filled with the tantalizing aroma of roasted meat. Easter put some finishing touches on the pork, potatoes, and turnips she had left simmering on the hearth before leaving for the rally. With the added thickener transforming the broth into perfect gravy, it was cooked to tender perfection. Her hearth-baked bread had a thick crust on the outside with a moist, soft sponge in the middle. Few in Herkimer were as skilled a cook as she, of that Easter had no doubt. Her secret ingredient for her bread, dried wild sage, gave it a fragrant, earthy smell and taste that, when spread with sweet cream butter, made the roast and bread duo a memorable experience.

She placed the feast on the table. On the right side sat her attentive admirers, the Conklin brothers. On the left was Harriet, and at the far end, her father. As the hostess, in Ma's absence, she gracefully took the chair usually reserved for Ma. The anticipation on Will and Jacob's faces made her spine tingle with pleasure. It was evident they couldn't decide if they were more enamored with her or the meal she had effortlessly prepared, while managing the store, attending the rally, and flirting with them endlessly throughout the day. She bowed her head and folded her hands as Pa said grace, then peeked at William out of the corner of her eye as Pa carved the roast. If they were excited about this, just wait until they saw the blueberry pie she had cooling in the pantry.

"Ahem, as you know, your father fought alongside my cousin Robert and me in the war," Philo announced as he served the roast.

Will and Jacob nodded respectfully. Jacob smiled to himself, as they had heard this story many times.

"General Jackson was a prominent figure in winning that war," Philo continued. "William, your brother says you favor Jackson for president. With your father, a Federalist like myself, that surprises me. Do share with us what you like about the man."

Will gave Easter a quick smile and responded, "Well you see, sir, it is like this. I really like the idea of tariff protection Jackson and Van Buren want to pass against the cheap imports from other countries that are hurting our goods in the north. This should help my father's farm and your own store, I might add. As you heard today, Jackson is a man of the people. He fought alongside the common man just like you and my Pa against the Brits. And, Jackson believes every man has a right to vote, not just rich men and land owners. He grew up on a farm, fought in the Revolutionary War when he was only thirteen, and knows what it is like for a common man to scratch out a living and raise a family. If Jackson gets in he'll clear out the Natives and open up cheap land for homesteading in the west. Any man with a strong back and a dream can make it rich out west if Ol' Hickory gets elected." With a glint in his eye, Will nodded with certainty. "I intend to make my way out west to seek my fortune."

Philo listened thoughtfully. Will reminded him a lot of himself when he was that age. Against his own father's wishes he had left Connecticut and gone west to the Mohawk Valley to seek his fortune—and found it he had.

Philo noted that Easter seemed to hang on Will's every word. Harriet appeared a bit bored with the conversation.

"And you, Jacob. Where do you stand now that you've heard Van Buren's promises for Andrew Jackson?"

"Well, sir," Jacob responded, "I'm still of a mind for Adams, but I do want to hear what my father thinks on the matter. I tend to vote alongside him in such things." Jacob looked smugly certain that Philo would like his answer best.

After all the chatter at the dinner table and ample second helpings of Easter's blueberry pie, the Conklin brothers politely tipped their hats and went on their way.

The sisters went about their evening chores. Easter gathered up scraps and went out to the hog barn to feed the pigs. Pa liked to keep a couple of hogs at the mercantile to consume any scraps and occasionally trade in well-cured hams. The animals greeted her with good-natured squeals. She'd paused for a moment to watch the beautiful pink clouds as the sun set behind the barn, when she noticed Will Conklin heading towards her from the side of the house.

"I forgot to leave a couple of Gazette editions for your Pa," Will announced as he approached. He tipped his head to one side with an engaging smile. Easter smiled back at him batting her eyes. He was such a handsome man. There was something about his scent that made her want to move closer. She imagined running her hands along those strong, muscled arms of his.

"Can I help you with that?" Will asked. He took the scrap bucket from her, his eyes twinkling.

Easter's lips were moist and slightly parted. Her eyes wandered over his body. She could tell Will found her attractive. He was fidgeting on his feet. "I was just getting ready to feed the pigs and Pa's horse. You can come along if you want." With a faint smile

Easter pivoted on her feet, confident Will would follow, and headed for the barn.

Harriet slowly ambled out back on her way to dump the waste water. Chores were almost done for the night. Tomorrow was Sunday, and it would be delightful to catch up on gossip about the political rally at church. Having personally witnessed the rally, Harriet would have plenty to share, and, of course, Pa would be sharing his opinions with anyone willing to listen.

The town took pride in the limestone Protestant Church, which had stood there since 1767. Her grandfather, Aaron Hackley, had played an instrumental role in building that church, which undoubtedly granted them some standing in the congregation.

Harriet heard something peculiar and paused, trying to locate its source. Giggling… it sounded like Easter, and it seemed to be coming from the barn.

Will Conklin gazed into Easter's eyes. She was silent now, gazing back, bold and inviting. He had been teasing her and making her laugh most of the evening, taking his time. Will was certain she was an innocent girl. She enjoyed flirting, and he had seen her do it quite often. He needed a life partner to help build his dream of his own thriving farm in the new western lands, and Easter ticked all the boxes. She was pretty, smart, sturdy, raised by parents in the remoteness of the Mohawk valley, and well-versed in survival. The blend of township sophistication with that of a savvy frontier woman was the perfect recipe for a pioneer wife. He had witnessed her effortlessly lift barrels of grain off of a freight wagon that could make most men groan under the weight. Clearly, she was unafraid of hard work, and her father trusted her to run the mercantile on her own.

Will touched his finger to her cheek and traced it softly down to her chin. Their lips mere inches apart, he could feel her breath. Easter softly pressed her lips to his, their bodies easily melding together like a custom-fitted suit. He paused for a moment and gazed into her eyes, tenderly stroking her cheek.

"Easter, you gotta come with me out west," Will blurted out. He wished he could bite his tongue; this was not how he intended to propose to her.

"What?" Still feeling flirtatious, she smiled sweetly and tilted her head to the side. She liked Will a lot—more than anyone she had ever met. Lounging in his arms like this was certainly an enjoyable experience. He had such exhilarating dreams for the future. This was not the first young man she had kissed…he was a good kisser. "You and me out west? Pa wants me to wait until I'm at least eighteen to get married."

Will replied softly, "You let me worry about talking to your Pa, all right? Just say yes. I'll be heading west in the spring, and I want you by my side. Easter, I…you…we would be good together."

Harriet stood, mouth agape, as she audibly gasped at the scene visible through the barn boards. Her sister was entwined in Will Conklin's arms. Will and Easter instantly stepped apart and looked in her direction. Realizing she had been discovered Harriet began backing up hastily. She whirled around, nearly tripped, and then ran like a scared rabbit to the house.

"Harriet! Wait, Harriet!" Easter gave Will a concerned look, "You should probably go."

"Easter," Will called to her as she dashed toward the house in pursuit her sister. Dang. This was not how he wanted any of this to unfold. No answer from her, not even a maybe. And now Harriet might be tattling to Philo on them and giving everyone the wrong idea about his intentions. He was uncertain whether he should leave or stay and try to talk to Philo. What a mess. Well, leaving was probably the best course of action. Best let everybody calm down and return in a few days to test the waters…

A flushed Harriet stormed into the house and marched straight to Pa announcing, "Easter and Will are sparking in the barn. She was kissing him."

Easter burst into the house to find Harriet and her father eyeing her accusingly.

"Easter, what is the meaning of this?" Philo demanded.

"Pa, I don't know what Harriet said, but Will and I, we were just..." She glanced at her feet and shook her head. Easter's dander was up, and she was furious with Harriet for spying on her.

She put her hands on her hips and blurted out, "Pa, Will is a respectable man from a good family. You know his father well. He wants me to marry him and for us to build our own farm out West. And I want to go. He's going to set out in the spring." It all came out so fast Easter could hardly believe her own ears. Spurred by the excitement from the promises at the rally and her attraction to Will, she had made a split second decision. She folded her arms defiantly and stared back at her Pa. Well there. I said it, she thought. I guess I mean it too. Me and Will Conklin, out west. Our own farm. Our very own homestead...

Philo responded with shock and disapproval. "Easter, you cannot be serious," he said. "You cannot simply up and leave with Will. What kind of life do you think you will have out there? It's savage and empty. You'd be carving out a homestead from scratch, with nothing."

"I believe in Will," Easter snapped back. "He has a plan, and we're not gonna let hard work or fear stop us."

Philo started to respond and then stopped himself to study Easter. There were so many reasons why this was madness...and yet she had this unwavering spark in her eye. She was echoing what she had heard at the political rally. He could see she had caught the fever inspired by Jackson's vision to chase her dreams, just as Philo had from President Jefferson's publications when he and Almira were wed; their aspirations had truly come to fruition. Cousin Robert had that wanderlust about him, as well as Soolee with her nomadic Native heritage, so Easter surely came by it honestly. In Philo's heart he knew the future lay in new communities west for those brave and strong enough to heed the clarion call. Settlers who were first and successful in this race would have their pick of prized locations. Easter was strong and capable. If anyone could make a go of it, she and Will could.

Philo offered a wry smile and a nod, his eyes closing briefly as he began to accept the thought of this new venture. The young were so fearless these days. So many of Easter's cohorts were voicing similar aspirations.

His daunting challenge, now, was to figure out how he was going to break the news to Almira: that their daughter would be joining the ranks of countless others ready to risk everything in pursuit of fortune and adventure on this new daring sprint westward...

1829 – Jacksonians

Thou go, dear wife! a woman soft,
And not too brave to shake
At sight of wolf or catamount,
Or many-rattled snake

ONE YEAR LATER… Easter - 16, Will - 20

Despondent was the only way to describe President Andrew Jackson's mood as he sat at his desk. This should have been a time of celebration and elation, having finally achieved what he had tirelessly pursued for years. Instead, he found himself ensnared in a quagmire. His beloved wife, Rachel, had passed away shortly after the election, and today marked the first anniversary of her death. The ongoing drama surrounding his cabinet members only served to reopen wounds he thought had healed.

Andrew's mind wandered back to those early days in office. Rachel's health had already been fragile, deteriorating under the weight of political mudslinging and relentless gossip from Washington's elite during the campaign. Grief-stricken, she couldn't be consoled, and her melancholy had sapped her will to live.

Andrew had always regarded his role as a "military chieftain" as his most significant duty. One of his favorite books was The Scottish Chiefs, a tale of the virtuous, patriotic Scottish warrior, William Wallace, who had also lost his beloved wife. Wallace had filled the void in his heart with a bloody crusade, ultimately securing his heroic place in history.

In that spirit, following Rachel's death, Andrew had devoted himself entirely to being both a father and a leader for his country. Determined to act for the benefit of the common man, he refused to yield to the whims of the elite. Rachel's niece, Emily, took on the role of First Lady, while her husband, who was also Rachel's nephew, became Andrew's personal secretary. Their presence brought him comfort. Emily, in particular, bore a striking resemblance to Rachel, and she skillfully hosted parties and other First Lady affairs.

But now, it seemed they had come full circle, reminiscent of Rachel's torment. The Washington elites had set their sights on another political couple: Andrew's close friend and Secretary of State, John Eaton, and his new wife, Peggy. Peggy's late husband had served in the US Navy, and while he was away, John and Peggy had developed a close bond. After Peggy's husband took his own life, the couple hastened the mourning period and married, igniting a fresh whirlwind of intrigue.

Madam Floride Calhoun, wife of the Vice President, spearheaded the ostracism of the Eaton couple from Washington society. Rumors of a passionate affair prior to the husband's suicide provided ample fodder for newspapers hungry for scandal. Invitations to parties and other social events pointedly excluded the couple, whose names should have rightfully topped such guest lists.

Regrettably, in this senseless feud Emily, in her role as First Lady, sided with Floride and her band of bitches. The Eatons found themselves expressly barred from presidential social events. This ludicrous snub not only interfered with Andrew's ability to govern but also caused him endless distraction as he witnessed Peggy's anguish, which painfully echoed Rachel's descent into despondency. While his cabinet should have been focusing on national affairs, whispers, knowing looks, and rolling eyes seemed to take precedence over governance. Andrew had heard rumors that the party was considering supporting Calhoun for the presidency instead of granting him a second term.

Andrew narrowed his eyes as he noticed Calhoun approaching

down the hallway. Their party was no longer the Democratic-Republican Party. The fierce mudslinging during the election between John Quincy Adams and Andrew had caused a rift; the Democratic Party sided with Andrew, while Calhoun and Henry Clay had formed a new "Whig" party.

Eaton had assisted Andrew in drafting his upcoming speech to Congress, announcing that their provisions for Native removal from new western lands opened for settlement had been agreed upon in recent treaties. The truth was that there were a few British and French claims Andrew planned to oust from those lands as well—by acquisition or force. He was determined to fulfill his campaign promise: The lands were meant for American settlers, and he would ensure that anyone who would not assimilate would be removed.

Andrew was fed up with Calhoun. They rarely saw eye to eye on anything. The bastard was every bit a gossipmonger as that bitch wife of his, no doubt attempting to tarnish Andrew's reputation in a bid for power. These Washington elites had made the Eaton couple's life unbearable. Andrew seriously contemplated disbanding his entire cabinet to rid himself of Calhoun's supporters. In their absence, he planned to rely on advice and counsel from personal associates: Van Buren, two prominent editors of influential newspapers, his nephew, and those loyal to him from his days in the military.

John Calhoun paused for a moment as he approached President Jackson. With his piercing stare and hands planted firmly on his desk, the man resembled a mountain lion poised to pounce, his Vice President being the prey.

How could a man associated with countless scandals become the President of the United States? A man who, without authority, had declared martial law and seized control of New Orleans, executed mutineers in the field, invaded Florida without proper authorization, killed British subjects, married a bigamist, and brutally murdered a disarmed opponent in a duel…

Calhoun had borne the brunt of Jackson's temper on several

occasions. He had hoped they could move past all this nonsense. Jackson should have fired Eaton at the first hint of gossip. The truth was that behind the scenes Henry Clay had fueled much of the rumor-mongering. Clay despised Jackson for various reasons and delighted in provoking those close to him. He mockingly called him "King Andrew Jackson," comparing him to King George III of England for the endless executive orders he issued, bypassing elected officials. Clay had organized a new party, separate from the Democratic Party, called the "Whigs," for those who shared his opposition to Jackson.

Regardless, Calhoun had come to offer a compromise—a quid pro quo. He had come to discuss, yet again, tariffs—specifically, the modification of tariffs. While Jackson's European tariff policies had been beneficial for small farm economies, it had hurt the large production farms in the south. The stubborn man had already vetoed Calhoun and Clay's bill to support the construction of a freight road through Kentucky, connecting the southern states to the north. Jackson insisted it was obvious that the project was meant to enrich a private company and benefit only one specific state, hence the veto. It had been a slap in the face to Calhoun and Clay.

Jackson constantly belabored his vision of humble farmers purchasing small 40 acre tracts from the government for $1.25 per acre without addressing the economic impacts. Such a policy would draw away laborers who were needed to grow manufacturing in the eastern states by inspiring dreams of their own chance at wealth. Jackson casually dismissed the senators' arguments as elitist. He spewed his favorite quote at them: "The great can protect themselves, but the poor and humble require the arm and shield of the law." In any case, Calhoun and Clay wanted something in return for this plan of Jackson's.

Let's see how reasonable he might be with the offer Calhoun had in his pocket. Henry Clay had gathered supporters for a bill to restrict the sale of western federal lands. With northern and southern backers, they had enough votes to override a presidential veto.

There it was: Tariff modifications to Clay and Calhoun's satisfaction and road construction in exchange for Jackson's ability to continue his vision of western expansion...

******

Easter paced on the deck of the flatboat, deftly avoiding the numerous crates and sacks that comprised the vessel's freight. They shared this massive barge with three other families. One group consisted of three brothers and an Irish comrade, heading for the mines near Galena in Illinois. Easter and Will's destination was Marion Township in Monroe County, Ohio. The flatboat would deliver them far enough down the Ohio River to Jackson Township, allowing them to bypass most of the land travel, and they would make their way from there. The third family, the Thompsons, was a married couple with two teenage sons and a seven-year-old daughter, also destined for homesteading. All would be disembarking at Jackson Township in Monroe County. The aspiring miners would cut across Ohio to reach their Illinois destination.

After Andrew Jackson won the election, Will and Easter had married, made meticulous plans, purchased and sent their homesteading supplies by freight to await them at the end of Lake Erie, and finally headed west via the Erie Canal. Everything had happened so swiftly. Ma and Pa had been hesitant at first, but Easter had fallen for Will, and Will was leaving. It was now or possibly never, and so they had relented.

Will had a dream: a commodity farm in Ohio. The land was affordable and fertile. President Jackson had cleared out the tribes. Thanks to his service in the Revolutionary War, Will's neighbor had been granted some land warrants in the area known as the Seven Ranges and had agreed to sell Will a 139-acre parcel for $1.00 per acre, payable with future earnings from their farm. This was at an even lower price than the federal land sale President Jackson had initiated.

Pa conceded their vision had a good probability of success.

With the completion of the Erie Canal, goods farmed in Ohio would have a robust transportation route along Lake Erie up to the canal, which could get the goods eastward for sale and trade.

In this new age, there were numerous ways to travel: by steamboat, in some cases by train, canal boats pulled by mules, or the old-fashioned way with wagon and oxen. It was a matter of choosing the most economical route that would get their supplies where they needed to go. The modern canal travel was faster, cheaper, and less risky than journeying with oxen and wagon over the rugged Appalachian trails where anything could happen. Will was so knowledgeable about such matters. To succeed, one's farm had to be close to one of the main waterways—the Mississippi, Ohio, Missouri, or Illinois Rivers—in order to reach the eastern ports through the northern Great Lakes via the canals. It was the optimal way of the day to travel and trade. Will believed that in Ohio they would make their fortune.

Together, they were living their dream.

Their first goal was to build a sustainable farm that would see them through the winter. The following year they would have extra produce to sell and pay off their debt.

During the first few weeks they had taken a flat boat, powered by mules, from Rome in New York to Lake Erie. At first the journey was exhilarating. Every time they came to a town there would be a bridge. The bowman would announce "Low bridge, everybody down," and all the people on top of the boat would duck to avoid being knocked over as they passed under the bridge. Occasionally, someone would leap off the bridge onto the boat, hitching a ride to the next town.

It was fascinating to witness the first set of tiered locks that enabled the flatboat to traverse hills. They began with entering the lock level with the canal, with the lock being closed behind them. Then, someone would open the water fall that filled their lock, floating them higher until the water level reached the next tier. This process was repeated until they were at the top of the hill, continuing on their way down the long, narrow, man-made ditch with the mule maintaining a steady pace.

It all felt so modern. Easter could envision their own farm goods making their way back to New York from their new homestead in Ohio on these very same flatboats someday.

She and Will had become utterly enamored with each other. When they married, they spent so much time in each other's arms that she was already well along with her first child by the time they embarked on their journey west. As her belly grew, they talked about the many strong sons they would have that would help them on the farm.

Once they reached Lake Erie, the trip across had been straightforward, but arranging and negotiating a shared flatboat with other travelers at a reasonable price for their freight took longer than anticipated. That worried Easter, too. One thing she excelled at was numbers. Working at the mercantile had honed those skills. Easter was fairly certain that the flatboat trip had dipped into their savings more than Will admitted. They had brought many supplies with them, including two oxen to pull their wagon for the final leg of the journey and eventually help plow the fields. Easter was fairly certain there wasn't enough left to cover the cost of seed. They had promised future earnings as payment, which meant, with no financial buffer, a single bad or missed crop could shatter their dream.

At Lake Erie, Easter had wanted to take the trail with the oxen and wagon to save on the fare. That was the plan until the Gear brothers entered the picture. The oldest Gear brother, Hezekiah, had orchestrated the whole arrangement. He had taken a liking to Will after learning that his father had fought alongside their militia in the same war. Hezekiah convinced Will and the other family to join forces with his group, which included his two brothers and his Irish friend, Thomas Wallace. Those bound for mining, rather than pioneer families heading for farming, required fewer supplies, if they were self-sufficient and content to walk much of the journey. As a result, the farm couples could fit more supplies on the boat. Easter tried to dissuade her husband, but he would not hear of it, given her "condition."

Easter now realized that these pains she had been feeling in her belly most of the day, meant that her baby was coming on this flatboat. It was so frustrating; she would have much preferred the trail. There was no privacy. To accommodate everyone's supplies and livestock, they had forgone the typical cabin enclosure for sleeping. Having grown up in the wilds of the Mohawk Valley, Easter was no stranger to sleeping on the ground and found it easy to curl up with Will on a blanket spread over straw.

The crew consisted of a single flatboatman who knew the route quite well and would be picking up some freight at their destination.

Will was shooting dice with the Gear brothers and their Irish comrade as he did most evenings. The trio had seen advertisements for miners in an eastern newspaper, inviting any able-bodied man to come to Galena. They were a ragtag lot with meager supplies and often walked the shores to catch game as the boat drifted.

Easter was pretty certain one of them was responsible for her missing rooster. She had three of the fancy brown Italian hens her father had given her. Her Italian rooster was to be the foundation of their flock at their new farm. She frowned, so disappointed. There was plenty of game in these remote lands, but the brothers couldn't wander too far from the banks or they might lose track of the flatboat, so sometimes they went a couple of days between cooked meals, subsisting on hardtack. Easter was certain they had helped themselves to her rooster. This only added to the resentment Easter already harbored for this lot. If it had not been for them, she and Will would be happily on the trail with their nest-egg intact. Hezekiah had even tried to put ideas into Will's mind about mining instead of farming, which was so infuriating.

As they journeyed down the river, Easter had supplemented supplies by foraging. She had been happy to fix the men more than a few meals with the game they caught, along with her tubers and wild rice, but their selfish consumption of her rooster had left her vexed. The pain in her belly and back allowed her little patience, and her ire rose with each contraction.

She studied the Irishman, Thomas Wallace, as he approached, evidently tired of the dice game. Typical of the Irish he was not a tall man like Will. He was a bit shorter than Easter and quite handsome with his heart-shaped face, bulging muscles, and red highlights in his honey-brown hair. His strong broad shoulders, warm disposition, and kind smile made him a welcome travel companion. Thomas was a story teller. His endless tales of Ireland, travels in the States, and work on the first-ever railroad kept her amused for hours. Well-liked by everyone, he went tirelessly about daily chores on the boat, never complaining when he did more than his share. He had told her that Hezekiah had some family back home he planned to send for once they settled in.

Easter put her hands on her hips and demanded sternly, "Thomas, which one of those rogues took my rooster?"

Thomas lifted his hat and scratched his head, appearing to study the banks of the river, watching Easter out of the corner of his eye. He liked this lass and her husband quite a lot. He couldn't imagine a more perfect woman to have at your side while seeking your fortune in these wild lands. Weighing the friendship he had forged with the Gear brothers against his new Conklin friends was difficult, but he had no reason to lie.

"Well, lassie, here's the thing. I'm not saying one of those lads didn't sneak your rooster off the boat, cook it, and eat it, and I'm not saying one did."

Easter watched as the Irishman tilted his head to one side grinning with that dimpled smile of his. He always made her feel pretty, even in her late state of pregnancy.

"Well, if they told me they were that hungry I would have gladly cooked them up something that did not include my farm stock," Easter snapped back.

"I have no doubt of that, lass," Thomas replied respectfully. He noticed the way she was holding her back and wincing. He had witnessed family members in labor more than a few times to recognize the signs. "Would you like me to ask Mrs. Thompson to come over and sit with ya?"

Easter snorted, still angry, and feeling a bit of rage rising.

Thomas had been around enough Irish women to know this little lass was definitely getting her dander up. He stepped back a bit as he watched her narrow her eyes, focusing on the men at their game. Then she put her hands on her hips and raised herself to her full height, which was very impressive indeed, easily an inch or so taller than himself.

"Will!" Easter's voice almost sounded like a roar. It commanded everyone on the boat to take notice. The men stopped mid-roll of the dice and focused on the source.

"Ahhhh…" Easter followed with a moan and then began to pant, leaning into her first heavy labor pain with her hands supporting her belly. Thomas stepped back not sure what to do. Will came running like a scared rabbit, leaping over the crates to her side.

"Easter, honey, are you okay? Is it the baby? Is it coming now?"

Thomas noted the raw fear in Conklin's eyes as he watched his wife breathing deeply with her eyes closed. He was obviously frozen, not knowing what to do.

"Take her arm and steady her, lad," Thomas offered. "They'll be more than a few of these pains for her to get through before the babe comes. I've witnessed me dear cousin go through this a few times."

Will glanced at Thomas with a thankful nod and gently guided Easter onto a crate as she breathed through the last of the contraction.

At last Easter got her breath again. "Will. Will, one of those Gear's stole my rooster," she ranted loudly, focusing her attention on the brothers. The elder Gear held her gaze. The other two had their eyes on the ground, seemingly ashamed. Well at least that was something. She felt another contraction coming and bellowed as it hit.

"I want my rooster back!" she screamed at the top of her lungs. She had tears of anger streaming down her face as she breathed through her next contraction. The baby was coming fast, much faster than she had ever thought possible. She slid down on the bottom of the flat boat and snarled, "Will, you go get my rooster back now, or I'm gonna get my gun and shoot those thieving bastards, do you hear me?"

At these turn of events Thomas took his hat off and scratched his head, backing up a bit.

"Ahem, Mrs. Thompson, ma'am, d'ya think you could come over here and sit with Mrs. Conklin for a bit. I think the baby is about to arrive."

As Mrs. Thompson approached Easter looked up at Will, who stood there staring down at her helplessly. "It was to start my flock, Will." She gasped and panted while Mrs. Thompson took her hand and called to her daughter for a bucket of water.

"Go get my rooster from those Gears; go get him back."

Thomas patted Will and guided him back to the Gears.

Will rubbed the back of his head as Easter hollered, announcing another contraction. He looked at Thomas then faced Hezekiah. Thomas offered up, "Ahem, well we all know the lass's rooster is gone. Women can get quite out of their minds during child birth don't ya know?"

"I don't have the woman's rooster," Hezekiah Gear responded flatly.

"Well, we all know that, but we all know that one of ya took it," Thomas retorted.

Hezekiah shrugged his shoulders and studied the bank.

"Listen, I like you, Hezekiah, and I like your brothers. But ya know, I believe that little lass when she says she is gonna shoot someone for stealing her rooster."

Thomas studied Will, who was looking completely despondent as he replied, "Easter does have quite a temper. I'll see what I can do after the baby comes, but…"

Everyone was uncomfortable. Hezekiah started glaring at the spot where Easter and Mrs. Thompson were attending to the birth. He folded his arms stubbornly.

"Nobody knows what happened to the damn rooster; it probably flew overboard. Will Conklin, are you telling me you can't control your own woman?"

Thomas tilted his head impatiently. Everybody knew the rooster was safely penned in a crate with rest of the chickens and could not be released without some kind of human assistance.

Will responded with a dark look, first at the brothers and then at the place where his wife was giving birth. They could get by without the damn rooster. There were more important things, like forging friendships and contacts with other settlers they met along the way. Things were not off to a good start. Easter was very opinionated and had brought a couple of books with her that her father had given her on homesteading and farming. She was constantly quoting them to him. He did not need any books to tell him how to farm. He was lighter on cash now than he had planned, having overspent on the flatboat trip. He'd actually considered changing strategy and following the Gear brothers to the mines in Galena to earn a bit more, but Easter would not hear of it. They had already invested heavily in their homestead, and she insisted that switching their plans now could ruin them financially. She spouted numbers and dollar figures at him, like bullets, until he finally conceded. And now she had insulted the Gear brothers by threatening to shoot at them. He glared in her direction again. Easter was pretty stubborn and determined to get restitution. But, as her husband, it was his job to take care of her. He thought about what Easter's Pa would likely do in this situation. Philo certainly would not likely allow such an indignity. In fact he would likely be quite blunt about it. A confrontation it was to be then…

"So Daniel," Will addressed the middle Gear brother, as he rubbed the back of his neck, glancing over his shoulder at Easter. "Did you take Easter's rooster?" Will folded his arms and looked at the man. Logically the middle brother was the likely suspect. The youngest was more of a pup who followed his brothers around, doing their bidding. Hezekiah was too dignified for such an act. Daniel was acting sullen and shifty, refusing to meet Will's gaze.

Will's irritation grew. All the man had to do was own up and offer to pay. He gave Daniel's shoulder a shove. "I'm talking to you, pal."

Daniel immediately puffed up and shoved Will back in the chest with both hands. "You keep to your business, and I'll keep to mine," he seethed.

The quick rise in temper was a surprise to everyone. Will, anger mounting, pushed him hard in the shoulder again. "How about you just answer the question, Daniel. Did ya take it? You took it, didn't you. Why don't you just admit it?"

Thomas became alarmed as the mood turned dark. A confrontation on this small vessel did not bode well for anyone.

Hezekiah tried to intervene, "Look, Conklin, anything could have happened to the rooster."

Will quickly retorted loudly, advancing again toward Daniel. "Anything could have happened to the rooster? We all know what happened to the rooster. Daniel stole it. Daniel is a God-damn thief!"

At that, Will grabbed Daniel by his shirt and pulled him forward. Daniel threw a punch which grazed Will's ear. Will got in two quick punches to Daniel's gut before Thomas and Hezekiah pulled them apart. Hezekiah held Will in a bear hug with his arms pinned and Thomas pushed Daniel back.

"Just hold up here, hold up, all right?" Hezekiah growled.

As the two men calmed down they exchanged bitter glares like a pair of wolves circling each other.

Thomas, decidedly on the Conklin's side in the matter, decided to intervene.

"Tell ya what I'm gonna do," Thomas announced, "Hezekiah, I appreciate you and your brothers bringing me along for the work in the mines. I'm thankful and looking forward to the work. I'll pledge to get the lass a replacement for her rooster, Will, she knows it's gone for good. I travel light on me feet. I'll secure you one when we get to Jackson Township, if not before, and then I'll catch up with Hezekiah and his brothers in Galena when we finish our business." Thomas offered the men his finest Irish grin, the dimples in both his cheeks and his glowing face slowly easing the tension.

At last, Hezekiah shrugged his shoulders and sat with his brothers to resume their dice game. Will and Daniel continued to exchange embittered glances.

"Thomas, you don't have to..." Will rubbed the back of his neck again shaking his head. Easter deserved restitution from the Gear brother.

Thomas interrupted, "The little lass has made me more than a few home cooked meals on this trip. I am delighted to return the favor in this wee small way. It will take her mind off her troubles and allow her to focus on the wee babe."

In conclusion, Thomas offered Will a swig of whiskey, which he eagerly accepted, happy to put the conundrum behind him. The two drank well into the night, serenaded by Easter's bellowing, and at last to the sound of a strong newborn's wail.

1830 - An act of removal

This massacre, this horrid crime,
To baulk this wicked plot!
My parole given!, by Heaven I could,
I Would, regard it not.

LESS THAN A YEAR LATER...

Nestled in the backwoods of Tennessee, Elizabeth observed her husband as he sat by the stone hearth, a gentle fire casting a warm glow throughout the room. At forty-five years of age, David Crockett had accomplished more than most men could ever dream. As a war veteran, former magistrate, town commissioner, and now a multi-term congressman representing Tennessee, his presence was striking. Tall, lean, and clean-shaven, with a straight nose and inquisitive eyes, David commanded attention wherever he went. Although he could converse in plain language with ordinary folk, he was actually quite articulate and studious.

When not attending to his congressional duties, David often donned comfortable leather pants, a home-spun shirt, and moccasins, just as he was dressed at this very moment. Elizabeth rarely saw him in his formal congressional attire: a starched white shirt, black waistcoat, cloth trousers, fine leather boots, and a matching silk vest. Handsome as he was, David had a gift for storytelling that captivated everyone he encountered—a talent that endeared him to his constituents.

Elizabeth still held on to the hope that their family might one day achieve affluence. David had even hinted at aspirations of running for president; however, a few ill-fated business ventures had left them struggling with debt. The devastating flood of 1821 had washed away their gristmill and distillery, setting them back considerably. Undeterred, David continued his political career, fearlessly championing what he believed was right, even when it meant facing the most powerful men in the state and the nation.

David was reading a letter for at least the fifth time. His thick furrowed brow and down-turned lips betrayed his concern about the contents. The letter was from Chief John Ross, a representative of the Cherokee nation. David was one of a few in congress that supported the Natives' position.

"Problems, Davy?" Elizabeth gently prodded. Their children were tucked in bed and it was relatively quiet. Elizabeth ran a tight household and cherished her couple of hours of solitude in the evenings. When David was home, it always disrupted her routine. As her second husband—her first having been killed by the Creek —Elizabeth was accustomed to managing things on her own. She wasn't sure if she preferred his presence or absence more…

"Well, things are looking pretty hopeless for Chief Ross," he replied.

David gazed thoughtfully at Elizabeth, a sad smile on his face. His wife was a beauty, and he cherished her company. Her independence suited them both. Elizabeth was capable of running their farm and raising their six children singlehandedly when David was away. Three children were from David's previous marriage, two from Elizabeth's, and one they shared. This visit home would be brief, and he was sorely distracted by the president's intensified removal efforts. Soon, he would have to return to Washington.

It was a rare occasion for a letter to reach him at their home in western Tennessee. David's wanderlust often found him traveling far and wide. When not attending to congressional duties in Washington, he could be found on a long hunt, visiting neighboring forts, acting as a scout soldier, or even guiding settlers further west in search of more affordable land.

David took a sip of the whiskey his wife had discreetly poured for him and pondered the letter before him. John Ross was a dear friend. He was the son of a mixed blood Cherokee mother and a Scottish father; as such, he was well spoken in both the Cherokee language and English.

Chief Ross himself was a business man at heart. In his younger days he had built a trading post and run ferry services. In fact, the majority of the Cherokee council that had negotiated treaties were men like Ross: those of mixed heritage, English speaking, and well educated. David's compatriot, Sam Houston, the former governor of Tennessee and a confidant of President Jackson, had joined Chief Ross in speaking in favor of Cherokee rights. Sam and his Cherokee woman also ran a trading post and had a deep interest in advocating for the Natives.

As part of the Cherokee National Council, Ross had labored tirelessly to negotiate borders, land titles, and rights for the Cherokee Nation. John Eaton, Jackson's minion, had dealt the first blow. Eaton informed Chief Ross that President Jackson would be supporting states' rights, extending local laws over the Cherokee people and taking precedence over federal statutes.

But the worst blow had come recently. Despite opposition from David, Senator Henry Clay, and a few others, this insidious bill had passed. On May 28, 1830, the Indian Removal Act had been signed into law. Now Jackson would begin systematic negotiations with tribes to cede their lands in exchange for money and other government lands that, for the most part, were wastelands nobody wanted anyway. Granted this would pave the way for more lucrative lands for settlers out west and accelerate Jackson's westward expansion vision, but what about the human cost to the Natives? Jackson's position was that relocation served their best interests, as remaining in settled or soon-to-be-settled lands risked their extinction.

David's thoughts turned to his time serving under General Jackson alongside his comrades, Sam Houston and John Ross. He never could have imagined back then that their futures would lead them to their current positions: David as a Congressman, Sam as the former governor of Tennessee, and John Ross as the chosen chief and primary representative of the Cherokee Nation. Their relationships with this president were indeed complex and fraught with tension.

Over time, David had come to believe that Jackson was stubborn, vengeful, and prone to physical violence. It wasn't that there weren't other statesmen with a penchant for violence; rather, it was crucial to know which individuals might be inclined to inflict personal harm in response to a heated debate. Jackson was such a man and had proved himself so many times before becoming president. Sam Houston was such a man as well…

The former president, John Quincy Adams, was not one to resort to violence, nor were the Jeffersonian presidents—Monroe, Madison, and Thomas Jefferson himself.

Granted, Jackson had roared like a lion at the country's powerful elites when they sought to buy up the cheap government lands and sell them at a profit. If allowed, it would have not only gouged the pioneers but also prevented those with few assets from achieving their own independence out west. Many eastern elites did not want these inexpensive lands luring workers from their coastal manufacturing enterprises. In the face of Jackson's opposition, the elites had indeed backed down.

What pained David greatly was Jackson's willingness to see these lands going to greenhorn Germans, Swedes, Irish, and other European immigrants while denying the American Natives. They not only knew the country like the back of their hands but had also lived alongside colonials for well over a hundred years in some cases. Often, local natives assisted these new settlers in survival and proved to be invaluable neighbors.

When a soft tear spilled down one of David's cheeks, Elizabeth walked over, stood behind him, and put her hands on his shoulders. Silently, he took her hand as he read the letter yet again. It reflected Chief Ross's admiration of Jackson since his boyhood and recanted his service alongside Jackson during the war. With regret, Ross now felt Jackson's policies toward Natives was unrelenting and indeed ruinous.

David's days as a frontiersman, soldier, and scout for the army had held fewer heartaches than this life of politics. He yearned to don his coonskin cap, pickup his long rifle, and head out west to somewhere so remote the politics of the day could not reach. His primary focus thus far had been on getting folks fair prices and access to government land sales, but now there was this. Although most folks from Tennessee supported the act, David felt it unconscionable. His honor was at stake and thus his vote against. He loathed Jackson for these callous, dehumanizing acts.

In the letter Ross thanked Crockett and Henry Clay for voting against the bill, a vote so unpopular in David's home state that it would surely cause him to lose his seat in Congress. It also announced that the Chief would be challenging the law in the Supreme Court.

"Chief Ross says here he thinks my constituents might support my position." David snorted, "Whoa doggy did he get that wrong."

He paused for a moment then declared resolutely, "Regardless, he'll fight like hell. John Ross is not one to go quietly into the night."

Elizabeth nodded in silence and squeezed his shoulders again.

Jackson would certainly have a fight on his hands, but ultimately the majority and prevailing winds of opinion were on his side. There was no doubt who would emerge as winners and losers...

1831 - Den Lul Brune Hoens

The cheerful robin's sturdy note,
The gay canary's trill,
Blent with the low of new-milked kine
That sauntered by the rill.

LESS THAN A YEAR LATER...
Easter – 19, Will – 23, Phoebe – 7 months

The tall dry grass swayed in peculiar patterns, defying the stillness of the gentle morning mist. In fact, there was no wind at all to stir it, and yet it moved. Two observers watched these strange patterns, each unaware of the other.

It was not easy to sneak up on Erielhonan Long-Tail. As a skilled hunter, he preferred the art of the sling to the violence of war. His woman had tasked him not to come home without something specific, and he was on the hunt for it. Drawn by the distinctive gobble of a large bird, he now approached with caution, knowing full well these creatures were quite savvy and not easily ambushed. With his sling at the ready, Erielhonan focused on the rustling field. The contented purrs of the feeding flock assured him they were not aware of his presence. With the amount of swaying grass it was likely multiple bird families had gathered. Erielhonan needed a male, and precision was crucial.

Suddenly, the flock's purring shifted to shrill yelps. He hadn't moved, so something else had startled them. With astonishing speed, a woman burst from the tree line, expertly whirling a sling over her head. Erielhonan could only gape as she dashed into the scattering birds. Akin to a wolf, she lunged at something, but the tall grass obscured his view. All he knew was the woman had an infant strapped to her back, and from what he could tell, was white. Having missed his chance at the prey, he was curious and decided to take a closer look.

As Easter's stone struck the male turkey, she could tell it was merely stunned. Wasting no time, she sprinted to the thrashing bird, pinned it down, and swiftly severed its head with her small hatchet. The turkey was an impressive size. It would certainly make a hearty dinner with leftovers to spare. Grinning with delight at her prize, she could not wait to get it home and dressed. Her focus was so intense she failed to notice the Native man approaching. As she stood up, he seemed to materialize before her, a silent statue studying her thoughtfully. Her smile faltered.

The man stood a couple inches shorter than Easter, his long dark hair streaked with gray, partially pulled back by a pair of feathers that draped gracefully. He wore a fringed leather tunic without sleeves, his muscles rippling with each gesture. Around his neck hung an intricate bone disk, its pattern carved around a central hole. A double-wrapped belt held a beautifully beaded pouch, hinting at valued possessions within. He wore no paint. The leather leggings and beaded moccasins gave him a civil appearance, absent the fear a war-painted Native might inspire. Although armed with a hatchet, club, and sling, Easter felt no fear.

Amid the flock's chortles, the pair stared at each other until finally little Phoebe, on Easter's back, broke the silence, jabbering and cooing while attempting to chew on a strand of her mother's hair.

The Native man nodded in greeting, and Easter nodded back. He appeared curious but not threatening. She quickly scanned their surroundings, confirming he was alone, likely hunting, just like her.

She spoke to him in her mother's Algonquin tongue and was relieved when he understood her. They could communicate.

"Greetings, brother. How are you on this fine day?"

"Goodly, sister. I was at hunt... but you got the bird first," he motioned to her catch.

Easter smiled, lifting her turkey, "My aim ran a bit low, he almost got away. I just stunned him."

"Hmm," the Native responded, "I have never seen a white woman hunt with a sling before."

"An Algonquin woman taught me to hunt when I was young," Easter replied.

The Native man glanced at the ground and towards the trees where the bird chatter echoed, "My woman told me not to come home without Father Neyhom. She wants the meat and the feathers." He good-naturedly shrugged at Easter.

Recognizing Neyhom as the Algonquin name for turkey, Easter said, "Well, here." She quickly knelt, cut the wings and tail from the turkey and handed them to him. "There was only one father with that flock. You can catch Sister Neyhom for the meat, and your woman can still have these feathers."

The Native man's face broke into a broad smile, "Many thanks to you. I can save face with my woman now. I am Erielhonan Long-Tail."

Easter returned his smile, "I am Easter, and this is little Phoebe Ann."

The Native man nodded once more, holding up the feathers, then turned and walked silently through the grass following the distant sounds of the turkey flock.

As he vanished, Easter's curiosity stirred. She'd seen no signs of a village nearby, but these wilds were vast, and they might be just passing through. If she crossed paths with Erielhonan Long-Tail again their meeting would likely be less happenstance, and she could glean more information without seeming rude.

"All right Phoebe, let's get this bird home and on the hearth. We want to cook it slow so it will be tender."

Upon reaching the tree line, Erielhonan Long-Tail paused to look back at the white woman. Tall and confident, she hoisted the large bird over her shoulder and strode in the opposite direction. Her steps were resolute yet silent, and despite her youth, she seemed well at home in the woodlands. It was rare to find a young white woman navigating the forest on her own, let alone with a baby on her back. The fact that she spoke a Native tongue fluently was astonishing. He wondered if her man approved. She was certainly well skilled with her sling. Regardless, this would make a fine story to tell around the campfire, and he would be delighted to hold up the feathers she had gifted him for any who did not believe his tale.

Easter expertly arranged her hearth, stacking two Dutch ovens for dinner with little Phoebe Ann secured to her back. She stepped outside the one-room cabin to gauge the time left before sun-down. Just as she had learned when she was young, she placed both hands on top of each other and then again on top of the horizon, taking away fingers until the sun rested at the top of one. Each finger was about fifteen minutes until sundown. Six fingers remained— roughly an hour and a half. Will and Thomas Wallace would return home just before sundown, ready to wash up, and she would ensure their meal was freshly cooked, hot, and delicious. Satisfied, she stepped back inside and adjusted the coals.

When they first married she and Will had dreamt of the sons they would raise that would help them build their homestead in the wilderness, and then their first born turned out to be a girl. Will, however, took it in stride, "If she is as strong as her mother she is worth two sons put together."

Upon arriving in Jackson Township the previous September, Thomas Wallace, true to his word, had secured her a rooster from one of the locals in town. Not only that, he had grown so fond of her and Will that he offered to stay and help them get started in exchange for just room and board. Easter had been right: Will had fallen a bit short of seed money, but she came up with another way to obtain their planting seed.

At first, Will was quite irritated with her fixation on her chickens. When they secured their land in the fall, they had to live out of the wagon, as Easter had insisted that the first structure built be a sturdy henhouse to protect her new flock from predators. Now, she had a healthy flock of laying hens scratching in the garden by day and roosting in their secure henhouse at night. Not only did they enjoy fresh eggs for breakfast every day and the occasional roast chicken dinner, but they also had a valuable commodity to trade with the mercantile during their monthly visits to church. It wasn't a significant income, but it added a touch more richness to their lives than they might have otherwise experienced.

She had traded with a Danish neighbor who lived about three miles from them one good laying hen, a copper pot, and a couple of fine wool blankets her parents had given them when they got married for some wheat and corn for both flour and planting. The man, Lars Hansen, had taken a liking to her and threw in a young ewe and one of the pups from his herding dogs to boot. He was quite taken with "den lul brune hoen," which, he told her, was Danish for "the little brown hen." She was one of Easter's three best layers brought all the way from Herkimer that had started her flock. This little hen was descended from a strong European stock. Hansen had a good eye and was very keen on improving his own flock.

The pup she named Ned, after her father's favorite workhorse. Hansen told her Ned's mother was a Buhund, a breed preferred by the Danes as a working dog. Now it was spring, Ned was mostly grown and well tutored, with Hansen's help, to protect stock when they foraged during the day.

Easter had taken some of the wheat to the grist mill in Long Bottom. The owner of the grist mill, one Jake Stone, had turned the wheat into the most beautiful flour she had ever seen. With the progress Will and Thomas were making, their new fields would soon be ready to plant, and next September she would be proud to make bread from their own home grown grain. From her recent count, her next baby would be born sometime in September as well, hopefully a son. But for now they were still focusing on building a sustainable farm for their growing family.

Most folks in the area were growing corn, but Easter had

convinced Will to plant one field in wheat. Although corn would be more sustainable for the farm in terms of feed for the livestock and the family, according to her Pa's farm journals, wheat was purported to be a better cash crop, and they needed that money to pay off the land.

Her father continued to send her cut-outs from his Gazettes. One of his favorites was John Skinners American Farmer. Pa paid four dollars a year for his subscription and always posted a copy in the mercantile for locals to come and read. It covered all types of modern ways of farming like new crops, improvements in tillage, fertilization, crop rotation and drainage, how to pick the best breeding livestock, all kinds of things. Will was not always interested in her ideas, but his ears perked up when she read some of the authors of the views and essays were none other than Thomas Jefferson and James Madison.

For the most part the journal reported on agriculture and methods that produced the best results, but occasionally there would be some political matters that might affect a farmer's welfare, reminding the farming community not to become apathetic. It was important to stay active in obtaining legislation to protect their interests. The journals stressed that cheap, safe, and quick transportation was indispensable to the prosperity of the farmer and informed farmers when better routes to market became available.

Only this last week she had entertained Will and Thomas with a ladies section in the journal where Skinner invited "Farmeresses" to post their recipes, household hints, poems, and other items of interest, calling out examples of the contributions of women to the home and farm. It made Easter proud to be part of this cohort.

Easter had planted a patch of flax near their shack, which was already starting to sprout. Her ewe was ready to be shorn and would be able to breed this year. So, by next year, with twins God willing, she would have three sheep, and likely more if she could trade some fine ground flour for a couple more of Hansen's young ewes. With Ned's help, Easter was a fierce protector, and so far no predators had succeeded in pilfering her stock. With the flax and the wool, she would be able to make homespun cloth for family clothes, farm sacks, cordage, and other items they might need.

In the mean time they were still mostly living off the land. Easter did most of the hunting and foraging, with Phoebe Ann strapped to her back in Native style. There was no end to wild game. Meat and hides for their homestead were not a problem. She had even tanned some hides for new shoes, warm water resistant shirts, and pants. This allowed Will and Thomas to focus on building the initial cabin they would live in the first couple of years and clearing the land.

And now suddenly they were at the point where they had three good fields almost ready to plant. Without Thomas, they would have had only one field; Easter was certain of this. Thomas Wallace had been a true godsend. And she made damn certain he had tasty meals for his troubles, along with comfortable moccasins and gloves for everybody.

Easter grimaced at the sun, which was now at two fingers. Just as she had predicted, Thomas and Will were cresting the hill with the oxen.

Thomas watched as Easter waved warmly. Will, however, remained unresponsive, so Thomas took it upon himself to return her cheerful gesture, as usual. He couldn't smell what was cooking, but his mouth watered in anticipation. Conklin seemed to take for granted the remarkable partner he had in Easter. In Thomas's travels he had seen more than a few settlers starving or barely scratching out a living, failing in their pursuit of their dreams, graves from women dying in childbirth, and mostly farmers with no wives at all. To be living among a warm loving family with a woman and babe, with home-cooked meals was a true blessing. It nurtured his aching soul. He sorely missed his family. He missed his homeland of Ireland to which he could never return. Mostly he missed his dear Ma.

Easter was pulling her weight more than any woman he had ever met—cheerful, even thriving. They had warm meals every evening, and she managed the homestead single-handedly. Conklin indeed was a fortunate man. Thomas couldn't help but imagine the babe at Easter's waist and the small shack they were approaching belonging to him. Ah, dreams were the stuff men were made of, his dear Ma used to say. He would have his own, someday. That wee babe on Easter's hip would make some man a fine wife with Easter bringing her up for sure.

Thomas was fascinated with Easter's ability to use the wilds of this country to support the family. Although he had been raised on a farm himself, it was an Irish farm. Living off of the wilds wasn't something someone of recent European descent really knew how to do. He had been taking note of Easter's example, preparing to emulate her ways when he would eventually be on his own again.

"Hello, darlin', what's that amazing smell coming from your hearth?" Thomas grinned warmly at Easter.

She frowned a bit when Will didn't even look at her as he and Thomas unharnessed the Oxen and settled them. She figured he must be in a bad mood.

"A roast turkey I snared in the hickory grove, some wild rice, and cornbread." Easter replied with a smile.

"Ah, I can't wait, lass." Thomas beamed at her.

Will approached Easter, scooping up a cooing Phoebe Ann into his arms. He winked at Easter, still saying nothing, and went inside.

Conklin was an odd man, Thomas mused. In Ireland a man kissed his wife when he left for the day and when he came home. This man was cold, except for when he bedded the lass. Thomas had always been taught that a lass was like a flower. You needed to keep her watered with affection or she would wilt and her beauty fade. He hoped that fate would not befall Easter.

Thomas's feet were starting to itch for the promise of work in Galena. It was time for him to move on and seek his fortune. After all, Father Rathmore had taken great risks on his behalf, and it was now his duty to make something of himself. Following the spring planting he would be heading to Galena to catch up with the Gears and try his hand at mining. He had heard tales of generous wages paid in glistening silver, the perfect means to earn his own nest egg. The American dream was slowly taking root in Thomas's mind. There was no reason an Americanized Irishman, like himself, couldn't possess a homestead of his own, akin to the Conklin's. In addition to aiding this family, his months of toil on the homestead had taught him the skills needed to carve out a place of his own.

All that remained was to gather enough coin to register his own claim. While many pioneers were resorting to squatting, Thomas craved the security of owning his land outright, free from the fear of someone seizing the soil he had labored to transform from untamed wilderness into a thriving farm. America was not Ireland, where the common man had no choice but to pour his sweat and blood into enriching the estates of wealthy landowners.

Recently, one of the newspapers Easter enjoyed perusing had announced that the Indian Removal Act, signed into law by President Jackson, had unlocked even more fertile lands for settlement in the territories further west. Thomas was resolute in his pursuit of the American dream, not only for himself but also in the hope that, against all odds, he could persuade some of his Irish kin to join him someday.

Later in the evening, after Thomas and Will had indulged in a hearty meal, they sat by the fire, watching as Phoebe Ann crawled from one person to the next. With pride, she pulled herself into a standing position, awaiting the expected applause. She would be walking soon, Easter thought. Best to get Ned taught to keep her herded up with the rest of the stock. She smiled to herself.

Glancing over at Will, she noticed him eyeing her with trepidation. Something was amiss.

"What is it Will?" Easter asked patiently.

Will glanced at his wife and then into the fire, dreading the conversation to come.

"We don't have enough wheat seed left to plant that field you wanted," he confessed.

"What do you mean? I saved some in a barrel in the root cellar. We have enough."

"I had to trade it a while back. I didn't mention it. The two ploughs cost more than I expected. I needed a bit more coin for some supplies... to clear the fields."

Thomas held his breath. Easter had her heart set on that field in wheat. Conklin pilfering her wheat seed without asking would likely ruffle her feathers.

"I'm going to take a nice walk in the night air," Thomas announced and quickly darted out the door.

Easter was silent. She felt a rage brewing in her gut. Everything had been planned. He had taken her wheat and not asked. "What supplies?" she inquired, her voice tinged with darkness.

"It's none of your concern, Easter," Will replied sharply.

"None of my concern, Will Conklin? None of my concern? Then how do you expect us to pay off the land next fall, Will? What if he won't wait and all this work we have done will be for nothing? He could sell our improved land to someone else. What if he makes us leave and we have to start over, with no money? What if—"

Will interrupted. "Easter it's done. I'm not ask'in. I'm tellin' you, it's done and gone. We'll figure it out during harvest."

At that Will abruptly walked out of the house.

Later Easter crawled up into the loft with Phoebe Ann. She could hear Thomas and Will outside. They had built a fire and were drinking whiskey. She wondered, with a hint of bitterness, where they had procured it in this remote place, and if that was the "supplies" Will had alluded to. Lying there, she pondered the situation.

At last she made a decision. Desperation gnawed at her, and she knew what she had to do.

******

Lars Hansen was plowing his last field in preparation for planting. He was fortunate to have three strapping sons to help him in the fields: fifteen, twelve, and ten years old. Sadly they had no daughters to assist his wife, Frieda, around the homestead. Lacking in women folk to talk to, Frieda often succumbed to melancholia and loneliness. It pained Lars to see his normally robust wife in such a sad state. Sometimes, her sadness would linger for weeks. Once, he and his sons returned from a hunting trip to find Frieda delirious and gravely ill in her nightclothes. She had stopped eating and become manic from the isolation. The farm animals roamed about, unfed. It took nearly a month of tender care to dispel Frieda's melancholia and help her recover. Now, Lars was afraid to leave her alone.

A doctor suggested it could be symptoms of encroaching prairie madness, a condition experienced by some women settlers who couldn't bear the solitude and harsh environment of homesteading compared to their previous, more civilized lives. The doctor had tried bleeding Frieda to alleviate the perceived illness, but it had only worsened her condition. A mild case of prairie madness might involve a woman taking to her bed and hallucinating. The doctor told him of more extreme cases, with some women committing suicide or needing to be confined in an attic or asylum for good. There was a well-known instance of a man returning home to find his wife had killed all of their children due to such an affliction. The thought of Frieda possibly losing her mind permanently was utterly terrifying.

Frieda's face always brightened when their nearest neighbor, Easter Conklin, appeared on the horizon for a visit. Easter hadn't been by in a while. Curiously, she always seemed to come to Lars's mind just before she materialized. He glanced up the hill...and sure enough, there she was. He smiled at the Viking-like figure approaching him across the field. Easter was every bit as tall and strong as his Frieda, although his wife's features were much fairer, with the blondest of tresses.

Easter carried her babe on her back, a sack of something in her hands, and intriguingly, her finest lul brune hoen tucked under one arm. She must be hoping to trade for something special. Lars had tried to coax her out of that particular hen since he'd traded for the last one. He grinned from ear to ear as Frieda came running out of their well-established farmhouse, her face brimming with childlike delight and waving a greeting.

After visiting with Frieda for a while, Easter approached Lars with her proposition. She knew that her lone chicken, along with leather gloves, pants, and a shirt, wouldn't suffice for a barrel of good wheat seed. Prepared to offer labor as well, she acknowledged her desperation. The walk to this homestead was quite long, but she was determined.

Lars thoughtfully observed Easter after listening to her offer. He had planned on planting another field this year and possessed just a bit of extra seed. They both knew that one chicken and the leather goods wouldn't be enough for this barter. He could hear Frieda humming in the cabin as she made flatbread and tea. Her mood had shifted dramatically from despondency to joy. This visit would cheer her up for a day or two, but then she would likely return to her gloomy disposition. Lars didn't want to discourage Easter's friendship by disappointing her. Frieda needed the companionship that only another woman could provide. Suddenly, he had an idea...

"I know the seed is important to you, Easter, I do, and I want to help you. But I have to be fair to myself and my family as well."

Easter nodded, feeling ashamed that she couldn't offer more. Her mind raced, considering what else she might do to sweeten the deal. But then Lars made a surprising offer.

"My wife has been very lonely out here, and she's been struggling quite badly with melancholia. How about we trade the wheat seed for your leather goods, two of your lul brune hoens, and on top of that, you make the trek to our farm once a week or so for the next three months to visit Frieda? It would help her to feel less lonely."

Easter mulled over the offer and knew that she couldn't afford to turn it down. They shook hands on it with Easter feeling both elated and deeply concerned for Frieda's well-being. Whispers among settlers told stories of remote homesteads sometimes robbing women of their sanity, particularly those accustomed to more populous eastern lifestyles. It made Easter quite sad to think that Frieda could succumb to such a fate and made her determined to do everything in her power to help.

******

That evening, when Will and Thomas returned home, Easter was not at the door waving to them. As they went about their business, they smelled dinner cooking as usual. A barrel sat next to the door. Will peeked inside, running his hands through the fine wheat seed and narrowing his eyes.

Thomas observed that it appeared to be at least some seventy pounds of grain. It was no small task to get home without a stock-animal to help. He wondered how far she traveled to fetch it, and with a babe on her back no less.

"Easter," Will demanded as he entered the house. "Where did you get it? Did you borrow on it?" His eyes were narrowed and accusatory. At this turn of events Thomas was happy to wait outside. That Easter was surely a stubborn lass for sure.

Will glowered at Easter as she set plates on their home-hewn table and ignored his question.

At last he demanded again, "Easter, were did you get it?"

"I traded Lars Hansen one of my little brown hens that I brought with me from Herkimer along with some leather goods," she responded flatly. "There should be enough there to plant one field. He was short on seed, so I owe him the last hen as well. I'll be taking her over to him tomorrow." A solitary tear crested the corner of Easter's eye and slid down her cheek. She sighed and continued on with her chores.

Will paused for a moment, his sullen accusatory demeanor slowly transformed into regret and remorse. Suddenly Will swept her up into his arms and hugged her close. Tears streamed down Easter's face, and he held her while she cried. She had fought so fiercely to bring those chickens from Herkimer to the homestead, keeping them alive all winter. She had insisted on building a fortress for them first, while the rest of them slept on straw under the night sky. And now she had traded her last little Herkimer brown hen away.

"I'm sorry Easter," Will whispered softly in her ear. "I'm sorry." Will looked like a sad, conscience-stricken little boy. Easter couldn't resist him.

"I have their offspring, Will." she sighed. "After all, they're just chickens. It's not like I traded Phoebe Ann away." She looked up into his eyes and giggled, "And now you can plant a field of wheat, just like we planned." She felt a warmth spread in her belly and down her spine with the thought of the reconciliation they would share later, in bed.

Will chuckled and stroked her hair, "Just like you planned, you mean. Easter, you are so damn stubborn. We'll plant it. And it won't dare not grow with you watching over it. Anyway, a barrel of seed seems a bit much for a couple of chickens and homemade leathers."

"I also agreed to visit Frieda once a week for the next three months and stay with her when Lars and the boys go hunting."

"What?"

"Frieda gets melancholia in a bad way occasionally. It cheers her up when Phoebe Ann and I visit. That was Lars's price for the seed. We won't owe them anything more."

"Huh..." Will replied, scratching his head.

When Thomas heard the cheerful voices he peeked inside and asked, "Everything okay folks? We ready to eat?"

Will and Easter broke into fits of laughter, and they all settled down for their well-earned dinner.

Easter thought back on when she was fighting to keep her chickens alive on the long trip to Ohio. She had no idea how valuable they would end up being.

It was remarkable to think that those cherished feathered creatures had proven crucial in rescuing her family's homestead, future and livelihood; her lul brune hoens...

1832 - A Man's Worth

So when the Night puts on her robes
Of sad and sable hue,
A host he sends, of shameful strength,
To oust that noble few

ONE YEAR LATER…

athed in moonlight, Blackhawk and his Sauk warriors rode across the river, their hearts ablaze with bloodlust from their recent victory. These battle-hardened men had fought alongside the British during the War of 1812 and bitterly opposed the latest increase in white settlers' intrusion and the Native border decrees that had arisen since then.

Recently, the white men had demanded that Blackhawk's people stay west of the Mississippi, completely out of what they now called the state of Illinois. Though Blackhawk had initially complied, his ancestral connection to the Illinois Native lands gnawed at him like a festering wound. He couldn't help but resent the prosperity the whites reaped from his homeland.

His formidable band included warriors from the Fox, Potawatomi, Kickapoo, and a few from the Ho-Chunk Tribes. In total, he had mustered nearly a thousand warriors to participate in the skirmishes. However, their numbers had begun to dwindle, and they had fractured into smaller, scattered bands. The whites had started organizing militias. Troops from the regular army were being summoned to defend and expel "the Native incursions." It was a story Blackhawk had witnessed time and time again. Well-versed in the art of white warfare, he smiled grimly as one of his braves rode by, brandishing a British flag—a potent reminder that they did not recognize that the Great Father in Washington had any right to dispose of the Sauk's tribal homelands.

Bit by bit, these settlers had chipped away at what once belonged to the tribes. Before their arrival, a natural rhythm had governed Blackhawk's people. In summer, they tended corn until it was knee-high. Then, while some elders and women fished and gathered reeds for mats, others journeyed to the mines. The young men went west to hunt buffalo and deer. Come autumn, they would reunite and trade dried meat, lead for making paint, dried fish, corn, and mats. The lands and waters around Rock Island had been the best farming and fishing grounds for his tribe for as long as anyone's grandfather could remember—until the whites built their fort on the island, just a stone's throw away from his ancestral village. That marked the beginning of the end.

Blackhawk would tolerate no more of these affronts. A steep price would be extracted from those who had dared to venture deepest into his sacred homelands.

******

Thomas Wallace settled himself into the small military encampment at Dixon's Ferry in Illinois. He sat down upon a rock and pulled off one boot. With a knife in hand, he attempted to bend a nail that had been poking him. He was so disappointed that his fine walking boots, purchased in Chicago, had failed him so soon. Thomas traveled light, relying on his legs and feet for transportation, his long rifle and knife for protection, and the foraging skills Easter had taught him for sustenance. The roll of scrip he'd earned from his work on the railroad supplied his modest needs as he continued to seek his fortune out west.

While passing through Chicago on his way to Galena, Thomas had learned about the Native uprising. The Indian Removal Act, which President Jackson sought to enforce through treaties with Native chiefs, had been met with resistance from some of the more obstinate tribes. Horrifying tales of brutality inflicted upon white settlers by Natives convinced Thomas that his safest option was to join one of the local militias that had assembled to repel the incursions.

Now at Dixon's ferry, his group had joined forces with a militia under General Samuel Whiteside, a reputed veteran of the War of 1812 and an experienced Native fighter. With rumors of the regular army enroute to assist them, it was very unnerving for an Irishman such as himself.

This journey, thus far, had been quite hair-raising. When passing through the central part of Ohio, Thomas thought he had gone mad when witnessing a terrifying spectacle of nature, which the Native scouts described as "the dead man walking": an incarnation of the Great Wind Spirit, Oonawieh Unggi. Near Xenia Township, powerful winds formed two colossal swirls reaching skyward, their dusty bases resembling feet. Their swirling limbs connected up to the massive thunderclouds above. Petrified, Thomas had taken shelter under hillside rock for a full day. It was all too easy for a superstitious Irishman to imagine a giant figure controlling the staggering, wind-driven legs from above the clouds. It felt as though the earth itself was as enraged at the pioneers as the Natives were for invading its pristine lands. Thomas had seen small dust devils on the prairie before but never these mountain-sized whirlwinds that swooped up and carried logs, rocks, and trees in their wake. And now, he faced the wrath of frenzied Natives attacking homesteaders. It made him yearn to flee back to the Conklin farm as swiftly as his legs would allow. But the promise he had made to Father Rathmore back in Millstreet—to build his own home with a proper Catholic family—gave him the courage to press on.

"How are you doing, soldier?"

Thomas looked up to see a gangly tall man standing over him. At once he recognized their young militia captain, Abe Lincoln, and jumped to his feet with one bare foot dangling in the air to avoid muddying it.

"Well sir, thank you sir, I'm fine, sir," Thomas responded somewhat awkwardly. Captain Lincoln was around the same age as Thomas, in his early twenties. According to the other men, this captain lacked military experience, much like the rest of them.

Lincoln replied good-naturedly, "Well, Irishman, if you are fine then you are doing better than the rest of us. We're all on edge."

Thomas displayed his engaging dimpled smile and shrugged his shoulders. "Truth be told, sir, I've only met a couple of Natives since I arrived in America. I was just on my way to try my hand at the mines at Galena. I, ah, are we going to be engaging them, do you think, sir?"

Lincoln paused a bit and responded, "Well, General Whiteside says that Major Stillman is scouting about with a force of men to see if they can locate Blackhawk's war band. We'll know more when they get back. For now, we are waiting for the main army reinforcements to arrive."

Captain Lincoln patted Thomas on the back. "Get yourself something to eat and try to get some sleep."

Thomas nodded and sat back down on the rock as the young Captain moved on to offer support to the other soldiers in their garrison.

******

Blackhawk slowly paced through the scattered Native encampment. A few communal teepees caught the rain, creating little rivers through the muck and mud. The whites called this place Old Man's Creek. Despite his cold and hungry state, Blackhawk could still summon distant memories of warm summers when vivid wildflowers blanketed the banks of the stream, their perfume irresistible to bees. Fattened horses grazed in spring grasslands while happy Native villagers went about their day with the smells of home-cooked meals over tribal fires wafting through the air, prepared by brightly beaded Native maids.

Abruptly he was snapped out of his reminiscing. Two of his young warriors, rain dripping from their hair and weapons, ran towards him. The fear in their faces told the story: White soldiers were approaching.

Blackhawk was weary. He closed his eyes. He would send emissaries and negotiate a retreat back across the river. They had made their point. The young ones did not possess the same passion for this fight that burned within him. It was time to leave this white man's Illinois country. It was no longer his homeland. The whites seemed to have chased away his ancestors' spirits with their never-ending encroachment.

******

Thomas awoke to the sounds of metal clanking and shouting. He crawled from under his blankets and started pulling on his boots, his eyes wide with panic, trying to understand. Were they under attack? Mother Mary, and Joseph, what was going on? He spotted Captain Lincoln amidst the chaos, motioning the men to come with him.

"Sir," called Thomas. "What is going on? What—?"

Lincoln stood his full six-foot-four height and barked out commands. "You men I have chosen, come with me." For a moment his eyes rested on Thomas, pointed at him, and motioned him to follow. "The rest of you stay here."

Captain Lincoln's small troop dashed over to their horses and mounted up.

Lincoln announced, "Blackhawk's war band ambushed Major Stillman's troops. Nobody knows how many were killed, but the Indians have the troops on the run. We're going with General Whiteside to look for survivors."

Thomas's preferred method of travel was on foot, and he had never once imagined traveling as a militia soldier on horseback in search of murderous Natives. Fear gripped his heart as he rode with the party into the dusky dawn. All he could do was watch the men around him and try to imitate their behaviors. Everyone was quiet and appeared steadfastly dedicated to the task at hand. Only snorting horses and hooves clipping rocks announced their passing.

As the sun slowly turned dawn into day, the party slowed.

Lincoln motioned to his men to the front, and Thomas fell in beside him. Something had been discovered up ahead. And then Thomas saw…eerily still bodies in contorted positions were strewn across a small hill. Again Thomas looked to his comrades—sharp eyes were scanning the hillside and trees all around the ghastly encampment. Silently, Lincoln moved forward and motioned to his men. Thomas mimicked the behavior as best he could. From the pacing and circling of the troops on their horses, Thomas could tell they were searching for any stray Natives that might be lingering, perhaps even trying to draw them out. The bright morning sun only accentuated the grisly scene. Most of the dead were missing pieces of their scalp, and many had been hacked and mangled, likely by hatchets. Blood was spattered and pooled all around, and buzzing flies were gathering.

Thomas had heard of such Native practices but had never borne witness to them until now. He wondered if the deeds had been done to them alive or after death. One of his comrade's stepped off his horse and began to retch.

"Nothing here, captain," a soldier reported from the ridges above. "They're long gone."

For a minute Lincoln was silent as he surveyed the dead. At last he announced, "Ahem, you men," motioning to Thomas and four others, "time to bury the dead."

With the imminent fear of a battle now relieved, Thomas found comfort in finally being assigned something he was competent at —digging holes.

******

The Sauk warriors and their allies shadowed Blackhawk as he wove in and among the war band. They were traveling across their homelands at a quick pace. Everyone was elated. Blackhawk had led them to victory against the white troops. When he had sent emissaries to the soldier camp bearing white flags to sue for peace, some of the warriors observed from the ridges above. The whites had cowardly attacked the peace emissaries, and in response Sauk scouts started firing back. Eventually, the entire war band had come to their aid, chasing and killing any whites that could not outrun them. It had been glorious. They had taken many scalps, and the warriors displayed the bloody flesh proudly on their weapons.

Blackhawk brooded glumly as he traveled with his dwindling band of warriors and their families. His people had stamina; they were brave. The hunger in their bellies hadn't been satisfied in days, and it weakened them. This battle at Old Man's Creek had not been not his intention. The whites would certainly gather a force to take revenge. It was Blackhawk's turn to run with his people and find a suitable place to possibly make a stand or perhaps slip back across the river into lands nobody wanted, for now at least. He noticed a few of his Sauk warriors with some Potawatomi riding in from the east with a couple of white female prisoners—more trouble, no doubt. He told his scouts to send word for the warriors' families and elders to make their way south, near the secret Dancing Grounds by the Maquoketa River, and stay there. Blackhawk wanted them as far away from this final battle as possible. Avoiding the massacre of innocents might save his tribe from the genocide that would surely be sent in retaliation from the Great White Father in Washington.

******

Hezekiah Gear needed workers, and not just a few. Originally, he had arrived in Galena to work in the mines, hoping to earn enough to start a homestead. However, after observing the ease at which certain mine owners were amassing fortunes, he decided he wanted the same for himself. He and his brothers had come to this place at the most opportune time. Recent incursions of miners on Winnebago native lands had resulted in the lands to be taken and the tribes pushed across the Mississippi River.

Fortune struck when, after a few short months of digging prospect holes, they had discovered and filed their claim for one of the largest lead deposits of the day. Government lands with mineral deposits were not for sale, only for lease. That made one's investment quite small, and from what he had observed, it was very problematic to get lessees to pay up. Sometimes less successful mine lessors could be coaxed to work his mine for coin.

Creating the initial mine shaft was taking more time than Hezekiah cared for, so he was desperate for workers. There was no shortage of cheap land in these parts. Labor, though, was scarce, and only those offering the most attractive wages and working conditions were rewarded.

Galena was a bustling town. Muck and mud ruled the streets, while the smells of man sweat and animal feces pervaded the air. The clatter of hammer and nail served as a lively serenade to the town which was bursting at the seams with fortune seekers.

Hezekiah stood at his usual viewpoint, just down the hill from John Dowling's Trading Post. It was a fine two-story stone building that John had built with his son, Nicholas, some five years prior. Goods were easily delivered by steamboat these days. They came up the Mississippi and into the Fever River, bringing goods right into Galena. John kept his store well-stocked and was a master of supply and demand. The man had quite a nose for what would be needed months in advance, ensuring those very goods would be available in his store for purchase.

Gazettes from the east adorned the windows of John's store, enticing potential customers to linger. Just about everyone in town passed through those doors, and Hezekiah found it the perfect place for prospecting potential miners to come and work for him. Retaining workers, however, was not easy. More often than not, they would decide, as he and his brothers had, to go off prospecting for their fortunes on their own, leaving him short of workers once again.

Hezekiah glanced at a group of youngsters with slates under their arms. They were obviously heading to the town church, which doubled as a schoolhouse for local children during the week. He had considered trying to tempt some of them with the promise of coin for a bit of work, but then decided his popularity might suffer. Hezekiah had grand plans; once he made his fortune, a man like him could become prominent, perhaps even run for some type of political office. Maintaining appearances was as important as accumulating wealth. His wife was finally enroute from back east with two of their children, who would soon be joining those same youngsters at school. He glanced back at the trading post just in time to see a sturdy looking young man entering the front door. Obviously someone new in town—perfect!

Thomas Wallace paused for a moment as he stepped into the trading post. Even in this early time of the day the place was clean, well-stocked from floor to ceiling, and ready for business. A diligent young lad was storing canned goods atop a long, wide counter hewn from an enormous tree. Bright Native blankets were neatly stacked alongside staples that any man would find appealing.

Thomas had seen quite a bit in his travels across this new country. He had learned to expect the unexpected, but nothing had prepared him for Galena. The town was bursting at the seams with excitement. He had thought it would be similar to the northern Chicago Township he had passed through. That place had been somewhat swampy and modest in size, with folks living their lives at a slow, easy pace, save for the fear of Native incursions.

Once again, under these new circumstances, Thomas felt fortunate to be alive. Captain Lincoln had discharged a number of soldiers when they reached the Apple River Fort. Most of the wayward Native forces had been reduced and were now on the run, soon to be captured. Luckily, none of Captain Lincoln's troops had engaged in battle. The worst had occurred at the Davis Settlement. Several white families had been massacred, including women and children. Two young girls had been kidnapped. They were rumored to be held by Blackhawk himself. Messengers had carried the news to various settlements, and stockades were erected so people could defend themselves against the Natives. It was said that a $2,000 reward had been offered for the girls' safe return.

Galena seemed somewhat oblivious to the explosion of

violence in the countryside. Miners and shopkeepers went about their business around town. Thomas supposed it was the mining fever spoken of by some travelers he had encountered. A prospector's fear of missing out on a once-in-a-lifetime ore-strike kept them working long hours for days on end with no rest, blind to the toll on health and wellbeing, let alone any hazards that may be lurking nearby.

"Hello, sir, my name is Nicholas. Let me know if I can help you with anything. We take coin, approved scrip, or trade goods."

Thomas smiled and tipped his hat. A sign displayed above the counter reiterated what the young man had just said. "Thank ya, lad. I'm gonna look around a bit if ya don't mind."

Nicholas returned a smile with a friendly nod and resumed his work. He noticed the Irishman pausing before the front window where his father had all the latest gazettes posted, apparently able to read. Nicholas found it interesting that most folks raised in the East, who had recently migrated, seemed to have no problem reading or counting coin. Those who had sprung from the early pioneers in the area typically did not like to trade in coin because they could not read, write, or count it. But regardless, everyone understood a fair trade, and that was what the Dowling Trading Post was known for in these parts. Whether furs, grain, ore, or coin be the currency, the Dowling Trading Post traded at a fair price to both Natives and any nationality of whites.

The variety of nationalities in this remote place was quite intriguing. Nicholas had met migrant Scots, Irish, Swedes, Germans, and Englishmen, besides the multi-generational Americans that had spawned from the original settlers or colonials from back East. The glint in their eyes was all the same—a chance for any of them to strike it rich. Some dreamed it would be from mines, others working in a trade or as shopkeepers, others as farmers. They all shared the same dream and had taken the same bold risks his father had made to make their fortunes. The more settlers arrived, the more the government pushed the Natives further west.

Transporting goods to market had become much easier now that the steamboats were making it all the way up the Mississippi River and into the Fever River, right into Galena. There were plans to build a steamboat landing dock, but for now, the steamboats would simply beach long sturdy wooden ramps for offloading cargo and passengers.

Everyone was a bit uneasy with the local Native trouble. The incursions had been close by but not in Galena. It was on everyone's minds. There had been a town meeting about the girls who had been kidnapped and families slaughtered. It certainly had unnerved him and everyone he knew.

Thomas studied one of the listings on the window. There was an advertisement for surveyors.

Surveyors Wanted
Top pay in gold coin and land scrip.
Must know how to read, write,
and cipher enough for the purpose.
Apply at the land office to Jenifer T. Sprigg, under contract to William Clark, Superintendent of Indian Affairs, War Department, for subdividing the Half-Breed Reservation for public lands in Lee County.

Above the listing for the surveyors was an unsettling announcement:

$2000.00 reward
for the safe return of the Davis girls,
kidnapped by Blackhawk's British warband.

Thomas supposed they specified "British warband" to distinguish the errant Natives from the friendly ones who had been fighting alongside the soldiers and militia. These allies provided negotiation assistance as well as scouting information about the troublemakers' whereabouts. It had taken Thomas a while to understand the differences among the local tribes. Many tribes in the area wanted no trouble and were up in arms over Blackhawk's warring behavior. It was fascinating to try and comprehend the politics of the Natives. Apparently, during the War of 1812, just as many Natives had fought with the Americans as those who had fought with the British. Both sides had long memories and to this day still warred against each other.

During his travels, Thomas had the opportunity to chat with Captain Lincoln about his ambitions. The captain hailed from New Salem in Illinois and was descended from early English colonists. He had held various jobs, including working as a rail splitter, a shopkeeper, a postmaster, and a land surveyor. Captain Lincoln was planning to run for the Illinois General Assembly.

Thomas could still hear Captain Lincoln's advice: "You know, Thomas, with your education, you could work as a surveyor. I've done it myself. It's a well-respected trade, pays well, and you could earn some land scrip. Once these Native disputes are behind us, it would be much better pay in the long run than working in the mines. Prospecting for your own mine would be quite a gamble. There are those who do it, and for a few, it pays off. But miners' work is hard-earned and less profitable than that of a successful farmer, for sure. A farmer's family will never starve in these parts. Let me give you a tip. A day's work from a learned man out west, or any man for that matter, is worth quite a bit, more than one can buy an acre of land for these days. Men are scarce; women are scarcer, and land is cheap. You are a smart man. Use your smarts wisely."

"Thomas Wallace, I do declare, fancy running into you in this place."

Thomas jumped at the sound of his name and turned around to see none other than Hezekiah Gear, his former traveling companion, walk towards him with a warm smile, his hand out in greeting.

"Hezekiah Gear, lad, what a sight for sore eyes." Thomas took his hand and shook it warmly.

As he worked, Nicholas eavesdropped while the two men exchanged pleasantries. In this vast country, in his father's small trading post, he had seen many such reunions. Once settled successfully, former neighbors and extended family often wrote home to coax folks they knew to come join them. Germans settled with Germans; Swedes with Swedes; Irish with Irish. Many local subsequent generations had forgotten their original roots and just identified as true Americans. Most everyone seemed to get along, although curious about some of the odd behaviors settlers brought with them from their homelands.

Now that Hezekiah Gear had struck a rich claim, he did a lot of business at the Dowling Trading Post. Nicholas had instructions from his father to provide certain customers with the best of service, although everyone was treated with respect. One never knew which broke settler or miner might turn out to be the next rich man. Nicholas waited for a pause in the conversation. Mr. Gear was notably trying to persuade the Irishman to come work for him immediately.

"Ahem, Mr. Gear, let me know if you need anything," Nicholas interjected when the opportunity arose. For a moment, both men looked at Nicholas, and he received a curt nod from Mr. Gear.

"Well, Hezekiah, it is quite nice to see a friendly face, in this remote place. I was hope'n I would run into you, indeed I was. I am looking forward to seeing that claim of yours as well, and I'll be out to take a look at it, now that you told me where to find you." Thomas paused for a moment rubbing his chin, scanning the goods in the trading post. His eyes rested back on Hezekiah who was staring at him intently like a wolf stalking prey. He remembered what Captain Lincoln had told him about a man's worth out west...

"You must come and stay with us Thomas." Hezekiah coaxed. "Granted, we are still lodged like badgers. Humble burrows in the hillside keep us dry and warm for now, but I'm having a house built in town for when my wife arrives with the family."

"Your wife is traveling to Galena right now?" Thomas inquired, somewhat in disbelief.

"Yes, I know the Native uprising is disturbing, but I'm sure that will be quelled by the time she gets here. And she will be coming up the Mississippi by steamboat. It's all very safe."

Thomas rubbed his chin. "Don't they need to stop on shore periodically to cut wood to fuel the steamboat on the trip up?" Having witnessed some of the results of the slaughter and never having met Hezekiah's family, it still bothered him that he would take such a chance. The folks in this town seemed so removed from the violence.

"I'm confident they'll get her up the river safely," Hezekiah stubbornly replied.

Thomas looked down at the ground and nodded. Certainly it was not his business, but still…

"Well, Hezekiah, I've some business to do about town. I'll be out to see you once I get settled. Could you point me towards the land office?"

Hezekiah tilted his head to one side, very curious. He wondered if the Irishman was planning on prospecting himself rather than working, like he had originally planned.

"Happy to escort you there myself," Hezekiah replied.

As the two men walked out the door, having heard the full conversation Nicholas could not help himself. He rushed over to the window to see what the Irishman had been looking at before Mr. Gear had interrupted him. There it was:

Surveyors wanted…
Apply at the land office.

Nicholas smiled to himself. A man was worth more than a pretty penny that could do that type of work. If he had the abilities, they were certain to hire him. Mr. Sprigg, the chief surveyor himself, was a Scot. The Irishman would likely be back for supplies, and with this Native uprising there would probably be land scrip bonuses. From what Nicholas knew, the surveyors had already crossed the river so the Irishman would need to catch up to them. Mr. Sprigg's back-ordered surveyor's chain had arrived. Nicholas would send it along with the Irishman to ensure he would be awarded a very warm welcome.

The following morning, after visiting the trading post, Thomas made his way on foot towards the Mississippi River. His new employers had given him a map of where to find the survey gang, some coin for supplies, and coin for the ferry between Illinois and the Dubuque mines area. Thomas had decided to save the coin and swim. He could make a quick raft to carry his supplies and clothes and had no fear of traversing the waters himself. God had gotten him this far, and he was certain his fortune lay across that river.

Once Hezekiah had learned of Thomas's plans he had endlessly tried to dissuade him, even pronouncing the Native uprising as a reason not to go, having dismissed it as a risk to his own beloved family. Hezekiah was persistent and would not take no for an answer. Thomas told him he would consider it and come take a look. Hezekiah expected him to show up at his claim this afternoon, but Thomas would be well across the river and on his way to earning his own land. Those working on the survey gang would have first chance to pick the best of the best land.

He imagined the delight on his family's faces, back in Ireland, once they learned their little run-away brother was a land owner in America... This was an actual chance to make his dreams come true.

******

William Stanbery, a congressman from Ohio, stepped out of the boarding house onto the cool evening streets of Washington City.

For comfort, his fingertips confirmed a pistol was tucked easily accessible under his coat, a habit he'd acquired since his speech on Indian Affairs at the House of Representatives ten days prior. Stanbery glanced around, ensuring it was safe to venture forth as had become his recent custom.

He hadn't anticipated that his speech would incite violence upon himself. It was merely politics. He and his fellow Whig Party members were incensed by President Jackson's position on the nation's banks, which had caused them significant financial hardship back home. They hoped to weaken Jackson by attacking his good friend, one Governor Sam Houston, who was in town with the Cherokee delegation. Three years earlier, Houston had resigned as governor of Tennessee. His current role, representing the Cherokee, was perceived as Houston's reentry into politics as Jackson's ally.

So much controversy was swirling around Jackson's Indian Removal Act. For his enemies, it was basically Jackson's vulnerable underbelly at the moment. On behalf of Ohio, Stanbery had denounced the act's weaknesses and failures while calling out officials, like Governor Houston, as corrupt, accusing him of attempting to profiteer from food ration contracts. As his close friend, this insinuated Jackson's duplicity and incompetence. Once Stanbery's remarks were published in the newspapers, Houston became incensed, stalking Stanbery's known haunts and proclaiming to many that he would have satisfaction. Having never met Houston, Stanbery could only rely on rumors that he would be no match for this formidable frontiersman. Stanbery was aware that Jackson sometimes insinuated violence should be visited upon those in Congress who opposed his policies, inviting attacks by private citizens. Many were on edge these days.

As Stanbery walked up the street, the hair on the back of his neck bristled at the sudden sound of footsteps approaching from behind. He whirled around, all at once face to face with a man he suspected must be the source of his trepidation: the former governor from Tennessee. Towering over six foot tall with a broad-shouldered muscular build, the man was dressed in a formal evening suit which framed a vest made from some type of spotted animal skin. Rugged features, thick sideburns, and an intense gaze conveyed a force to be reckoned with. As his brow furrowed, jaw clenched, and his lips pressed tightly together in a scowl, his fierce eyes burned with anger and indignation narrowing and fixating on Stanbery. The man was indeed in a savage mood.

"Are you William Stanbery?" Sam Houston demanded, one hand clenched around a cane and the other opening and closing in a fist. His eyes were blazing with fury.

Stanbery's throat constricted with fear, rendering him speechless. He managed a nod and then the towering figure bellowed, "Then you are a damned rascal!"

Stanberry scarcely had time to raise his arm in defense as Houston's cane swooped through the air, striking him repeatedly. The next thing he knew they were on the ground, rolling in the dirt. Stanbery finally managed to loosen his pistol, shove it into Houston's chest and squeeze the trigger, only to hear a disheartening empty click. This only served to further enrage Houston, who continued the beating until, at last, his rage subsided. He abruptly turned and stomped righteously away, leaving Stanbery badly injured and bloodied in the street.

******

President Andrew Jackson was beyond provoked. But then, being provoked had become an almost constant state of being. The small band of Sauk warriors headed by Blackhawk had their exploits plastered all over the eastern newspapers. People were having second thoughts about heading west, fearing not only death but also torture, mutilation, and kidnapping by savages. The treaties resulting from his Indian Removal Act were proving more difficult to carry out than his generals had anticipated–specifically, the removal part. Some tribes absolutely refused to vacate the lands and had resorted to vicious retaliation, sparing no one. Even women and children had been slaughtered.

At first, he'd had General Atkinson take the lead from the local Illinois militia, but the Sauk warriors were running circles around him. So Jackson sent General Winfield Scott to take command. Now, he had reports from the field that an outbreak of cholera had struck Scott's soldiers on their way west, and his some 1,000-strong force had been reduced by almost two-thirds. It had been over a month since his last report.

Jackson's secretary of war, Lewis Cass, entered the office with a new update, "I have great news, Mr. President."

"Well, let's hear it then."

"The local militia caught up with Blackhawk's band when they were crossing the Wisconsin River. With Ho-Chunk scouts they killed a bunch of them. Our armored steam boat cornered Blackhawk at the mouth of the Bad Axe. We pounded his warband with cannon fire until General Atkinson's men came in from the rear, cutting off retreat. The few who escaped were finished off by the Sioux. We took a few prisoners, but they were mostly women and children."

"And General Scott?"

"Still recovering in Chicago, Mr. President. He will be giving relief to General Atkinson as soon as he is able," Cass replied.

"And Blackhawk?"

"Still at large, sir. But he has no warband left. He's on the run on the other side of the Mississippi. Our boys will get him."

"Let General Scott know we'll be pushing them further west. I want them at the very least 40 miles west of the Mississippi. When he catches the rest of them, we'll sign a treaty, give them some coin—let's say 11 cents per acre—and they will relinquish the usual—rights to plant, hunt, or fish."

"As you say sir."

Relieved that these skirmishes finally seemed to be under control, Andrew turned his thoughts to his good friend Sam Houston, who had, yet again, gotten himself into a spot of trouble. An Ohio congressman had publicly maligned Sam's motives as an emissary for the Cherokee, to which Sam had retaliated by beating the man nearly to death with his cane. After all, Sam's reputation and honor were more important to him than his very life.

What a backstabbing cutthroat of a place this legislature had become. Adversaries had immediately labeled Sam as a dangerous western savage and had him arrested for contempt of Congress. From Andrew's perspective there were more than a few other such loud-mouthed congressmen that deserved to be Houstonized as well. In any case, Andrew was determined to get Sam off with a mild rebuke, but it was high time Sam was distracted from the Cherokee situation. The chatter from Texas about independence from Mexico was growing louder. Andrew needed Sam out of the way, and Texas was indeed a good distance from the Indian affairs at hand. With some encouragement, Sam's future, momentarily soured, could indeed be turned around if the right strings were pulled. Given their friendship, Andrew was happy to do the pulling.

On another note, although Andrew admired Sam's compatriot, David Crockett, this congressman was constantly at odds with Andrew's policies and had become downright intolerable. His fearlessness and sense of humor was admirable, but it was time to put the man in his place. Andrew would make certain Crockett's political aspirations in Tennessee were quashed and see if they could point his nose towards Texas as well.

******

From his small log house, Thomas gazed with pride and admiration at his field of corn, which stood taller than a man could reach. Over a year of surveying had earned him enough funds to return to the land office in Galena to register his tracts and pay in full with land scrip. After trading with some of his neighbors for lands a bit further west, he had settled on this bountiful soil on the banks of Lytle Creek in an area known as Makokiti, a Native name for one of the local springs.

Thomas and a few of his neighbors had finally finished assisting Father Samuel Charles Mazzuchelli in erecting a log house Catholic Church. There were already a few Irish Catholics in the area with large families. What they were most excited about was the chatter of the school that would soon follow.

Thomas's greatest aspiration was to persuade some of his kin in Ireland to undertake the voyage to America and seek their fortune here, in Makokiti. Throughout his journeys he had penned many letters detailing his escapades to his brother, John, to share with the family back home. Now that he was well-established and settled, it was time to pen new letters of his success, with an actual postal office nearby from which he could receive letters. He also harbored hopes of enticing the Conklins to consider a move from Ohio as well. Ever since his stay with them, Thomas had regarded them as kin. Though the Ohioan lands were indeed suitable for self-sustainable farming, the fertile plains of Makokiti promised far grander opportunities. He desired such prosperity for Will and Easter, just as he did his siblings across the sea.

Thomas seated himself beside the glowing hearth and arranged the blank sheets of parchment before him. He knew what he wanted to say, yet the precise phrasing eluded him. Thomas knew the thought of making the journey across the ocean and through the wilds of America was daunting. He knew that his family would be afraid, but he hoped that his words would be enough to convince them that the risk was worth it.

He picked up his pen and began to write.

"Dear John and Family,

I hope this letter finds you all well. I miss you more than words can say. Life in America has been hard, but God has seen fit to let me prosper. I can now call my farm successful with an abundance of crops I grew with my own sweat that I have sold and which earned me extra coin. I own all of my land free and clear. Many Irish have homesteaded here in this land they call Makokiti, and we have built a wonderful community.

Our latest accomplishment is a sturdy log house Catholic Church. Next we will build a school. There is just one thing missing: more Wallaces to take their place in the pews.

To own your own farm, to grow your own crops, and to no more be under a landlord's thumb is what I want for you. Come to me here in America. I know that the journey will seem difficult and that you will be afraid, but I promise you that it will be worth it. I know that you can make a good life for yourself here, God willing.

I can send you money for the sea fare with instructions how to travel. And I can meet you part way to escort you the last leg of the journey. I can help you file a claim, stake out your own farmland, and build your own homestead. Please…just come.

Tears fell on the letter as he said out loud, "I miss you all terribly, and I want nothing more than to be reunited with my family."

Instead he wrote:

> *Your loving brother,*
> *Thomas*

Thomas knew it might take a bit of time for them to make up their minds, and possibly many more letters. He was up to the task and would send as many as it took: describing the trip for them, what they would see, how they would travel, what adventures they would encounter along the way, and the beautiful lush countryside they would live in when they arrived. He was a stubborn man and would keep writing until his family and the Conklin's became so inspired by his stories that the prospect of adventure and fortune would make them all brave their fears. Some day they would take that first step, one after the other, embarking on that endless journey west, until at last they found themselves here, alongside him, in this paradise he now called home…

1834 – A Tennessee Congressman in Ohio

"I'm that same David Crockett, fresh from the backwoods,
half-horse, half-alligator,
a little touched with the snapping turtle;
can wade the Mississippi, leap the Ohio,
ride upon a streak of lightning,
and slip without a scratch down a honey locust;
can whip my weight in wild cats,
and if any gentle- man pleases, for a ten dollar bill,
he may throw in a panther..."

TWO YEARS LATER...
Easter - 22, Will - 26
Phoebe - 4, Anna -3, Mary - 1
Aminadab - 3 months

It was a dewy morning in July1834 when the steamboat, Hunter, as if weary from its journey, ran out of steam and drifted onto the shores of Jackson Township for repairs. After a late night of carousing at the local roadhouse, David Crockett was reminding himself that he was sitting in his accommodations on his way to Cincinnati, Ohio, via steamboat from Pittsburgh. He had been traveling at a breakneck pace, covering the distance from Philadelphia to Pittsburgh via the new Pioneer Fast Line which encompassed both train and canal passages. It took a mere three and a half days—a trip that once took a staggering twenty-one days. The nation's transportation network was expanding with astounding speed. Crockett shuffled through his papers, fingering the travel flyer for the Pioneer Fast Line—a souvenir he intended to share with his constituents back home. From Pittsburgh, one could embark on steam or flatboats, journeying to a myriad of destinations.

This whirlwind North and Down East tour had multiple objectives. One aim was to promote the book he had recently co-authored, both to cement his image as he wanted to be remembered and to earn a much-needed income to settle his debts. Flamboyant narratives of his life, written by others seeking profit and fame from his unique reputation, had already circulated—some rooted in fact, others in pure fiction. These accounts, however, failed to capture the essence of the man he sought to portray as a potential candidate on the Whig presidential ticket. Why else would a congressman from Tennessee be visiting other men's districts?

David's book not only entertained readers with his many daring exploits as a scout and pioneer but also recounted his stories of service as a colonel in the Tennessee Militia, a devoted congressman, and notably, his involvement in the War of 1812 and the Creek Wars under General Jackson.

It was no coincidence that David retraced portions of President Andrew Jackson's Northeast Tour from the previous year, although not venturing quite as far west. Senator Henry Clay had meticulously arranged a well-coordinated route and orchestrated events for David. Speeches drafted with key Whig talking points accused Jackson of acting like a king rather than a president who served the Constitution. After all, "King Jackson" had vastly exceeded his authority by ordering funds to be removed from the National Bank, pushing it to the brink of insolvency. Moreover, the Whig platform emphasized support for tariffs to shield farmers and booming manufacturers from foreign competition. A select group of influential Whigs believed David might challenge General Jackson's narrative as the "other" renowned Democrat and frontier hero. Though the Whig Party was relatively new and somewhat divided, they were auditioning several regional favorites for the nomination. With his widespread popularity, David harbored aspirations of becoming at least a vice-presidential running mate, if not more. This tour would surely showcase his broad appeal.

Senator Clay was traveling this leg of the journey with David to get a pulse on the rural folk's views in person. There was nothing Henry and David liked better than pressing hands with farmers.

At every event, transcripts of David's speeches were distributed to local newspapers as well as those back east, which eagerly published them. Such was the thirst so many folks had for tales of frontier heroes' adventures.

David picked up his book and perused some of the passages he had penned on his opposition to Jackson's Indian Removal Act:

...of this second term, I saw, or thought I did, that it was expected of me that I was to bow to the name of Andrew Jackson, and follow him in all his motions, and mindings, and turnings, even at the expense of my conscience and judgment. Such a thing was new to me, and a total stranger to my principles. I know'd well enough, though, that if I didn't "hurra" for his name, the hue and cry was to be raised against me, and I was to be sacrificed, if possible. His famous, or rather I should say his in-famous Indian bill was brought forward, and I opposed it from the purest motives in the world. Several of my colleagues got around me, and told me how well they loved me, and that I was ruining myself. They said this was a favourite measure of the president, and I ought to go for it. I told them I believed it was a wicked, unjust measure, and that I should go against it, let the cost to myself be what it might; that I was willing to go with General Jackson in everything that I believed was honest and right; but, further than this, I wouldn't go for him, or any other man in the whole creation; that I would sooner be honestly and politically damnd, than hypocritically immortalized. I had been elected by a majority of three thousand five hundred and eighty-five votes, and I believed they were honest men, and wouldn't want me to vote for any unjust notion, to please Jackson or anyone else; at any rate, I was of age, and was determined to trust them. I voted against this Indian bill, and my conscience yet tells me that I gave a good honest vote, and one that I believe will not make me ashamed in the Day of Judgment. I served out my term, and though many amusing things happened, I am not disposed to swell my narrative by inserting them. When it closed, and I returned home, I found the storm had raised against me sure enough; and it was echoed from side to side, and from end to end of my district, that I had turned against Jackson. This was considered the unpardonable sin. I was hunted down like a wild varment, and in this hunt every little newspaper in the district, and every little pin-hook lawyer was engaged. Indeed, they were ready to print any and every thing that the ingenuity of man could invent against me.

...Look at my arms, you will find no party hand-cuff on them! Look at my neck, you will not find there any collar, with the engraving

MY DOG.

Andrew Jackson.

But you will find me standing up to my rack, as the people's faithful representative, and the public's most obedient, very humble servant, DAVID CROCKETT.

David took immense pride in his book and the Whig message. In his mind, Senator Henry Clay and his followers were honorable men, while Andrew Jackson and his acolytes were anything but.

Throughout his travels from state to state, David was astonished at the leaps and bounds which had been made in logistics and transportation. The route he had recently taken from Pittsburgh now provided a new, low-cost canal route to Philadelphia equal to a mere two days' wagon drive. New York legislators claimed the Erie Canal would carry all the produce and merchandise from the west. Yet, after witnessing the newly completed Pennsylvania Canal firsthand, David could not fathom why anyone south of Pittsburgh would risk their wares all the way around to New York via the Great lakes.

In Cincinnati, he planned to laud this remarkable achievement and, once more, denounce Jackson and his minions. David reviewed a segment of his speech, tailored for the Ohio audience:

…But in 1834 what do we see? We see ourselves arrived at a crisis when one man can hold the sword in this hand and the purse in that, and bid defiance to Congress and to the nation. That man is Andrew, the first king of this country. A king we wouldn't think so hard of across the Atlantic. But to have a king in our own country, putting up his will against the whole country, and declaring, that unless two-thirds of Congress will vote for a measure, he will veto it, is worse than George the Third or any other king of England would dare to do. My friends, it would cost him not only his cap, but his head with it!

But, with Andrew the First, it is my will, my secretaries, my Congress, my government, my PEOPLE. This is the ' great Roman patriot.' This is the 'hero of two wars.' This is the 'greatest and best' of mankind, the great 'Tennessee farmer.' Where is the retrenchment and reform he promised? Has he done it? Gentlemen, I myself was one of the first to fire a gun under Andrew Jackson. I helped to give him all his glory. But I liked him well once: but when a man gets too big for his breeches, I say Good bye…

…I will show the people how Andrew Jackson is surrounded by a set of the most cursed scoundrels that ever moved; and the old man suffers himself to be a perfect tool in their hands, to deceive and ruin the country, and to destroy its peace and harmony. But I for one love my country. I'll speak my mind; I'll proclaim the truth, and the people shall know what I've seen and heard.

His conclusion read:

May the Whigs increase in numbers and grow in strength, and send one to represent them that can serve his country, instead of being the tool of a party.

And then, to his empty hotel room, David declared aloud, "And perhaps that might just be one humble Congressman from Tennessee, Colonel David Crockett."

A rough knock on his door jostled David back to the present.

"Yeah, what?" David responded, feeling no need to rise up

from his comfortable seat to open the door.

Henry Clay sauntered into the room, hands on his hips, appraising the evidently hungover congressman.

"We're in luck. There is a county fair being held here today of all days. We're gonna go try out that speech of yours on some of the locals while they get the steam boat operational."

"Where are we again?" David asked, rubbing the back of his neck.

"Jackson Township."

"And we're gonna try and turn these folks against Jackson?"

Henry shrugged and lifted his hands.

"Right is on our side. Let's get this information out to our honest critics and see what happens."

"Well, best case is we get heckled... worst case, tar and feathered?"

Henry grinned broadly and replied, "Just put on your best country boy charm and you'll be fine. You're one of them, after all."

David stood up slowly and grabbed a box of his books.

"Well, maybe I'll get a few sales out there and win some folks over. Who knows?"

Easter and Will stood amidst the scattered crowd at the county fair with their infant son, Aminidab, just three months old, on Easter's hip and Phoebe Ann, now four, perched on Will's shoulders. They had left their two younger girls with neighbors to enjoy this trip to town. This was the first fair and cattle show they had ever attended in this place that had become their home. It was astonishing to see the number of people assembled, transforming the usually sparse town into a bustling array of booths, farm animals, performers, and contest hubs. Prizes ranged from four to eight dollars for the best exhibits. Contests included best bull, heifer, buck, and ewe, while women vied for best woolen cloth, table linens, and bonnets. Easter had brought linen woven from her own garden crop to compete, and the surprise appearance of these renowned political figures was the icing on the cake.

Upon arriving in town, the first thing they heard was that the famed frontier hero, Davy Crockett, and the distinguished Washington Senator, Henry Clay, were to give political speeches at the fair. After dropping off a few items, Will and Easter hastened to ensure they were in attendance. Both politicians, known for their strong opinions and charismatic personalities, attracted a fairground teeming with eager listeners. Crockett, the former colonel, Tennessee congressman, and folk hero, took the stage first. He spoke about the dangers of Andrew Jackson's leadership and the need to protect the rights of the common man from his tyranny. Jackson, Crockett argued, was ruling from Washington like a king, demanding that senators and congressmen—elected by the people —do his bidding. Although many laughed at his folksy yarns and jokes, the political portion of his speech was met with jeers and boos from the crowd, many of whom were Jackson supporters.

As they listened to the speeches, Easter glanced sideways at Will, who audibly gasped and shook his head in disbelief. It reminded her of the political speeches back in Herkimer Township the night Will had proposed, except, of course, rather than nodding and cheering, he was scowling.

Next up was Henry Clay, a senator from Kentucky and a leading figure in the new Whig Party. Clay spoke about the dangers of the Jackson administration, the importance of protecting American industry and frontier farmers with foreign tariffs, and expressed his opposition to President Andrew Jackson and his policies. While there were a few cheers for the protective tariffs, his anti-Jackson rhetoric was also met with resistance from the crowd.

Will booed and hissed along with his neighbors, most of whom folded their arms and shook their heads. The event ended on a sour note, with locals obviously feeling disappointed and dejected that their hero was criticized by these famous figures. The crowd quickly dispersed, hurrying off to various competitions that were preparing to be judged. A few folks approached the politicians to shake hands and personally debate their positions.

Will announced, "Easter, we're land owners out here, and what these politicians do affect us. I'm gonna go speak my mind." He handed Phoebe Ann to Easter and promptly approached the group, pushing his way forward. Quite surprised, Easter followed.

Crockett and Clay turned to greet what appeared to be a local farmer and his young family. The couple introduced themselves as settlers who had recently moved to Ohio from the east, inspired by President Andrew Jackson's policies. While respectfully shaking their hands, the farmer, one William Conklin, originally from a colonial family in New York, told them that he was disappointed by their speeches and wanted to know more about their views on issues affecting settlers like themselves.

Henry Clay observed the couple attentively as Crockett unleashed his down-home charm. Swiftly steering the conversation towards crop cultivation and the upcoming methods to transport their produce eastward for sale, Crockett had the pair chuckling and exchanging tales in no time.

"Whoa, doggy! Who's this pretty little filly?" Crockett reached down, scooped up their inquisitive young daughter, and engaged her in a chat about her contributions to the family farm.

"Well," the little girl answered, "I gather eggs in the mornin', let the sheep in the barn at night, help weed the garden sometimes, and…and…watch my two little sisters a whole lot so Ma can get her chores done." She glanced at her parents for approval.

The couple beamed as the folk hero complimented their healthy children and the picturesque countryside. Crockett certainly possessed a gift for connecting with people, one on one.

Henry Clay thoughtfully pondered the impromptu stop they had made in this remote locale. As always, such stops proved invaluable for understanding the prevailing sentiments. It reminded Henry that politicians' perspectives did not always align with those of the general public. The Whigs' political grievances against Jackson held no significance for these folks.

The challenges of settling on new land, the importance of

safeguarding land rights for pioneers, and the need for improved infrastructure to support their livelihood were their primary concerns. This couple were staunch supporters of Andrew Jackson, and they praised his policies, echoing the campaign messages that portrayed him as a true champion of the common man. They genuinely believed Jackson's leadership had enabled them to pursue their dreams of a better life on the frontier.

Both men pledged to convey the couple's concerns back to Washington, and David gave the young woman an autographed copy of his book to express his gratitude for their insights.

Easter smiled as she cradled the book David Crockett had gifted her.

Will hoisted Phoebe Ann onto his shoulders and grinned at Easter, quite pleased with himself for having spoken his mind. A wave of pride in his family and their budding farm swelled within him. The respect these politicians had shown him and his family left a lasting impression. It made him feel valued in the political decisions being made back in Washington, almost if they were being made specifically for his personal aspirations.

Easter's thoughts were captivated by the vision the politicians had painted for them of the new, faster, cheaper transport methods through the new east-west Pennsylvania canals. Their future seemed brighter than ever.

1842 - A Profitable Wife

The fritil' butterfly, the bee,
Whose early labours cheer,
And point the happy industry
That marks the opening year

TWELVE YEARS SINCE EASTER AND WILL'S
ARRIVAL IN OHIO...
Easter - 29, Will - 33
Phoebe - 11, Anna - 10, Mary - 8, Mahala - 5
Aminadab - 6, Billy - 4, Elijah - 2

Disgust flitted across Phoebe's face as she watched her younger sisters vanish into the distant forest edge. This left her with more than her fair share of chores to complete, as well as overseeing her three young brothers, Elijah, Billy, and Aminadab. Ma had ventured into town for a couple of weeks with some trade goods, and Pa was laboring in the fields. At ages two, four, and six, keeping track of the boys was relatively easy. They were sweet and tended to trail behind her like loyal pups.

The girls, however, were a different matter. Supervising Mahala, Mary, and Anna, aged five, eight, and ten, felt akin to herding chickens. As the eldest of the Conklin brood at eleven years old, Phoebe wasn't averse to using a switch on them if they caused her too much trouble. It wasn't that they were naughty; rather, they were easily distracted and somewhat mischievous. Anna and Mary were constantly brimming with ideas, while Mahala possessed an unyielding stubbornness that could not be thwarted. Fleet-footed like a rabbit, she trailed Anna and Mary everywhere, knowing they couldn't outpace her even if they tried. Consequently, the trio was inseparable.

That morning, Anna and Mary couldn't stop chattering about honey. Anna had noticed some particularly active bees in the area, and another idea had taken root in her mind.

"Ma's Irish friend said it was true, Phoebe. If I can get Ma some honey to trade, maybe we can get some cotton cloth and silk ribbon for new church bonnets."

Phoebe replied dismissively, "Ma's friend lives in the Iowa territory, way out west. This is Ohio. It's a fool's errand and a waste of time. Pa will be cross if he comes home to unfinished chores. Besides, farm girls like us have no business wearing fancy cotton bonnets with ribbons to church."

In the evenings, Ma often read and reread letters from family and friends. She was especially fond of the Irishman's letters—one Thomas Wallace—who had aided her and Pa when they first homesteaded in Ohio, but that had been over a decade ago. Nevertheless, Thomas Wallace's letters arrived faithfully at least twice a year, delighting them with tales and adventures of his life homesteading further west. In absentia, he was often cited within the household as an authority on various topics and disputes.

Ma was particularly excited because, in his latest winter letter, Thomas announced his eldest brother, John, was bringing his family all the way from Ireland to homestead in Iowa, and they would stop for a few weeks on their journey to visit the Conklin family. The Wallace clan could arrive at any time, and so it was important to make sure the farm kept plenty of supplies on hand for the extra mouths to feed. Both Pa and Ma were eagerly anticipating the extra hands to help with new field preparation during the visit. Food had never been a problem in their valley. Although they never had a crop fail, even if one did, the ample wild game and forage in the surrounding hills ensured there was always food for any with a strong back.

Anna pouted. "If we can trade a bunch of honey for coin, Pa won't fret over a few late chores. Besides, the boys can help you. To use Thomas Wallace's trick he learned from the Natives, it takes two of us to find the bee hive. I need Mary to help, and a bee is a bee no matter where it lives. They all fly in a bee-line back to their nests. We can do this." Her face had been so obstinately grim, as if their very lives hinged on the success of this ridiculous scheme.

Phoebe had a daunting list of chores for the day: making butter, baking bread, milking cows and turning them out, gathering eggs, cleaning pig and sheep pens, weeding the garden, picking early spring greens, fetching water from the creek, and catching up on laundry. She needed Mary to supervise the younger ones with some of the lighter tasks, so Anna and Phoebe could tackle the heavier chores and prepare dinner later. They would be eating cold pancakes for lunch. Pa wanted them to start tilling another field for a larger house garden, given that everyone was growing and consuming more. They had a surplus of wool that needed carding and spinning, but that could wait, with the little ones lending a hand when the time came. What Phoebe truly desired was to simply go fishing. She craved fresh fish rather than the salted stuff stored in the root cellar casks, and she just loved fishing.

"Okay, fine. Go search for your honey, but take Ma's gun with you and bring back something for dinner. And you're in charge of chores tomorrow so I can go fishing," she yelled after her sisters as they scampered across the fields, not needing any further encouragement.

Shaking her head as the girls vanished from sight, she turned to her brothers, "Okay. Aminadab, gather eggs in the basket and put them in the root cellar. Billy, watch over Elijah. Your job is to keep an eye on him and play near the garden to scare away crows while I work, all right? If you see any crows or coyotes, send Badger and Bear after them." She smiled as the boys nodded their heads in agreement. No debate; they were so much easier to handle than the girls. And, of course, their farm dogs, Badger and Bear, would watch over the boys as well as the livestock. If Anna returned with rabbit or pigeon, Pa would be pleased at the fresh meat. Besides, everyone knew Pa was more lenient about chores than Ma. With Ma away, Phoebe might even persuade Pa to join her for a fishing trip tomorrow. Sometimes being in charge was gratifying, but more often than not, it entailed a great deal of work and worry.

******

Will Conklin guided his oxen down to the creek that meandered through their land for a well-deserved midday break. It was time to eat some of the cold pancakes Phoebe had sent with him for lunch. Will and Easter's lives had settled into a well-structured routine. In their first year, they managed to earn a modest sum off of the wheat fields, thanks to Easter's persistence. After Thomas Wallace moved on, the babies started coming each year. One man working the fields was enough to maintain a sustainable farm for the family but not much more. They fed the corn to the hogs, which they smoked for meat. They also raised potatoes and wheat as well, most of which the family consumed to get through the winter. Hogs and wheat served as cash crops when they could grow a surplus, which hadn't been frequent.

Easter had devised a plan with some neighbors to pool their smaller grain surpluses. By doing so they were able to strike a deal with Mr. Kemple, who owned a mercantile in Jackson Township and could ship the combined large surplus through Pittsburgh via the Pennsylvania canals to the east for a premium price, minus his commission. This method was far faster than sending goods north through the Erie Canal to New York and a fraction of the cost. After the neighbors divided the profits, they managed to accumulate a little bit for a few extras as well as monies saved into their nest egg—an investment to purchase more acreage, boost their yield, and possibly hire help if any could be found.

As it stood, they were technically squatting on part of the land they farmed, as they didn't own all of it. Will wasn't as skilled as Easter at saving money. Something at the mercantile always seemed to catch his eye, and, much to Easter's annoyance, he would squander their savings on it. He suspected Easter had hidden a secret stash of savings, as she hadn't been bringing home as much money as she used to from town, always grumbling about increased competition from the influx of new settlers in the area.

When Easter wasn't creating trade goods herself, she had the older girls working on them. When a trip to town was imminent, the fruits of their labor would be assembled and admired. These goods included muffs made from any available fur, buckskin gloves and mitts, oak staves for crafting casks, and, if the timing was right, a surplus of butter and eggs. Easter also consistently made extra linen aprons, bonnets, and ladies' undergarments for trade, using the flax harvested from their quarter-acre plot each year.

Will paused and rubbed the back of his neck as he thought about Easter. He sorely missed her warm body against his in their bed when she was away on her trips to town. It would be a relief to finally hold her in his arms again when she returned.

Suddenly, a single gunshot pierced the quiet valley. On high alert, Will stood and scanned the tree line around him. It was probably just someone hunting, but the nearest neighbor was a couple of miles away, and this shot sounded alarmingly close. Then he heard screams—shrieks, actually—and the snapping of bushes. Something was rapidly approaching through the forest. The shrieking grew louder, multiple voices joining in. Fear gripped his heart; it sounded like his girls. Abandoning his oxen, he sprinted toward the noise, just as three of his daughters burst from the tree line. To his surprise, they raced past him, heading for the creek, wildly waving their arms around their heads and shedding their shifts. Mahala reached the water first, followed by Anna and Mary. Their screams and splashing frightened his oxen, who stampeded across the field as the girls continued their frenzied display.

"Girls!" Will demanded. "Girls, what in God's name are you doing?"

Mahala turned to her father. Her little lower lip stuck out and was quivering. She sat down in the creek, the water reaching up to her waist and began rubbing mud on her arms and face. "Anna," she whimpered, then declared loudly and accusingly, "Anna made the bees mad! Anna made the bees very mad!"

"Bees?" Will tilted his head and moved closer. Now calmer,

both Mary and Anna followed Mahala's lead, applying mud all over themselves. At least the shrieking had stopped, although somber moods now held them captive. Mahala and Mary both eyed Anna with extreme irritation. Anna stared steadfastly at the creek, guilt etched on her face, remaining silent.

"Anna, what happened?" Will asked gently. They all seemed calm now, and he found the situation a bit amusing, although he noticed several welts on their bodies that would likely be sore for a few days.

"I'm sorry, Pa," Anna said softly. She sighed with deep regret and glanced toward the forest from where they had come. "I dropped Ma's gun. I need to go back and fetch it." She clenched her fists and began marching toward the tree line. She had only recently been allowed to carry the gun on her own, and she feared Ma would revoke that privilege now.

"Oh no you don't, young lady. First you are going to tell me what happened."

Anna halted, peered at her father then stared at the ground.

"Well. It seemed like a good idea at the time. We were using Thomas Wallace's trick for finding some honey. You catch a few bees, then let them go at exactly the same time in different spots, watching which way they fly."

Will was curious now. "Go on."

Encouraged by her father's interest, Anna continued. "Well, it actually worked. Tell him Mary."

"Yeah. I took my bees to the other side of the field from Anna, and we let them go at the same time. They flew in a straight line, and we ran after them to where they crossed paths," Mary confirmed.

Anna resumed, "We found a huge hive, Pa. Lots of honey, but there were too many bees to get close." Anna looked at the ground again, ashamed.

"Anna shot the beehive with Ma's gun to scare away the bees," Mary announced.

"Anna made the bees very angry, and they started stinging us and they chased us," Mahala finished the story.

Will started laughing so heartily that tears filled his eyes. He rolled onto his back literally howling with amusement. Anna and Mary smiled sheepishly. Mahala maintained a stern expression. "It's not funny. It hurts," she said flatly, rubbing the bumps on her legs and arms with more mud.

Will calmed down, still smiling at his girls, "Well, it's a lesson well learned, I guess. A nest of bees is akin to General Jackson's army. You girls were the British, firing into their army. They chased you away just like 'Ol Hickory chased the British down the Mississippi to New Orleans." Will howled with laughter again.

Mary glanced down at her legs submerged in the creek and giggled. Anna brightened up a bit and peeked at Mahala to see if there was a chance for forgiveness. Mahala folded her arms stubbornly and looked away, refusing to give in to her father's mirth. But Mary and Pa's laughter proved infectious, and soon they all surrendered to it. Pa and Ma loved to tell stories about their grandfathers' time in the New York Militia and all kinds of tales about General Jackson. Anything relating to General Jackson's antics was told and retold in their household.

"Just give me a minute to round up the oxen, and then we'll go get your Ma's gun and have a look at your honey tree. We'll mark it with the Conklin brand so everyone knows it's ours. And I'll show you how to make the bees go to sleep so we can get honey from it without riling them up. Good job, girls." He grinned as bright smiles replaced their formerly grim expressions. "If we're lucky, there will be enough for your Ma to trade at the mercantile in town. And that will make her very happy."

******

Easter pulled the wagon to a stop in front of the Witten farm in Jackson Township to check for mail. She had some letters to post to her father and to Thomas in Iowa, letting him know how excited they were for his brother's visit. Although anything could happen on the journey out west, travel was much safer and more reliable than it had been in years past. James Witten, the township's postmaster, was also a good source of local gossip.

The Brigman farm, further down the valley, was her next stop. Centrally located, it hosted the township's schoolteacher and a charming hewn-log schoolhouse with a dirt floor. With plank benches and a wood stove, the building also served as a venue for monthly Presbyterian Church services, which Easter's family occasionally attended. Easter wanted to arrange her children's scholastic testing with John Musser, their new schoolteacher. The last time they had spoken, he mentioned using the "Lancaster Principle," a method he had learned while studying back east. It was the first formal teaching approach to reach their county, and many were excited about it.

In his schoolroom, students with the same mastery level in certain subjects sat together. To prove a student had completed a level of study, a mastery test was applied. Children with higher mastery levels than others assisted in teaching. He called them "monitors." Some of his monitors were willing to visit local farms to teach what they had learned, assigning lessons for younger children to work on at home. Monitors who passed special exams received badges as a reward, sparking quite a bit of competition among the children, who loved wearing their badges to church to show off their mastery.

Easter had her children practice reading, writing, and ciphering nightly, hoping that each would pass the age-appropriate mastery levels when tested. She planned to request one of Mr. Musser's monitors to visit her farm for testing and lesson recommendations and hoped that Anna and Phoebe might even earn badges as monitors. Local farms were generally generous when monitors came to test and tutor their children.

Her next stop would be Mr. Kemple's mercantile. Like Easter's father, Mr. Kemple always posted a variety of newspapers in his store for local folks to read. Many neighbors would gather on Sundays before and after church to discuss news and politics. Mr. Kemple also coordinated some of the commerce and shared crop trade for Easter and her neighbors.

Their farm was a good three-day-wagon-ride into town, which made planning for each journey crucial. In spring, summer, and the milder parts of fall, most of the family journeyed into town at least once a month for church, and made other smaller trips as needed. Camping trips along the way were usually supplemented with hunting and gathering, swimming in local watering holes, and occasionally chatting and trading with long-time neighboring farms they passed on their way.

******

Hannah Wallace rested her hands on her pregnant belly, feeling the fluttering of a babe curious about the new world it found itself in. She wasn't due for another three months by her estimation. They had been traveling for four months, and the conception had occurred just before their voyage to America. Her youngest, Catherine, just over a year old, had made the voyage in surprisingly good health. Her son, John, named after his father, was eight, and her middle child, Julia, had just turned five. Little John and her husband were at work reassembling the wagon that had been offloaded from the flatboat they had traveled on, along with some supplies. In any case, John's pioneer brother, Thomas, planned on coming to meet them at his friend's farm and travel with them to Iowa for the remainder of the journey.

Thomas's letters had assured them the land in Iowa was unparalleled in beauty and fertile soil. The chance to become landowners and successful farmers with his help was there for the taking, if only they could be brave enough to surrender to the spirit of adventure. Hannah and John were the only Wallaces daring enough to give it a try. The others would wait breathlessly for word from them when they reached Iowa.

Raw fear had plagued Hannah during the first few legs of the journey. So much was new. She had never in her life traveled outside their small town of Millstreet in Ireland. Aboard the ship, when she saw the land disappearing from sight, with nothing but water before them, it was all she could do not to scream out loud in terror. After a few days of seasickness, she had adjusted to the swaying of the ship better than most, and her children had not suffered at all. What Hannah was unprepared for was the difficulty she faced when they finally made it to New England and were safely ashore. Who knew that legs once adjusted to the sea had to relearn how to walk on unmoving solid land?

The colonial towns of America reminded Hannah a bit of home. It wasn't until they started up the Erie Canal and left civilization behind that raw fear set in again. Just like the sea, there was an endless expanse of land before them. How anyone found their way anywhere in such a raw, untamed place was unclear to her. The occasional towns they passed through slowly calmed her. Amazingly, they reached every travel point Thomas had described, moving on to the next leg until at last, they found themselves floating down the Ohio River on a flatboat with other families, all healthy, well-fed, and none the worse for the journey. It was surreal.

And now, here they were in Jackson Township, landing safe and sound where they were to seek out the Conklin farm, which would provide them lodging until Thomas came to fetch them for the remainder of the journey.

Hannah surveyed the flatlands and rolling hills around her that promised more of the same—dirt roads heading hither and yon into an empty expanse of never-ending land. She made the sign of the cross. God had gotten them this far safely. The flatboat had deposited their goods and left them. The operator had been a very quiet fellow, and none of their travel companions knew anyone named Conklin. Her family was the only one of their group to land in this place.

Although at first it looked deserted, as she walked up the hill she could see a few buildings. She scooped up Catherine and took Julia by the hand as she studied her surroundings. A couple of chickens scurried past one building, and she could hear voices in the distance. What appeared to be a gristmill was alive with the sound of stone grinding. She decided to go up and explore.

Upon entering the gristmill, no one was in sight. A steady stream of water turned the stone, which appeared to be grinding someone's grain. Catherine and Julia were as quiet as she, imitating their mother's wide-eyed gaze as they took everything in.

Upon exiting the mill, Hannah noticed some buildings up the hill that looked to be some type of mercantile with storage. A freight wagon was out front with a pair of large stock horses waiting patiently, watering themselves at will from a trough. As she approached, one of the horses turned to inspect her curiously, water dripping from its chin. Apparently satisfied that she and her children posed no threat, it returned to drinking with its companion.

Hannah was unsure if she should go inside, not knowing who she might run into in this remote place. She huddled by the corner of the building, wondering if she should wait for John, when all of a sudden, the door opened, and a very tall, stocky woman emerged with a barrel on her shoulder. She easily deposited the barrel in the wagon and immediately went back inside. Startled, Hannah looked at her girls, who were as wide-eyed as she was. It seemed seeing astounding things in this new land was becoming the norm. Immediately, she made a decision. She took a deep breath, gathered all her courage, and marched into the building. As her eyes adjusted to the darkness of the room, she noticed a man gazing up at her from a counter, a pen in his hand. The large woman was squatting down, putting some things in a basket. Both immediately stared at Hannah curiously.

"Anything I can help you with, ma'am?" the man inquired. The large woman rose, brushing her hands on her skirt as she regarded Hannah.

Hannah's throat constricted, and she froze. She had almost believed she and her family were alone in this place, and being confronted by strangers all by herself was overwhelming. All she could do was gape at them, like a fish out of water. She felt Julia tugging at her sleeve and glanced down at her daughter.

"Ask dem about da peeples."

Hannah nodded hurriedly but couldn't find her voice. She

looked desperately at Julia, who bravely turned to the strangers, stepped forward, and asked with her childish, high-pitched Irish brogue, "Ello, mister and missus, we'd be lookin' for some peeples by d'name of Conklin, might eeder of ya know dem be chance? Me fader's name be John Wallace and his brudder Thomas be a friend of da Conklin's. And dis is me ma." Julia finished with a charming dimpled smile.

The man's face broke into a warm grin, and he replied, "Well, little missy, welcome to our town. You've indeed found what you're looking for. This is Easter Conklin herself, right here."

At this turn of events, Hannah still had not recovered her voice and gawked back and forth between the man and the woman.

Suddenly, Easter's voice boomed. "Oh, my Lord! You're Thomas's family? Jesus, Mary and Joseph, we're so happy you made it!" Easter laughed and cried simultaneously, her emotions overflowing. She opened her arms and swept up Julia, who beamed with pride for having spoken up. The next thing Hannah knew, she and Catherine were enveloped in Easter's warm embrace, making her feel that, at last, perhaps she was no longer a stranger in a strange land.

After reuniting Hannah and her girls with John and little John, Easter helped them stow their supplies in one of Mr. Kemple's outbuildings. She was glad to have the Wallaces' company on the three-day journey home. Easter even allowed little John to drive her wagon for a while as she used her sling to catch a couple of rabbits for dinner.

Easter found Hannah somewhat hard to read. The young woman was petite and quiet, often casting nervous glances in Easter's direction. Her girls seemed like miniature versions of their mother, with reddish-brown hair and freckles sprinkled across their noses. John, on the other hand, was boisterous and flirtatious, much like Thomas. She could sense his exhilaration now that he and his family were so close to reaching their destination.

Their first night's encampment was in a spot Easter favored, a flat grassy meadow with a small stream that pooled into a natural swimming hole. Will had hung a rope from the tree for the kids to swing into the water which was still there, and Little John and Julia were taking full advantage of the fun.

Two Dutch ovens simmered a generous dinner of rabbit stew and dumplings over a campfire. John hobbled the horses so they could graze while keeping an eye on his swimming brood. Later, they would make beds under the wagons and get an early start in the morning. Finally having Hannah to herself, Easter, ever the candid soul, asked plainly, "Hannah, is everything all right? Is there anything you need? Anything I can help you with?"

Hannah stared at the fire and glanced at Easter, unsure of what to say. Everything was so overwhelming. She had never seen a woman do the things she had seen Easter do that day: a woman all by herself in the wilderness, driving a wagon, procuring and loading supplies, negotiating with Mr. Kemple for storage, guiding them across remote hills and valleys to her home, and hunting for their dinner, no less.

Easter observed Hannah's struggle and said, "You've come quite a ways, all the way across the sea to a new country. You must be quite dazed with everything being so new. I can't imagine how I would feel if I crossed the sea and landed in Ireland." Hannah looked at Easter and nodded, still remaining silent.

"Well," Easter added, "Enjoy this quiet while you can. With my seven little ones at home and your three, it will be quite a lively household."

"Now that will be a welcome for sure," Hannah blurted out. She managed a faint smile. "I miss…well…I thought where I came from we were country folk, 'ya know? This place…America, is so much unlike anything I could ever imagine." She shrugged and shook her head. "You've made me feel welcome, Easter, and I thank you for that. But I'm either scared out of my wits or numb inside. Sometimes I think I'm losing my mind," she trailed off in a whisper.

"Uncivilized is what the Swedes call it," Easter responded. "We have a group of both German and Swede families living nearby, if you can call being a half-day away nearby. Occasionally, a family from their old country arrives, coaxed here by kin or former neighbors. The children adjust quickly, as do the men, but it seems harder for the women. They tend to long for their homelands and struggle to embrace their new home. They all call it the same thing: uncivilized."

"I can't imagine ever thinking of this huge, massive, beastly land ever being as dear to me as my beloved emerald island," Hannah replied softly, a tear trickling down her cheek. She glanced at John playing with the children and whispered, "I wish we had never come. I wish we had stayed home. I wish…" Hannah's words dissolved into sobs, and she found herself swept up in Easter's warm embrace once more.

Easter held her for a while and then said softly, "Hannah, if you are with your children and your husband, if they are happy, healthy, warm, and well fed, wherever that may be…then that's home."

Hannah nodded and sighed, wiping her tears away.

"You'll get used to it, I promise. There is never a dull moment out here, and the opportunities for those willing to work hard are endless. Make your new home into what you want it to be. You'll meet new neighbors, build a family, and learn to love your new home every bit as much as your old one, I promise you. You already have an upper hand with your brother-in-law having his homestead well established and waiting for you. Just get used to one thing. The only thing out here that never changes is that things are always changing and surprises are endless. Try to keep a sense of humor about it." Easter laughed and went back to tending dinner. Hannah sighed and smiled, finding Easter hard to resist.

Suddenly Easter froze, staring over Hannah's shoulder and slowly rose to her feet. Hannah looked over her shoulder, yelped and immediately ran to stand behind Easter.

John was coming up from the swimming hole with Julia in his arms and Little John trailing behind, and froze as well. Across the stream was a small group of Natives. One was on horseback, and the rest were on foot. To both John and Hannah's amazement, Easter stepped forward, raised her hand with her palm open towards the group, and spoke in a language they didn't understand. The one on horseback approached, raised his hand, and appeared to engage in conversation with Easter.

After some back-and-forth conversation, the Native dismounted, and the group followed Easter back to the fire. Hannah felt her throat constrict yet again and was certain she would faint at any moment. John looked very intent and still.

"John, Hannah, don't be worried. These are Native Wyandots. They're headed to some lands the government granted them in the south—travelers, just like you. I've crossed paths with the older fellow a few times over the years. He's been a good neighbor. He had to stay behind with their sick grandson until he was well enough to make the journey with the rest of their tribe. I invited them to eat with us. We have more than enough. I'll just toss a few more potatoes and carrots in our stew."

Hannah was yet again dumbstruck and looked at John for any sign of what to do. He simply shrugged, placed his hands on his hips, and stared at the approaching Natives. There were six in total —an older man, accompanied by three women and two children, a boy and a girl. The children, who immediately began to gather firewood, appeared to be around the same age as Julia and Little John. The elderly woman, her hair as white as snow, wore a full lynx pelt draped around her shoulders, complete with the head, feet, and tail. The two younger women, their raven-black hair cascading down their backs, seemed about Hannah's age. They appeared more frightened than Hannah felt, hiding behind the elders.

The Native women were all clad in leather shifts with knee-high leather boots tethered by rawhide strips, and they carried large rolled packs. Frayed beaded patterns adorned the hems and boots, hinting their clothes had seen better days. The old man's leather tunic, adorned with a generous amount of fringe, missing bits here and there, had somewhat soiled leggings and boots. His headdress was stuffed with multicolored plumed feathers of all colors— reminiscent of headdresses Hannah had seen depicting ancient druids in Ireland. Each of them wore a round bone disk with a hole in the center, intricately carved, suspended from their necks. Hannah noticed their obvious self-consciousness under her scrutiny.

Suddenly, Hannah's fear dissipated. These people seemed to be more afraid of intruding on her and John's camp than anything else. Their humanity was so real and Hannah instinctively felt she had nothing to fear.

Easter went about cooking and kept chattering in the Native tongue with the elders while all of the Wallaces gaped at their guests. When the little girl brought in her firewood, Julia decided to make an overture, "Ello, lassie, I'm Julia. It's very nice to be meetin' ya and yer family...and what might be your name?"

The Native girl retreated and buried her face in her mother's shift. Julia stepped forward and squatted, crouching down with her hand outstretched as if coaxing a timid puppy. "Awwww. Da not be afeard; I won't bite ya, little lass." Easter smiled as Julia flashed the little Native girl a dimpled grin that immediately reminded her of Thomas.

"Julia, leave her alone. She's afeared." Hannah had suddenly found her voice. Clearing her throat, she looked at Easter and decided to reach out to these people herself, unsure if they would understand her. Speaking slowly and gesturing with her hands, she introduced her family. "We are all very happy to meet'cha. We are the Wallace family. I'm Hannah, this is me husband, John. Dat there is Little John, and of course, Julia ya met. And me babe is Catherine." Hannah noted their fascination as they followed her gestures, feeling certain they understood. John smiled, admiring his wife's newfound courage.

The elders returned their smiles, nodding, and the old man began to speak in halting English. He gestured at the ancient woman. "Yodagent, She-Who-Saves." Then to each of the younger woman: "Tse'sta, Good-One; Gyantwaka, One-Who-Plants;" then the boy, "Dekanawida Two-Rivers-Running;" then the little girl, "Wáhta, Maple-Tree;" and at last, he placed his fist on his chest, "Èrielhonan, Long-Tail."

With introductions over, everyone seemed more at ease. Over

their shared meal, the children bonded and somehow found a way to communicate and play together.

Easter was delighted with how everything had unfolded. If Will had been with them, he would never allow her to invite the Natives to join them. He never seemed to understand that they had so much knowledge about the territory due to their nomadic lifestyle. If treated kindly, they were happy to share the latest gossip and were valuable trading partners. In any case, there were very few Natives left around, with all the removal treaties that had been going on. For the most part, they were harmless, friendly, and often carried valuable home remedies they were willing to share.

From what she gathered, Erielhonan Long-Tail's woman was a healer. It seemed that every time Easter crossed paths with Erielhonan, he was always running an errand for Yodagent. The woman seemed very confident and would likely be open to trade.

And now the Wallaces would have some pleasant stories to tell about the friendlies they had met—a fitting introduction to the West.

Later Hannah and John fell asleep under their wagon, and the children slept with Easter. The Natives' bedrolls were scattered around the fire.

When they awoke the next morning, the Natives were gone, leaving no trace they had ever been there, save for a crackling fire and a stack of firewood to help prepare their morning meal. They left a few trinket gifts for their hosts—a charming corncob doll for Julia and a few small satchels containing Native remedies for fevers known to afflict the area, which Easter had inquired about. All in all, the gifts were worth far more than the rabbit dinner they had shared.

Julia held up a foot-wide wooden disc with beaded sinew woven in the middle and feathers trailing below. "What is this?" she asked, holding it in the air. "One of them left it with my shawl."

"That's a dream catcher," Easter replied thoughtfully. She

assumed Yodagent must have left it for Hannah, as she had noticed the elder woman studying Hannah during their shared dinner the night before. Yodagent must have recognized her troubled spirit. It was curious John had no idea his fragile wife was in such emotional distress.

"The Natives use it to encourage good dreams and keep you from having bad ones," Easter explained matter-of-factly as she loaded up the wagon. The truth was that this was used by Native healers to help heal the mind when someone was mentally disturbed. Typically, many hung inside a shaman's circle hut. But Easter wasn't about to reveal that to everyone.

Before long, they were off. After another two more uneventful nights, home was just over the next hill.

******

Anna was the first to catch a glimpse of the two wagons when they crested the hill above their home. Seeing multiple heads in the wagons, she let out a whoop of delight. Surely the Wallaces had finally arrived!

"Pa, Phoebe, Marrrrry, Mahala, Ma's back with company!" She took a breath and yelled, "Aminadab, Billy, Elijaaaaah!" With that she took off running up the hill, determined to be the first to greet the Wallaces. She could hear the pounding of her sisters' feet behind her and her brother's calling hellos as Ma's wagon came down the hill followed by the other.

Easter pulled her wagon to a halt and grinned at her brood swarming up the hill through the north wheat field like a herd of bounding deer.

Hannah, John, and the kids stood up in their wagon, waving and smiling at the eager family approaching them. Hannah gazed at the beautiful homestead, larger than their rented cottage back home. A neatly planted house garden promised vegetables that would ripen in stages to keep the family in fresh produce throughout the spring, summer, and fall. Beyond the home was a healthy field of flax that, when harvested, would keep the women busy all winter spinning and weaving homespun clothes. It was truly a self-sustaining farm of which any landowner would be proud. John and Hannah hoped, against hope, that they would someday have something like this of their very own.

Suddenly, the children were wildly climbing into the wagons, and Easter was swarmed by her children with hugs as they looked through everything to see what she had brought back. Introductions happened fairly quickly, as none of the children could sit still for very long. Immediately, Anna grabbed Little John's hand and led him out of the wagon, bounding back down across the field, determined to be the first to introduce Little John to Pa.

A busy afternoon was spent unloading the wagons and getting the Wallaces settled into their living spaces. Finally, dinner was made, everyone was fed, and it was time to lounge in front of the fire in the house and share news and gossip from town.

First, a very proud Anna announced her honey tree find and was rewarded with praise for her resourcefulness. They all had a good chuckle about her initial attempts at retrieving the honey herself, the mishaps and mad dash to the creek, the stampeding oxen, and finally, the branding of the honey tree as owned by the Conklins.

"We all make mistakes, Anna, but your actions brought us a valuable surplus we can sell for coin. And Phoebe managed the farm so you and your sisters could do your foraging. The rest of you kept the chores going. You have all done well," Easter concluded as Will wrapped her in his arms with a warm grin.

John offered, "Will, ya mentioned that you were farmin' some adjacent land that ya did not have title to yet. Some news we heard back east may be of interest to ya. Some folks on the flatboat were sayin' President Tyler had passed some type of Homestead Act that would allow anyone who was squatting who had improved the land to purchase it at a very low price."

Will raised his eyebrows in surprise. "We'll have to look into that for sure."

"Wait until you see how much coin we got this time," Easter

whispered, her eyes gleaming with excitement. "Our grain did well back east. Our share is quite more than we expected. We got 40 cents a bushel."

Will nodded thoughtfully at Easter's news. She always amazed him when her crazy ideas resulted in these unexpected successes. That was 10 cents more per bushel than they could have gotten locally.

A profitable wife surely was something he had not even mused about. Knowing all he knew about her background when they'd married, he had anticipated a sturdy pioneer wife and partner in Easter. Survival in these parts proved easier than most thought. Wild food was plentiful and sustaining a family on the frontier was attainable with determination and grit. Surpluses to sell, coin, and men for hire were scarce.

Easter had blessed him with three strapping sons who soon would be sturdy farmhands and four scrappy, hardworking daughters, all blessed with robust health. She had proven herself to be very savvy at trading and was pretty much self-sufficient. She had far surpassed his expectations, although it was obvious she did not realize it; indeed she had become a cornerstone of their farm's success. He gazed down at her with a tender, possessive smile, and drew her head against his chest, caressing her hair. It carried the scent of hay and wildflowers, which never failed to arouse him.

Easter was a profitable wife, indeed.

1845 – Manifest Destiny

What's the cause of this commotion, motion, motion,
All the country through?
It is the ball a-rolling on
For Tippecanoe and Tyler too.
And with them we'll beat little Van, Van, Van,
Van is a used up man.
And with them we'll beat little Van…

FIFTEEN YEARS SINCE EASTER AND WILL'S
ARRIVAL IN OHIO…

Julia Gardiner Tyler, the wife of President John Tyler, was a vibrant woman some thirty years his junior. At a mere fifty-one years of age, Tyler was the youngest man, to date, ever to serve as president. They married during the second year of his presidency, another first. Alas, John had not won a second term.

John had to run this last race as a third-party candidate. The senator from Kentucky, Henry Clay, had run on behalf of the Whig Party, from which John was now estranged, and James Polk had run for the Democratic Party. Toward the end of the campaign, Andrew Jackson himself had personally asked John to withdraw his candidacy so they could deliver a crushing defeat against Clay, and so he had.

Julia was hosting a private tea for the incoming First Lady, Sarah Childress Polk, and Dolley Madison, the widow of President Madison and her cherished friend. Only the previous year, Dolley had returned to living in Washington, endeavoring to sell some of her deceased husband's papers to raise money for her struggling plantation. Due to her popularity and connections, Dolley had been granted an honorary seat in Congress, allowing her to witness debates in person. She often engaged in witty repartee with the gentlemen on the Hill during intermissions. Her gossip was a delightful source of entertainment.

Interestingly, Dolley had always been a close friend of Henry Clay; in fact, they liked to call each other "cousin," despite having no blood relation. With John's estrangement from Clay, Dolley had not taken sides. Whoever Dolley happened to be with at any given moment always seemed to be her most favorite person. It was one of the many reasons she was so well-liked. Undoubtedly, Dolley had known James and Sarah Polk from political circles over the years, and all three had close affiliations with the former president, Andrew Jackson.

At the moment, Dolley was immersed in a lively conversation with Sarah and appeared to be enjoying it immensely. Sarah Polk was an attractive woman who possessed the unique ability to look stylish even while dressing modestly. Given that Sarah was an devout Christian, both Dolley and Julia were curious if White House entertainment would be served "dry," as they say, for at least the next four, if not eight, years. Would the place be open to the people or restricted to only those with wealth and influence?

"Well, Sarah, you must know that Henry Clay is in quite a tizzy over losing the election to your husband. This was no less than his fifth attempt, with three actual runs. He is quite beside himself," Dolley said, tilting her head with a half-smile.

"I doubt Henry Clay will be a tolerable fellow for some time to come," Julia added as she refreshed each lady's cup. They all nodded, sharing a moment of amusement.

Julia glanced at Sarah as she quietly sipped her tea. All present knew that this particular lady, having a comprehensive education and no children, played a very active role in her husband's ambitions and politics. Sarah had adeptly navigated the position of First Lady when her husband was governor of Tennessee and was now ready to assume a similar role on the national stage. It was said that she would continue her role as her husband's private secretary, reviewing and prioritizing all his correspondence.

Dolley mused over the unwavering support Andrew Jackson had given to Polk's campaign. Certainly, Jackson held a long grudge against Henry Clay, but Dolley knew all too well that Sarah Polk had been involved with Floride Calhoun in the infamous Petticoat Affair that had ostracized Jackson's favored couple, the Eatons, in the first year of his presidency. Henry Clay had fueled the gossip as well. The scandal had paralyzed Jackson's ability to accomplish his goals for months. Back then, Jackson had referred to the women involved as a "witch's coven." Clearly, Sarah had been forgiven. Such were the shifting tides of vengeance and clemency in Washington.

"I am curious how you will manage White House hospitality, Sarah. Do tell. Will it be exclusive parties or the people's house?" Dolley inquired.

Sarah scrutinized the two ladies. She had their undivided attention. They were members of a small club now—all wives of presidents. Some of this club remained involved in politics every bit as much or more than their husbands, well beyond the tenure of the office. Some were glad to be rid of the place once their service had ended. Both Dolley and Julia seemed to thrive in and out of the limelight, and in that, they were all kindred spirits.

"We are Jacksonian Democrats through and through. Western expansion will continue to be a priority," Sarah stated firmly. "As for our new home, it will be the people's house, albeit in a more temperate Christian climate."

"No card tables then, I take it?" Dolley teased.

Sarah smiled politely at Dolley's mischievous grin. At seventy-seven years of age, this well-respected lady had worn black since the death of her husband in 1836. There was very little teasing Dolley could not get away with, as she was so beloved by those in Washington. Sarah knew she and her husband would likely be relying on Dolley's politicking skills and prestigious presence at parties and events to help gain influence in the months ahead. To achieve some early goals, they would need assistance reaching across the aisle to some disgruntled Whigs, specifically one Mr. Henry Clay. In that, Dolley was just the person to help.

"Well, I am hoping I can count on you two to support the fundraising effort for President Washington's monument." Dolley continued, "As you know, the Monument Society has been trying to secure enough funds to begin construction for quite some time."

"I can assure you, my husband and I are equally committed to the monument, and we will indeed push to secure initial funding as well as support your private events to raise money for the effort," Sarah replied. Both she and James were quite aware of Dolley's interest in this project. It would be a modest down payment for Dolley's support.

"Splendid!" Dolley replied, her eyes gleaming with determination. She was well aware that there would likely be favors traded to achieve the ultimate goal of breaking ground. Her fervent hope was to see the cornerstone set before drawing her last breath on this earth…

President John Tyler reviewed the bill before him, determined to fulfill his final duty during his last few weeks in office. In his mind, the fact that he had even served as President of the United States was nothing less than divine intervention.

Tyler had been chosen to run with William Henry Harrison on the Whig Party ticket as Vice President solely to secure the Virginia vote. Harrison, leaning more towards abolitionism, needed southern votes to win the election, and Tyler was well known for his southern roots and politics.

They had won a hard-fought race against President Van Buren of the Democratic Party, who had followed the two-term presidency of Andrew Jackson. As Jackson's successor and Vice President, Van Buren had won his first presidential term riding on Jackson's coattails. Van Buren had maintained Andrew Jackson's expansion policies and most of his cabinet during his term. Through Jackson's Indian Removal Act of 1830, and with some nineteen treaties negotiated under Van Buren, there had been many instances of violent, forced removal of thousands of Natives occupying treaty lands.

To resonate with the common man, the Harrison-Tyler ticket used a log cabin and hard cider as campaign symbols. They even minted metal tokens for circulation that displayed an image of a log cabin and the phrase "the people's choice." Out of several frontier hero candidates, the Whigs had chosen Harrison to compete with the Jackson patriotic narrative. Some chatter suggested that the former congressman from Tennessee, Colonel David Crockett, was a better choice, but in the end, Harrison's story held more appeal. Harrison's father had been one of the signers of the Declaration of Independence. Harrison himself had served in the War of 1812, commanding the army in the Northwest Territory. He had also served as governor of the Indiana Territory and fought a famous battle against Natives at the Tippecanoe River. This feat had been used in their popular campaign slogan "Tippecanoe and Tyler, too."

Not long after winning the presidency, Harrison contracted a fever and died, making Tyler not only the first president to hold the office without being elected to it but, at 51 years of age, the youngest as well. With a long career in politics and an almost religious sense of duty born from his predecessor's untimely death, Tyler had immediately stepped up to the challenge.

It had been a rocky road. He was dubbed "His Accidency," and most of the Whig-affiliated cabinet resigned after he took office. Nevertheless, Tyler had taken hold of the reins as a working president, not just a placeholder.

Although he had achieved a few foreign policy treaties with Britain and China, Tyler's primary focus was on the Manifest Destiny of the American people. Just five months into his presidency, he enacted the Preemption Act of 1841, allowing squatters already living on new public lands to purchase sections at $1.65 per acre before they were offered for sale. Ten percent of those sales were allocated to the states, targeted for investment in roads, bridges, canals, and railways—anything to make the way west more accessible for their expanding nation.

At last, Tyler's vision of annexing the Republic of Texas as a territory was about to become a reality. Texas had been recognized as a sovereign republic in 1837 when they had won their independence from Mexico, with Sam Houston serving as their president. Now, nine years after Texas had become an independent country, signing the bill before him would set the annexation into motion. The incoming President, James Polk of the Democratic Party, had agreed to seal the deal.

As college roommates, Tyler's father had been a good friend of Thomas Jefferson, the third president of the United States. Who could have ever imagined that his son would someday join the presidential brotherhood as the tenth?

Given Tyler's refusal to compromise his principles, Senator Henry Clay had convinced the Whig Party to ostracize him. Essentially, Tyler was a president without a party. He had even renamed his Virginia plantation "Sherwood Forest," cheekily implying that he was proud to be "outlawed." Just as in the story of Robin Hood, the preemption laws he signed supported the common man pioneering in the west, not wealthy investors seeking cheap land to resell at higher prices.

Tyler's vision, much like Thomas Jefferson's, was for each American to have the opportunity to become a self-sustaining farmer. This would be achieved by populating new lands as the United States continued to expand westward. Tyler had worked tirelessly for the last two years to bring about this Texas annexation. President-elect Polk, a protégé and longtime ally of Jackson, promised it would not end with Texas. Polk had his sights set on the Oregon Territory and the expansion all the way to the Pacific Ocean...

1848 – Banditti of the Prairie

Yes, away to the prairie, whose bosom, though wild,
Is unstained by oppression, by fraud undefiled;
From the wrongs that surround us, the home of our rest,
Let us seek on the wide, rolling plains of the West.

EIGHTEEN YEARS SINCE EASTER AND WILL'S
ARRIVAL IN OHIO...
Easter - 35, Will - 39
Phoebe - 17, Anna - 16, Mary - 15, Mahala - 12, Esther Malinda - 4
Aminadab - 14, Billy - 12, Elijah - 9, Moses Rueben - 6, John Bunyan - 1

oger Mills, the captain of the steamboat Blackhawk—aptly named after an infamous Native war chief—sucked on his corn cob pipe as his crew replenished the wood supply that would carry them to their next stop along the Mississippi. Among the passengers, one particular family had kept his crew, and himself for that matter, unusually entertained. The mother of the brood traveled without her husband, a circumstance not uncommon in these parts.

Pioneer families' menfolk often journeyed ahead to carve out the homestead, secure a food supply, and build shelters before sending for the rest of their kin. The country was pulsating with movement as countless settlers ventured westward to seek their fortunes.

This spirited Conklin woman, at the head of the family, reminded Roger of his former sergeant-at-arms in the militia. When she barked out orders to her children, they gave nary an objection and carried out said tasks with great haste. It was, however, the affection and humor among them that was engaging, and there were some beauties in the bunch that, in some communities, would already have been married off.

With her sharp, ever-roving eyes, Mrs. Conklin observed everything on board: scrutinizing the banks for movement, vigilantly watching her children, and seizing every opportunity to hunt, trade, or gather. A few military personnel on this trip were eager to deliver supplies to the soldiers at Fort Atkinson, a temporary resting place for the Winnebago Indians as they relocated to their new reservation. Old habits, however, died hard; some of the Native people still traversed the land, hunting and trading on the territory now reserved for pioneer families.

Roger chuckled as Mrs. Conklin bartered with the sergeant, offering her services and those of three daughters and two sons to help procure wood and game, as well as cook meals for the remainder of the journey, in exchange for a few crates of military rations.

"Me and my kids have homesteaded in the wilds of Ohio these past seventeen-plus years. We have strong backs and are talented foragers. You won't be disappointed." Easter confidently rested her hands on both hips, looking the sergeant straight in the eye.

The sergeant studied the lady and her small workforce with skepticism, shrugged his shoulders and replied, "You do honest work and we'll give you two barrels each of corn and wheat seed." The promised seed was part of the supplies for the Winnebagos, who were expected to take up farming on their new reservation. However, with only two men currently gathering wood for fuel, the additional help could save them a day or two of travel. In his opinion, it was well worth it. His mouth watered at the thought of home-cooked meals.

Delighted with the agreement, Easter immediately assigned jobs. At 16 and 17 years old, Anna and Phoebe were every bit as tall and sturdy as Easter, with Mary not far behind. Aminadab, now 14, and Elijah, now 12, were lean and gangly, yet strong and wiry, fully capable of assisting their older sisters. Mahala, also 12, was tasked with watching over Moses, Esther, and John Bunyan, who were 6, 4, and almost one year old, respectively.

Counting her payment in advance, Easter was confident that with the military supplies, the seed she'd brought from last year's garden staples, and her John Chapman apple tree saplings, she and Will could plant a robust garden for the fall harvest—provided they had fields to plant in.

Her most recent letter from Will mentioned that none other than Thomas Wallace himself was helping to prepare their fields in a little township called Otter Creek, just as he had twenty years ago when they had homesteaded in Ohio. And, just as she had back then, Easter traveled with her best laying hens and a rooster. As the fiercest of her brood, she entrusted Mahala with watching over the small flock. All of her children had heard the story of how Easter had lost her first rooster when they had traveled from the Mohawk Valley to Ohio.

Roger chatted with the sergeant as they watched the Conklin family expertly set to the tasks at hand. The younger ones supervised the babies onboard while the older ones swarmed the banks with their mother. He observed the nearly grown girls and a teen boy chopping wood, while the smaller ones foraged for what appeared to be tubers and wild rice. A couple of the children trotted into the forest carrying slings similar to those used by some of the local Natives and, after a while, returned with rabbits and squirrels in tow. The family reminded him of the tribes—how they were at one with the land in a place they had never been yet seemed to intuitively understand. It was fascinating to watch.

The Conklin family enjoyed lively debates about a few frontier heroes they had read about in newspapers. It was a pleasant distraction for Roger and his men to listen in on the discussions as they went about their chores. The older girls and young Elijah favored Davy Crockett, mainly due to stories from a genuine autographed book their Ma had gotten from Crockett himself, as well as newspaper fables. Elijah tended to carry the book on his person quite often and quoted from it occasionally. His Ma had even fashioned him a coonskin cap with a fluffy tail hanging off the back, akin to what the famed frontiersman liked to sport.

The older boys preferred Daniel Boone because he was not only an Indian fighter and captain in the Revolutionary War but had also worked as a surveyor along the Ohio River. There was a lively discussion about the statesman, Henry Clay, due to his recent run for president and support of farmers, settlers, and western trade; however, they finally agreed that he had not participated in heroic battles nor pioneered anywhere, disqualifying him for consideration. Besides, young Billy Conklin pointed out, Pa didn't think much of Henry Clay because he was emphatically anti-Andrew Jackson. The same could be said of Davy Crockett, given all the anti-Jackson speeches Pa complained about and had even heard in person when Davy visited Ohio. This, Billy stated, should make Daniel Boone the winner, but his siblings playfully heckled the boy down on that argument.

All the young Conklins seemed to feel they were every bit as adventurous as these famed frontier heroes who had explored and pioneered before them.

From the riverbank, Easter helped the girls stack wood, occasionally noting the whereabouts of John Bunyan who was held safely in Mahala's arms, as instructed. Mahala was steadfast and reliable. She had quite a temper when riled, but it was usually for a just cause.

Will had headed to Iowa when Easter was pregnant with their tenth child, leaving her to choose a name. One of her favorite books, sent to her by her father, was John Bunyan's The Pilgrim's Progress. Easter had read it many times to the children, and each one of them, in turn, had read aloud some of the chapters as part of their schooling. Anna suggested John Bunyan as the name, and to everyone's delight, their new sibling was named after the famed author. Easter doubted Will would mind; he was always overjoyed when a new son was born. Not that he didn't love his girls, but he wanted strong farmhands and preferred the girls to stick with more traditional tasks for women. Until the boys were old enough, it made sense to divvy up chores among all able-bodied family members, girls or not.

As such, her girls would be the epitome of a farmer's dream life partner. Hired help was scarce, so neither she nor Will were in a hurry to see their older daughters married off anytime soon. Easter planned to find strong, well-established farmers with successful homesteads for her girls, and she would accept nothing less.

When they left their farm in Ohio, Easter and Will received two dollars per acre plus another twenty for the already-built homestead, along with stock and wagons. They transported three wagons of their belongings down to the river and loaded them onto a flatboat. From there, Easter's brood floated down the river to the Mississippi, where they transferred their belongings to the steamboat Blackhawk. Just as they had when they traveled from the Mohawk Valley to Ohio, they took the safest, cheapest, and most modern transportation of the time.

Having gotten to know the captain, Easter was confident he would be willing to put them ashore at Bellevue along with their supplies. From there, Will and Thomas would come to retrieve them and bring them to their new home in Otter Creek Township. With loaded wagons, the journey from Bellevue would take a full day. Thomas had written that the town's name meant "beautiful view" in French. Everyone was eager to see if it lived up to its fancy name.

Easter had pondered long and hard about their decision to move to Iowa. The rugged, hilly terrain of their Ohio homestead hadn't offered the fertile soil found in the flatter part of the state. Their German and Swiss neighbors had transformed their land into productive and profitable dairy farms, collaborating in a thriving cheese-making business. Will had been too stubborn to change his ways, so their farm had rarely achieved surpluses beyond providing a comfortable subsistence. Their dream was a commodity farm, and now, with their expanded family, they had the manpower to fulfill this dream in the right setting. With the growing population in Ohio, they had decided to sell their land to the dairy farmers and seek their fortunes further west in lands that

Thomas Wallace touted as a farmer's dream—where the corn grew taller than a man's height. As icing on the cake, their new home would be in Jackson County, Iowa. Will felt this was a lucky sign, given it was named for the president who had inspired them to move west.

Captain Robert studied Easter Conklin as she herded her family back on board with all their prizes in tow. She had a rough prettiness about her. Years of pioneering and child-rearing had etched lines in her face, but they were friendly lines.

"None of that!" She commanded sternly as the boys started playfully pushing and shoving dangerously close to the edge of the boat.

Captain Robert chuckled as the boys immediately came to attention, fidgeting and awaiting their next orders. Bellevue was where Easter had asked him to deposit the family and their cargo. An Army run to Fort Atkinson typically did not include a stop in Bellevue. The place had a bit of a tarnished reputation due to a nasty shootout that had occurred some eight years prior. There was a lot of bad blood between a couple of political factions in town, and it was suspected that some had ties to the outlaw gang known as the Banditti of the Prairie.

Easter, for her part, remained vigilant, keeping a watchful eye on her brood as they prepared for the next leg of their journey. As the steamboat churned down the river, with the Conklin family and their cargo aboard, the sun dipped low in the sky, casting a warm, golden hue over the rippling waters—an inspiring sign of adventures that might lay ahead.

******

Edward Bonney stroked his stubble as he followed his comrades on horseback up the rugged Native trail. They were headed back north to Bellevue, having used some of his expertly crafted counterfeit scrip to buy quite a few supplies down south. After securing delivery of the supplies via a steamboat to Bellevue, the group now traveled back upriver the same way they had come to take advantage of some opportunities spotted on the way down.

Edward had more than a few regrets about leaving his thriving livery business in the north to infiltrate this gang. They were a ruthless bunch, yet quite sophisticated. Like a wolf pack, they identified the vulnerable targets with the highest reward factor. The suspicion that one or more of them had been connected to the murder and robbery of a wealthy, well-connected colonel was what had aroused multiple states' ire, resulting in the high bounties placed on their Mormon heads.

Edward had a history with the Mormon community in Nauvoo, Illinois, where he had spent time on the council, which was where this gang hailed from. The town of Nauvoo had a charter that forbade the county sheriff from entering the place—a fact many bandits took advantage of. When Edward's Mormon friend Joseph Smith and his brother had been killed, their new leader, Brigham Young, had Edward removed from the council. One could only assume, given he and the only other two Gentiles on the council of fifty were removed, that they were no longer welcome in that community. So Edward had moved his family to Lee County, Iowa, and opened what had become a very successful livery business.

Over the past few years, nefarious groups had sprouted from the Nauvoo area that considered themselves above the common man. More Mormon in word rather than deed, they drank, shared secret oaths, and stole from the Gentiles. While tithing a good portion of their takings to the church temple, they attempted to bring other young, impressionable converts into their gang.

Although the church coffers grew, the public was warned that their leaders did not sanction stealing and that the church would not tolerate thieves. Ultimately, most had been excommunicated but still considered themselves "chosen saints," and believed that stealing from Gentiles was sanctioned by God. The town and surrounding areas became so inhospitable that Brigham Young had moved the majority of his followers to territories in the southwest to begin anew.

The most notorious gang in Nauvoo had been dubbed the banditti of the prairie, but contrary to their name, they rarely rode together as one. Edward had come to learn that, instead, they roamed counties throughout the Mississippi valley across territories and states—horse rustling, robbing, and counterfeiting—ultimately bringing resources back to loosely connected family circles mostly residing between Nauvoo in Illinois and Bellevue in Iowa. Stealing was a way of life for some of this gang. The ones that robbed as retribution for real or imagined misdeeds against them tended to be the most dangerous.

Bounty hunting was a side business for Edward, both lucrative and rewarding. It was the thrill of the hunt combined with his reputation as an exceptional investigator that kept him in this game. The livery business provided a reputable cover, allowing him to pursue this passion with a semblance of respectability. His knack for freelance catching and bringing these so-called rogues to justice, along with the evidence to convict them, had earned him admiration from more than a few sheriffs and marshals.

Having taken their formal "prayer of vengeance" to infiltrate the gang, Edward had pledged to kill any members who violated their secret oaths, as well as help any and all gang members who found themselves in trouble. These people were well-known for taking vengeance out on the families of those who dared violate their oaths. This was dangerous business, and as such, he was being very cautious.

Although the Illinois Militia had extinguished the most visible portions of the gang, like rodents, pockets of them had resurfaced. Edward had been hired by the law to root them out. Today he rode with the Hodge Brothers, Amos and Ervine, and one Bartholomew brother, Abram. Both families had members convicted in the murder of the Colonel, and as such, they followed in their older brothers' footsteps, preying on the vulnerable. Now that he knew their hiding places, he had sent word to the law to meet him in Bellevue, hoping to take them prisoner. So far, he had gathered enough evidence to put them away for a long time at Rock Island.

They would be in good company there; the place already housed some of the banditti.

As the boat chugged its way up the river, Anna and Mary sat with their legs dangling over the edge, taking a well-deserved break. They had helped Ma feed the crew and soldiers, as well as making some very fine mixed berry pies from their foraging, of which the soldiers were happily taking seconds. Dishes had been washed, and it appeared no more chores would be needed before the boat moored along the shore for the evening.

Suddenly, Anna felt Mary sharply poke her in the ribs. Noting Mary's intent gaze, she immediately saw the source of her sudden trepidation. Anna's hair stood on end as she observed the group of four men on horseback, standing so still as if carved from stone, gazing down at them as they paddled up the river.

"Go tell the Captain," Anna whispered without moving. Normally, they were excited to see strangers, but Anna felt as if she had been staring down a wolf pack on the hunt. Like a scared rabbit, Mary ran to the other side and hollered, "Captain Robert, Captain Robert!" When he stood up from eating his pie, she pointed at the ridge.

"What do you see, girl?" Captain Robert asked, confused.

Mary looked back up to the ridge then back at Anna.

"They went down the back-side of the bank," Anna announced.

"A bunch of men on horseback staring at the boat," Mary answered. "I don't know…They didn't look right." Anna nodded in agreement.

Captain Robert cocked his head and studied the ridgeline. He had been around these girls long enough to know that they were not likely to have imagined anything. He would certainly talk to the soldiers about setting extra guards this evening, just in case. Even as remote a chance it was that the girls' intuition was right, the supplies they carried would be valuable loot to banditti or Natives. He had been a bit too complacent on this trip. It was time to focus. His eyes narrowed as he studied the river turns up ahead in his mind's eye, guessing where the best place might be for an ambush of some kind. Given how well-armed they were on this trip, any banditti would have to be pretty foolish to attack them, and now with the girls' sharp eyes alerting the crew to their presence, a sneak attack was no longer in the cards.

As they rode down the hill away from the river, Amos gave his brother a sly wink, "Purty, huh?"

Ervine smiled wryly, running his tongue over his lips, nodding. Neither of them had taken a wife, and seeing the two beauties on the steam boat up close like that had made them take pause. Women were rare in these parts. It was nearly impossible from the glimpse they had gotten, not to be drawn to see more.

"That's the Blackhawk. It's carrying our supplies," Edward stated. "It's well armed. It's carrying military supplies as well." He certainly did not want to have to witness robbery, murder, and kidnapping with this crew. He was pretty sure they had some robbery planned before they reached Bellevue.

"Well isn't that lucky?" Amos retorted, "We'll have to make sure we get home in time to meet the boat and get our supplies personally."

Ervine grinned again in agreement.

Edward noted that Abram kept his eyes down, stoic as ever. He seemed a bit softer than the others, as if he rode with them reluctantly. What was left of Abram's family was imprisoned at Black Rock. The Hodge brothers had taken him in because he was from the Bartholomew family. Loyalty was thick with these people, but Abram seemed to have an ethic and empathy about him the others lacked. Edward dismissed the thought. It didn't matter. Abram had chosen to ride with the banditti and would be convicted of their crimes along with the Hodges, regardless.

******

Anna, Mary, and Mahala walked the picturesque hillside meadow near the river, foraging for dinner. It was late afternoon, and it had been a couple of days since they'd spotted the men on the shore. With no sign of them, convinced that any thought of robbing the riverboat had been outweighed by their obvious ability to defend it, the captain was no longer worried.

Anna glanced at her sisters as they scurried here and there. It was a nice break to get away from the river boat for a while. For their whole lives the three of them had been like a little sub-tribe in their family. Where one was, the other two were almost always nearby. At twelve years of age, Mahala was just a little shorter than her sisters but still sported the lean, gangly frame of youth with solid, square shoulders. She was the scrappiest in their family, and few dared to tempt fate by crossing her. Mahala was a fair but a vengeful thing. Mary was always temperate and easily followed her sisters. Anna had always been the benevolent leader of the bunch. Their older sister, Phoebe, was so much like Ma that they had learned to avoid her to have any real fun.

As a symbiotic force, the three traveled like natives. Silent as the land around them, they were ready to let loose a slingshot if some unlucky game caught their eye. Mary was a bit ahead of her sisters. As she came to the top of the hill she decided to stroll down a bit. Suddenly, she froze. Below there was a small homestead with two saddled horses outside. Mary had only gotten a glimpse of the men from a few days before, but the horses looked very much like the ones she had seen. The noise coming from the cabin sounded like someone was ransacking the place. She blinked her eyes a couple of times to be sure of what she was seeing. It chilled her to the bone. A pair of very still, naked feminine legs were protruding from the cabin doorway. Suddenly, they began to slide from view as if someone within was pulling the limp body inside.

******

Abram spotted the young woman just as she stepped over the edge of the meadow. He was in the trees, standing guard for the Hodge brothers as he always did. Their new comrade, Edward Bonney, had made it clear to the gang that he only participated in counterfeiting and not any violent illegal activities. Counterfeiting was so specialized and valuable that this arrangement was easily acceptable, and so when this opportunity arose, he had been sent ahead to meet up with the gang later.

Abram felt a lump in his throat when he saw the young woman staring down at the Hodges' horses. The Hodges would not want any witnesses, and who knew what they might do if they caught her. As a lookout, his job was to warn them of her presence and capture her immediately. Earlier, he had heard a solitary scream coming from the cabin below, followed by silence. Murder was not beyond the Hodges to eliminate witnesses. Gratefully, Abram had not heard more than the single scream; he hoped perhaps the victim was only rendered unconscious…

As he stalked the new arrival, he momentarily glanced down the hill to see if anyone was with her—nothing. It appeared she had just strayed away from the riverboat. It was probably moored nearby for the evening. The gang would have to move fast to get out of here. Her kin would certainly come looking if this young woman did not return.

****

When they saw the man silently creeping towards where Mary had disappeared over the hill, Anna and Mahala immediately dropped to the ground. He glanced down at them. Luckily the tall grass hid them well. They could see him, but he could not see them. He turned and disappeared in the direction Mary had gone.

"What do we do?" Mahala mouthed at Anna.

Anna's eyes were frozen on the hill. Who knew what could happen to Mary if they ran back to the boat for help? She could be hurt, kidnapped, or worse. In an instant she made a decision.

Anna whispered, "Stay here. If I don't return you run back to the boat. Okay? If you see anybody, stay hidden."

Her eyes wide with worry, Mahala nodded.

******

A shriek rose in Mary's throat when she was grabbed from behind, but before she could sound it a large hand covered her nose and mouth. She was shoved to the ground and pinned with her hands behind her back, someone's rough knee on her backside. She felt someone's breath on her neck as she struggled.

Abram whispered, "Goddammit, hold still. Don't make a sound. I'm not going to hurt you. Hold still! If they hear you, things are going to go in a rough way." Abram was desperately trying to hold onto the wench, but she was a lot stronger than she looked. He let up on her mouth so she could suck in air, ready to cover it again if she made noise…She was keeping quiet but still struggling. He rolled her onto her back, pinned her arms over her head, and sat on her waist to hold her down. Face to face with her now he put his fingers to his lips. "Shhhhhh." Her eyes were quite captivating, but she was listening now. Her hair smelled like wildflowers. He shook his head to focus and glanced down the hill. The Hodges were still inside.

"Listen to me. We don't have much time," he whispered.

Mary nodded her head. She was terrified.

"You stumbled into something here. You need to forget it. You never saw this. You never saw us. I'm gonna let you go. You're gonna skedaddle out of here. But if you tell, they will find out and hunt you and your family down. These are a dangerous, vengeful lot. Understand?"

Mary nodded. It felt as if her heart would pound out of her chest. The lifeless legs she had witnessed was proof enough.

"Promise you won't tell?"

Mary nodded again.

And that is the last thing Abram remembered. Something struck him from behind and everything went dark.

When he woke up, the Hodges were leaning over him.

"Abram, what the hell? What happened? Geez, who did this to you? Did you see them? Did they see us?" Amos had a savage look in his eye. Ervine was standing up scanning the hillside.

Abram reached back and touched the back of his head. There was a huge lump there. Someone had hit him from behind.

"Ugh, it was some Injuns. I came up on one. Another must have hit me from behind. Did they take my horse?" Abram added to re-enforce the Injun story. He did not want them to suspect anyone else. It looked like the young woman had escaped. Hopefully she would keep her mouth shut like she had promised. Abram did not ask the Hodges what had taken place at the homestead. In truth, his conscience already weighed heavy upon him. The less he knew about their actions the better.

******

Mahala leaped to her feet as she saw Anna and Mary sprinting down the hill. In unison the three of them ran without stopping until they were almost in sight of the boat.

"Wait," Mary gasped breathlessly. "Wait, I have to tell you something." They all came to a stop.

The three of them looked over their shoulders and all around to confirm no one pursued them.

Mary held her forefinger up to let them know she had to catch her breath. She had their attention.

It had all happened so fast. When she saw Anna in the background come up behind the man who had pinned her, it took everything she had not to look. She had held his gaze while Anna slammed him in the head with a rock. Mary wondered if the man was even still alive after that. It took both of them to roll him off of her, and then they took off running for their lives.

"We can't tell," Mary finally announced.

Anna studied her sister. She had never seen her so intent. Fear and determination was what she saw.

Mahala and Anna remained silent, waiting for Mary to continue. This was nothing any of them had ever dreamed of experiencing. How could they not tell?

"The man. He said he was going to let me go. There were some men down below. I think they were robbing a homestead...or maybe something even worse. He said if I told, they would find out and hunt us down. They are a very bad lot."

She held her sisters eyes so they would understand how important this was.

"He said we never saw him, we never saw any of it. You have to promise, promise with all your heart. You can't tell."

They all paused for a good minute to process all that had happened. At last Mahala nodded solemnly.

"They were the men we saw from the shoreline a couple of days ago, weren't they?" Anna whispered.

Mary just stared back at her silently.

"Okay. Okay. I promise, I won't say a word," Anna confirmed.

When Easter saw the girls return she noticed right away something was a little off. It was almost dark, and she was starting to worry. It was a relief to see them climb on board, even though they were empty handed.

"Everything all right?"

Anna, Mary, and Mahala kept their eyes on the ground and all nodded as they silently went on their way. Phoebe watched curiously as well. The girls finally settled on some gunny sacks and stared at the bank, glancing back from where they had come. As she held John Bunyan on her hip Phoebe wondered what they had been up to. They were such a secretive bunch. Who knew what mischief they might have gotten into?

******

Abram followed on horseback as Ervine and Amos drove the

wagon down to the shore where the steamboat had landed near Bellevue. The soldiers bustled about, unloading freight as Edward Bonney conversed with the captain, who was having the cargo sorted into piles for transfer.

After the cabin robbery, they had hastened up to Bellevue because Amos and Ervine were still determined to get a closer look at the pretty girls on board. As they drew near, Abram immediately spotted four of the ladies, one of them quite young, gazing in their direction. He recognized the girl he had briefly encountered at the robbery scene. Her expression was inscrutable; she had obviously kept her promise and was now deeply and justifiably suspicious of them. He glanced at the others, wondering which one had clubbed him.

Anna whispered to Phoebe, "Those are the men we saw at the shore on the way upriver."

Phoebe noticed her sisters were quite agitated. Mahala had one hand opening and closing as she stared at the men. Mary was frowning. Anna was unreadable—hiding something. And then Phoebe saw it. One of the men rubbed the back of his head, smiled, and shrugged at Mary. Mary shrugged back and looked down. They had met; Phoebe was certain of it.

Ma had been engaging in lively conversation with Mr. Bonney and the captain before his comrades arrived. She seemed to have taken a liking to him, gleaning valuable information about the roadways and travel times. Phoebe edged closer, holding John Bunyan on her hip, to listen in on their exchange.

"Well. Mr. Bonney," Easter bantered, "From all of your travels it sounds like you know these parts like the back of your hand."

"I do indeed, Mrs. Conklin," Edward replied relishing the company of ordinary folks after spending so much time with his unsavory comrades. "I have not met Thomas Wallace or your husband, but Abram there has worked for the Wallace brothers a few times. I reckon with your wagons, you'll be reunited with your husband in a day and a half or so, given the time of year." Edward smiled at the delight on the woman's face.

"Thank you kindly, Mr. Bonney."

Easter had an idea. She was so close to seeing Will again that she couldn't wait any longer. Hoping against hope, she approached Edward Bonney's comrades to see if she could persuade them to help. Edward Bonney seemed like an upright member of the community, so she felt comfortable that his comrades would be as well. This Abram fellow had even worked for Thomas. She trusted Phoebe could manage the family on her own for a couple of days with assistance in securing lodging.

Edward chatted casually with the captain, keeping an eye on the Hodges and Abram. Mrs. Conklin was conversing with them as they loaded their cargo onto the wagon. It was late enough in the evening that the Hodges would likely stay in town for the night before heading back north. If all went as planned, the marshal would have a posse nearby, waiting for his signal. Suddenly, he noticed that Amos was nodding at Mrs. Conklin and shaking her hand. Now they were unloading the wagon. He hurried over to see what was going on.

"Change of plans," Amos announced with a grin. "We are going to help this nice lady get her family and their freight into town while she heads out to fetch her husband on their homestead. He's stayin' with Ol' Thomas Wallace up by Otter Creek. Abram here is gonna show her the way."

Abram was taken aback by the sudden turn of events. He doubted the Hodges would risk a confrontation with the Wallace brothers and their Irish neighbors by hurting this family. There were plenty of witnesses to everything unfolding here. More likely, they wanted time alone with the daughters to court them properly.

The younger Conklin brothers were thin, wiry, and seemed entirely obedient to their mother and sisters—unlikely to cause any trouble. It was curious that the mother would trust her family to complete strangers, but that was not unheard of this far out west. The Hodges and others like them preyed on such people. If only Amos and Ervine knew that one of them had witnessed their recent robbery…

When Anna gave Phoebe a silent look of alarm, Phoebe motioned her to the back of the boat. As they strolled, Anna whispered, "She can't go with them. They are a bad lot. I can't tell you why. You have to stop Ma." Phoebe regarded her sternly and handed Anna the baby.

"You and your secrets," she hissed, abruptly turning and headed back down the ramp.

As Phoebe approached Ma and the men, she put on her warmest smile and swayed her hips slightly. The men gazed at her and doffed their hats. "Ma," she said, still smiling at the men, "Can I talk to ya for a minute?" Easter and Phoebe strolled down to the beach, with Phoebe casting one more flirtatious look over her shoulder as the men followed her with their eyes.

"Ma, those are the men Anna and Mary saw on the river the other day."

"I know that," Easter responded, "Edward Bonney told me they rode their horses up the river for some business and checked on the riverboat a couple of times because they had freight on board."

"Ma, we need to steer clear of those men. Something happened with Anna, Mary, and Mahala. They saw something. I don't know what. But Anna told me they are a bad lot. She means it Ma," Phoebe continued. "One of the soldiers told me there are a lot of banditti around these parts, especially in Bellevue."

Easter frowned. It would be just like Will to disregard such rumors for a more convenient, faster travel route for their freight. She had heard whispers of bandits but had thought them mostly tall tales. Easter had learned long ago to trust her instincts. She glanced sidelong at the men. Edward Bonney she trusted; he suddenly looked extremely uncomfortable, glancing between her and his comrades. Mr. Bonney appeared quite vexed, in fact. The Hodge brothers, on the other hand, seemed a touch too gleeful for her liking. Perhaps she had been misguided.

She headed back to the wagon with Phoebe following and folded her arms. "I guess the baby is feeling a little poorly," Easter announced. "I won't be heading out to Otter Creek today, that's for sure. We'll get that freight stored and then get a couple of rooms in town for the night. Perhaps you fine gentlemen can point us to a boarding house of some kind?" Easter and Phoebe beamed at the men, whose smiles had suddenly vanished.

Phoebe stepped forward. "It is so nice of you to help us with our freight." She raised her hands and motioned to her brothers, who promptly came running down the ramp and proceeded to help finish loading the freight.

Easter took note of Mr. Bonney's sudden relief.

Easter settled her family into two rooms at a boarding house in town and followed Edward Bonney's recommendation for storing their freight securely at the local livery. Once everyone was fed, she planned to sit down with Anna, Mary, and Mahala to uncover what the girls knew.

******

At Edward Bonney's behest, the bartender poured shots of whiskey for his three comrades. Edward tipped his hat to his surly mates and said, "Be back in a bit," and exited the saloon. Two of his comrades appeared displeased with Mr. Bonney; one even moved away to sit alone by the window.

The Red Rock Saloon was having a slow afternoon, which worked in his favor. The marshal had discreetly paid the bartender and informed him that these men were desperadoes soon to be ambushed and captured. Any damage to the premises would be reimbursed. So, for now, the bartender's job was to simply go about his business, stay out of the way, and enjoy the show.

As the men drained their glasses, the bartender refilled them as instructed by Edward Bonney, who was footing the bill. These men were eager for drink as they had been on the road for quite some time.

Abram took a small sip of whiskey, observing the Hodge brothers guzzle theirs down. With Edward Bonney covering the expenses, they were eager to get their fill. In another hour, they would likely be too intoxicated to reach their room unaided. Abram realized it was time to distance himself from this gang. With their business here concluded, they would be heading across the river back to northern Illinois. It would be easy for him to slip away under the guise of checking on relatives at Black Rock prison.

Seeing the Conklin family had awakened a yearning for a more normal future—one with a wife, family, and a homestead built with his own two hands. The Hodges' practice of taking what others had earned through hard work held no satisfaction for him, and their hypocritical religious justifications rang hollow.

As the bartender poured Abram a second drink while the now-jovial Hodges were on their fourth, he noticed a man glancing furtively across the street. Following his gaze, he saw two well-armed men with rifles staring at the saloon. Meeting the bartender's eyes, the man quickly looked away and moved back to the bar. Abram stood up and surveyed the streets. Three more men with rifles were approaching the saloon.

"Heads up!" Abram stated loudly. "It's a trap. We've gotta move out."

Like coiled timber rattlers, the Hodge brothers abruptly went from jovial to drawing their pistols. They joined Abram at the window. Amos narrowed his eyes at the bartender, who hastily ducked down behind the bar. Their horses were out front.

"Goddamn. It is a trap. Goddamn Edward Bonney. We have to get out of here now before they're ready," Amos hissed, counting the armed men he could see. They were still getting into position. Suddenly, Amos charged over to the bartender, grabbed him by the scruff of the neck, put his gun to the man's head, and ordered, "You walk out to the middle of the roadway, look down yonder, point out of town, and yell they went out the back. Keep yelling it until the shooting starts. Do anything else, and I'll shoot you dead, you understand?"

The bartender's eyes were as round as saucers. He hadn't expected to get involved in this. Terrified, he obeyed Amos's orders, moving toward the door.

******

At last, with all her errands completed, Easter was prepared to question the girls.

"I listened to you girls today and turned down a guide who would have had me half way to your Pa by now. You need to tell me why."

The girls stared at the floor silently. These three were as thick as thieves—a formidable trio, indeed.

"Do I need to take a switch to ya?"

One by one the girls raised their arms to accept punishment.

Anna sighed as she held out her hands for Ma to switch—a small price to pay to keep them safe. Easter shook her head in disbelief. Suddenly, they heard someone bellowing in the street. They all rushed to the window to see what was happening. Gunfire erupted, and Easter yelled, "Everybody get down. Get on the floor and stay down!"

Easter peeked out the window to see the Hodge brothers and Abram galloping their horses out of town, guns raised. Moments later, several men on horseback pursued them, guns also raised. Her girls inched up beside her to watch the astonishing scene. When they were finally out of sight, all Easter could do was stare at her daughters, dumbfounded, wondering what might have happened if she hadn't listened to them.

"Okay. Okay. I don't need to know. Maybe someday you'll tell me. But I don't need to know now." She wrapped all three of them in her arms and held them tight far into the night.

The next morning at breakfast, their hostess shared the gossip about the gunfight.

"Edward Bonney is a bounty hunter. He set up the Hodges and Abram Bartholomew to get arrested by some marshal when they arrived in town. Apparently they belong to a gang of murderers and thieves." She nodded knowingly. "Edward Bonney infiltrated their gang to get the evidence to convict them along with keeping tabs on their whereabouts so they could be captured. So far they have eluded the posse," she concluded.

Easter thought about how close they had come to being entangled with these dangerous people. Surely angels had been watching over them throughout this long journey. All that remained now was to get them through the last leg of their trek to Otter Creek.

******

Well north of Bellevue, the Hodges and Abram had ridden all night and swum their horses across the river into Illinois. Well-versed at eluding a posse, they knew the ins and outs of the Native trails that had traversed these parts for hundreds of years. By navigating from a hard, rocky surface to a slower pace in the river itself, they left no trail to follow. With a downstream exit from the river, they had easily evaded their trackers for now.

Abram pulled up his horse and announced, "I'm thinking we should split up from here."

Amos Hodge scowled in return.

"If they do catch up to our trail and it's split, we'll be harder to track. And I have some business up at Black Rock," Abram stated unemotionally.

Amos pondered for a moment and then without word nodded his head and pointed his horse northeast towards home.

As the brothers rode away Abram considered, with all his trepidation, how easy the split had been. Perhaps they considered their shared fates in the acts committed insurance enough to warrant trust, but then, they had all trusted Edward Bonney and look where that had led.

When they were out of sight, Abram rode his horse down river until he was close to Bellevue and crossed back over the river, now well behind the posse. There was one more thing he wanted to do.

******

Thomas Wallace paused to take note of the rider approaching the edge of his field. It appeared to be the nice young lad he had hired to help him in his fields a couple of times last year—one of the Bartholomew brothers from the Mormon community. A troublesome lot for the most part, but this young one had shown promise at one time, anyway. And who was Thomas to judge, given his own origins in this country?

"Top of the mornin' to ya, Abram. What brings you out this way with your horse lookin' so spent?" Thomas placed his hand on the horse to wipe some of the sweat away. It was obvious the animal had been ridden hard.

"Got into a bit of a jam in town," Abram grinned back at Thomas. He'd always liked this man. "I wanted to let you know I ran into a family in Bellevue by the name of Conklin. The woman said her husband was staying out here with you. Ya might want to go in and fetch them. There are a few hard folks hanging around town."

This elicited an even larger grin from the Irishman. "Bless you, Abram. We'll head in for them right away. Ya hungry? Help yourself to some food and rest inside," Thomas offered.

"Nah, I'm in a bit of a hurry. I'll be off." Abram tipped his hat and rode off as fast as he had come.

Thomas leaped in the air, let out a whoop, and then ran to get Will. If they left now, with a quick pace, they could reach town a little after dark.

1849 – The Dancing Ground

To the wide, rolling plains of the West let us hie,
Where the clear river's bosom immirrors the sky,
On whose banks stands the warrior so brave,
Whose bark hath alone left a curl on the wave

ONE YEAR LATER…
Easter - 36, Will - 40
Phoebe - 18, Anna -17, Mary - 16, Mahala - 13, Esther Malinda - 5
Aminadab - 15, Billy - 13, Elijah - 10, Moses Rueben - 7,
John Bunyan - 2, Thomas Didamus - three months

Will was quite surprised that his family had so many local bachelors keen to assist in establishing the Conklin farm. Certainly Thomas Wallace and his brother had been the most generous contributors, but other established local families such as the Aherns and the Sades had thrown quite a bit more shoulder into it than Will himself had ever done for new neighbors back in Ohio. Eventually he noticed the subtle glances of admiration these men cast towards his older daughters and realized their intentions—to court them as frontier wives. He mused at his good fortune. A house, a barn, a root cellar, a bunk for the boys, and two fields cleared had been their opening bids. Easter's carefully preserved nest egg was hardly touched, ensuring funds for seed, stock animals, as well as possibly a modern plow, and maybe even a store-bought stove.

Their homestead was becoming a paradise. A sweeping field led up to the house, perched on a gentle hill overlooking Lytle Creek, which provided clean, flowing water year-round. The eighty-acre property boasted patches of timber teeming with game and ample space for hogs to roam. The L-shaped log house featured a stone fireplace for heat and cooking, as well as a long bench-lined table for meals. It felt gratifying to refer to their dwelling as a house rather than a mere cabin. A ladder led to the younger children's sleeping quarters in the gabled section of the house—an ingenious idea from Thomas Wallace. This arrangement afforded Will and Easter a private room at the back of the L, separated by a blanket. The older boys' well-finished bunkhouse, complete with its own small warming hearth, proved to be a clever addition.

The entire place smelled of fresh-cut wood. Windows on the front and sides of the house were protected with shutters that could be opened to admit fresh air and sunlight. Easter already had planted a well-tilled kitchen garden, brimming with sprouting seedlings. Will's next project was a larger root cellar, though it could wait for now. The neighbors had helped them dig a small one that, while cramped, could store enough provisions to last the winter. Thomas had even gifted them a charming flat-paneled outhouse adorned with a crescent moon cutout, delighting Easter, Anna, and Phoebe. With three acres of cultivated land, a milk cow in the barn, and a planted flax field for fabric, the Conklins were well-equipped to thrive in their new home.

His family was settling into a rhythm with the land and homestead. The younger children busied themselves with chores and playing in the woods, while the older boys toiled diligently in the fields under Will's watchful eye. Easter and the older girls had begun producing goods for sale and family use, utilizing resources from the land and animals. It was a fresh start for everyone, with the tantalizing prospect of Will Conklin's dreams finally materializing.

During their time apart, Will had nearly forgotten how much he yearned to hold Easter in his arms each night. They sent the children to bed early most evenings, savoring every moment spent making up for lost time. Easter was already well on her way to having another child, and Will was certain it would be a boy...

******

The soft, furry red creature nuzzled Mahala's chin as she carried it to the new pen, set at a safe distance from the family farmhouse.

A couple of weeks earlier, Mahala had discovered the lifeless mother fox while foraging for berries. As she examined the animal, having never seen a fox up close before, a high-pitched whimper caught her attention. Tracking the sound, she found an injured pup, likely harmed by whatever had killed its mother. Mahala's family was initially curious about the tiny creature she brought home—except for her father, who warned, "When it's grown, it'll kill all your Ma's chickens."

Ma helped her patch up what appeared to be a broken hind leg along with stitching up an open wound on the chest, instructing her to keep her special salve on it to promote healing. Mahala named her newfound companion "Whiskers." The pup's expressive eyes and twitching whiskers seemed to communicate with Mahala, and Whiskers showered her with affection during meal times. Mahala grew deeply attached.

Once it became evident that Whiskers would likely recover, Ma agreed that the fox should be housed away from the farm until it was strong enough to be released. "When Whiskers is grown, she'll need to manage on her own and forget about us. It's for the best," she said.

Mahala built a sturdy, shaded hickory pen a half-mile from the house, close to where she had found Whiskers' mother. Though she would be heartbroken to part ways with the fox, Mahala was overjoyed that Whiskers had healed so well. The warmth of such mutual affection was a new experience for her, one she hadn't previously considered. As much as it pained her to think about releasing Whiskers in a few months, she wanted what was best for her little friend.

Carrying Whiskers towards the edge of the woods, Mahala passed Ma's new Iowa kitchen garden. Having helped tend their

Ohio garden for years, she observed similarities in its layout and plants—distinctly different from their crop fields. Ma always planted "the three sisters": corn, pole beans, and winter squash. The corn provided a ladder for the beans to climb, while the squash sheltered the mound where they all grew, retaining moisture and tolerating shade. Alongside a variety of cooking and medicinal herbs, tubers, and greens, Ma had also planted her favorite garden flowers. Some deterred pests with their scent, while others, like the bee flower, attracted pollinators. Ma waited for nature's cues to plant certain seeds, observing birds and animals and chatting with local Natives about such matters—when Pa wasn't around. Each year, Ma relocated the garden, as planting the same crops repeatedly in the same spot invited pests to ambush the plants.

Finally, Mahala reached Whiskers' new crate. She placed the little fox pup inside, scratched her chin, triple-latched the crate, and trotted back home.

Once she was out of sight, a shadowy figure emerged from behind a tree and approached the crate.

Whiskers peered up at the looming silhouette of an unfamiliar human.

The following day, Mahala happily walked down the trail, carrying a pail of water and food to replenish Whiskers' supplies. As she approached the thicket where she had left Whiskers, panic set in—the pen's door was open, and Whiskers was nowhere to be found.

Mahala dropped the pail and examined the pen. The triple latches she had installed hadn't been chewed through; a human must have interfered. Her bottom lip quivered as she thought about the brace still attached to Whiskers' healing hind leg. The little pup wasn't old enough to hunt for herself. Mahala immediately focused on the tracks surrounding the pen, discovering flat-soled shoe prints too small to belong to her father or older brothers. She immediately suspected Billy, who had echoed their father's sentiments about Whiskers and the chickens.

For a moment she panicked, calling out to the forest,

"Whiskers…Whiskers…Whiskerrrrrrs!" Then she realized there was no telling how far Billy might have carried off the pup.

Mahala spent the rest of the afternoon trying to track Billy and search for Whiskers. The rough rock hid the trail in many places. She tried a circular pattern beginning at the pen and went around in a large corkscrew. Using this method she was able to pick up the trail a couple of times. With the apparent meandering of the abductor, she realized the futility and headed for home to find Billy.

Billy was sitting on the fence next to some penned hogs. He had just finished feeding them and was feeling very smug at having disposed of Mahala's "stupid" fox pup. It had been easy to release the thing and dispose of it a good half day from the pen. The pup made no noise when he placed it on the ground. It had merely darted into the forest, and Billy felt well rid of the thing. He was certain Pa would be happy about the outcome.

The sun was setting behind the house, and it was almost time for supper. All at once he saw Mahala headed for him from across the barnyard, her eyes blazing with fury. Without a word, she punched Billy in the face, knocking him into the pigpen. Scrambling to his feet, he felt Mahala jump on his back and shove his face into the corncobs littering the ground. She smashed his face into the cobs over and over until suddenly Anna appeared and intervened, pulling Mahala away. His face was wet with blood, too numb yet to feel any pain. Billy angrily rolled onto his back to see Anna holding a struggling Mahala by the waist, trying to calm her down.

"He took Whiskers! He took Whiskers!" Mahala cried out over and over. Finally she stopped struggling and turned to weep in her sister's arms. Billy had never actually seen Mahala weep before. For a moment it made him forget the damage she had done to his face. Anna glowered at Billy, and he realized there would certainly be no denying this. The best he could do was to own up and say he thought it was for the best.

After a couple of weeks, those in the family who had taken Mahala's side had stopped glaring at Billy and Mahala had ceased casting vehement looks his way. Tensions had eased and Billy was up in the north field spending the day clearing a patch of rocks for Pa, in preparation for tilling the next day. Any rock stuck in the till would cause Pa to stop and clear it, so this was a tedious but important task. Billy worked very hard, putting in a full day of sweat and toil. At the end of the day he surveyed the field one last time to make sure he had not missed anything. Proud of his accomplishment, he trotted off for Lytle Creek to wash up before heading home.

As Billy disappeared from view, Mahala entered from the edge of the woods, donning her mother's sturdy deer-skin gloves. She was determined to work through the night if necessary, her resolve unwavering.

In the morning, Billy trailed behind as Pa led the team out to the north field. He had assured Pa the previous night that the field was thoroughly cleared. All the while, he imagined the pride that would fill Pa's eyes upon seeing his meticulous work, but as they reached the edge of the field, Pa stopped, cursed, and glared at Billy. Pa was livid. Billy rushed up to see what the problem was, only to find the entire field strewn with stones, as if he hadn't lifted a finger the day before.

"You're a lazy, no-good, little liar, Billy Conklin!" Pa said, his voice rising with anger.

"Pa, I don't understand it. I cleared it. I swear I did."

"You get your little ass out there right now. I reckon you're still too young to be trusted with a man's work," Pa scolded. "You'll' get a switching when we get home. For now, I've wasted half my morning. Get out there and help me clear them rocks. Maybe I can get a third of it tilled before sundown."

Later that evening, as promised, Will took Billy behind the woodshed and administered five hard whacks with a hickory stick before silently walking away. Dumbfounded, a tear slid down

Billy's cheek as he rubbed his sore backside. He suddenly noticed Mahala, who had been watching the punishment from beside the barn. Her face was impassive, but she locked eyes with him and tilted her head to one side, as if taking in his punishment and loss of pride.

In that moment, Billy realized Mahala had moved the stones back onto the field—clearly additional retribution for disposing of her fox pup. He was certain no one would believe him if he told. She had put in no small effort to sabotage his work. This was something he would certainly have to ponder. It made him angry but at the same time, it made him wonder if it was worth it to contemplate retaliation…

******

Ansel Briggs, the first governor of Iowa, surveyed the Native encampment situated a mere three miles from his home in Andrew Township, Jackson County, Iowa. The village, a bustling hub of women, children, and elders, stretched before him. A local man, Mr. Shinkle, accompanied the governor along with Ansel's political advisor, providing background on the place. Mr. Shinkle held no animosity toward the village, which was precisely why he had been invited to guide Ansel around. The governor sought to hear both sides of the story.

"At one time, this was stomping grounds for Chief Blackhawk himself," Mr. Shinkle shared. "There's a huge ceremonial circle up yonder, hidden by a bunch of tall cedars with just one way in; hard to find unless you know what you're lookin' for. They used to have some wild Injun dance parties up there, but that was a long time ago. All the warriors are long gone. I've lived alongside these people for nigh on twenty years; never had no trouble. They've got some ol' burial grounds up that-away." Shinkle pointed to some distant hills. "But this place? Nothing but women and old folk left. They don't bother nobody. They like to trade, fish, and hunt a little. That's it. They keep to themselves. I'm guess'n some of the settlers just don't like the idea of them being there."

Ansel observed that this was typical of the dwindling Native villages remaining in his state. Most Natives had been rounded up and placed on lands specifically reserved by the government through treaties. Their nomadic nature, however, was not easily stifled. Young men had mostly fallen in battle, and those left spent their time hunting to provide for the primarily fragile population waiting in camp.

Ansel's thoughts drifted to his recent marriage. His political adviser had introduced him to his mother-in-law, Frances Carpenter, an attractive, educated, older widow with three children still at home: the eldest, a 17-year-old boy, and two girls aged 7 and 10. Single women of suitable age were scarce in the west, and Ansel, having been alone for a long time, hadn't hesitated to marry a woman slightly older than himself. The local newspaper had printed a scathing opinion on the union—alongside other recent prominent marriages—calling it an attack of the "Winged God," referring to Cupid, whose insatiable thirst no bachelor in Iowa could escape. While Ansel laughed heartily at the piece, Frances had been incensed and scowled for days.

Ansel learned early that Frances had quite an opinionated, sharp tongue. She insisted the surrounding settlers were very bothered by this encampment of wayward Indians and, as governor and a member of the community, he should ensure that it be eliminated.

Ansel officially became governor on December 28, 1846, when President Polk signed Iowa's statehood bill into law as the first free state west of the Mississippi. Polk's opponent, Henry Clay of the Whig party, had given him a tight race. The presses printed slanderous gossip against both Polk and Clay, turning the election into a contest of who could amass the most scandalous anecdotes about the other. Across the country folks consumed the printed vitriol and falsehoods like moths to a flame. In the end, an abolitionist and Liberty Party candidate had attracted just enough votes in New York to push Polk over the top with electoral votes. Had that candidate not been in the race, Henry Clay might have won. Who could say how Clay would have prioritized Iowa's statehood? Regardless, Iowa's citizens could now vote for president and elect representatives to Congress.

In October of that same year Ansel had beaten his Dubuque lawyer opponent by a mere 247 votes. Such was the way of politics and the winds of the printed press.

Ansel noticed Mr. Shinkle's narrative seemed to have reached its conclusion.

"Thank you for your input, Mr. Shinkle, we're going to look around ourselves for a bit if you don't mind. The information you have given us is quite helpful."

"Sure thing, Gov'nor."

The two men watched as Mr. Shinkle rode away, their mood somber. This scenario had played out many times before. Now that the village had caught the attention of the local settlers, its safety was in question. For Ansel's future political viability, the only real questions were where to move them and how soon…

******

"I bought you a gazette," Will announced as the wagon rolled up in front of the new barn. There it was—that spark in Easter's eyes whenever she caught wind of fresh news. It pleased him to see it on her face, especially with the new baby, a son—a sixth boy, added to their brood. Will Conklin would become the envy of every man in Otter Creek Township with successful crops and strong sons to help bring his produce to market. The future was so bright.

Easter snatched the gazette from his hands and began combing through it, their babe on her hip. Will stepped off the wagon and scooped up little Thomas in his arms as he coaxed a smile from the child's cute, pudgy face. Easter's babies were always strong and plump. Unlike many homesteaders, they had lost only one baby during their marriage. The west could be a brutal place for youngsters to survive infancy.

"Our governor got married!" Easter announced with a grin as

her children swarmed the wagon, looking for any hidden loot given Will's return from Bellevue. "It says here Governor Ansel Briggs married a widow by the name of Frances Carpenter. She has three children of her own, so with the son from his first marriage, that makes four."

"Only four?" Will lifted his eyebrows, grinning back at his wife.

"They live right here in Jackson County, in the town of Andrew down near the Maquoketa River."

"What does Maquoketa mean, Ma?" Elijah, now ten years old, inquired.

Easter looked thoughtfully at her young son. He was always interested in Native comings and goings. She had seen him regularly fishing with some Native children on the banks of Lytle Creek, which fed the larger Otter Creek for which the township they homesteaded in was named. Will had been so surprised at Elijah's sudden talent for fishing when he abruptly began bringing home strings of bass, bullheads, and sunfish, all of which required different methods to catch.

More recently, during her long walks foraging, she caught sight of Mahala, now thirteen, and Moses, now seven, joining the group. Will did not approve of the children interacting with the Natives, so she had not mentioned it. Easter always enjoyed chatting with the occasional Fox or Sauk Natives she ran into. This was a wild place, and Easter felt it was better for the children to learn to coexist with the land and its creatures rather than be at odds. Such thinking was a very Native point of view, but then...for a moment, Easter flashed back to her times foraging in the woods with Soolee, a habit she had continued most of her life. Elijah had an essence about him that reminded her of that formidable lady. He was a bit darker than the rest of her children, with midnight hair and a touch of brown in his tree-bark eyes.

Easter allowed herself to ponder that neither Will nor anyone else outside her parents' family had any idea of her Native heritage. Easter remembered once when Pa had ordered china-head dolls for her and Harriet from an import catalog. When Ma opened the crate, one was broken, and she announced that one was Easter's. Easter had always wondered how Ma knew hers was the broken one and not Harriet's. The thought produced a grim smile. Harriet had quickly lost interest in the thing, and so Pa had put it on display as an oddity in the mercantile. The cornhusk dolls her girls and the local Natives played with were certainly more durable and easily repaired, although the Natives tended to bury or burn theirs in the spring. Some Native lore regarded the dolls as the Corn Spirit, one of the Three Sisters that ruled their planting methods, and so they were returned to the ground in the spring, with new dolls made during harvest—usually with no face, as Native lore dictated.

Easter certainly recognized Mahala's connection to Elijah. Although she was closer in age to Billy, those two were like oil and water. An unspoken conflict between them had begun in their youth and never quite resolved. Billy was the spitting image of Will, which is why they had named him after his father.

Mahala's stubborn and curious ways made her crave adventure. Elijah was adventure incarnate, always asking the most unusual questions, which sometimes earned him a switching from Will. It was as if Will was trying to beat what he considered unusual ideas out of him, the part of Elijah that Mahala adored the most. Even as a baby Elijah was always very sensitive—more like her girls than her other boys. She had named him Elijah Friendly, for he was such a loving, quiet babe. She could see him as a young man with a future—not stuck in old ways.

Easter smiled at Elijah. As usual, all the other kids perked up when he asked a question, and this one did not seem to draw their Pa's ire. They were all curious to hear her answer as well.

"Well, the Natives actually call it the Maquaweutaw," Easter said, and shaped her hands into claws, as if to pounce. "It means… there are bears."

Elijah's laughter erupted instantly. His reaction time always seemed faster than the rest, and his infectious laughter soon had the others joining in.

"Leave it to Injuns to be blunt and to the point about naming a place," Will snorted.

The next part of the story made Easter pause. She wondered if that was why the number of Natives had appeared to increase in the area lately. A village had been emptied out near the Maquoketa River. Her eyes immediately went back to Elijah. Intuitively he met her gaze.

"It says here they emptied out the Native village down that way. Locals complained, and the governor had them evicted."

Elijah tilted his head to one side and looked thoughtfully at the ground. Easter was sure the Native young'uns he had been hanging out with must have told him something. Someone like Elijah would certainly someday make a better governor than the one that had just evicted the poor Native families from their ancestral homes in the Maquoketa.

"That land belongs to the settlers. It was ceded years ago back during the Blackhawk War," Will said flatly. "Those Injuns were the ones squatting. They should've been moved out long ago."

Elijah took the news about the Maquoketa village with quiet introspection. He continued his chores, unloading the wagon with the others, exchanging silent glances with Mahala and Moses. Once Ma and Pa were out of sight, the three slipped away and headed towards the woods.

"Do you suppose that's why Mingan Gray Wolf has been bringing new friends to our fishing hole?" Mahala asked.

Elijah responded with a shrug. Mingan was roughly the same age as Mahala but a bit shorter and quite lean. The last time the Conklins had visited their secret spot, Mingan had brought six other Native children with him, all fishing and not very friendly. A couple of them were a little older than Mingan. Elijah's plan had been to do some fishing and a little swimming. Even though Mingan was his usual friendly, good-natured self, they had not stayed due to the dark looks and churlish behavior of Mingan's comrades.

"Well, they sure weren't very friendly," Moses remarked, stating the obvious, "Especially given it's our land they were fishin' on."

"I supposed if someone kicked us out of our home, I would not like them much either," Elijah replied.

"We didn't kick them off their home," Moses retorted.

Mahala interjected, "I'm sure Mingan knows that. But some of them see all settlers as the same, just like some settlers see all Natives as the same."

Elijah considered his sisters word's. Sensible; that's what he admired so much about Mahala. She was not much for emotion except for when she got trifled with, but she could always be counted on for her levelheadedness.

The trio crested the hill above their fishing hole and paused for a moment. Elijah imitated a bird call, and they all waited and listened. Sure enough, the same bird call was returned from below, indicating Mingan Gray Wolf was indeed there and signaling his location. The Conklin children wove through the brush and headed down to the creek. Mahala was especially curious about Mingan's friends. Two of them were girls and seemed very adept at fishing. They had constructed a V-shaped area with rocks and appeared to be herding fish into the V for easy spearing. Mahala was eager to get a closer look at this technique. A couple of younger ones used fishhooks made from bone, baited with some kind of flesh. Fishing lines of bark were tethered and left afloat while they played on the shore.

******

Billy Conklin rounded the edge of the barn just in time to see his siblings slipping into the woods. That bunch had a secret fishing hole they wouldn't share with anyone, and it irked him. Mahala never missed a chance to play a mean prank on him. The last one had been particularly annoying, as it had earned him a whipping from Pa for a lie he didn't commit. In that, Mahala had gone too far. Billy was determined to get even.

******

Elijah and Mingan Gray Wolf sat together on the shore, watching Mahala try her hand at spearing fish with her new Native friends. This second visit, gifts of Ma's hardtack was all it took for the Native newcomers to forge a bond. Moses played with the younger ones on the shore, seeing who could hit a target closest with their slings.

Mingan jumped to his feet and motioned for Elijah to follow him up stream. The two walked in comfortable silence for a ways and then paused at a large pool to practice skipping rocks in the water.

"Tomorrow, some of us are heading back down south to the Maquaweutaw," Mingan announced in his slow, steady English. He was quite good at speaking it, having been raised near white settlers and traders all of his life.

Elijah tilted his head and thoughtfully replied, "Aren't you worried the soldiers might come and chase your people out again?"

Mingan snorted. "They can try. We're good at hiding."

The boys continued tossing rocks for a while.

"In any case we are not going to stay. We are just going down to dance one more time in our sacred grove and get some stuff we left in caches. When they made us leave there was no time to retrieve it. The rest of my people are heading west. After we get what we need we will be heading west to meet up with them."

Elijah stopped chucking rocks and studied his companion.

"So, my friend, this is the last we will see each other for a very long time."

Mingan returned Elijah's thoughtful gaze, and then they continued skipping rocks.

Elijah felt a pang in his heart as he processed this news. He had gotten so accustomed to meeting up with Mingan these past several weeks that the prospect of him leaving had not really crossed his mind. This friendship had brought him a lot of happiness—something he had not realized was missing until now, and it was about to vanish as suddenly as it had appeared.

"Well." Elijah sighed deeply. "I'm going to miss fishing with you."

"You should come with me to see our sacred dancing grounds. It's just a day's travel. There are catfish in the Maquaweutaw that are as big as baby buffalo."

Elijah smiled at his friend; such a thought, such an adventure.

"I don't know. I'm not sure I can."

Some rocks tumbled down the hill from above, and the two looked up to see Billy sliding down the hill coming towards them.

Elijah felt a knot in his gut. Billy was bigger than both of them and would likely be brutish. Pa didn't like Natives hanging around, and Billy was always one to mimic Pa in everything.

"So this is what you have been up to?" Billy demanded loudly as he approached. He puffed up his chest and clenched his fists in outrage. "Fishin' with Injuns on our land?"

Elijah whispered to Mingan, "That's my older brother. He's a bit of a bully. I'll keep him busy. You better fetch your friends and go."

They clasped arms for a moment then Mingan turned and trotted quickly back down stream. He glanced over his shoulder to see the older boy reach Elijah and push him hard in the shoulder. It made him angry, and he stopped for a moment, then, weighing possible outcomes, continued on his way. Settlers hating Natives was not new to him. Over time, his people had learned a hard lesson that in such confrontations melting into the forest was the best and only response. In any case, it was a good thing he and his people were leaving tomorrow. The elders had sensed a bad wind heading their way, and it was time to be on the move.

Elijah held his temper while Billy kept pushing him around the clearing, hitting him in the shoulder, hurling insults like bullets. Keeping him occupied while Mingan left would ensure Billy did not find their secret fishing hole and allow Mingan to make a dignified exit.

"Wait until Pa finds out you've been hanging out with dirty Injuns. Li-jah," he taunted.

"He's my friend," Elijah responded flatly, staring into his brother's eyes.

At that, Billy gave him a mighty shove to the ground, sending his coon-skin cap flying, and kicked dirt at him. "Conklins don't make friends with Injuns."

Elijah replied firmly, "Ma talks to them and trades with them."

Billy scowled at his brother trying to think of a retort and finally said, "It's what Pa says that matters."

The boys heard someone approaching and turned to see Mahala coming up the trail with an ample string of fish in her hand and a pole over her shoulder.

"Where'd you get that fish?" Billy bellowed accusingly.

Mahala snorted at Billy, reached down, and pulled Elijah to his feet, handing him the string of fish and pole. While Elijah retrieved his treasured cap, she put her hands on her hips and silently stared Billy down as he clenched his fists in anger, hoping against hope he would give her a reason to punch him.

They were barely a year apart, and Billy wasn't keen on trying to push Mahala around the way he did Elijah. Her retribution was…well, dreadful to say the least, and she was not one to back down. She could throw a punch equal to any of her brothers.

"Just wait until Pa hears. Just you wait," Billy hollered as he turned, heading for home at a quick pace.

Will was irritated. Easter had gone to the neighbors until tomorrow. He took a second swig of whiskey out of his jug as he thought about how it seemed like she was always gone when foolish stuff came up with the kids. It irritated him that Elijah had been withholding information, more than it did the why. Billy's tattling about Elijah's friendship with this Native had closed with, "And Mahala was with him," but Billy conceded he had only seen Elijah with the Native. Will did not want his children interacting with the Natives. He took another swig of whiskey. There was too much animosity with most folks towards Natives in these parts, and he did not want people to get the wrong idea about his family. Many still remembered savage exchanges during the Blackhawk war, and some even had kin that were killed. There was nothing he could do about Easter, but he could lay down the law with his kids. He would have to make an example of Elijah so his siblings would think twice before having friendships with these people ever again.

He leaned against the barn, whittling on a thick hickory stick, determined to give Elijah a whipping he would not soon forget. Will looked up to see Elijah suddenly in front of him, so silent had been his approach. He was in his coon-skin cap, standing a few feet away, holding his string of fish, observing him whittle the switch.

Will sighed, stood up, approached his son, and announced loudly, "Conklins don't make friends with Injuns." Then he bent Elijah over his lap and began to rhythmically switch his legs and buttocks expecting his ten year old son to cry out. When no noise came from his son he began to hit harder and harder until at last something caught his arm. He looked up into Phoebe's distressed face as she held his arm tightly. Her siblings fanned out behind her.

"Pa, don't ya think that's enough?"

Will was a bit dumbfounded at the intervention, then noticed he had broken through Elijah's clothes with the switching and his son had soiled himself. His coon-skin cap had fallen to the ground. Will let him up.

Elijah was still holding his string of fish, ever silent, eyes wet with grief, almost as if something or someone had died. He made no effort to retrieve his cap. The rest of the children were silent as well. Even Billy looked glum.

Phoebe led Elijah off to wash him up. Will let out a sigh and took another swig of whiskey, as he stared at Elijah's cap in the dirt, wondering yet again why this all had to happen when Easter was away.

******

Easter rode down the ancient Native trail with Mahala. This trail, used by tribes for centuries, was now trodden by settlers and soldiers as well. A part of her was angry, while another part nagged with worry. The third part kept watch on the trail for signs of travel to ensure they were on the right track.

She'd brought a pack horse, a couple of rifles, and quickly gathered supplies that would last a few days. Their quarry had a three-quarter day head start and was traveling quickly. Easter glanced back at Mahala, who sat comfortably behind her with her hands on both her thighs. Her eyes were bright, taking in every detail, and she was becoming adept at spotting signs of the group they were tracking.

Easter tried to make sure that each of her children had an equal chance to go on overnight trips into town. When Will went, he mostly took the older boys. It was important to Easter that all her children were well-versed in wagon travel and setting up an ad-hoc camp. With the older ones trained, Will seemed to forget that the younger ones had to learn from scratch as well.

At thirteen, Mahala was well-trained in almost all aspects of homesteading, foraging, hunting, and camp travel, but with this opportunity, she was learning to track Natives. If one could track Natives, one could track virtually anything or anyone. The Natives could leave little trace when they chose to, but in this case, they did not seem worried about being followed. From what Mahala had told her, it was likely a younger group anyway. Even so, there wasn't much sign. One had to know what to look for.

At first, Mahala had gone to Anna, who immediately brought the issue to Easter. Elijah had run away, angry at the punishment Will had doled out when Billy tattled about his fishing escapades with the Natives. Elijah had told only Mahala that he planned on traveling with his Native friend south and then heading back east to look up his grandparents and find work. Elijah said if Davy Crockett could live on his own at thirteen years of age, as it was written in his book, he could, too. Mahala had sat on the information most of the day. Will was working the fields. Easter told everyone she and Mahala were taking a trip to see a neighbor who was expecting a child and would be back in a couple of days. She instructed Anna to say, if Will asked about Elijah, that Easter had taken him with her. Even with their late start, they had covered several miles before sundown the night before.

By Easter's estimates, they would likely be camping near the Maquoketa River that evening, hoping to catch up to Elijah the following day.

******

Wearing only buckskins and moccasins, Elijah reveled in the feeling of the leather against his skin. Their group consisted of four elders and five young teenagers, including Elijah and two girls. As soon as Elijah had joined Mingan for their journey, the elders insisted he wear Native attire to avoid drawing attention. Having learned some of the Sauk language, Elijah could comprehend most of their plans as they chatted during the trip south.

They had traveled quite quickly, obviously knowing the trail like the back of their hands, as Ma would say. Upon arriving near their former camping grounds, the Natives visited the caches as planned. Some contained dried meat and fish, while others held treasured items valuable for trade and comfort during their travels: freshwater pearl beads, spoon shells carved by ancient ancestors, and paint supplies ground from local Galena ore.

Everything was packed up and put onto travois for transport. They would spend the night here in their sacred dance grounds before heading west. Tomorrow, Elijah would part ways with Mingan Gray Wolf, but for today, they were going fishing in Mingan's special spot on the Maquaweutaw that had fish as large as baby buffalo. Later, Elijah would dance alongside his Native friends around the campfire under the stars, just like their ancestors.

******

Captain Pierce Nelson from Fort Atkinson scanned the horizon as his small troop set up camp. They were making one last sweep of the area to pick up any stray Natives that had given the main troop the slip when they rounded them up and took them to the reservation.

The truth was, quite a number had faded into the wild woods of Iowa when they had been kicked from this area. Old habits were hard to break for these people. Now that things had settled down, Pierce's commanding officer had assigned him to comb through their ancient stomping grounds and gather any strays.

From a distance, he could see one small campfire not far from the river. Given its visibility, it was likely not one of the tribes, but regardless, they would check it out in the morning.

What intrigued him more was what he could hear. Raising his hand, he signaled for his men to fall silent. Everyone held still.

From the hillside vantage point, Pierce understood why the Natives cherished this place. As the sun vanished beyond the horizon, it bathed the ancient trees in a golden light, casting long shadows that, from this viewpoint, resembled spirit guardians. The river sparkled like jewels as it caught the last rays of sunshine. A pair of bears attempting to fish seemed to be enjoying great success. A gentle hum from some kind of insects drifted across the valley, but that wasn't the sound that captivated him—There it was: just a hint of Native singing and drums.

"Hear that?" he asked one of his soldiers, who smiled grimly and nodded.

******

Elijah watched curiously as Mingan meticulously fashioned a sharp barb at the end of their second long pole, before notching the tip to secure the rope.

"We tie a rope around the end. We will come at him from two sides and spear him, then tie the ropes to the trees on either side of the creek. Hopefully it will hold him still long enough to finish him off with the shorter spears."

"Where did you learn how to do that?" Elijah asked, intrigued.

"Actually from this big blond Swede settler who was passing through."

"Not from your grandpa?" Elijah chuckled.

"Fish is so plentiful we don't need the really big ones. So, no, we use smaller spears and fish traps. This Swede told me in his home country they used to catch a fish many many times the size of these grandfather catfish with this technique. It works, but I'm not sure I believe him about the size of the fish he caught in his home country."

"Whales," Elijah suggested, "He must have been talking about whales."

"Don't tell me you are going to lie to me about the size of the fish from your homelands as well."

Elijah thought for a moment. "These are my homelands. I was born here, and so was my Ma and Pa. I've read about whales in a book, though. But I've never seen any fish in person as big as a baby buffalo."

Mingan shrugged. With the spears and ropes prepared, it was time to stalk grandfather catfish.

They paced cautiously along the bank for several minutes. The sun hung low in the sky, casting its final golden rays upon the water. Grandfather catfish's belly would make him hunt for food before night was upon them. The same light that aided the boys to stalk their prey was used by the catfish as well.

And there it was. A massive, shadowy figure, larger than a tree trunk, emerged from the depths, moving with deceptive grace. In unison, both boys leaped from the banks, plunging their spears deep into the creature, using their own weight to anchor them. The mammoth catfish responded with a violent thrash, flinging Elijah around like a rider on a wild bronco.

"Let go of the spear!" Mingan shouted.

Just as Elijah let go, the fish made another violent thrash, flinging him with a mighty splash into the water.

As he came up for air, he saw Mingan pulling his rope to the opposite bank and remembered his task. Elijah grabbed his rope, scrambled up the bank, and secured it around a tree. Pulling it tight, he tied it off and surveyed their handiwork. The barbs held fast, and the mighty catfish was ensnared.

Both boys beamed at each other in delight as they whooped and leaped on the banks. They and their comrades would surely feast well that night.

******

As their ancestors had done for generations before them, the small Native troop gathered wood for their bonfire, adorned their faces and bodies with paint, arranged hollowed-out logs to serve as drums, and prepared for the moonrise. When Elijah and Mingan Gray Wolf entered the dancing ground from the secret trail pulling a massive creature on a travois behind their horses, everyone rushed to see what prize they had brought for that night's celebration.

The moon ascended steadily to mid sky. With the drums pounding and the Natives' rhythmic song, Elijah began swaying up and down alongside his comrades. The girls had decided to cook enormous chunks of the fish as they might a buffalo haunch, so it hung over the fire on spits, sizzling and crackling as the fat dripped into the flames. Elijah tried to etch every scent, sound, and sight of this place into his memory. He closed his eyes, feeling a deep sense of peace. Suddenly, Mingan nudged him in the ribs, offering him a large piece of fish. Both boys hadn't realized just how famished they were after their long day. And now, it was time to celebrate and bond…

The next morning, Elijah shook off his drowsiness and began packing up as, one by one, his friends exited the dance grounds. All was quiet. It was likely the last time anyone there would see this place, at least for a very long time. The night before, as the moon rose above them, Elijah had danced alongside his new blood-brothers around a blazing bonfire. When everyone had exhausted their dancing, the Elders told ancient stories about how the world was formed and how the people came into being. As they awoke in the morning, it seemed as if Elijah's eyes had barely closed in slumber. Time had flown by so swiftly.

Breaths formed silky puffs in the early morning chill. Elijah marked into his memory the expansive flat camp, encircled by tall, thick cedar trees that concealed its existence from anyone who didn't know the secret entrance. He imagined the tribe at its peak and the many teepees that must have once stood during celebrations. Mingan Gray Wolf had told him that the warrior chief, Blackhawk himself, had greatly favored this place.

The Elders began leading the way down a narrow trail. Some of the girls were packing up the enormous leftover bones from the grandfather catfish, no doubt to craft spearheads or fishhooks. Elijah pulled a prized gift from the decorated leather pouch in his pocket and examined it more closely. Mingan had given him a beautifully embellished bracelet to present to Mahala as a token of friendship. Her friends had fashioned it from some of the prized water pearl beads and ancient spoon shells they had retrieved from the caches. It made him wonder if he would ever see his sister again to give her the gift.

Elijah bowed his head, a tinge of sadness washing over him as he felt a small ache in his heart for his own bunkhouse bed and the aroma of Ma's breakfast biscuits. Determined to maintain his friendship with Mingan and see his plan through, he reminded himself of what Davy Crockett had said in his book: "I leave this rule for others when I'm dead, be always sure you're right, then go ahead!"

******

Easter and Mahala were just breaking camp when they heard the sound of gunfire. Shouting echoed from a large grove of trees not far away, the same direction from which drums and singing had emanated the night before.

"You stay here," Easter ordered Mahala as she grabbed her rifle and leaped onto her horse.

******

Captain Nelson observed from atop his horse as his men tied up the Natives. It had been easy to spot them emerging from the thicket, given the sounds that had betrayed their position the evening before. A few gunshots into the air had effortlessly subdued the group. He was somewhat disappointed at the makeup of the prisoners: a few Elders and some young teens. Not much to brag about but better than nothing. He would have his men escort them to the reservation.

"Cap'n," one of his soldiers called and pointed down the flats. A determined-looking woman was riding hard and fast towards them, carrying a rifle. Certainly it was unusual to see a white woman by herself out this far. That was probably the fire they had seen the night before; perhaps she had been out hunting with her husband. She had likely been drawn by the gunshots.

As the woman pulled up, she took one look at the captain as if to take his measure, then turned her attention to the prisoners.

"Howdy, ma'am," Pierce offered. "Sorry if we startled ya. Just rounding up some Injuns that strayed off the reservation."

The woman climbed off of her horse, gave him quite a fierce look, and moved towards the captives. A couple of his men stepped in her way and looked to the captain for guidance.

The woman literally pushed one of them flat on his back and elbowed the other as she stepped in front of the prisoners, inspecting them. Then her eyes settled on one.

"Elijah?" the woman said and reached for one of the young heathens.

His men recovered and grabbed the woman by her arm. That's when Pierce heard the cock of a gun, and it wasn't from his men or this woman.

"You take your hands off my Ma."

Pierce turned around to see a young white girl with a cocked rifle pointing right at him.

"Take your hands off my Ma!"

Pierce motioned to his men to let the woman go and said, "Easy now, girl. Don't get too excited, you don't want that gun to go off accidently now."

The woman was cutting the bonds from one of the young Injun's hands.

"This is my son," the woman stated flatly. "He ran off to go fishing with his friends. It was a mistake. I'm taking him home."

Pierce glanced at the young girl who still had a bead on him. She was as steady as a rock. He looked back at the standing young'un all dressed in Injun leather, looking at the ground sheepish as if in very big trouble and ashamed. Yep; tan but lighter skin than the rest. Hair cropped below the ears; dark, but glints of red could be seen in there.

"All right. Let that one go," Captain Pierce announced. He noted that his men looked mightily relieved. This mother and her daughter were quite a formidable pair, and none of them wanted to be known for going up against a couple of white women.

"Ma," the girl said still holding the gun on the captain. "We can't let them take Mingan Gray Wolf. He's our friend; and the others—they're his family."

Easter studied Elijah, who had tears streaming down his cheeks. She pulled him close, and he wrapped his arms around her.

"I'm sorry, Ma. I'm sorry."

"I know," Easter replied as she surveyed the motley, skinny group of prisoners.

"Mahala, put the gun down, now," Easter ordered.

Mahala lowered and uncocked the gun, still holding it ready, just in case.

"Ya know, young man," the captain started to lecture, "If it weren't for your Ma showing up here when she did you'd be on your way to the reservation with these Injuns. Your family would never know what happened to you."

Easter tilted her head sideways, sizing up the captain.

"My name is Easter Conklin. This here is my son, Elijah Friendly, and of course my daughter Mahala, whom you have already met. We have an eighty-acre homestead up in Otter Creek Township."

Pierce tipped his hat, "Captain Pierce Nelson, ma'am."

"Well Captain Pierce, I'll let the Mayor know up our way that you helped us and ask him to write a letter on our behalf to Governor Briggs. He'll put a good word for you in with the governor I'm sure." Easter had never personally spoken with the mayor of Bellevue or any other mayor for that matter, but she wanted this captain to think she had in case he was getting any nefarious ideas. Without giving the captain any more time to think, she ushered Elijah and Mahala onto their horse and gave a quick wave as they turned and rode away. When they breached the hill they stopped for a moment to look back at the troop.

With heavy hearts Elijah and Mahala gazed upon their bound friends below.

Elijah pulled his coon-skin cap out of his bag and placed it back on his head where it belonged. In anguish he pleaded, "Is there nothing we can do, Ma?"

Easter scrutinized her children. It was a hard lesson. They had spent a lot of time bonding with these Natives through fishing and forest play. Inconsolable was the only word to describe Elijah and Mahala.

"The law says this particular folk have to stay on the reservation. When they leave, their lives are in jeopardy and potentially forfeit. It may not be fair. It may not be right, but it is what it is."

In truth what the captain had said was a fact. It was a miracle they found Elijah. They might never have known what happened to him…

******

Captain Pierce looked at his remaining prisoners, four Elders, two girls and two teens, hardly worth the trouble of the six days of escort to return them where they belonged. It occurred to him it might be easier to shoot them, collect a bounty, and claim they had resisted. However, that damn white woman might indeed relate her story to the mayor, who might ask questions about the prisoners' destination. He did not need any accusations of slaughtering Injun children and Elders on his near-perfect military record for sure.

******

Easter glanced back at Elijah and Mahala as they rode happily together on the pack horse. They would spend the night on the trail and be back home by tomorrow late afternoon.

"Elijah, everybody at home thinks we went to see Mrs. Ethel, who is in a family way, and you came along to help with chores, chop firewood, and such. Nobody else knows you ran off except Anna, and we're going to keep it that way. Okay?"

Easter stopped her horse and made solemn eye contact with her children to make sure they understood this was a pact. Both of them nodded in agreement.

"Great. Okay, you two need to rustle us up something for dinner. We're out of supplies. This took longer than I expected. Stay near the trail, but you'll be going hungry if you fail."

By the end of a day of leisurely travel there were three rabbits and a turkey hen hanging from the pack horse, some wild rice in Mahala's trail bag, along with a perfectly ripe batch of gooseberries.

This last night of their journey they would have quite a feast.

Things could have turned out much worse. Elijah had become a master fisherman from the whole affair, and Mahala could now add Native tracking to her homesteading skills.

Elijah looked over his shoulder at his sister and said, "Me and Mingan Gray Wolf caught a catfish as big as a baby buffalo."

"Really?" Mahala's eyes widened.

"Yeah, he had whiskers longer than Pa is tall." Elijah pulled a bracelet out of his pocket, placing it on Mahala's wrist. It was quite intricate and long enough to wrap around four times obviously meant for special occasions. "They made it for you," Elijah added.

Mahala held her wrist up in the air to admire the gift. A great bit of detail had been carved into the beads and bits of ancestors' spoons that made up the pretty thing. It made her heart twinge as she remembered her friends with their hands bound, captives of the soldiers.

"Best you keep that hidden from your Pa," Easter warned.

Mahala stoically nodded and sighed.

Elijah thought about the feast that night and dancing around the fire with his Native friends. No one would ever be able to take his treasured memories, not even Pa.

If Elijah had not traveled with Mingan, he would never have known they had been captured. Now, he could only hope that Mingan Gray Wolf and his comrades would somehow escape and safely join their family out west.

The cherished memories of his time with Mingan Gray Wolf would be forever overshadowed by the haunting image of his friend and comrades captured, shackled, and force-marched to that dreaded reservation—a place they deemed a prison for both body and spirit. What a bittersweet conclusion to this treasured friendship…

1850 – Of Compromise

But know that fear is not the brand
That marks the coward slave;
'Tis conquered fear, and duty done,
That tells the truly brave

ONE YEAR LATER…

On the second floor of the presidential manor, the Oval Room provided an intimate space for family gatherings. President Millard Fillmore and his wife, Abigail, sat within, captivated by their eighteen-year-old daughter's graceful performance on her harp.

An enormous Persian rug, with hues of burgundy and cream, adorned the hardwood floor. Tall ceilings necessitated a roaring fire, its warm glow illuminating the room. To protect her instrument from the heat, Mary and her harp sat near the bay windows, cracked open to admit a breath of fresh air. Shadows of the girl and her harp danced on the floor in mesmerizing harmony. Abigail's love for literature was evident in the book-lined walls, and Millard knew she yearned for funding to establish a grand library which guests could enjoy. Ornately carved overstuffed chairs and settees were arranged in cozy groups, rendering the room a comfortable haven.

Millard's private secretary entered discreetly and whispered in his ear, careful not to disrupt the moment. "Excuse me, sir, the honorable Senators Henry Clay and Stephen Douglas have arrived."

With his gaze fixed on his daughter, Millard replied in hushed tones, "They can wait." The secretary departed as unobtrusively as he had arrived.

The senators had come to discuss the never-ending saga of slave versus free states—an urgent matter that threatened to rend the nation asunder yet again, if one could believe the newspapers. Ever since the original founding fathers wrote in the Declaration of Independence that all men were entitled to life, liberty, and the pursuit of happiness, the enslaved had been debated. Each time a new state was admitted to the union, this story played itself over and over like a worn out political song.

With the new territories recently won by the Mexican-American War, new states would join the union if a compromise could be achieved.

For now, Millard allowed himself the pleasure of sitting beside his wife, savoring the sublime performance. As the melodic notes danced through the air, they stirred memories of bygone days. He and Abigail had met while she was teaching at the Academy of New Hope, and their marriage had blossomed into a partnership of equals, united in intellect and love. Abigail, his bedrock, surpassed the wisdom of most men he had ever encountered. For a moment he wished it was appropriate to have her on his arm during this discussion with these opposing senators as a gentle voice of reason in the room.

Stephen Douglas, a lawyer and Democratic Senator from Illinois, sat next to his colleague, Senator Henry Clay of the Whig Party, as they awaited their meeting with the President. Henry's frequent rasping cough hinted at a frailty that concerned many. It was evident this aging statesman was weary to the bone. At seventy-three, Henry stood a lean six feet tall, his gray hair and pallid complexion contrasting sharply with the intense intelligence in his blue eyes. Always impeccably dressed, he wore a smartly tailored dark suit and waistcoat over a well-starched white shirt, adorned with a frilly white cravat. His square jaw and large mouth seemed perpetually poised for eloquent oratory, captivating audiences regardless of their political leanings.

In truth, the Whig Party was composed mostly of older statesmen, while the Democratic representatives boasted a younger generation. Following months of debate over how to organize territories ceded after the Mexican-American War, no consensus had been reached. Though Henry had opposed the war, it resulted in a near-doubling of the United States' landmass. Henry himself had lost a son to the conflict. While part of him seemed to have perished with the young man, he had stepped up to the challenge and proposed a sensible compromise.

One of Henry's primary opponents was President Zachary Taylor, a fellow Whig. But with Taylor's untimely death, Vice President Millard Fillmore, had become the thirteenth president.

Texas, emboldened by its victories in the Mexican-American War, insisted on expanding its borders quite a bit into the newly acquired lands. Many in Congress believed the vast territory should be divided into multiple territories, and Senator Calhoun, representing the southern states, insisted that none would be free states. The political atmosphere was charged, with both Whigs and the Democratic Party in conflict over slavery and statehood. Though no one was more skilled at negotiation than Henry Clay, they remained at an impasse, with both sides digging in their heels.

Sensing that the President would be some time, Stephen initiated a conversation. "The president and I support your vision, Henry; of course you know this."

Henry wearily replied, "Yes, and yet you don't."

Stephen shrugged. "The differences are not vast. Breaking your legislation into pieces makes it more palatable."

"You underestimate the carrots that are in play, my friend," Henry replied with the hint of a smile.

Henry's compromise was indeed full of carrots, which is why Stephen and the president were in favor. It proposed a smaller Texas state border in exchange for a federal payoff on state bonds and other loans. The plan would admit California as a free state, create the new territories of Utah and New Mexico with residents voting on the issue of slavery, and negotiate further compromises on slave laws and trade. Mexicans in the region would gain the opportunity to become citizens. Having won over key figures like Sam Houston, a former Texas president now serving as a Texas senator, Henry's compromise could bring about lasting change.

The founding fathers were surely celebrating from the heavens as their sea-to-shining-sea dreams for this once modest nation were on the verge of coming true, with borders that would now stretch from the Atlantic to the Pacific.

Stephen chuckled softly. If only Henry would compromise on his compromise...

Henry listened to the faint sound of a harp wafting through the presidential manor. The delicate notes stirred memories of his roots. Though Kentucky had been his home for years, his mentors were from his time in Richmond, Virginia, during an early renaissance in performance art, music, and politics. Having earned his law license as an intern with the Virginia Attorney General, he had become Henry Clay, Esquire.

Stephen interrupted his thoughts. "Henry, I've always wondered how you became such an eloquent speaker. Truly, there is no one in Congress who can captivate an audience like you." He smiled.

Henry chuckled. "Oratory is indeed a vanishing art in Washington. I honed my skills as a young lawyer in Virginia. I used to attend court sessions and theater performances to learn from some of the most talented lawyers and actors of our time. You have to think of yourself as a stage performer. To sway people's minds, you must first captivate them and stir their emotions, much like the enchanting notes of that harp, but with the spoken word."

Stephen nodded. Indeed, listening to Henry Clay present his case was very much like going to the theater. He had heard that Henry spent his early days as a defense attorney representing common men. Though these cases paid little, this reputation had endured. Undoubtedly compromise was Henry's specialty. He was celebrated for promoting the possible and avoiding the unattainable, but above all, he was a master at captivating and swaying his audience.

"They say in your younger years you were quite passionate and even challenged some of your fellow statesman to duels," Stephen inquired.

"Well," Henry replied, "Luckily no one was injured, and it was the impulsive folly of my younger self." He smiled. "Alliances and the well spoken word hold far greater influence than petty violence."

Henry thought about the issues at hand. This noise over slave and free states grew a little louder each time it raised its ugly head. A split of the union was always threatened. A compromise was to be had for the relentless. One needed to focus on what all held in common, which was commerce and fair competition. The northern and southern states quarreled endlessly about this topic, akin to sibling rivalry at the kitchen table, all wanting a greater share of the American pie. He wondered how much gentler the nation might have been if they had elected more presidents like himself or David Crockett, who had pushed for amicable treatment of the Natives, rather than the mix of Jacksonian minded successors that had followed Andrew Jackson. Crockett's political aspirations had ended with his infamous death in Texas at the Battle of the Alamo.

A wise man had once told Henry that the country's agriculture, manufacturing, and commerce should work together in harmony. The manufacturers on the coast always feared that inexpensive frontier lands would empty their mills of workers. The massive plantation owners in the south worried about competing with the smaller, more efficient frontier farmers. Such plantations depended on slavery. The western farmers competed by building cooperative communities that needed goods to flow to and from the east for greater prosperity.

The glue that tied them all together was tariffs to protect American goods from cheap imports, more immigrant workers to fill up the factories, and government investments in the banking system, roads, railways, and canals to facilitate the flow of goods. This united these competing factions into a well-balanced American System, which had been Henry's lifelong pursuit.

Henry was tired in both body and spirit. A persistent cough had tormented his lungs for weeks. Over the years, he had lost all his beloved daughters and three sons—four, if one counted his tormented son Theodore, who languished in a Kentucky mental asylum. Each loss had chipped away at his very soul. At least his grandchildren offered him some solace. They, along with their peers, would shape the future of this great country—if only capable legislators could soothe the divisions.

Henry longed for rest and the comfort of his wife in Kentucky. This Stephen Douglas was a skilled orator, level-headed, and well-connected. He had made it clear that he was ready to take up the baton and work with all sides to achieve Henry's vision.

The harp's music had ceased, and shortly after President Fillmore entered the room. Henry rose to his feet and greeted him with a handshake.

"Gentlemen," President Fillmore began, "I know you've been diligently fighting for this, but let's reiterate our objectives. We must find solutions that unite all sides—slave and free. We have effectively doubled our country's size. It's crucial that we maintain unity. Just think of it, gentlemen—if we don't, we risk losing everything. Let's establish these new borders in a way that everyone can accept."

All three men nodded in agreement. They were united in their conviction. Henry understood deep within his soul what was needed during this critical moment. He was determined to forge a partnership with his political opponents to insure compromise came to pass—even if it was the last thing he ever did.

If it meant splitting up his bill into smaller pieces, so be it.

1850 – Of Brides

It is done, the words are spoken,
Words that bind you heart to heart;
Whom the Lord hath joined together
Neither life nor death can part.
Hope and friendship, joy and sunshine
Hail you both on every side,
They are singing happy greeting
To the bridegroom and the bride.

~

Sleep on, oh, statesman, sleep
Within thy hallowed tomb,
Where pearly streamlets glide,
And summer roses bloom.

SAME YEAR...
Easter - 37, Will - 41
Phoebe - 19, Anna - 18, Mary - 17, Mahala - 14, Esther Malinda - 6
Aminadab - 16, Billy - 14, Elijah - 11, Moses Rueben - 8, John Bunyan - 3, Thomas - 6 months

Father Perrodin slipped from under the covers of his feather-tick-bed onto the wooden floor of his small log cabin. This humble abode served as the rectory for Saint Patrick's Parish in the Garryowen settlement. When he'd first come to this place it was called the Makokiti settlement, named for a local river that bordered the area. However, after building a log cabin school and acquiring a proper teacher, the teacher suggested renaming these lands in honor of a beloved area in Limerick, Ireland. This Gaelic name, which meant "Eoin's Garden," was associated with a twelfth-century church dedicated to St. John the Baptist by the Knights Templar. The Garryowen name certainly brought smiles to the faces of the Irish immigrants, both those who stayed and those who merely passed through. The Irish, being a superstitious lot, found the auspicious name inspiring for their community.

Today was a special day. Father Perrodin would be presiding over the marriage of one of his favorite Irish parishioners, Thomas Wallace. This hardworking man had lent his strong arms and portions of his ample harvest to help build the log church and support the parish. Tales were shared around hearths of the forty-foot-long beams, hewn and raised with sweat and brawn by Thomas and his neighbors to create this place of worship.

With fourteen unmarried men in the area and less than a handful of unmarried women, a frontier wife was a rare treasure. Thomas's chosen bride was neither Catholic nor Irish, but under his guidance, she had been baptized and agreed to raise their children in the Catholic faith. Thus, they could be married with the sacrament.

Mass was held at the Garryowen church of St. Patrick on the second Sunday of each month. Today, the second Sunday would include the nuptials. When Father Perrodin first arrived in this place, there were few roads—mostly Native trails and military routes—and he had felt incredibly isolated. The winters were cold and damp. As a gentle country Frenchman, Perrodin was not much of a horseman. In these wilds, he longed to visit his family home in France. Eventually, the bishop purchased a horse and gig for him, enabling him to attend to flocks in more distant locations like Dubuque, South Fork, and Iowa City. As the years went by, his soul set roots in this land, and it was here, in his humble log cabin that he now called home.

******

Phoebe stood on the steps of St. Patrick's Church near Lytle Creek, watching her mother straighten Anna's white lace collar on her black linen dress. Ma had painstakingly sewn intricate details at the cuffs and hem, with the help of a Danish neighbor highly skilled in embroidery. Peeking out from the bottom of the dress was an ingenious stiff linen broom-type trim that helped keep wet mud from creeping up the hem. This fine dress would last Anna a very long time, and Phoebe was certain it would be the envy of many at church.

Thomas Wallace's sister-in-law, Hannah, had given them yardage from a bolt of fine linen she had brought all the way from Ireland. There was enough to make dresses for all the girls, with deep seams and hems that could be let out as they grew. However, theirs did not have the fine detailing and lace that adorned Anna's wedding dress.

Anna held a beautiful spray of spring wildflowers that Mahala and Elijah had picked fresh from the fields that morning. Pa wore his half-smile that always appeared when he was amused, chatting with one of Thomas's friends and the man who was now Phoebe's husband, Thom Sade. Thom kept glancing Phoebe's way, as if keeping an eye on her—a habit she found slightly annoying. She held their three-month-old son, Nathaniel, on her hip. Thom Sade had a successful, established farm when they wed a little over a year ago. Pa had arranged everything, and Phoebe was glad to have her own home and family. There was not much love between her and Thom Sade, having only met him a few times before they married. Their wedding had been simple, officiated by a justice of the peace. Thom Sade was a staunch Protestant who often preached at the church in the Iron Hills in the south of Jackson County near their farm. He was not a mean man, but a bit cold—as was their bed.

This Catholic church was lucky enough to have a pipe organ, which had been brought in all the way from New York, donated by the Aherns, one of the more successful Irish families in the area.

That Anna was to marry Thomas Wallace himself was something none of them could have ever dreamed of on their trip to Iowa. What sealed the deal, Pa said, was the day Thomas was served biscuits and gravy on the Conklin farm while Ma was on a trip to Bellevue. Thomas had mistaken them for Ma's biscuits, and when Pa told him Anna made them, Thomas had quite fallen in love right then and there.

Anna had quite a different story to tell, of course. "Phoebe, he makes me laugh. He brings me flowers. He tells me all kinds of stories about Ireland. He is so kind. He never gets grumpy, like Pa, and he is so affectionate. He holds my hand all the time."

There was quite an age difference between the two, just as there was with Phoebe and Thom Sade. Ma had been a bit uneasy with the idea at first, but Pa had assured her, "Well educated homestead wives are a commodity out west. A man should be well established with a working farm of his own to house his wife and raise a family. Anna will be well taken care of with Thomas, as Phoebe is with her husband." Ma couldn't help but agree.

The Conklin farm had thrived with the help of the Sade and Wallace families. Barely a year into the homestead, they had reaped quite a harvest, with a well-established log house, barn, and bunkhouse for the growing boys. Certainly this had a lot to do with their suit for the Conklin daughters. The Conklins were lucky indeed to have such good friends and neighbors.

Anna looked radiant with happiness. Thom Sade and Daniel Ahern, dear friends of Thomas's, stood next to him and Pa, smiling and shaking their hands. Out of the corner of her eye, Phoebe noticed Thom Sade and Pa both kept glancing at Mary and nodding their heads while chatting. It made her quite uneasy. There were a few unmarried Sade brothers likely looking for wives as well. The thought of Pa planning Mary's fate without her input did not sit well with anyone. Phoebe and Anna had made conscious decisions, but Pa seemed to be trying to railroad Mary without asking for her opinion.

"Have you heard the news of the new territories admitted to the union?" Thom Sade asked.

"I heard the abolitionists were getting their dander up and

Calhoun was yelling about the southern states seceding if he didn't get his way." Will Conklin cynically smiled.

"Well, the Old Coon, Ol' Henry Clay pulled it off. The deal is done. California is admitted to the union, and we've two new territories north of Texas: Utah and New Mexico. Instead of war and secession, folks are talking about heading west for cheap land and cattle ranching."

"Never been a fan of Henry Clay; I've always been a Jackson man," Will replied, shrugging. "I'm surprised he's still alive. He must be old as heck by now."

Thom Sade smiled and said, "Well, the way I see it, his import tariffs make sure the eastern states buy our goods at a fair price. He's had his nose in tariffs a lot over the years. I voted for him in '44 for president when he ran against Polk."

Will nodded as he watched Anna and Phoebe chatting. Time had passed so quickly, and their families were expanding. The future looked quite bright.

The small church was easily at full capacity, with the Wallace and Conklin families filling the front few pews. The Conklins were not Catholic, but nonetheless, members of this congregation had come by wagon from some twenty miles around. After the ceremony, there would be an afternoon picnic with smoked pork and other fixings to wish the newlywed couple well. It was to be a happy day indeed.

All at once, it was time to go into the church. As Thomas offered Anna his arm, Phoebe peeked back over her shoulder one more time to give Anna her most supportive smile. Anna was about to become a wife in a real church wedding. It was all so exciting!

******

Thomas Wallace lifted his hat and scratched his head while watching Abram Bartholomew stable the team after a long, hard day in the field. The young man had been working for Thomas in exchange for room and board for quite a while now. Thomas

205

enjoyed having Anna's family visit frequently, and her younger sisters would often pop in and stay with them for a few days.

Anything that brought Anna joy brought Thomas joy as well. Already in her first pregnancy, she glowed with health and vibrancy, promising an easy birth. Waking up to Anna in his bed each morning filled Thomas with a euphoria he had never imagined possible. The age difference between them seemed insignificant; they were not only passionate lovers but had also become the very best of friends. After their marriage, Anna had quickly organized and transformed his home, making it as warm and welcoming as the hearth he'd seen at Easter's. It was as if the fruits of his labor all these years in creating this homestead had finally been rewarded by divine providence with a young incarnation of Easter—everything he admired in a woman. In the name of the Father, the Son, and the Holy Ghost, surely he had now satisfied the penance for murdering the Peelers in Ireland, a task Father Rathmore had assigned him some twenty years before. Thomas had never been happier in his entire life.

Abram had avoided arrest long enough that, with the Hodge brothers convicted and in jail, the charges against him had been dropped. Abram had a chance to start a new life away from the troublemakers he had previously associated with. Much like Thomas when he had arrived in America, young Abram did not have many prospects. He would need to find a job that paid actual money to secure a stake and start a family.

What concerned Thomas was Anna's sister, Mary. The last few times she visited, Thomas noticed Mary and Abram spending quite a bit of time together. Mary would often chat with Abram in the barn, they went on walks together, and the last time she was there, Abram gave her a ride back home on his horse. Romance was brewing. Thomas knew how much Easter had her heart set on a well-established farmer for Mary's hand. Such men were plentiful in Jackson County, while frontier wives like Mary were not. Abram would not be a welcome choice. In fact, Thomas worried that Will Conklin might come after Abram with his gun and make Mary a widow if Abram married her.

As Abram came out of the barn Thomas waved him over.

"Abram, I've been meaning to talk to ya about somethin'."

"Yeah, Thomas, sure thing, what's up?"

"I wanted to show ya this posting in Bellevue for a mill worker. It pays a fair wage. It's probably time you start thinking about moving on now that most of your trouble is all settled."

Abram took the posting and glanced through it.

"Are you not happy with my work, Thomas?" Abram inquired.

"Of course, of course I am, it's just that with the missus in a family way, and her family coming over quite a bit, I'm looking at making a few changes around the place. Ya know how it is..." Thomas explained, avoiding Abram's gaze.

Abram studied his Irish friend, who was not displaying his usual dimpled smile. It was evident that Thomas did not want Abram around his wife's family, and it was probably Mary he was concerned about.

"Sure thing, Thomas. I'll pack up my things and leave in the morning if that's okay."

"That'll do. That'll do," the Irishman replied.

"And thanks for the tip on the job," Abram added.

"Sure thing, lad. I'll stop in and check on ya when next I'm in Bellevue." Thomas held out his hand to Abram to make it clear this would be their last conversation on his farm.

Abram grasped his hand firmly and turned to pack up his things.

The next morning, Abram headed straight for the Conklin farm, intending to watch for Mary and let her know he was leaving. They had grown quite fond of each other, and she enjoyed hearing him talk about his plans to go to California. He was determined she would become his wife. He just needed to earn some money to set them up in a small room in town before they could gather enough for a wagon and supplies to seek their fortunes out west.

******

Mary headed down to the creek to fetch water. Her feet were bare, and she had on a plain homespun dress with long sleeves, no collar, and a slightly soiled matching apron. At mid-morning, all of the early chores were done, and she was fetching water for later. A faint smile graced her face as she thought of Abram. On the day they had first met, he had saved her and her sisters' lives from the Hodge brothers, like a knight from a fairytale. She was grateful that Anna's blow hadn't killed him.

She felt comfortable in his arms, and kissing him was delightful. Her belly felt warm, and her spine tingled just thinking about it. Mary was slightly shorter and more petite than her sisters, but she still stood taller than many men. Her long, dark brown hair was usually styled in a braided bun to keep it out of her face while doing chores, but today she had left it loose.

Abram was nearly as tall as Pa and had striking golden hair he kept cropped short. His square, masculine face was always clean-shaven, and his clothes began each day spotless. She loved running her hands over his muscled chest and arms. His broad shoulders tapered down to a slim waist, perched atop a sturdy set of long legs. His blue eyes, framed by golden eyebrows and eyelashes, always looked at her with attraction and kindness. She couldn't help but wonder if they might have a future together, although she knew both Ma and Pa would disapprove. They wanted a farmer with an established homestead, like Thom Sade or Thomas Wallace. But Mary wanted someone young and vibrant like Abram.

When she reached Lytle Creek, she waded out and decided to sit on a rock in the sun. Quiet moments to herself were a rare commodity now that Phoebe and Anna were gone.

Abram spotted Mary as soon as she left the house. He shadowed the tree line, watching her saunter down to the creek with a sweet smile on her face. She was alone; his timing was perfect.

She was surely a pretty thing; prettier than her sisters; pretty much prettier than any girl he had ever seen. Her thick, dark eyelashes and eyebrows framed deep green-brown eyes that enchanted him. Her hair, usually kept in a bun, cascaded in untamed, dark brown curls falling all about her shoulders and back. Her chiseled features and tiny waist reminded him of storybook fairy tales his mother used to read to him when he was a child. The first time he had kissed Mary, her soft, moist lips had ignited a passion he knew he would never tire of. As she sat on the rock with her feet in the stream, tossing her hair to one side, he stepped forward.

"Mary."

"Eek!" Startled, Mary jumped to her feet, slipped on some rocks, and fell sideways into the stream, drenching half of her dress and part of her hair.

Seeing Abram standing by the stream, laughing at her, made her a little angry. "Abram! Why'd you sneak up on me like that?" she asked, exasperated, wading towards the shore and wringing out her hair and dress.

"I'm sorry, I'm sorry." Abram chuckled, extending his arm to help her out of the creek. "I didn't think you would fall in like that. I wasn't trying to sneak up on you. I just had to see you."

Mary smiled up at him, fluffing her dress and removing her wet apron, "Well, now we'll just have to sit here in the sun for a while so I can dry off."

They sat on the bank together, remaining silent, watching the sun sparkle off the stream and the birds flit among the rocks. Finally, Abram gathered his courage, "Mary, I'm leaving Otter Creek and moving to Bellevue. I'm going to get a job at the mill there and save up a nest egg for heading out west to California."

Mary looked into his eyes as he spoke, while Abram stared at the stream.

"The thing is, Mary, I want you to come with me as my wife. You don't have to make up your mind now. Once I get my job, I'll come back and fetch you. We can get married by a preacher in Bellevue."

"Ma and Pa will never agree," Mary said flatly.

They paused for a long time. He put his arm around her, and they kissed for a while. She leaned her head into his chest as he wrapped his arms around her.

"I'll be back in a month. Pack your things and be ready, okay?"

Mary looked up into his eyes and nodded.

A month later, Mary told Ma she was going to stay with Anna and Thomas for a week and left to rendezvous with Abram a little way from the farm. A small sack of clothes, a few supplies, and a new cake of soap were all she brought with her. She stopped by Lytle Creek to scrub herself from head to toe, then put on her Sunday dress.

As she picked a few flowers along the bank, she imagined the trip west, walking alongside her own prairie wagon, foraging for meals while Abram managed their team with his horse tied behind. Their team would consist of oxen. Ma had told her mules were strong and could travel at a good pace but tended to be temperamental and easily startled. Oxen would eat poor grass and possessed remarkable strength. With three pairs to pull their wagon, they could get out of just about any fix they might encounter. Oxen could be pricey, though, as they had to be castrated when young to make them docile and grow large enough for strength. They might need to mix their team and use a couple of female cows.

As she walked to the hill where she was to meet Abram, Mary imagined the names she would give her team: Jenny, Hazel, Jake, Rover, Thomas, for Anna's husband, and Mule, just for fun.

Abram stood just below a hill, concealed by trees, anxiously awaiting Mary's arrival. He was nervous she might change her mind. She was late; they were supposed to meet at sunrise, and it was already halfway to noon. Suddenly, his horse pricked up its ears and snorted, gazing at the tree line below. As Mary emerged, a warmth tingled through Abram's entire being. He had never seen anyone so beautiful. Mary's hair, still slightly damp, caught the sun as her soft, natural curls bounced while she waved and scampered up the hill to meet him.

Together, they rode into Bellevue, got married by a preacher, and settled into a small room at the bar near the mill where Abram was working.

Money was going out faster than it was coming in with the rent on their small room. Abram bought a prairie wagon with a broken axle and no canvas situated on some empty land outside of town. His plan was to repair it, purchase their supplies, and head west.

Three weeks into their marriage, Abram and Mary began to quarrel almost every night. Mary was unhappy, miserable in the noisy, dirty, and dusty town. There was little for her to do, as she was not living on a farm, and Abram refused to let her get a job. Just barely making ends meet consumed every penny Abram earned.

******

Abram returned home after a long day at the mill to find a note from Mary, stating she had gone home to visit Ma and Pa and would return in a few days. The message left him feeling sick to his stomach. What if she didn't come back? She had told him she despised living in town and found it absurd that he expected her to wait around in their cramped room all day while he worked, only to share a brief night together before he left again in the morning. He hadn't thoroughly considered their plans; his primary goal had been to secure her as his wife and figure out the rest afterward. Abram tried to reassure Mary it would only be for a few months, but the truth was, oxen could cost as much as twenty-five dollars at the very least. It might take him up to a year just to earn enough money for one of the sturdy creatures.

Abram's thoughts drifted back to his days with the banditti, when they pilfered supplies and animals from the surrounding homesteaders. It was undoubtedly hard work, but it was an easier and faster way to achieve their goals. He shook his head, determined not to fall back into that dreadful lot, nor drag Mary into it.

A few days later he came back to the room to find Mary waiting for him. They silently melted into each other's arms. Finally Abram asked, "How'd it go?"

"Well, Pa would not even look at me, let alone speak to me. Ma was very glum, but she said she hoped we will be happy together. She's excited about our trip out west. Look, she even gave me a Dutch oven and some cooking utensils. She told me to let her know what she could do to help."

Abram managed a smile, admiring her small treasures. Beneath his façade, he was unsure of what they were going to do.

******

After over two months of marriage and with no progress on the wagon, Mary's patience wore thin. It was as if her dreams had vanished into thin air. That night, she and Abram had their worst fight ever, resulting in him spending the night elsewhere. Mary finally decided she would move into their wagon, whether it was ready or not. The next morning, she packed her sack, rode out to the prairie wagon, and left a note for Abram explaining where she had gone.

Her first night was spent under their broken-down wagon, the stars and moon as her only companions. Mary was well-versed in living out of a wagon, building fires, foraging, and hunting. Her plan was to create a small homestead at this temporary "squatter's" site, enabling them to live more cheaply and fix up the wagon to pursue their dream. She was confident Ma would help her scrounge up the few supplies needed to establish a self-sustainable routine. Despite their short marriage, Mary already longed for Abram's large, warm body next to her. She cherished their intimate moments together and wondered if she could endure seeing him only on weekends…

Abram arrived the next afternoon, visibly distressed. After some heated arguments, he finally conceded that Mary would live at their wagon homestead during the week, and he would return on weekends to work on the place.

******

Over a year later, a new routine had settled into the Conklin farm. Older sisters no longer dominated the family routine, and the boys now outnumbered the girls.

Mahala held little Thomas, almost two now, on her hip as she watched Malinda, now seven, and John Bunyan, now four, playing in the grass. She scanned the horizon for a sign of dust announcing the older boys and Pa's wagon were close to home. Cooking meals and watching the little ones was not her favorite thing to do, but the duty fell to her with Ma away. She had been somewhat spoiled when her older sisters were around, as they took care of most of the mothering and cooking. Most of Mahala's fifteen years had been spent adventuring with her older siblings, fishing, hunting, and foraging, with the fruits of her labor praised and turned into a meal by her older siblings or Ma. With Ma away, Moses, now nine, did a few chores around the place in the morning and then disappeared to either catch up with Pa or to stay as invisible as possible to avoid extra chores, occasionally allowing Malinda to tag along. Right now, Mahala could use his help to fetch some water, but he was nowhere to be seen.

"What's that smell?" Malinda asked wrinkling her nose and lifting it to the air. "It's coming from the house."

"Shite!" Mahala shrieked. She ran inside to see her bread scorched black and a rancid burned smell coming from the bottom of her stew. The Dutch ovens had been left too close to the hot coals for too long.

"Damn it to hell!" she exclaimed loudly. She placed Thomas on the floor and pulled the scorched food from the fire.

"That's cursing. I'm gonna tell Pa," Malinda announced loudly.

Mahala turned to see Malinda holding Thomas Bunyan's hand, standing in the doorway with wide eyes, taking in the chaos.

"You just shut your mouth," Mahala menacingly ordered her sister. "You want me to box your ears?"

Malinda's lip began to quiver, and she put her fingers in her mouth.

"Then you just keep your mouth shut and watch Thomas and John Bunyan while I get dinner ready."

Malinda took John Bunyan's hand and sat him down with Thomas on the floor. She watched Mahala go about what was usually Ma's duties, looking miserable. It made her feel sad. She offered, "I'm sure it will be fine. We can just cut off the black parts."

With her hands on her hips Mahala frowned at her sister. Malinda shrank a bit and looked contrite, so Mahala shook her head and returned to her work. Hopefully, Ma would be home soon. All her hard work in the kitchen today was completely ruined. Her ungrateful family was sure to complain loudly about the quality of her dinner, not noticing the washed dishes, swept floors, fresh picked vegetables, weeded kitchen garden, milked cow, and the hundreds of other chores she had performed that day besides watching the little ones. This situation was unbearable. She belonged out working the farm and hunting alongside her brothers. Mahala was certain that she could accomplish more in a single day than any of them could in three.

******

Will Conklin shook off his sleep as he walked out the front door of their house. Things no longer ran smoothly when Easter was away. He sat down on the porch to put on his boots. The noise level in the house had diminished significantly now that his three oldest daughters were married off and in households of their own.

Mary had defied him and Easter by running off with Abram Bartholomew. This man had some questionable run-ins with the

214

law, had very little means, and earned a meager wage as a mill worker, which was barely enough to keep them fed. Rumor had it they were living in a dilapidated covered wagon, squatting on some vacant land near Bellevue. It made him angry just thinking about it. Certainly, he and Easter had started out in a covered wagon, but they had a nest egg, supplies, a plan, and a destination. This Abram fellow had nothing but aspirations and a low-paying job at the mill.

Phoebe had recently given birth to a second son, and Anna her first just one month later. His girls were proving themselves every bit as capable as homestead wives as Easter. Thom Sade had surely hit the jackpot marrying Phoebe, as had Thomas Wallace in marrying Anna. Both men were quite a bit older than their strong, capable, new frontier wives. Both men had well-established, sustainable farms that won them the right to such wives. This Abram Bartholomew had nothing to his name.

Easter was over at Anna's place for a few days, helping with the new baby. There were just two daughters at home now, Mahala and little Esther Malinda. Will frowned a bit as he thought about what had happened between him and Mahala the night before. The girl could surely be difficult when she had a mind to. His mouth watered when he thought of the breakfast cakes and stews Phoebe, Anna, and Mary used to cook up, equally as good as their mother's. Mahala did not have the same talents at the hearth as her sisters. Granted, she had just turned fifteen, but in these parts, so rare with women, some felt fifteen was a fair enough age for marriage. Such a girl should be able to run a household without burning dinner.

In any case, when Will had come home last night, dinner was burned. The young'uns shoveled it in regardless, but Will had complained. Mahala had gotten smart with him, and he smacked her so hard she flew off her stool. Will was not sure what got into him. If Easter had been there, it would have never come to that. The kids respected their Ma more than they did him. Will was tired, out of patience, and not up for the disrespect that girl hurled at him.

Mahala was nowhere to be seen this morning, but Aminadab had prevented another altercation by fixing breakfast for everyone. The gruel was nothing compared to Phoebe's hotcakes or Anna's cornbread, though. His mouth watered yet again, thinking about his older daughters' cooking.

He sighed and reached down to pull on his boot…They were wet and had a rancid smell of urine about them. What the hell? Will frowned. He noticed something appeared to be moving inside of it. "Ahhh! Jesus!" Will screamed, throwing the boot and jumping back. There was a damn snake in it. His eyes narrowed and scanned the tree line. This dangerous prank had Mahala's handiwork written all over it…

******

Anna waited patiently with Mahala by the shore in Bellevue. This place was not a favorite of hers. After three-plus years of making Otter Creek her home, Bellevue had grown quite a bit, but still attracted the roughest of characters. Today, she would see her sister safely aboard the flatboat that would take her to her new position as a laborer in the household of one Mr. Thom A. Holmes in Minnesota.

Ma and Pa had said their goodbyes at home, and Anna had left her baby with them while she and Thomas gave Mahala a ride into town, to her new life. Phoebe's brother-in-law, Bartlette Sade, had helped Mahala find the position. Things had become quite impossible at the Conklin home. With Phoebe, Anna, and Mary's marriages, Mahala was the only woman left in the household besides Ma. Pa did not have many left to vent his foul temper upon.

Mahala was not one to take slights lightly, and her latest and last act of defiance had been to put a timber rattler in one of Pa's boots while watching the encounter from a nearby tree. Not only that, she had peed on them to ensure her ire was well remembered…peed on Pa's boots; Anna shook her head in disbelief.

After Mahala had hightailed it off to stay with Anna and Thomas, Pa fumed for days. In that, Pa and Mahala were much alike—a long memory for any slight, real or imagined.

Now, Bartlette Sade, Phoebe's brother-in-law, had taken quite a shine to Mahala. Anna secretly thought, even though Bartlette was quite a bit older, he was waiting for Mahala to come of age to ask for her hand. Bartlette found Mahala's temper charming and always made her laugh when the family got together.

In any case, Bartlette's acquaintance, Mr. Holmes, was starting a new settlement in the wilds of Minnesota. He was a man of means and good reputation, with a trading post under construction. They would be traveling on the Wild Paddy flatboat, with a number of hired help. Scoring Mahala as a servant was a rare prize, and they were assured she would be safe, well cared for, and paid a decent wage. Anna left word at the mill for Abram that Mahala was leaving. She had no idea if the message would get to Mary in time.

Thomas was chatting with Mr. Holmes while the freight was being loaded onto the boat.

Anna had helped Mahala pack the night before. Mahala's belongings consisted of a single knapsack of goods with a respectable Sunday dress tucked inside, along with a bar of soap, some hardtack, her secret bracelet in its special pouch her Native friends had given her, and a blanket. She wore the rest of her clothes as layers: a sturdy hat, long johns, a day dress, a warm overcoat, knitted wool stockings, and laced shoes. Ma made sure each of her children had a respectable set of clothes.

Mahala stood a little shorter than her three older sisters but still a good height for a woman. Her face was a bit rounder, and her eyes always serious, flitting here and there, never missing any detail. Her very dark hair, as usual, was styled in a braided bun. She was strong and sturdy. This Mr. Holmes was getting a good worker.

Anna studied Mahala from the corner of her eye. She stood with her head held high, stoic as ever, showing no emotion, but Anna knew her well enough to know she must be hurting. With the discord at home, neither Ma nor Pa had batted an eye when she announced she was leaving on this Minnesota adventure.

"Mahala!" a voice shouted.

In unison, they both turned around to see Mary galloping wildly towards them on a saddleless horse, gripping it with her thighs like a Native, her dress flapping with the horse's gait. She pulled the animal to a stop and leaped into her sisters' arms. All three of them clutched each other.

"I was so scared that I would miss saying goodbye," Mary cried out, breathing heavily. For a moment, all three girls just stood in a circle, grasping each other.

Mahala finally broke the silence. "I hate Pa," she declared flatly.

Anna looked at the ground, "I know."

Mary offered, "He can be pretty hard to forgive sometimes."

"You remember what Ma taught us, and never let anybody run roughshod over you," Anna said with tears in her eyes. "And if you don't like it there, you come home. We'll send someone to fetch you."

"And write often so we know you're all right," Mary added.

Mahala felt doomed as she looked into the tears of love in her sisters' eyes and nodded.

With some final hugs from her sisters and a hearty bear hug from Thomas, she picked up her sack and headed down to the flatboat. Anna and Mary watched as their little sister climbed aboard the boat and it slowly headed upriver, her destination: the remote wilds of Minnesota. Thomas wrapped his arms around Anna and Mary as tears streamed down their faces. They stood silently together for a long time after Mahala and the Wild Paddy disappeared from sight.

"If she doesn't write I'm gonna go fetch her," Anna declared.

"She'll be fine. She's scrappy just like her sisters and her Ma," Thomas retorted. "And if she doesn't write, Bartlette Sade will go fetch her." Thomas winked at Anna and Mary, coaxing smiles from their tear-stained faces.

******

Mahala shivered as she watched the last hints of Bellevue disappear from view. She was heading upstream amongst the wilds of the Mississippi River on a boat powered by men's muscle, pikes, and a couple of sails. She wasn't cold, but leaving her family behind after having lived with them her entire life was suddenly terrifying. The day turned into a night of camping onshore, much like her trip on the Blackhawk steamboat with her family from Ohio to Bellevue. With the more familiar routine, she became more at ease, almost a bit excited. She was off to a new life. With every passing mile, there was a new scene to discover. The day-to-day drudgery she had left back home was already beginning to feel surreal.

After a few days' travel, they finally turned onto the Minnesota River and would soon reach their destination. It was a settlement called Shakopee. Mr. Holmes had built a trading post, and Mahala would be doing all types of odd jobs for him along with other workers. Her parents were assured she would have respectable quarters with another family in their cabin: a Mr. and Mrs. Haywood and their daughter.

Mahala had been mostly ignored by the crew on this trip, although she noticed an occasional curious sideways look.

A little past noon, some Natives on horseback appeared onshore and started matching their pace. No one paid them any attention. Suddenly, as if out of nowhere, the settlement appeared before them. The boat was beached, and the men began to unload.

Closest to the beach on the rise of a hill was a large, two-story log structure, obviously the new trading post. Several smaller log structures were sprinkled around the muddy settlement with all kinds of characters wandering around. There were Natives dressed in full buckskin, settlers, a couple of soldiers, white trappers, a few dogs, but no children anywhere. Quite a few open fires attracted clusters of different folk. Hearth smoke from around the bend of the place hinted more structures might be found there.

"That cabin yonder is where you'll be staying," Mr. Holmes announced as he pointed up the muddy bank to a small log cabin at the edge of the encampment.

Mahala gathered up her things and stood waiting.

"Don't just stand there, girl, go on up, introduce yourself to the Haywoods, and get settled in. I'll expect you tomorrow an hour before sun-up at the trading post to help with chores. In the meantime," he gave her a half smile, "explore a bit and get your bearings. Don't stray too far from town by yourself."

Mahala nodded, feeling very small, and started up the hill towards the Haywoods' cabin.

"Benjamin." She heard Mr. Holmes holler. An older man, about her father's age, was coming down the hill.

"This here is Mahala Conklin. I promised the Haywoods some supplies for putting her up. Show the girl around town a bit and deliver those supplies, please."

"Sure thing," Benjamin replied.

He tipped his hat to Mahala and motioned her to follow. "I'm Benjamin Shumway, ma'am. At your service."

It felt a bit odd for Mahala to be called "ma'am." She studied him and the area surrounding her intently as they walked. There were quite a few men and no women in sight. A number of the men wore Native adornments along with typical settler clothes. With their darker complexions, she suspected they might be some of the "half-breed" settlers and traders she had heard tales about.

"I've been helping Thom Holmes out with his trading post, and he pays me with supplies, which I trade as well. I have a homestead built not far from here."

Mahala was feeling a bit more comfortable with Benjamin chattering away at her. He reminded her of Elijah and didn't seem a bit fazed that she wasn't chattering back. It suddenly occurred to her that she would be able to wear her special Native bracelet out in the open in this place. No longer would she need to limit her behavior by her parents' rules. It was an odd feeling.

"We almost have the second floor sleeping rooms completed in the trading post. There is a missionary at the very end of town and some log cabins that have goods stored in them, from which we also trade. There's some nice calico, blankets, powder, beads, and lead. We get a lot of good fur from the local Natives."

Benjamin noticed her looking at the black arm band he and some of the men around town were wearing.

"The grand senator from Kentucky, Ol' Henry Clay, has finally passed away. Bells have been ringing all over the country to mourn the old man. People are wearing black armbands to honor the way the Old Coon stood up for us frontier folk over the years."

Mahala glanced at his face to see him smiling at her with obvious interest.

"Would ya like one? I have extras."

Mahala immediately nodded. She imagined her family back home would be wearing such armbands as well. Although Pa had never been a fan of Henry Clay, most of the rest of her family surely was. She stopped and held out her arm as Benjamin affixed it carefully.

"There ya go," he announced as he finished. He walked over to a supply pile and picked up a crate. He turned to Mahala and motioned with his head to follow him.

"You are not much of a talker then, huh?"

Mahala shrugged her shoulders.

"Well, then, you'll fit right in here." Benjamin smiled again. "The Haywoods are up this-a-way."

1853 – Of SNAKE!

Vile reptile!
Base as vile, and cowardly as base;
A straight descendant thou of him, methinks,
Man's ancient foe, or else his paraphrase.
...For there is nothing mean, or base, or vile,
That is not comprehended in the name
Of SNAKE!

THREE YEARS SINCE THE GIRLS WED...
Easter - 40, Will - 44
Esther Malinda - 9, Julia Etta - newborn
Aminadab - 19, Billy - 17, Elijah - 13, Moses Rueben - 11, John Bunyan
- 6, Thomas - 3 years
~
Phoebe - 23, Anna - 21, Mary - 20, Mahala - 17

Will Conklin sat for a long time on his horse, surveying the encampment below. The teepee to the right was absent the cheerful, brightly painted Injun pictures on the outside one normally would expect to see. That and the fact that there was a broken down covered wagon, missing two wheels with a corral and a shed next to it, made it clear that this was pretty much a settlers' encampment. Obviously these people were down on their luck, or why else would they be living out of a teepee? The wagon wasn't even decent enough to live in. They were using it for storage.

Smoke rising from the teepee hinted that the occupants could at least keep warm and cook. A substantial pile of chopped wood beside the shed promised to fuel fires through the winter months. Why Abram Bartholomew kept his wife in a place like this was beyond Will's comprehension. For God's sake, the horse had better accommodations.

The buck strapped to Will's packhorse was originally intended for his own family. They had sufficient supplies to last until spring, Easter had seen to that. Still, Will relished those few winter months when the farm was asleep. Like the leafless deciduous trees and hibernating bears, it did not need constant attention. This allowed him to indulge in some leisure activities; specifically hunting, visiting neighbors to hear the latest news, and chat about next year's planting.

This particular hunting trip had taken Will near Bellevue. Something in his gut made him worry about Mary, and he had decided to pay her a visit. Will had only seen her a couple of times since she married this fellow. Abram was still not a welcome addition to the family from Will's perspective.

As Will approached the encampment, he was met by a suspicious Mary emerging from the teepee with a loaded rifle. Her fierce scowl melted into a warm grin when she recognized her Pa. It seemed she didn't even have a dog for company while her husband was away.

"Pa!" Mary shouted and waved as he rode up.

Will returned her smile and dismounted, sizing her up. Mary wore a big warm buffalo robe, and had her hair styled into a bun, much like her Ma, so there was no mistaking her for an Injun for sure. Her beaming countenance betrayed no hint of unhappiness. He swept her up in his arms and swung her around.

Mary noticed the buck on his packhorse. "What are you doing hunting this far from home?"

Will shrugged, "A wanderlust got into me. We have plenty of meat at home. I've been on the trail a few days and am missing your Ma's biscuits somethin' fierce. I was hoping I might trade this buck for some of yours; they're every bit as good."

Pa flashed a boyish smile Mary had not really ever been the recipient of before. It was quite charming. He was treating her like an adult, tugging at her heartstrings. She did miss them all quite badly, and they did need the meat. Abram was still working at the mill and didn't hunt, so any food they didn't have to buy could contribute to their nest egg. He might not be pleased about accepting the meat, but she was not about to turn it down.

"Deal. You can hang him on that tree yonder. Cut off some choice steaks, and I'll cook those up for you too," Mary beamed at him before disappearing into the teepee.

Will's smile vanished, replaced by a scowl. Abram had almost two years to fix this wagon and get them on their feet. Easter told him Abram refused to even build a cabin because, from his perspective, they were about to depart for California at any moment and did not want to set down roots in this place.

"Did you hear that Mahala got married?" Will asked, entering the teepee with the steaks.

"What?"

"Yep. Your Ma got a letter from her. Mahala married a Minnesota farmer named Benjamin Shumway. Their homestead is near St. Paul, and they have a son. She's been quite the busy lady since she left home," Will said, grinning.

Mary shook her head as she tended the coals and Dutch ovens. Letters from Mahala had been few and far between. She'd received only one, saying that Mahala was well settled, had made friends, and was happy. Her sister was so independent and already had a son. Mary hadn't written much to Mahala either. Ma served as their gossip hub, keeping tabs on everyone. Mary felt happy for her sister, wondering when she and Abram would have good news to share. Abram was a dreamer, but not much of a planner or saver.

Will spent the night in his daughter's teepee, well-fed and warm. Abram usually stayed in an inexpensive bunk in Bellevue during the week and came home on weekends. In the morning, Will awoke to Mary cooking breakfast on a griddle, just as she'd done at home. The bed had been warm blankets over a thick, clean mat of straw—certainly better than sleeping on the ground by a fire. The modest dwelling was well-organized for cooking, crafting leather goods to sell, spinning, and weaving. Easter likely provided Mary with flax and wool from the farm. But compared to Phoebe and Anna's homesteads—and probably Mahala's, too—it nearly brought Will to tears. Mary deserved better. What if she had a baby in this place? It was absurd!

******

The Red Rock Saloon in Bellevue had a reputation. Not only did it house women "of the right kind" for solicitation, but it also offered, for a price, various nefarious services. The town had become somewhat tamer in recent years, with the worst gunfights occurring in the 1840s. Although most notorious thugs were no longer around, intimidation and bribery could still be bought, along with various types of thievery.

Emma Johnson was a lady that could broker such things. The bartender routed such prospective customers her way, and she would provide a kickback in return. Being discreet and delivering as promised was what kept her in business. Anything less could land her in jail as a co-conspirator, and so she was more than careful to ensure safe customers and as reliable workers as one could expect in such a business as this.

Years of homesteading had etched lines into Emma's face. She was plain and plump. When her husband injured himself so severely that he couldn't work on the farm, they moved into town. Now, Emma was the sole breadwinner.

Her mouse-brown hair was styled in a bun, like most settler women. She wasn't the type to catch a man's eye or draw attention while serving drinks or polishing glasses. This was intentional. While the other girls, "of the right kind," wore fancier, more revealing clothes and spent time on their hair to compete for patrons, Emma's goal was to observe, make casual friends, and catalog her acquaintances. She also connected people in need of reputable business contacts, like flatboat owners offering freight services or traders looking to swap goods. Her legitimate business provided cover for her more illicit dealings. Business was business, and Emma was an astute businesswoman.

Sitting across the table from her right now was a paying customer nursing his fourth whiskey. A farmer wanted to broker a "discreet hunting accident." His target was a local mill worker with few ties. Emma knew the right pair for the job. With winter slowing things down, they were bored and likely to accept a few pieces of silver for the task. The mill worker had a young wife, and the farmer wanted to make her a widow. It needed to appear beyond suspicion; perhaps a snakebite or a fatal encounter with his horse. Emma took the silver and watched the man leave. In the winter, snakes moved slower, but timber rattlesnakes could still strike quickly. If the mill worker fell into a snake pit while hunting, it could indeed prove deadly…

******

The bonds that gripped Abram's arms were tied over his shirt. Odd that these men had done it this way. It was almost as if they did not want to cause any injury to his wrists. With the sack over his head, Abram had no idea where they were taking him. He carried nothing valuable to steal. He suspected they were part of the Mormon Nauvoo gang, finally exacting their revenge, still bitter over his departure from their ranks. Those were ones with a long memory, and vivid stories of their revenge were hair-raising to say the least.

He heard muffled voices say, "We're to make it look like a hunting accident."

If Abram did not have a gag stuffed in his mouth to silence him, he could have responded, "But I don't hunt. My wife does all the hunting. I work in the mill…"

They had jumped him on his way home from town. Abram had no chance of escape, no warning. He desperately hoped they weren't after his wife, too.

Suddenly, Abram found himself on the ground, his bonds being cut. He swung at one assailant but missed, then found himself tumbling into some sort of pit. An ominous rattling forewarned the impending strike of many snakes…and then the strikes began.

Abram leaped and danced, trying to evade the serpents, but it was futile. Each bite swelled and discolored his skin. He screamed and clawed at the pit's sides, unable to climb out, as two faces watched from above.

Abram's heart raced, and his skin began to tingle, as if needles were poking him from the inside out. The snakebites seemed endless, and the figures above blurred, while his labored breaths weakened. An overwhelming fatigue pulled him to his knees, as if he weighed 500 pounds.

At last, in the end, as he lay on his back, Abram gasped into the darkness, "I don't hunt…"

******

Easter, Phoebe, and Anna escorted Mary away from her husband's grave as the men shoveled dirt over his rough-cut wooden coffin. Thomas and Will had constructed the thing.

Mary was numb, her heart utterly broken as if it had died with Abram. She was in the depths of despair, having wept for days. She continued to weep, even though her eyes had no moisture left for tears.

It had taken the search party a couple of days to find Abram's body after he went missing. It seemed to be a freak hunting accident: He had shot a deer and, while gutting it, fell into a snake pit camouflaged by fallen limbs. Mary told anyone who would listen that Abram didn't hunt…

His horse had somehow found its way home, the only witness to the tragedy. A pity it couldn't talk.

Easter knew full well that Abram did not hunt, but it wasn't something many people knew. A man wouldn't brag about his wife doing all the hunting in their household.

"Ridiculous!" was all Will would say about the matter. "She's well rid of him in any case." He was quite insensitive to Mary's grief, but went through the motions at the gravesite. Everyone knew he had no use for the young man his daughter had married.

The unusual circumstances of Abram's death fueled gossip. Many in town thought it was likely Nauvoo gang retribution that had finally caught up with him, given the grisly scene and his history with the gang.

In any case, when Mary came back to live on the Conklin farm, there was something a bit too smug in Will's eyes for Easter's liking. She suspected he might know more than he admitted, but that was something none of them would likely ever know for sure...

1855 – Of Rye

I saw a youth in an evil hour
Beguiled by the tempting bowl;
And he deeply drank of its baneful dregs,
That burned to his very soul

FIVE YEARS SINCE THE GIRL'S WED…
Easter - 43, Will - 47
Esther Malinda - 11, Julia Etta - 2
Aminadab - 21, Billy - 18, Elijah - 16, Moses - 14, John Bunyan - 8,
Thomas - 6
~
Phoebe - 25, Thom Sade - 36
Nathaniel Jefferson - 6, William Harrison - 4, Mary Lucretia - 3, Franklin
Pierce - 1
~
Anna -24, Thomas Wallace - 49
John Claudius - 4, Esther Angeline - 3, Thomas Joseph - 1, David Jerome
- newborn
~
Mary - 22, Bartlett Emerson Sade - 41
Bartlett Emerson - 2, Mary Ann - newborn
~
Mahala - 19, Benjamin Shumway – 32
Emerson Bartlett - 3, Esther - 2, Mary Etta – newborn

orothy Meechum poured another round of her husband's rye whiskey for her guests, as Earl dealt the next hand for their draw poker game. A number of neighbors from Otter Creek enjoyed stopping by the Meechum homestead on their way to and from town. Earl's hospitality and his rye whiskey had become somewhat famous locally. Often, the men would linger in the barn, trading stories or playing cards with Earl's hickory-carved coin chips, which kept the competition amicable and the ladies at ease. Sometimes wives accompanied their husbands, as Easter and Will Conklin had today. Dorothy always had fresh baked goods on hand for guests, and she and Earl, being childless, genuinely relished the company.

Earl never tired of telling anyone who would listen the story of how he came to make his rye whiskey. During their homesteading days in Ohio, Earl had the good fortune to chat with the famed Tennessee congressman, Davy Crockett, on a visit to Cincinnati in 1834. Crockett, true to his larger-than-life reputation, had gone out of his way to converse with local farmers, as he had with Will and Easter at the county fair on that very same trip. After swapping tales at a nearby tavern, Earl and Davy found common ground in their interest in distilling whiskey. Crockett shared a few east coast recipes that incorporated rye rather than the pure white corn mix many frontier folks preferred for home-brewing. The concoction was supposedly a cousin-to-cousin hand-me-down based on President George Washington's rye whiskey recipe from his early commercial distillery: 60% rye, 35% corn, and 5% malted barley.

Earl's rye whiskey ingredients were all homegrown on the Meechum farm and ground at the gristmill in Garryowen. He had special copper pot stills shipped from the east, which he heated with open hickory wood fires to cook the mash. After fermenting in charred wooden barrels for just the right amount of time—sometimes up to a year—Earl's rye would be ready. Local farmers occasionally contributed their excess harvest grain to his little hobby. Of course, local preachers often sermonized on temperance and abstinence from strong drink, though many did not practice what they preached. Only a select group of neighbors were invited into the Meechum rye social circle, as it were. The last thing they needed was for a local temperance society to denounce them in town as sinners.

Will and Easter Conklin were among the select few Earl happily included in his rye whiskey circle. Easter presented something of a conundrum for Dorothy, who found herself both liking and loathing the woman. Earl shamelessly flirted with her, like he was doing right now, much to Dorothy's annoyance. The woman was like a sow, giving birth to a child almost every year, managing her bustling household and farm with infectious good humor and a confident swagger. On this particular afternoon, she had left her younger children in the care of her older ones and ventured to town with her husband. From Dorothy's perspective this woman seemed to have it all: an attentive husband, a successful farm, a passel of kids, and even grandkids already. Standing as tall as Earl and only a bit shorter than her husband, Easter was sturdy and solid with amazing stature. With time, many frontier women became permanently bent over as if carrying some invisible burden on their shoulders, but not Easter. In a frontier town, one might even consider her attractive. Even at her age, her dark chestnut hair showed no signs of gray, and her radiant skin, though lined, bespoke robust health. As they had come from town, she was dressed in a pale green dress with a soft peach flower print with pantaloons peeking out from under her petticoat.

Dorothy frowned at Earl's flirtations. He was drunk. They were all drunk for that matter. Even Will Conklin had taken the liberty of slapping Dorothy playfully on her backside, along with a sly wink, when Earl and Easter were distracted, but Earl was over the top tonight. She was extremely aggravated with him.

Earl slurred loudly, "Easter, darlin', you get prettier every time I see you. Will Conklin, how do you keep this lady of yours so good-lookin' with all those young'uns she's been raising up for you? Y'all got to be the luckiest man alive with such a woman."

"Earl, you stop. You know you don't mean it." Easter batted her eyes and grinned, visibly glowing under his compliments. She caught a glimpse of Dorothy shooting dark looks at Earl and quickly changed the subject. "Dorothy, you make the best biscuits and preserves in Otter Creek Township. Better than even mine, and that's saying something." Easter helped herself to another biscuit, glancing out the window. They would have to be going soon if they were to make it home before dusk.

Dorothy managed a half-smile at Easter's praise. The woman was certainly empathetic and agreeable most of the time. She enjoyed Easter when Earl's flirting was not encouraged for sure.

"Will, we need to get going." Easter stood up and poked Will in the shoulder. He had drunk so much he was almost asleep at the table. It was clear Easter would be the one driving the team home tonight.

"Earl, you might have to help Easter with Will there." Dorothy snickered a bit.

Easter rolled her eyes and smiled as they loaded a drowsy Will into the back of the wagon. "See you next time," she called, clicking her tongue at the team and heading out.

"She's quite a woman," Earl slurred has he put his arm around Dorothy.

"Why? Because she punches out kids like a brood sow and drives a team?" Dorothy retorted shaking off Earl's arm.

"Dorothy, honey I'm not comparing her to you. You're my one and only sweet-heart; just admiring Conklin's good fortune, that's all."

Dorothy snorted as she walked into their house, shaking her head, "Just shut up, Earl." She watched him stagger toward the barn, likely to spend the night drinking there. Although annoyed, she had enjoyed their evening with the Conklins. She supposed she could forgive Earl tomorrow. After all, passing out from drink and sleeping in the cold barn seemed a fitting punishment for being so insensitive.

******

Father Jeremiah Trecy was delighted to be baptizing yet another one of Thomas Wallace's children into the church. This one, barely three months of age, was the epitome of good health. The high survival rate and vigor of the children in his congregation always amazed him. In these Iowa wilds, people didn't become sickly or go hungry. Fowl, fish, and game were abundant, and each pioneer family was a bastion of self-sufficiency. If crops failed, they could hunt and fish for sustenance, raise and shear their own sheep—of which the wife carded and spun the wool or flax for clothing—while tending to her household garden. Those adept at foraging gathered berries, wild rice, greens, and roots. The isolation of most farms helped to prevent the spread of disease.

Father Trecy had taken over as the priest of St. Patrick's Congregation from Father Perrodin in 1851, spearheading not only the erection of a new stone church to replace the log structure, but he'd also had established a group of Sisters of Charity of the Blessed Virgin Mary in their own cabin to assist in teaching the local children. Although the sisters' living conditions remained quite primitive, they were steadfast in their devotion to the locals.

Only last year, the church construction had been completed, with stone quarried three miles south of Garryowen. To ensure the church would stand for generations, an architect and stonemason were hired, as the bishops and the Catholic diocese had done in the homelands of Europe for centuries. On Christmas Day in 1854, they had held their first official Mass within these hallowed walls.

This was Thomas Wallace's fourth child—one of three sons and a daughter. Little David Jerome Wallace would be one of the first babes baptized within these walls. Thomas had chosen well in his frontier wife, as the woman appeared quite capable of producing many more parishioners for the Church and offspring for this man.

******

Easter pulled out her Bible to record another name in her ever-expanding family tree. She wrote the year, 1855, at the top of the page. She was now a grandmother to—gasp—thirteen grandchildren, with two of her own children still under seven years of age.

Mahala had married Benjamin Shumway in Minnesota and now had a son and two girls.

Anna and Thomas Wallace had three sons and a girl.

Phoebe and Thom Sade had three sons and a girl.

After her husband's death, Mary had subsequently wed Bartlett Sade, which made Will quite happy, but the light had gone out of Mary's eyes. After Abram died, she didn't seem to care who she married and let Will arrange everything. It had all happened rather quickly. Now Mary had a daughter and a son from Bartlett on their well-established homestead. Two Conklin sisters had married two of the Sade brothers. Something in Easter's gut told her it should have been Mahala that married Bartlett, but that was water under the bridge.

Easter herself had given birth to another daughter, Julia Etta, who was now two. And she was pregnant again, a fact she had not yet shared with Will.

The only births Easter hadn't been able to attend were Mahala's, whom she hadn't seen since she left for Minnesota, and Anna's most recent son, David Jerome Wallace, who had arrived in November during a heavy snow. She finally got to meet him when he was almost a month old and quite chubby.

Easter mused on Mahala's marriage to Mr. Shumway. Bartlett Sade and Mahala had always seemed so fond of each other. If Mahala hadn't been so young, Will would have married her off instead of sending her to Minnesota. Yet Mahala had married soon after anyway and even named her first son with Shumway, Emerson Bartlett. After years of butting heads with Mahala, Will didn't look forward to any more daughters. Easter wondered how he would feel if their next baby turned out to be another girl.

With Mahala's survival skills, she would make Benjamin Shumway an exceptional frontier wife. One could only hope the man was good to her and appreciated his good fortune. There were no hints in Mahala's occasional letters to suggest otherwise, but Easter had no doubt Mahala wouldn't tolerate anything less than respect from her mate.

Picnics and family gatherings this summer would be boisterous affairs, with the children's laughter filling the air. Together, they could easily fill up a couple of wagons. Things were almost going too well. The following year promised to be a record harvest for the Conklins, in both family and crops. Corn and oats would likely fetch 10 cents a bushel, and wheat, 20 cents.

Their neighbor, Earl Meechum, had recently passed away. The morning after she and Will last visited, Dorothy found him lifeless in the barn, cradling a jug of his rye. He had died in his sleep.

Now Dorothy was looking to sell off some of the farmland. She couldn't afford labor to work it. Easter had negotiated a deal with her to buy forty more acres at $1.25 per acre on which they could plant wheat. The land wasn't contiguous to theirs, of course; it was next to Dorothy and Earl's place. Will would have to go a bit north with the boys to work it, but there was plenty of water, it was very fertile, and it was halfway to Anna's farm as well as the Garryowen Post Office and Washington Mills depot. With Lytle Creek close by, it was a prime piece of land. She wished they could buy more, but they needed ample seed money for spring. Perhaps she could work out a deal with Dorothy to sharecrop some of her remaining land.

It saddened Easter to think about Dorothy and Earl. For the past couple of years, she and Will had enjoyed stopping at their farm on their way to and from the stores at Washington Mill, monthly church services, and visiting Thomas and Anna. Earl's hearty backslaps and admiration for Will's good fortune in having strong sons to help on the farm always put a bounce in Will's step. Earl lamented his and Dorothy's misfortune of never having children of their own.

The Conklins' older boys were indispensable in working their expanding farm. Soon, they'd want to start families of their own, but that would require a nest egg. Will was counting on their dedication to the Conklin lands and might not take kindly to them selling their labor to other farms. But at some point, they would have to.

******

Will scowled at the plate before him; stew again. It seemed like every night this week they had venison stew. The boys were wolfing it down as fast as they could. He glowered at Easter and reluctantly began to eat. What he really wanted was a drink.

"Something wrong?" Easter asked.

"Seems like we could have a chicken or one of our hams once in a while." Will snapped back.

"We had ham yesterday, Pa." Moses offered.

"We did?"

All the kids nodded, and Easter looked at Will curiously. He had been growing increasingly forgetful and very temperamental—rougher than usual with the kids and downright nasty most of the time. It seemed like the only time he was in a good mood was when he drank, and that worried her. Perhaps it was a good thing that Earl had passed on. Will had spent a bit too much time at the Meechum farm, sampling Earl's rye. With luck, this next year of planting could be their best year ever.

Will reached for the salt and accidentally knocked it over, cursing. At the sight of spilled salt, Easter grabbed a bit and threw it over her shoulder, something she had learned from Thomas Wallace back in Ohio. The Irish believed that spilled salt was bad luck, and to ward it off, you must throw the salt over your left shoulder. Easter wasn't superstitious by nature, but it was better to be safe than sorry.

Aside from Will's foul temper, things had been going exceptionally well in their lives over the past couple of years, and it almost unnerved Easter. In any case, with another baby on the way, perhaps the promise of new beginnings would cheer up Will.

1856 – The Best of Times…The Worst of Times…

For there her sleeping children lie
Unconscious of her woe;
Her choking sobs may not be stayed,
For oh, she loves them so.

TWENTY EIGHT YEARS SINCE EASTER AND WILL WED; SIX
YEARS SINCE THE GIRL'S WED…
Easter - 44, Will - 48
Esther Malinda - 12, Julia Etta - 3, Nancy – new-born
Aminadab - 22, Billy - 19, Elijah - 17, Moses - 15, John Bunyan - 9,
Thomas - 7
~
Phoebe - 26, Thom Sade - 37
Nathaniel Jefferson - 7, William Harrison - 5, Mary Lucretia - 4, Franklin
Pierce - 2
~
Anna -25, Thomas Wallace - 50
John Claudius - 5, Esther Angeline - 4, Thomas Joseph - 2, David Jerome
- 1
~
Mary - 23, Bartlett Emerson Sade - 42
Bartlett Emerson - 3, Mary Ann - 1
~
Mahala - 20, Benjamin Shumway – 33
Emerson Bartlett - 4, Esther - 3, Mary Etta - 1

The year began with rumors of locusts. The older townsfolk reminisced about the swarm of 1841 that had turned day into night, with clouds of the horrid winged insects stripping cornstalks bare. Back then, that, along with the drought, had devastated local farms. The chatter had everybody spooked, but in the end, it turned out that the rumors were just rumors, and the crops this year looked to be record breaking.

Will and Easter pulled up in front of the Otter Creek Mercantile. They had various errands to run about town. The journey from home had taken a couple of hours. Most of the ride had been spent with little conversation between them. They would each spend about an hour running errands and making a bit of small talk here and there before heading home, with enough time to unload before nightfall. Easter had brought a bundle of leather goods and a basket of eggs to barter, along with some additional coin which she hoped would be enough to secure a respectable store-bought Sunday dress for Malinda. At twelve, she stood as tall as a grown woman and, with no older sisters at home to pass down their garments, needed something presentable for church and trips to town. Home-spun attire sufficed for daily wear, but Easter wanted her children to look their best on special occasions.

It was a welcome respite from the farm, especially for Easter who had recently given birth to little Nancy, now three months old and under Malinda's watchful eye for the day. Nancy's delivery had been smooth, and Easter had recovered swiftly. The infant was rather petite compared to her siblings.

Easter stepped down off the wagon while Will walked around the rear to open up the back. As he was unlatching the wagon Easter noticed something caught his eye. He was staring with intense interest, and then shot Easter a curt nod before crossing the street at a brisk pace. And then Easter saw what had him so distracted. The Widow Meechum was strolling down the sidewalk in a robin-egg-blue dress with a matching bonnet. Her white lace petticoats peeked out from her skirt as she strolled. She carried a basket loaded with some purchases. When Will caught up to her, he tipped his hat, took the basket from her, and chatted merrily as they ambled toward her buggy.

Laden with an armful of goods, Easter leaned against the wagon and sighed in exasperation. There she was, struggling to carry her items, while Will dashed off to assist Dorothy with her meager basket.

"Hello, Easter, deary, can I help you with anything?" Mrs. Sorenson, the store-owner's wife was standing at the entrance. At first, Easter was at a loss for words, but then she noticed Mrs. Sorenson's eyes flit between her and Will, who was engaged in conversation with the widow down the street. Was that a flicker of pity in the older woman's eyes?

Easter's gaze returned to Will, who was now grinning foolishly as he helped Dorothy into her buggy. For a fleeting moment she fancied Dorothy was smirking at her from afar. Shaking her head at the absurdity of her suspicions, Easter responded to Mrs. Sorenson, "Yes, indeed. I've brought you some of the usual for trade." She flashed a confident smile, handed over a bundle, and returned to the wagon for the remaining goods, all while stealing glances at Will, who continued to laugh and seemingly flirt with Dorothy Meechum. Easter reassured herself: He's just being friendly because she's all alone. After all, Earl had been a dear friend of theirs. It was only natural for Easter and Will to extend kindness to his widow...

******

Dorothy Meechum pulled the glass from Will Conklin's hand as he lay sprawled across her bar, snoring loudly. As usual, he had drunk himself into oblivion and was now sleeping it off, occupying valuable space at her expense. She didn't object to his patronage when he was conscious; it was just that he invariably ended up monopolizing a spot a paying customer might want when he succumbed to his stupor.

After Earl's death, Dorothy had mourned for a time before realizing she couldn't manage the farm without children of her own to assist with the labor. Hired help was too costly, so after selling off some acreage, she decided to convert her farm into a makeshift roadhouse. Folks were already accustomed to stopping by, so she started by selling meals. A few couples, single farmers, and farmhands became her initial customers for her home-cooked meals and, eventually, laundry services. Inspired, she began selling Earl's Rye, and soon "Earl's Place" became a popular, if somewhat unrefined, watering hole. As the ladies stopped frequenting the establishment, the men of Otter Creek Township and nearby Garryowen enjoyed the place, indulging themselves without their wives to restrain their spending. Dorothy quickly turned a handsome profit, ecstatic that her once-dire circumstances had given way to a thriving business.

A few months later, she decided to introduce a few working girls from Bellevue who were the "right kind." They assisted in serving her patrons and encouraged the men to purchase the girls drinks. Dorothy paid little heed to any side ventures her girls might have had; their liquor was diluted, and the men paid full price for it. She offered the girls a generous fifty percent cut from their drinks as compensation. The girls, in turn, were happy to earn a decent wage and retain the majority of their "extras." As a woman on her own, Dorothy had come to understand that business was business, and she was the only one who could improve her prospects.

It was true that a handful of men, like Will Conklin, had emerged as hard drinkers, but who was she to judge? Will had shown a fondness for assisting her around the farm and often treated her to drinks. She was lonely, and his attention was flattering, putting a spring in her step.

Dorothy welcomed Will's money and advances. Admittedly, a few women she encountered in town had begun casting disapproving glances her way, Easter among them. Many had even started avoiding her at church. However, Dorothy preferred her current circumstances, as opposed to becoming an impoverished widow, begging for handouts, or worse, shackling herself to the first man who would marry her. Pride swelled within her as her business flourished, and she ostentatiously deposited coin into the church coffers in front of everyone, as if to prove she was just as good, or better than, any of them.

"Hey there, Ira Edwards," she said, smiling sweetly at one of her regular customers seated at a table, engrossed in a card game. "Would you and your pal there carry Will here out to his wagon? He's a bit under the weather." She offered another smile and rolled her eyes playfully.

"Sure thing, Dorothy," Ira replied.

Dorothy watched as the men hoisted Will by his shoulders and legs, ferrying him outside. Her ultimate dream was to move her business out west to California. With throngs of men prospecting for gold and so few women, she envisioned a fortune in catering to their hunger, washing, and dispensing Earl's Rye, along with a smattering of simple luxuries. Eventually, she could hire enough hands to manage the operation rather than labor herself. That was her true aspiration, and the earnings from locals like Will Conklin would help make it a reality.

To her surprise, Will had surfaced as a frequent contributor to her ambitions. At first, it was a boost to her self-esteem when her flirtations elicited eager responses, considering how Earl used to cast admiring glances at Easter. As their flirting evolved into a more intimate relationship, Dorothy occasionally welcomed Will into her bed. A part of her found solace in the thought of Easter's jealousy and anguish when she found out her husband was cheating. After all, Earl had been quite fond of flirting with Easter and lamenting Dorothy's infertility in contrast to Easter's brood. Until recently, Dorothy hadn't realized how deeply that had wounded her. Earl had even flirted with Easter the night he died. Taking her down a peg or two would be gratifying. Payback's a bitch, as some of her working girls liked to say...

******

Betrayal and jealousy were words that one might use to describe Easter's emotions. From her perspective there were no words that would suit...this. Her trust in Will lay in shambles. To suspect him of chicanery and carrying on in front of the whole township caused raw wounds that could not be described by mere words. Easter was done making excuses for his behavior. Something alive, dark, and hurtful was eating her gut from the inside out and sucking her spirit to the point she was sure her heart might shrivel up and die.

In retrospect, she had noticed a hint of perfume on Will weeks earlier but dismissed it as an oddity not worth her attention. The fact that they hadn't been intimate since Nancy's birth had been unusual as well…

Will had begun frequenting Earl's Place after working in the north fields. Easter wasn't pleased about the increasing amount of time Will spent there, but he was stubborn, insisting his years of labor entitled him to relax with other local farmers.

In truth, quite a few local farmers spent time there; it had become something of a gentlemen's club. Easter had chosen to ignore this behavior, throwing herself into making their farm the success she knew it could be. With Will's increasingly idle ways, she had taken charge, making decisions and implementing her ideas. Now that Aminadab, Moses, Elijah, and Billy were old enough for a full day's work, she had multiple fields plowed, solid crop rotations, and year-round harvests planned, even venturing into milk and cheese production learned from the Danes back in Ohio. Their growing free-range hog sales brought in extra cash as well.

Lately, Will had developed the irritating habit of returning home from Earl's Place passed out in the wagon. Their loyal workhorse, Ned, led by his hungry belly, would bring him home and then wait patiently to be unharnessed, stabled, and fed. Will's drinking buddies would simply deposit him in the wagon and send Ned on his way with a swat to the flank.

Easter peered up the road to see the dust rising in the distance. There he was. With the sun nearing the horizon, she could see old Ned plodding up the road with Will slumped in the seat.

She had discovered a significant amount of their money missing from the seed tin, and her fury knew no bounds.

As Ned pulled up, Will stepped out of the wagon and stumbled to his knees. He reeked of Earl's Rye, and there was that faint scent of lavender—the kind Dorothy Meechum at the roadhouse favored.

Will clambered to his feet and spotted Easter, hands on her hips, glaring at him.

"Easter, honey, have one of the boys put up Ned, will ya?"

Easter's glare remained unyielding as he walked to the watering trough and splashed his face with water.

Will took his time, finally standing up straight. Easter's stare bore into him, obviously quite angry.

"You're drunk," Easter accused. "And there's money missing from our seed tin."

Will's anger began to smolder. Easter was always pushing him to do things her way, and he was sick of it. Yes, he'd taken some money from the tin, but he had worked hard and earned the right to spend it as he saw fit. Dorothy's roadhouse was his one refuge—a place where he could have some harmless fun a couple nights a week, flirting with the girls, drinking, playing cards with his neighbors, and occasionally sharing a little bump and tickle with Dorothy. It was a place where he could forget his troubles, responsibilities, forget the fact that he was growing old and still had young kids to raise and damnit, Easter had just recently given birth to yet another goddamn girl. He turned on her like a snake.

"You need to just shut up and keep your nose out of my personal business!"

"Personal business, Will Conklin? Personal business? We need that seed money to plant this spring, and you know it. We'll come up short next year. Not only are you giving that woman half our earnings, you been carrying on with her, haven't you!" It was more of a statement than a question. Easter had finally said it out loud. She paced back and forth in front of him, her anger mounting and her voice rising with each word.

Will merely glowered back at her.

"How are we going to get enough seed for two new fields and that new team we talked about for next year? And what about expanding the house and hiring extra hands like we talked about? How are we going to—"

Suddenly Will lunged toward Easter and caught ahold of her

mid-sentence. He grabbed her by the back of the neck, his hands squeezing like a vise, and started shaking her like a rag doll.

Elijah and Aminadab were in the bunkhouse. They had walked the oxen home when, earlier in the day, Pa had pointed his nose towards Dorothy's roadhouse. After a quick swim in Lytle Creek to wash off the dust, they had gotten the stock settled and were playing a lively game of dice. They often bet chores on the dice rolls—a nice way to pass the time and a chance to dump their tasks onto the least fortunate. Billy wasn't back from working yet. He was still out in the south fields with Moses.

"Can I play, too? Please?" John Bunyan asked loudly for the fifth time, while he held his pup on his lap, scratching his ears.

"You're not old enough to toss bales or catch and butcher hogs," Elijah responded patiently for the fifth time.

Aminadab smiled and glanced at John Bunyan.

"Go gather some pebbles. We can play for rocks later while Elijah does all my chores for me," He grinned as his latest roll pronounced him the lucky winner. Elijah groaned and fell on his side, while John Bunyan giggled at his brothers' good-natured competition.

Suddenly, they heard a commotion. The three boys jumped to their feet and ran toward the yelling coming from the barnyard. Rounding the corner of the barn, they skidded to a stop and gaped in disbelief as they watched their Pa shaking their Ma by the neck and then giving her a mighty shove to the ground.

Will stood glowering over Easter, breathing heavily, while she gasped and stumbled to her knees.

Easter couldn't believe what had just happened. As she sat on her knees a rage built up inside of her she had never felt before. Slowly, she climbed to her feet and with every ounce of strength in her body, punched Will in the chin, knocking him back onto the ground, out cold.

As he lay there, all Easter could think about was that this was the first time Will had ever laid hands on her in anger. She was so furious she wanted to kick him in the ribs. She looked up to see Elijah, Aminadab, and John Bunyan standing by the barn, completely still, mouths gaping and eyes wide in shock. These days, all the boys except for Thomas slept in the bunkhouse. Malinda, Julie Etta, and Thomas stood by the doorway, eyes as big as saucers. Billy and Moses were nowhere to be seen. Thankfully, baby Nancy hadn't awakened during the scuffle. She and Will had put on quite a show. Easter was fuming.

She barked out commands. "Aminadab, put up Ned in the barn and feed him. Elijah, help put away the wagon. All of you, leave your Pa alone. Don't touch him."

******

Lying flat on his back, Will Conklin awoke staring at a mid-morning sky. John Bunyan's mongrel pup was licking his face. Will's head was splitting, like someone had clubbed him. For a moment he tried to remember how he got here, and then it all came rushing back. He'd been lying here all night and well into the morning. He covered his eyes with his arms and swore, "Bloody hell."

Rolling himself over onto all fours he sat up for a moment to think. He looked around. None of the kids were in sight. The wagons and oxen were gone. The older boys were likely already up in the fields at work. Every bone in his body ached, as it did most mornings lately. Time was catching up with him. He was getting old and worn out. The monotony of spring planting, summer nurturing, fall harvesting, and winter angst over what he had not accomplished that year versus what failures might be waiting in the next, weighed him down.

His body was not what it used to be. The burden of using it to carve out a living for his younger children the way he had with the older ones held no pleasure. There were those in the valley who hired workers and managed them rather than using their own backs. Although his sons were a tremendous help, to prosper it took all of them putting in everything they had each year. Will was just exhausted, physically and emotionally. Farm work and the family no longer held his interest. He craved something more. Perhaps they had stayed too long in this place. Maybe they should think about moving further west...Dorothy talked endlessly about California and the opportunities the railroads would eventually bring. One had to make it there before the railroads and rising prices, just in time to reap the rewards. Father Jeremiah Trecy up in Garryowen was getting together a group to head further west. Many folks at the roadhouse were talking about it.

Last night was a distant nightmare. He certainly had made a complete ass of himself. The last thing he remembered was Easter hitting him on the chin and then blackness.

He massaged his jaw a bit and then slowly got to his feet. He had a lot to make amends for, and it was time to get to it. Will whistled for the kids. A few little heads and eyes peeked out at him from the barn. He motioned his hand to coax them out. It would be a team effort. He knew how to make Easter smile, and he would make it so.

As she fussed over morning biscuits Easter could hear Will outside, pounding away, working on something. She stretched her aching muscles and walked outside to take a look.

When Will saw her, he paused, tilted his head to one side, and shot her that flirty grin of his that had won her heart so many years before. He was working on the root cellar. She'd been asking him to expand it for months, and the younger kids were helping. John Bunyan stuck his head up out of the ground and waved at her.

"We're fixing up your root cellar for ya, Ma."

Thomas and Malinda bounced out of the root cellar and stood proudly beside their father, covered in dirt. Will grinned at her again, and she sighed. Suddenly, Easter found herself making excuses, telling herself that it was all a misunderstanding. As she indulged these thoughts, her pain subsided. In her heart, Easter knew the truth would return in full force to knock her back down, but for now, she would ignore it.

******

Fall harvest was just around the corner. Easter was dedicating this morning to completing their farm census sheet as required by the County Seat. The kids were already out and about their chores. Breakfast would be on their own this morning. After what she had been through the night before, she did not feel guilty. There was plenty of hardtack in the pantry to keep their bellies from rumbling until lunch. As she sat up, she felt a pain run down her spine. She rolled her shoulders a bit to loosen them up.

They had a bumper crop this year—the best ever.

The last few months had been quite trying between her and Will. The first few times they had danced this dance, she was in shock and disbelief. Surely it was a mistake on his part. Surely he didn't mean it. Finally, she had come to the conclusion that when he came at her swinging, he was really swinging at himself.

Being a marginally successful dirt farmer did not suit his dreams. After a long bout of drinking, Will would stew about his prospects and come swinging at Easter, who was not a willing participant. For the most part, she was quite strong and easily fought him off.

Every time Easter heard the sound of his wagon pulling up late, a knot in her stomach twisted and turned as she anticipated his entrance. Would he be in a loving mood this time or a brute?

Last night, one look at his face and she knew: The brute it was to be. Will demanded food. She'd had stew warming by the fire and put it in front of him, standing there in the cold, while the little ones, thankfully, slept peacefully. He grabbed her by her nightshirt, pulled her close, and asked her if there was anything she wanted to say. It made her angry, so she had hit him in the shoulder with the butt of her hand to get him to let go. Moses had carelessly left the firewood in a pile by the table, and in his ire, Will grabbed a piece and used it to knock the wind out of her. He pounced on her, punching a few times. She had managed to grab the firewood and hit him back, which quite knocked him senseless, and he stumbled off to bed.

This morning's bruises were a painful reminder of the night before.

Outside, she heard the familiar pounding of a man hard at work. Easter glanced out the window. Will and the young ones were working on the barn, replacing boards and shoring up the corral. It was always this way. After acting like a jackass the night before, the next day he and the kids would be hard at work, fixing something that should have already been fixed, plowing a field that should have already been plowed—payment made by Will for being such a brute the night before and aided by the kids, hoping to mend the discord.

These days, Will did not even look at her with that formerly endearing smile of his. It had become a tedious, vicious routine, like the endless bubbling water flowing along the sturdy banks of Lytle Creek, never diverting.

Although the surface bruises were a constant reminder, her internal bruises were far worse. Easter had never been one to shed tears. Of late, they flowed quite freely when she was alone. She had once loved this man dearly. As partners, they had carved out a strong, sustainable farm from this rugged country. Where had the love gone? Why wasn't this enough? The fact that Anna, Mary, Mahala, and Phoebe had families of their own and were not here to bear witness, gave her some solace. Those early years, though challenging, had been happy. Now when she looked at Will, there was a numbness inside her—emotional walls she had built brick by brick with each transgression, as if their love was being drained dry.

******

Elijah and Aminadab approached the roadhouse, spotting Pa's wagon sitting out front. Ma had sent them to fetch Pa, who had been gone for two days. They exchanged uneasy glances as they walked inside. In the dim light, they saw Pa sitting at a table, snoring. Dorothy, the only other person present, was polishing glasses at the bar.

"Glad you boys showed up," Dorothy said, placing her hand on one hip as she eyed the boys and then their Pa. "Put him in the wagon and take him home. He's been nothing but trouble—lost a bunch of money at cards and been drinking like a madman for two days."

Dorothy frowned when neither boy responded to her. They were obviously being disrespectful. She would make Will pay dearly next time she saw him, and set some local ire on those disrespectful sons of his as well. A few well-placed rumors among the more gossipy of her clientele would do the trick.

She watched Elijah and Aminadab roll their Pa into the back of the wagon. Suddenly, Will awoke and took a swing at Elijah, clipping him in the chin. A chaotic wrestling match ensued with the boys trying to calm Will down before they finally got him into the back of the wagon.

As the disheveled sons climbed into the wagon and pointed their horse towards home, Aminadab glanced over his shoulder with a resentful look that sent a chill down Dorothy's spine. She stood there while the wagon slowly disappeared into the distance, leaving behind a trail of dust. It occurred to her that she might be wearing out her welcome in these parts. She might just head out to California sooner than she had planned. In fact, with the nest egg she had accumulated, now was as good a time as any.

******

Anna basted the young suckling pig that would be the main course of their feast. Most of the children were at the upper field, running and playing as children do. The Conklins, Wallaces, and Sades were celebrating a very bountiful harvest.

Ma was roasting fresh husked corn over another fire, while the scent of her famous biscuits wafted from inside the house. Hannah

Wallace, Anna's sister-in-law, stacked some freshly baked apple pies on one of the tables. Everyone was dressed in their fancy black Sunday dresses.

This was going to be a wonderful celebration indeed.

A few family members were missing, most notably their host, Will Conklin. The Wallace brothers were freighting some of the harvest to Bellevue for sale back east. Phoebe and Mary's mother-in-law had just passed away, so they and their husbands remained at home in the Iron Hills down south. Two of the Sade brothers, James and Jesse, along with a neighbor, Ira Edwards, were present. Their labor had been shared, and so they would partake in the bounty celebration.

Elijah and Aminadab were missing, sent by their mother to find Pa.

Ma had a very sad look about her. Ma was not one to talk about her troubles, but Malinda had told Anna that Pa was always grumpy. Suddenly, Anna noticed Ma stiffen as she stared down the road. The creaking of a wagon could be heard. As the sun began to set, casting hues of gray and orange across the sky, Anna could see the boys driving the wagon with their horses tied behind. Sure enough, the boys had brought their Pa home—though it was obvious they had been roughed up, likely at Pa's hands.

Easter scowled at the approaching wagon. A few days earlier, Will had left to fetch some tools from the north fields and never returned. He'd been gone for two days this time without a word. Today, given the planned celebration, Easter had finally sent Elijah and Aminadab to fetch him, fearing he might be lying in a ditch somewhere.

More than likely, he was staying at the widow's house again. That woman's homebrew lured him like a siren. Her fancy clothes, piano music, and card games had drained more than half of the Conklin farm's earnings into Dorothy's pockets.

Will had become a specter of his former self, haunting her with memories of how things used to be. At first, his unexplained absences wounded her deeply, but then she found them a reprieve from his constant contempt. His absence meant peace and quiet with her kids and their farm all to herself. Sometimes, Easter secretly wished he would be lying in a ditch somewhere, permanently.

As her sons rolled up, Will staggered out of the back of the wagon and fell face-first to the ground, clearly drunk as a skunk. Easter's eyes narrowed.

"I'm gonna go tend the biscuits," she barked at Anna and disappeared into the house.

Will climbed to his feet and noticed Easter heading inside.

"Anna, honey, what smells so good?" Will grinned at his daughter as she shook her head and walked away. Suddenly, he noticed his neighbors and family and remembered today was their harvest picnic celebration. He'd let Easter down, yet again. He was so sick and tired of feeling like less than a man. Easter always picked up the pieces and carried on as if she didn't need him at all.

Will felt his ire rising. He glowered at the house, anger boiling up inside him. All he wanted now was another drink. There was a jug inside, but Easter was in there. He noticed the butcher knife next to the suckling pig and reached for it. There was no way Easter was going to come between him and his jug. He was tired of her telling him what to do. He had neighbors to party with.

Gripping the knife tightly, Will headed into the house.

******

Sheriff Joel Higgins tugged on his pants as one of the Sade brothers pounded on his door. It was early evening, and he was just getting ready for bed after a long day in the field.

"What's up, Jesse?"

"There's been a death up at the Conklin farm, you gotta come."

"A death?"

"Yeah." Jesse Sade looked deadly serious.

251

"Who?"

"You'll see when you get there."

Well, possibly Will Conklin had finally killed somebody. He was a hard drinker to be sure, and Joel had seen him at the widow's yesterday. Surprised the man had even made it home, Joel remembered that Conklin had lost quite a bit of money at cards and was in a foul mood when he left. Grabbing his gun and coat, Joel decided to pick up a couple of neighbors along the way for backup, as some of the Conklin boys had a surly reputation.

******

Aminadab watched the house intently. A low guttural wail was coming from inside. It had been bad. The situation was dire, and nobody knew what to do. They had simply reacted. Pa went after Ma with baby Nancy in her arms. Little Nancy screamed like a scared rabbit, and Aminadab could not erase the image from his mind. His father had turned on Ma just like a rattlesnake.

"None of you bitches are worth keeping! I'm done!" he had bellowed, approaching Ma with a butcher knife. Aminadab was certain his father, in his drunken state, intended to commit some heinous act. And now there was blood everywhere. Aminadab looked up as Jesse Sade approached with Sheriff Higgins and a small posse.

The posse paused upon arrival, hearing the guttural wails coming from inside the house. Sheriff Higgins solemnly dismounted, and the rest followed suit. Joel nodded to Aminadab Conklin.

It was dark outside, with several lanterns lit alongside a bonfire and a well-stocked picnic. The Conklin's daughter, Anna Wallace, and her sister-in-law stood by the barn, surrounded by the youngsters. They wore expressions of intense dread as they peered at the house. A couple of neighbors sat on the fence, and everyone was in stunned silence, even the little ones. Anna held the infant the Conklins had welcomed earlier in the year. A few of them had blood spatters on their clothes, including the infant.

"What happened?" Joel asked.

"Pa came home pretty cranked up," Aminadab responded. "I heard Ma and Pa screaming bloody murder, more than usual. Elijah ran inside and then hollered for me. The kids were outside except for Thomas and baby Nancy." Aminadab closed his eyes, shook his head, and took a deep breath. He couldn't bring himself to say the words that his Pa had yelled, the ones that made him rush to the house.

"Who got killed?"

Aminadab could not bring himself to say it. He looked at his hands. They were covered in blood.

Joel studied the young man closely. Aminadab Conklin was a man now, though quite thin. He stood tall like his Pa, about six foot four. Blood spatters covered his face and hands, and he was obviously quite traumatized.

Joel nodded again and walked up the stairs into the house. Easter Conklin had on her Sunday dress, with her hair in a bun, and was on her knees cradling the limp body of Will Conklin in her arms. One of the older sons, Elijah Conklin, knelt behind her, his blood-stained hands on Easter's shoulders in comfort. Tears streamed down the woman's face as she uttered a low wail. The place was a blood bath.

Will had a deep gash in his throat and appeared dead as a doornail...

1857 - July 11 – Of Courts and Trials, Jackson County, Iowa

Never give up, it is wiser and better
Always to hope than once to despair,
Throw off the yoke with its conquering fetter,
Yield not a moment to sorrow or care.
Never give up, though adversity presses,
Providence wisely has mingled the cup;
And the best counsel in all our distresses
Is the stout watchword, Never give up.

ALMOST A YEAR AFTER THE MURDER…

Easter - 45, Will - deceased

Phoebe - 27, Anna - 26, Mary - 24, Mahala - 21, Esther Malinda - 13, Julia-Etta - 4, Nancy - 1

Aminadab - 23, Billy - 20, Elijah - 18, Moses - 16, John Bunyan - 10, Thomas - 8

THE two Hackleys were traveling to Bellevue, Iowa, by railroad. Harriet sat next to her father. These events were so surreal. Her sister, Easter, had murdered her husband of twenty-eight years. Although the siblings had corresponded over the years, Harriet last saw Easter in person after the loss of her child, when she had returned to Herkimer to visit family and mend her shattered heart. In recent years, Easter's letters had grown increasingly somber, often alluding to her husband Will's melancholia and taking to drink.

Philo Hackley gazed at the endless prairie as he pondered

Easter's dire situation. He marveled at how the journey to Iowa had taken less than a week, a far cry from the journey that Easter and Will had made as pioneers for sure. The current president, Franklin Pierce, had significantly expanded the railroad's reach, with ambitious plans for tracks stretching from coast to coast.

It was kind of Harriet to take leave of her husband and children to accompany him. A boat ride down the Erie Canal along with the new train routes into Iowa had vastly shortened the journey. At his age he would not likely have made it otherwise. From Herkimer, Philo had helped Easter acquire the best attorney available. This particular attorney was an aspiring judge, so he had personal reputation at stake. It had taken almost a year for the trial to come to court. In the meantime, Easter and the boys had been allowed freedom to run the farm and tend her family.

Easter wrote Philo that Will's final resting place had been arranged by Phoebe's husband to be the Sade family plot in the southern part of the county. His remains lay in the Iron hills near Thom Sade's mother, along with some young Sade family members who had died in their infant years. This was far away from the Conklin stomping grounds and gossip in Otter Township, but close to those who would maintain the simple headstone in memory of better days.

In Iowa, the policy of allowing those accused of crimes to await trial while working their farms had grown increasingly unpopular. The thought was if such suspects were found innocent, in the meantime, it was not fair to let their farms go unworked and managed. Tensions escalated when a group of Jackson County vigilantes rounded up and hanged several individuals awaiting murder trials. Luckily, Easter and the boys had not been on their list. There were many in counties across Iowa that were angry justice had not been more forcefully served on the lawless and were fed up. People wanted safe communities. After the hangings, local governments had begun responding to the pressure with swifter justice.

When Philo and Harriet reached the Washington Mills station it would be just a little over a day's stagecoach to the Jackson County seat in Bellevue where the trial was to be held.

Philo thought back to simpler times when Easter was a little girl growing up on their farm in the rural Mohawk Valley. There were a lot more Natives around back then, counted as friend, family, as well as foe. For his young family, life had been fresh and just beginning. He had been in the midst of carving out his own future, having survived war and the first years of homesteading himself. Soolee, Easter's birth mother, had been quite a presence. For a moment he remembered that fateful day Soolee herself had dispatched a bear with a knife-blow to the throat, only to be savaged into a lifeless pile during the beast's death-throes...

Easter and Will had started out with such promise. The excitement of the new lands and an opportunity to carve out their fortune had been their dream made real.

The Hackleys finally reached Bellevue in the early morning, leaving just enough time to settle into their hotel before heading to the courthouse.

The courthouse itself was a stately building, a little out of place compared to the muddy streets and wooden structures that led the way. It was built in a colonial style, two stories of brick with a wide stone stairs and a bell tower. Quite a few people were already inside. The infamous tale of a murderess had attracted quite a few spectators.

Harriet took her father's arm as they climbed the stairs to the balcony. Easter's family was likely mingled with the crowd below. The incessant chatter made the hair on Harriet's neck stand up.

"She'll hang... hang for sure. Can you imagine any woman doing such a thing?" a man proclaimed from the balcony.

Walter Leffingwell, the defense attorney, shot the man a sharp glance, wishing he had more control over the rabble allowed to observe the proceedings. The entire courtroom and both balconies teemed with people, not only from Jackson County but also from neighboring ones. Everyone was titillated. Leffingwell took a quick inventory of the Conklin clan at the back of the room: all dressed in their Sunday best—the women in their starched black dresses, the boys all bathed and acting respectful, just as he had instructed them. They would be as much on trial as their mother. Many of them were key witnesses. It was crucial they appear respectable.

The jackass with the pre-trial verdict continued to announce his opinion. "Even if he was sniffing around the widow's place more than he should've, that was murder plain and simple."

Leffingwell noticed Easter visibly wince in her chair. Though a sturdy woman, the relentless negative chatter was taking its toll. He regretted not having prepared her better.

The courthouse in Bellevue provided a number of benches on the main floor with a banister separating the crowd from the prosecutor and defendant. They each had their own separate tables, with a large raised desk for the judge dominating the front. The tall open ceilings caused a bit of an echo when one raised one's voice. The jury's twelve chairs sat fully populated at the right of the prosecution in six sets of two.

Another spectator chimed in. "Well, you know William Conklin was a hard drink'n man, but Easter always had her family spit and shined and respectful, behaving in church. She midwifed for more than a few wee babe's in the township and…"

An old codger interrupted. "Even if Will Conklin was banging on the widow that is no excuse."

"They say those sons of his are a hard lot," another woman's voice chimed in.

Leffingwell glanced sideways at the jury, noting some shifting uneasily in their seats. They could hear the comments just as easily as Easter. With the judge running late, the trial was off to a rocky start. Among the jurors, Leffingwell noticed a prominent local businessman, Daniel Potter, whom he expected the judge would appoint as foreman. Potter appeared to be taking his duty seriously, shifting uncomfortably in his seat as he tried to ignore the chatter. At least there was that.

"The apple doesn't fall far from that tree," a woman said with a wry smile, nodding knowingly, "I have it on good authority that the older sons frequented the widow's roadhouse and had been seen quite inebriated…"

"Well," another voice interjected, "I heard that the two sons who helped her commit the crime had a brawl with their father at the roadhouse and had more than a few bruises to show for it…" The gossip-laced chatter continued.

Easter stared at the table in front of her as if her life depended on it. In some ways it did. Her attorney had coached her how to behave in the courtroom. It was important not to display too much emotion as there was no way to know how the jury might construe it. She needed to maintain an appearance of dignity and respect for the proceedings. How these strangers had the gall to act as experts on her family's personal business was beyond Easter; as if any of them could possibly understand what had unfolded. Easter herself could still not comprehend it all. Decades of marriage, fourteen children with the loss of only one babe, and numerous twists of fate had brought Will and hers to this sad conclusion. Easter had to pinch herself to be sure it was all not some bloody nightmare. She glanced furtively over her shoulder at countless faces. She counted many in the crowd as friends and neighbors. Others were curious spectators. Her own kin, who could easily fill two benches, huddled together at the back of the hall. Most of them were standing, only a few had found a seat. Each and every one was grim.

"Order! You will come to order now, people!"

Easter nearly jumped out of her seat as the judge entered the room, taking immediate command at his desk. Each strike of the gavel fueled her fear, and she marveled at her ability to remain outwardly composed. How much fear could one endure before one's heart simply gave up?

Until the judge's arrival, the boisterous debate in the courtroom had been deafening. Leffingwell welcomed the sudden silence, grateful that the judge's presence seemed to marginalize the spectators' opinions. Now, at last, the judge had the jury's full, undivided attention.

"Ahem," said the Judge. "All right then. Let's get started."

Emotionless yet stern was the only way to describe Judge Berkley. Thick wire rim spectacles sat at the end of his nose, hovering over a well waxed chestnut mustache. Middle-aged and balding, he wore a mildly tattered store-bought vest over finely pressed white cotton shirt with a gold chain hinting at a watch in his pocket. Judge Berkley maintained an air of confidence. He stared into the crowd as if to demand everyone's attention, and their attention he had. With bated breath they waited to hear the charges. Everyone was excited. The accused and her attorney sat at a small table to his right.

The jury, seated to the left of his large wooden desk, was arranged in two orderly rows. He had their attention as well.

"Members of the jury," he began, "The case before us is an indictment for murder; the State of Iowa vs. Easter Conklin, and two of her sons, Aminadab Conklin and Elijah Conklin."

Judge Berkley paused when chittering erupted anew. A stern look and a pounding gavel silenced the room, allowing him to continue reading the charges.

"The state asserts that Easter Conklin, Aminadab Conklin, and Elijah Conklin, of the county of Jackson, on the first day of October in the year of our Lord one thousand eight hundred and fifty six, at and in the county of Jackson, with force and arms in and upon one William Conklin, then and there being feloniously, willfully, and with their malice aforethought, did make an assault, and that the said Easter Conklin, with a certain knife of the value of ten cents which she, Easter Conklin, in her right hand then and there, had and held at the throat of her husband, William Conklin, feloniously, willfully and of the malice aforethought, did strike, stab and cut with the knife, with the striking, stabbing, cutting, did then and there give in and upon the throat of him, one mortal wound, of the length of two inches and the depth of four inches."

Judge Berkley paused for a moment at audible gasps in the room. It was one thing to hear gossip in the street, another to hear a legal accusation which many took as the absolute truth…

He continued, "Aminadab Conklin and Elijah Conklin on the day of their malice aforethought were present, aiding and abetting Easter Conklin in the felony to do and commit. The state's assertion is that Easter Conklin, Aminadab Conklin, and Elijah Conklin, in the manner and form aforesaid, then and there feloniously, willfully and of their malice aforethought, did kill and murder William Conklin, contrary to form of the statute in such cases made and provided and against the peace and dignity of the State of Iowa."

"This is the first trial in this case and is against the aforesaid accused, Easter Conklin. The honorable Richard S. Hadley is the Special Prosecuting Attorney of Jackson County, for the State of Iowa. The Honorable Walter E. Leffingwell is the Attorney for the Defendant."

The chittering started again. Judge Berkley paused to allow the jury to process his words, his eyes coming to rest on the defendant.

Stoic and solid she sat with her attorney, eyes fixed on the table in front of her. One would think with such charges she would be a bit frightened or show distress. Her dress was a pretty thing. Flowers printed on cream linen—this was a new method of creating cloth. He had bought such a dress for his own wife recently, and it did not come cheap. The lace collar and covered buttons definitely gave her an air of civility—hardly the image of a woman capable of such a heinous act.

Yet these savage lands had a way of transforming even the most civilized into savages. The judge had seen it time and again, though rarely in a woman. Before him sat a weathered, sturdy, and proud pioneer, clad in her Sunday best. Her long dark hair was pulled back into a flawless bun, and her face, though marked by years on the frontier, bore no lines of cruelty often observed in the accused. Thin lips slightly turned down, a strait nose with high cheekbones and a low brow could possibly hint at a Native in her lineage. Perhaps that was the source of the savagery in her actions. He glanced quickly at the court papers—her race was listed as white. Regardless, she was considered white in this community, so who was he to question?

Many pioneers with ancestors that had fought in the Revolutionary War had a bit of Native in them and hid it so their land would not be taken away. According to the papers her attorney had prepared, this lady's kin were a respected family from Herkimer, New York, a bedrock of early colonials. Her father was a successful farmer and mercantile owner, well respected in his township. Certainly she had been well raised. Someone mentioned her father had secured representation for her and had traveled all the way from Herkimer, New York to be here for the trial...

Judge Berkley cleared his throat. "Ahem. Will the defendant please rise?"

Although the words of the judge were not spoken with malice, Easter froze in her seat. She could not will her legs to move. She could not breathe. When she felt a gentle hand squeeze her elbow, she allowed it to guide her to her feet.

Intriguingly, the woman stood every bit as tall as her attorney, who was easily a six-foot man. Her shoulders squared, she blinked a few times as if to gather herself, and finally lifted her gaze from the table as her eyes seemed to peer into his very soul. There was something about her—an inner strength that hinted she had not given up.

"Easter Conklin, how do you plead to the charges as stated?"

"Sir," Leffingwell responded, "The defendant stands before you in her own proper person and pleads Not Guilty in manner and form as alleged. The defense will prove beyond a shadow of a doubt this act was committed in self-defense." At that the court erupted into a flurry, everyone talking at once.

As the judge's gavel pounded the table, Easter squeezed her eyes shut, willing it all to go away. She longed to turn back time, to return to the days when things were good between her and Will. She summoned the memory of those first sweet months when she had fallen for him in Herkimer. Will's brother, Jacob, and the surveyor, Hiram Ayres, had been vying against each other to escort her to the political rally back when Andrew Jackson was running for president. How different might her life have been if she had gone with Hiram and not met up with Will? Will had asked her to marry him that very night…

One by one the prosecutor called his witnesses: Malinda Conklin, Billy Conklin, Ira Edwards, Jesse Sade, James Sade, Anna Wallace, Hannah Wallace, and finally Sheriff Higgins. For the most part, they all told the same story. Will Conklin came home drunk. He followed Easter inside with a butcher knife in his hand. They heard the two quarreling loudly, and when things got out of hand Elijah, then Aminadab had rushed inside.

At last little Tom Conklin, barely eight years old, was called to the stand. He was frightened and could not speak without stuttering. When the prosecutor asked him what happened when his Pa was killed, he said, "M-M-M-Minadab held Pa by the h-h-hair while mam c-c-cut his throat."

Finally, the prosecutor rested his case and it was the defense's turn.

Leffingwell called Easter to the stand. Easter swore to tell the whole truth and nothing but the truth, so help her God. The entire room was silent as the defense asked Easter to tell her story in her own words:

"Will and I were friends of Earl and Dorothy Meechum. We would get together and play cards, the men would drink Earl's rye whiskey; you know, neighborly stuff. After Earl died, we stopped goin'. Then Dorothy turned their homestead into sort of a roadhouse selling Earl's rye whiskey and food. Will would stop off at the roadhouse after working the north field we bought from Dorothy.

"Will got into the habit of quitting work early and staying late at the roadhouse. A good chunk of our profit was going to the Widow Dorothy. When I complained, he got hot under the collar. He stopped speaking to me and acting all mean when he did say something. This wasn't my Will. The drink and that siren of a woman had changed him. He became more and more dark.

"On the day...the day of the picnic he'd been gone for a couple of days, and I sent the boys to bring him home. I was fixin' biscuits in the house for the picnic with baby Nancy on my hip. Will came in looking for a jug of whiskey. He couldn't find it. He was hollering to himself, banging some things around, stirring up his temper, carrying the knife he used for butchering our suckling pigs.

"Will said he was going to go back to the widow's for more whiskey and went to get money out of the tin. It was empty. First he accused me of hiding the money. Then he accused me of spending it on store bought dresses for the girls.

"He said he was going to end my interfering ways once and for all. He started circling me, waving the knife in my face. I told him to put it down before he hurt himself or someone else.

"Then Will said he was going to teach me a lesson I would never forget. He grabbed me by the hair. I took a hold of the hand with the knife and tried to wrestle it away. He punched me in the stomach. I lost my grip, dropped the baby, saw stars...and the knife coming towards my face. Then my son, Elijah, was behind him and grabbed his hand with the knife. The baby was hollering. Will let go of me and started in on my son, yelling he was going to kill him, pounding him with his fist while Elijah held onto the hand with the knife for dear life. Elijah hollered for Aminadab to help.

"The next thing I know Aminadab was there and grabbed Will's hand that was punching Elijah. The knife flew through the air. I got my strength back and jumped for it. Will was trying to get to it too. He was dragging the boys like rag dolls, hollering he was going to kill us all. I got a hold of the knife. I felt his grip on my hair again. I rolled around and struck at him twice with the knife. I missed the first time and the second time landed a blow; then I tossed it. The boys were still hanging onto him and Will was going for the knife again.

"Suddenly he started to slow down. He turned and looked at me, kinda astonished like. I could see...the blood...pulsing out of his neck from the knife blow. The baby was crying. The boys let go. Will touched his hand to his neck and then looked at his hand. It was drenched in blood. He looked at all three of us in disbelief and then just collapsed to the floor quivering…and then he let out a sigh and was still. I was laying on the floor. The boys were standing there with looks of horror on their faces. We were frozen, and then some of the little'uns started calling from outside. Poor little Thomas was cowering in the corner. He saw the whole thing. And that's when I realized…my Will was dead."

Leffingwell asked, "Easter, did you plan on killing your husband that day?"

"Of course not. It all seems so unreal…I still can't believe it all happened."

"Did you or your sons ever discuss killing your husband?"

"No, never. We were a family. Such a thing would never enter any of our minds."

Leffingwell concluded, "Your honor the defense rests."

The prosecutor stood up and studied Easter for a few moments before asking in an accusatory tone. "Easter, did you hide the money that was in the tin?"

Easter paused, her eyes downcast with remorse. "Yes sir." Then she looked him in the eye. "Yes, I did. We needed that money to buy seed for next year's spring planting. Will wasn't in his right mind and wasn't making good decisions."

"Isn't it true that Will would be alive today if you had just given him the money you had hidden?"

Easter glanced down at her hands, her voice soft, "I don't know."

The prosecutor approached Easter. "Isn't it true that you frivolously spent money on store bought dresses for your girls in the past? Didn't your husband have a right to be angry about that?"

Leffingwell interjected, "Your honor I object to the relevance of this question."

The prosecutor countered, "Your honor, this goes to prove that this lady antagonized her husband into his rage that day. A man has a right to say how money is spent in his own house."

The judge replied, "I'll allow it."

Easter continued, "Sir, yes this is true. A girl needs to learn to look presentable to get a good husband someday. Each of my daughters had one good dress to wear to church and God willing, it will stand-in as a wedding dress someday. My girls know how to plow, sew, cook, clean, pack up, and get a wagon ready for travel; they can keep their family alive on the trail and in the wilderness. They also know their manners, how to read, write, cipher, and act presentable in good company. They—"

The prosecutor interrupted, "So isn't it true that your spending on dresses dipped into your spring seed money?"

"No, sir. No. That was back in the previous spring after planting. We had plenty of money for a few extras. Will spent over seventy-five percent of our reserves drinkin' and gambling at the widow's through the summer." With tears in her eyes, Easter glared defiantly at the prosecutor.

"I was raised by my father, Philo Hackley, an owner of a respected mercantile in Herkimer, New York. From the time I was twelve years old until I married at sixteen years of age I helped my father in his mercantile. I know ciphering, cost of goods bought and sold, and accounting for expenses. I don't make those kind of bad finance decisions for my family. During most of our married life together Will left most of the expense planning to me."

The prosecutor regarded Easter with a sideways tilt of his head. He turned and walked slowly back to his desk, rifling through some papers before asking one final question.

"Easter. Isn't it true that you had your sons help you murder your husband that night to get even with him for spending the family earnings on another woman and jeopardizing your family's future?"

"No, sir, never," Easter took a deep breath, let out a sigh and shook her head "no" as she spoke. "Will lost his way that day. There was no planning anything. There was only madness and a horrible accident. Nobody wanted anybody dead. Will just lost his mind for a bit. I wish he was still here. I'm sure he'd have been sorry for what he done." Easter sobbed, and then got control.

"My Will was a good husband for many years. We pushed

through good times and bad, happy times and sad times together. He was not himself that day when he did what he done. It was the drink…He never would have done something like that if he had been in his right mind." Easter looked down at her hands as tears streamed silently down her cheeks. She shook her head no once more.

The prosecutor shuffled a few more papers in the hushed courtroom. The heavy weight of the emotional testimony filled the air. Finally, he announced, "The prosecution has no additional questions for the accused at this time your honor."

Leffingwell announced, "The defense rests your honor."

It was time for each attorney to present their closing remarks.

The prosecutor began. "We all feel empathy for the family in this case. The thought of the young Conklin children losing both parents under these circumstances is heartbreaking. They do have brothers and sisters who can take them into their own families and raise them, so push that from your minds. Facts are facts. Mrs. Conklin admitted to administering the murdering blow to her husband while her two sons held him defenseless. As to whether or not it was in self-defense we have only their word to the contrary. Little Thomas Conklin himself said, and I quote, 'Minadab held Pa by the hair while Mam cut his throat'.

"From the voice of an innocent we have heard what happened in that home that afternoon. We have heard countless renditions from people respected in the local community why Easter Conklin had cause to hate her husband. We heard from Easter herself how she liked to tell her husband how he ought to spend his hard earned money. A husband that slaps his bossy wife around once in a while does not give a person the right to commit murder. We have to send a message to other would be murderers that this community will not stand for such behavior. You must vote guilty as charged so this community can move on from this horrible event."

Leffingwell stood and studied the jury. Every single one of

them had their eyes glued on him, wondering what he would say. He cleared his throat and began. "Gentlemen of the jury, you are all members of this community. Many of you are farmers and pioneers, businessmen; all well respected. You all know firsthand what it takes to thrive in these savage western lands. We look for strong women in our frontier wives. How else will our children make it to adulthood? How else can our children thrive if we have to leave them under the tender care of their mothers while we toil in the fields or venture to new lands, then send for our wives to bundle up our household and follow?"

Leffingwell paused, observing the eyes of the jury. A couple of them scratched the back of their necks as if pondering his words. He continued, "In this regard, Easter has proven herself the epitome of what one wishes for in a frontier wife. She is strong, capable, and fiercely protective of her family. She has thirteen live children, four who are married to successful local farmers with children of their own. Easter has more than contributed to the success of their profitable farm while her husband was indisposed. Who here would not want such a wife?"

Leffingwell turned and walked back to the table, shuffling some papers, and noticed the jury glancing at Easter. She sat up straight with her sad eyes respectfully lowered. He continued,

"We do not deny the fact that Mrs. Conklin did indeed kill her husband. In our great state of Iowa it is not against the law to commit homicide against another in self-defense. William Conklin was the one who brought the weapon to commit harm against his family. He could have grabbed a piece of firewood, or a stick, or just used his fist as we have had testimony that he had many times in the past. Mrs. Conklin did indeed not want to kill Mr. Conklin. If he had a piece of firewood in his hand, it would have been that which she used to subdue his crazed rage, and he would probably still be here today. Mr. Conklin alone is responsible for his death on that terrible afternoon. In this case, the evidence is overwhelming and beyond the shadow of any doubt. You must vote not guilty."

*****

It was a solemn group of twelve that Daniel Potter sat among in the small room at the side of the courthouse. There were windows on two sides of the room, partially open to let in a gentle summer breeze. If the deliberation lasted long, Daniel was inclined to move the group outside, as the mid-summer heat was a bit stifling. Chairs and a table were the only furnishings. On the wall hung a painting of a triumphant Andrew Jackson, astride his horse in full military uniform amid a fierce battle. With no curtains on the windows, a few curious folks peered in from outside as they strolled by the courthouse.

Judge Berkley had assigned Daniel as the foreman of the jury to make sure the men kept on task and reached their decision by following his judicial instructions. A few of the men were farmers. A few, like himself, were business men in the community. Two were men that the local sheriff had pulled in at random from the Red Rock saloon when they came up short of twelve from those who were called to serve. A couple of farmers were talking about the upcoming harvest and what the price of corn might be. The others were avoiding eye contact with each other. Deciding this woman's fate was not a comfortable situation for any of them.

"Ahem," Daniel said to get their attention. The room quieted, and for a moment he squinted out the window while each took a seat.

"All right then. You all heard what the judge said. Let's get down to it and see what we have here." He paused and glanced around the room at the attentive faces. Even the last-minute draftees from the Red Rock saloon appeared engaged. Daniel was pretty certain what side he came up on. It was time to see where the others were at.

"So…is there anybody here who don't think Ol' Will Conklin got what was comin' to him?"

1857 Harvest - Of Stealing Children

And there she leaves her maiden choice,
Her husband, lover, friend.
Oh, were she woman could she less
To homely sorrows lend!

A FEW MONTHS AFTER THE TRIAL...
Easter - 45, Ira Green - 47
Esther Malinda - 13, Julia-Etta - 4, Nancy - 1
Elijah - 18, Moses - 16, John Bunyan - 10, Thomas - 8

Mariah Conklin stepped out onto the porch, eyeing the wagon kicking up dust as it approached the Conklin farm. Billy's sister, Anna, was at the reins, with her husband, Thomas, holding their youngest child on his lap. It appeared they had left the rest of their brood at home. Mariah snorted and glanced at the ground with disdain. They were likely here to meddle in Billy's affairs again.

Weddings were in the air for the older Conklin boys. Billy and Mariah had wed two months ago, and Aminadab was set to marry Mariah's cousin, Margaretta. Their fathers, the Edwards brothers, had been neighbors of the Conklins for years. Now that Mr. Conklin was gone, there was plenty of money to establish their own homestead—if only his mother would cooperate. But Easter was nowhere to be found. No one could locate her. Phoebe was watching over Billy's younger siblings while Easter was absent. Billy and Phoebe's husband were trying to manage the Conklin farm's fall harvest and crop sales. Billy was livid. He couldn't access any funds because his mother was the executrix. Someone had said she left the state with Ira Green, a longtime neighbor who had supported her through the previous year's turmoil. It was preposterous. Billy's five-year-old sister, Julia-Etta, claimed that Ira was going to be their new father.

Not only that, but Easter had told one of the neighbors she was of Native descent, sharing wild stories of roaming the woods as a child with her "real mother," learning to hunt and gather. Billy and Phoebe quelled the gossip by assuring folks their mother was a bit unhinged after all she had been through, but what was she thinking? She would ruin all their reputations before long.

When she was exonerated of Mr. Conklin's murder, Easter had been appointed to administer the estate with the bank lawyer overseeing her duties. Given her lack of transparency and the fact that she had vanished entirely, Billy and Phoebe's husband had joined forces to make Easter demonstrate why she shouldn't be discharged from these responsibilities.

They had no idea how Easter was managing the money. A couple of days ago, to access monthly stipends from Mr. Conklin's estate, Phoebe and Thom Sade filed for guardianship of the four youngest children: Julia-Etta, Nancy, John Bunyan, and young Thomas. With Easter's unstable state after the trial, it seemed right for Phoebe's husband and Billy to be solely in charge of the farm, ensuring the family income didn't vanish.

Anna and Thomas must have been informed by the lawyer. As they rolled to a stop in front of Mariah, both wore stern, accusatory expressions. Billy's brothers were out working the fields, and his younger siblings were with Phoebe and her family down south in the Iron Hills.

It was just her and Billy on the farm at the moment.

"Billy?" she called, "Anna and Thomas are here." Mariah watched Thomas and Anna climb out of the wagon and approach the house.

They stood a bit apart as Billy silently stepped out beside his wife, then slowly walked up to them. Mariah remained on the porch. Anna wore a starched, finely woven black dress adorned with tatted lace and a white collar peeking out at the neck—a style favored by the Conklin women. She donned it like battle armor. Anna was quite a force to be reckoned with, and Mariah had no intention of getting between the siblings. As an older sister, Anna had practically raised Billy, and Mariah could see him shrink a bit under her silent, accusatory gaze. Thomas, cradling his baby close, just looked at Billy and shook his head.

"The lawyer told us what you and Phoebe did." Anna shook her head, her eyes flashing with anger. "How could you do that to Ma after all she's been through?"

"It wasn't Phoebe; it was Thom Sade," Mariah caught herself and grasped her hands when Billy whirled around with a glare. She hadn't meant to get involved in this, but having been close to it all, she knew how much Phoebe was against it. Phoebe's husband and Billy had ignored her wishes.

"Sorry," Mariah said. "I didn't mean to interfere; just wanted you to know where Phoebe stood so you didn't get mad at her. She's doing a lot, takein' on your little brothers and sisters like she has, you know?" The truth was Mariah did not want Phoebe to get angry and send them all back to Billy, thus making them Mariah's responsibility.

Billy turned back to Anna. His face grew red with anger. "Yeah, Phoebe is taking care of Ma's young'uns, and I'm running the farm. Ma is missing. You and Mary are off busy with your own families. What was I supposed to do?"

Anna stood her ground. She had already sent word to Ma what was going on—better coming from her than the lawyer so she could be prepared. "How about just doing what you've always done and just run things until she gets back? How about not betraying her?"

"How am I supposed to run things without any money?" Billy replied, his voice rising in frustration.

The argument continued to escalate, with both siblings yelling at each other and throwing insults. Anna accused Billy of being selfish and greedy, while Billy accused Anna of being a know-it-all who was out of touch with what the farm needed to keep it afloat.

Suddenly, Billy lunged forward and grabbed Anna by the arm. When he saw the murderous look on Thomas's face, he let go and stepped back.

Thomas stepped between them, the babe, still in his arms dressed in his little hat, buttoned-up coat, and breaches, leaning into his Pa's chest. One small hand clutched his Pa's shirt, his eyes as big as saucers from all the yelling. Anna and Billy were both breathing deeply, glowering at each other like circling wolves. Thomas said quietly, "Well, the deed has already been done but that doesn't mean you're gonna get what ya asked for, Billy."

Billy glared at his brother-in-law. The man was as old as Billy's own father had been—gray-haired and weathered but wiry and well-muscled from years of farm labor. His black felt hat and fancy store-bought jacket, casually worn over work pants and well-oiled boots demanded the respect only a highly successful farmer could command. Billy felt like an errant boy standing in front of these two. It made him second-guess himself a bit. It had sounded reasonable when he and Thom Sade had discussed it, but now… maybe they had been too impulsive in their decision. Maybe they should have listened to Phoebe…

"Son," Thomas continued with his head tilted to one side, "Ya can just ask the lawyer to release ya some money until your Ma gets back. Give the man the bills and the receipts. Your Ma will make things right when she gets back."

Mariah felt relief as the soothing presence of Thomas and his sound advice seemed to calm everyone down. They certainly all had enough violence in this family to last a lifetime.

Thomas continued, "Just so ya know, we told that lawyer your Ma is fine, not to worry, and she'll be back soon to settle things."

"You know where she is?" Billy pressed.

Thomas turned to look at Anna, who had her arms folded, sternly staring her brother down.

"Well, I'm not saying we don't, but I'm not saying we do either."

******

Easter stood at the top of the hill overlooking Galena, Illinois. She breathed in the scent of late summer flowers and took in the beautiful rolling golden hills, bordered by the gently flowing Fever River. One's burdens could indeed be forgotten in this place, even if only for a few, fleeting moments. Ira Green had taken Easter on this trip to escape all the chaos.

Easter knew Phoebe's husband and Billy were conspiring against her. As two of Will's heirs, they wanted control of the farm and had an inflated view of what they believed to be their fair shares—the greedy little shites. They were convinced she could not manage the finances. Anna had told her everything. Anna and Thomas Wallace were unwavering in their support and loyalty. And now, Easter was certainly having second thoughts about leaving her young ones under Phoebe's care.

True, Easter had been numb and an emotional wreck after the verdict; nonetheless, she had always managed the finances and would provide a full account of all assets and monies for their ungrateful review. It wasn't worth it to her anymore. She would request that she be discharged as executrix and ask that, rather than one of these two selfish men gaining control of the money, the lawyer at the bank would be appointed as administrator of the estate.

Billy and Thom Sade had effectively proven they could not be trusted. As guardian of the child heirs, Easter would petition the court to grant a dollar per day for their upkeep, and ask the new administrator to pay her the sum monthly until the remaining assets could be divvied up. They would have decent clothes and would not go hungry. The lawyer told her that by Iowa law, as the widow, the dower, which was thirty percent of the estate including the house, would be Easter's and the rest split among the children. But certainly she wanted their profitable farm, which they had spent years pursuing with unfaltering persistence and backbreaking labor, to remain operational and intact. More land could be ceded to her adult children, but only if she agreed.

Mahala had written a letter, letting her know she and Benjamin were picking up stakes and heading west by covered wagon to California. They would seek their fortune there and, hopefully, Easter could come and visit them one day.

Ira Green wanted to marry Easter. He was not in good health and contemplating the end of his days, but he was very persuasive. "I don't expect much, Easter. You can have your own room; spend your money however you want. You will be Mrs. Ira Green. My name will protect you from gossip and bring you some peace of mind. You are the best cook in Otter Creek Township. A few home cooked meals a week and living amongst family again is more than I could ask for my remaining days."

Ira had such an engaging sweet smile. He reminded her of Thomas Wallace in her early years. Ira only wanted to make her happy. He had brought her across the river to Galena, where nobody knew her or her personal business. Since the trial, most folks in Otter Creek Township generally regarded her with distrust. Dark looks and whispers followed her everywhere, even into church.

For now, the river and waterways stood as a moat between her and all the pain still waiting for her back in Otter Creek. She closed her eyes and revisited the day the foreman stood up and announced the verdict.

"We, the jurors, find the defendant not guilty as charged in the indictment."

Each jury member had been polled for their decision. Not a single one found her guilty. They had been excused for less than an hour when they came back with the verdict. From a legal perspective she was completely exonerated.

With her acquittal the indictments against Aminadab and Elijah were dropped as well, but the victory felt hollow. They held an awkward celebration dinner with her attorney, her father, and her sister before they headed back East.

For a moment she pondered the question Elijah had finally dared ask her, days after her acquittal, in private when they were alone on the farm. With a tortured look on his face, he implored quietly, "Ma, when Aminadab and I had Pa pinned on the floor, why didn't you just run out of the house with the knife? Why did you stick Pa in the throat? I mean..."

For several moments, all she could do was gape at him. Finally, she responded, "Elijah, he roared like a crazed bear that he was going to kill us all. I was just trying to stop him. I was afraid for you and Aminidab. I was afraid of what he would do next. It was pure survival. I wish it had been different..." As she looked into his eyes with sorrow, she could sense he wanted more, but she had nothing left to say. "That's all I can tell you."

Elijah had nodded, eyes cast downward before hugging her and walking away.

A small part of Easter couldn't help but wonder if the thought of Will squandering their hard earned savings on Dorothy for months upon months and his abusive behavior at her protests, had caused her to strike harder, and considerably deeper...

But now, a sickness in her soul followed her everywhere she went. There was no shaking it. If only she could turn back time and somehow erase all the craziness that had transpired between her and Will during those last couple of years. Even now, she missed the way he would tilt his head to one side, shooting her that flirty grin of his that had won her heart so long ago.

Crazy enough, for a moment it was still comforting to make excuses and pretend it was all a misunderstanding. She closed her eyes, breathed in deeply, and willed it to be so; there it was—the pain subsided.

In her heart, Easter knew the truth would return in full force to knock her back down. But for now, she would just indulge these thoughts, feel Will's invisible arms hold her like he did back when their marriage was young, and just remember the love...

At last, she whispered softly to her audience of wildflowers, gently flowing waters, and the sun setting over the golden Galena hills, "I forgive you..."

Postlude

There was an old man, who Lived in a wood,
As you may plainly see;
He said he could do as much work in a day,
As his wife could do in three.
With all my heart, the old woman said,
If that you will allow,
To-morrow you'll stay at home in my stead,
And I'll go drive the plough.

But you must milk the Tidy cow,
For fear that she go dry;
And you must feed the little pigs
That are "within the sty;
And you must mind the speckled hen.
For fear she lay away;
And you must reel the spool of yarn
That I spun yesterday.

The old woman took a staff in her hand,
And went to drive the plough;
The old man took a pail in his hand,
And went to milk the cow:
But Tidy hinched, and Tidy flinched,
And Tidy broke his nose,
And Tidy gave him such a blow,
That the blood ran down to his toes!

A Profitable Wife

High! Tidy! Ho! Tidy! High!
Tidy! do stand still,
If ever I milk you, Tidy, again,
'Twill be sore against my will!
He went to feed the little pigs,
That were within the sty;
He hit his head against the beam,
And he made the blood to fly.

He went to mind the speckled hen,
For fear she'd lay astray;
And he forgot the spool of yarn
His wife spun yesterday.

So he swore by all the stars in the sky
And all the leaves on the tree
His wife could do more work in one day
Than he could do in three.

Postscript

When Easter was twenty-five, she was the mother of six children. Martin Van Buren (1837–1841), a Democrat and Jackson's former Secretary of State, was elected as the 8th President of the United States. With the economic depression of 1837 taking its toll, many were lured by vast expanses of low-cost federal land in new territories. The belief in Manifest Destiny—that it was the United States' divine mission to expand across the continent—served as a powerful incentive for westward migration. Van Buren continued Jackson's policy of Native removal, making way for ever-growing tracts of land for settlers. In 1840, the landmark case involving the Spanish schooner La Amistad reached the Supreme Court. Former President John Quincy Adams argued for the freedom of the African people on board, while Van Buren's government sided with the Spanish. The verdict favored Adams and the Amistad Africans, adding momentum to the growing abolition movement.

When Easter was twenty-nine, she was the mother of eight children. William Henry Harrison (1841–1841) had been elected as the ninth President. Following his untimely death, Vice President John Tyler (1841–1845) of the Whig Party assumed the presidency without an election as the tenth President. Tyler played a crucial role in the Preemption Act of 1841, which allowed "squatters" living on federal lands to purchase up to 160 acres at minimal cost before the land was offered to the public. Tyler's frequent use of his veto power rankled the House of Representatives, leading to the nation's first impeachment proceedings. A firm believer in Manifest Destiny, Tyler signed a bill initiating the annexation of the Republic of Texas.

When Easter was thirty-three she was the mother of ten

children. James K. Polk (1845–1849), a Democrat and fervent supporter of Manifest Destiny, was elected as the eleventh president. His inauguration marked the first swearing-in ceremony to be reported by telegraph. By this time, the United States' population had doubled since the American Revolution. Earning the nickname "Young Hickory" in comparison to President Jackson, Polk expanded the nation's territory significantly. He secured the Oregon Territory from Great Britain, which eventually gave rise to the states of Washington, Oregon, Idaho, and parts of Montana and Wyoming. In addition to ratifying the annexation of Texas, Polk's presidency witnessed the Mexican-American War, resulting in Mexico ceding territories that formed modern-day California, Nevada, Utah, most of Arizona, and parts of New Mexico, Colorado, and Wyoming. Though his attempt to purchase Cuba was unsuccessful, Polk saw Texas, Iowa, and Wisconsin admitted to the Union. In 1848, Easter and her family journeyed from Ohio to Otter Creek, Iowa, where her oldest daughter married a well-established, older Iowa farmer.

When Easter was thirty-seven she was the mother of eleven children. Zachary Taylor (1849–1850) of the Whig Party, served as the twelfth President. With the gold rush in full swing, California brimmed with opportunity. Taylor advocated for statehood for both California and New Mexico, but southern states opposed the idea due to concerns over slavery. In 1850, Taylor passed away from a stomach ailment. That same year, Easter welcomed her first grandchild and her second-eldest married a much older, well-established Irish immigrant farmer in Iowa.

When Easter was thirty-eight, Millard Fillmore (1850–1853) of the Whig Party became the thirteenth President. Though not widely popular, Fillmore ardently supported infrastructure projects, such as roads, canals, and railroads. He presided over the Great Compromise (also referred to as the Compromise of 1850), which Henry Clay helped negotiate. Between 1851 and 1853, Easter's family grew with the births of four more grandchildren. Her third daughter married an Iowa farmer, while her fourth daughter wed a Minnesota farmer.

When Easter was forty-one she was the mother of twelve children. Franklin Pierce (1853–1857), a lawyer, soldier, and politician, was elected the fourteenth President. Tragedy struck Pierce when his only living son died in a train accident. Despite this, he sent surveyors across the country to identify the best routes for transcontinental railroads and oversaw the passage of the Kansas-Nebraska Act. During his tenure, Easter welcomed seven more grandchildren into her life.

On Oct. 1, 1856, a harrowing incident occurred between Easter and her husband, forever altering the lives of their family. By then, Easter had thirteen children and thirteen grandchildren. Her four eldest daughters had families and farms of their own. Six sons and three daughters remained in the household. Her final child, a daughter, was born the year William Conklin was killed.

Despite this tragedy, Easter lived on, outlasting two more husbands and witnessing her older sons return unscathed from the Civil War. Easter lived through the administrations of nine more presidents, from James Buchanan (1857–1861) to Grover Cleveland (1893–1897).

Her children Elijah, Anna, Mahala, and Julia Etta each named a daughter in her honor, with Elijah even naming one of his sons Henry Clay Conklin after the famed statesman. Easter eventually ventured out to California to visit Mahala, who was rumored to have exacted revenge on horse thieves by hunting them down, shooting them, and scalping them (she purportedly nailed the scalps to her livestock corral). Mary outlived seven of her nine children and all of her siblings except Elijah.

Easter passed away on October 25, 1893, at the age of 81, having traversed her life under the governance of nineteen presidents. Though her final resting place remains unknown, it is whispered that she might share a grave with one of her approximately one-hundred-twenty grandchildren...

Main Characters

- Easter Hackley, 1812–1893
- William Conklin, 1808–1856; Easter's husband
- Philo Hackley, 1776–1859; Easter's father
- Thomas Claudius Wallace, 1806–1888; Elizabeth Anna's husband

    Fled from Ireland to US Mainland about 1821, when he was about fifteen   years old.
- Phoebe Ann Conklin, 1830–1910; Easter's eldest child, born in Ohio
- Elizabeth Anna Conklin, 1831–1917; Easter's second child, born in Ohio
- Mary Conklin, 1833–1926; Easter's third child, born in Ohio.
- Aminadab Conklin, 1834–1916; Easter's fourth child, born in Ohio
- Mahala Conklin, 1835–1909; Easter's fifth child, born in Ohio
- William (Billy) James Conklin III, 1837¬–1901; Easter's sixth child,   born in Ohio
- Elijah Friendly Conklin, 1839–1932; Easter's seventh child, born in Ohio

Minor Characters

- Elizabeth "Eliza" Conklin, 1840–1840; Easter's eighth child, born in Ohio

    Died as an infant. The only one of their children that did not make it to   adulthood.
- Moses Rueben Conklin, 1842–1909; Easter's ninth child, born in Ohio

- Esther Malinda Conklin, 1844–1908; Easter's tenth child, born in Ohio
- John Bunyan Conklin, 1847–1923; Easter's eleventh child, born in Ohio
- Thomas Conklin, 1849–1925; Easter' twelfth child, born in Iowa
- Julia-Etta Conklin, 1853–1923; Easter's thirteenth child, born in Iowa
- Nancy Conklin, 1856–1888; Easter's fourteenth child, born in Iowa

    She was born the year of Will Conklin's death.
- Almira Hackley, 1796–1872; Easter's mother
- Robert Hackley, 1775–1812; Easter's fictional biological father
- Sooleawa, 1775–1812; Easter's fictional biological mother
- John Wallace Sr., 1803–1882; Thomas Wallace's brother

    Immigrated with his family from Ireland to Otter Creek Iowa about 1845
- Hannah Wallace; John Wallace's wife
- Catherine, Little John, and Julia Wallace; John and Hannah Wallace's children
- Thomas (Thom) Sade, 1819–1916; Phoebe Conklin's husband
- Abram Bartholomew, 1830–1854; Mary's first husband and fictional banditti
- Bartlett Sade, 1813–1904; Mary's second husband; Mahala's fictional first sweet-heart
- Benjamin Shumway, 1823–1909; Mahala's husband
- Ira Green; Easter's second husband

Notes and Sources

Anon. Sketches and eccentricities of Col. David Crockett of west Tennessee. New York: J. & J. Harper, 1833.

Boney, Edward. The Banditti of the Prairies: A Tale of the Mississippi Valley. Philadelphia: T. B. Peterson and Brothers, 1855.

Boylston, James R. and Allen J. Wiener. David Crockett in Congress: The Rise and Fall of the Poor Man's Friend. Houston, Texas: Bright Sky Press, 2009.

Buley, R. Carlyle. The Old Northwest, Pioneer Period 1815–1840. Vol. I. Bloomington: Indiana University Press, 1978.

Carlander, Harriet Bell. A History of Fish and Fishing in the Upper Mississippi River. Bloomington: Upper Mississippi River Conservation Committee, 1954.

Cheney, Lynne V. James Madison: A Life Reconsidered. New York: Penguin Books, 2015.

Code of Iowa, Passed at the Session of the General Assembly of 1850–1. (Iowa City: Palmer & Paul, Sate Printers, 1851.

Crockett, David. An Account of Col. Crockett's Tour to the North and Down East. Philadelphia/Baltimore/Boston: E. L. Carey and A. Hart/Cary, Hart, and Co./William D Ticknor, 1835.

Crockett, David and Thomas Chilton. A Narrative of the Life of David Crockett. Philadelphia/Boston: E. L. Carey/Allen & Ticknor, 1834.

Crosby, Fanny J. and Mrs. Alexander Vanalstyne. Memories of Eighty Years. Boston: James H. Earle & Company, 1906.

Curzon, Sarah Anne. Laura Second, The Heroine of 1812: A Drama and Other Poems. Toronto: 1887. Project Gutenberg. https://www.gutenberg.org/ebooks/7228.

Ellis, Hon. James Whitcomb. History of Jackson County, Iowa. Vol. I. Chicago: S. J. Clarke Publishing Co., 1910.

Halliwell, James Orchard, Esq. The Nursery Rhymes of England. London: John Russell Smith, 1841.

Heidler, S.David and Jeanne T. Heidler. Henry Clay, The Essential American. New York: Random House, 2010.

History of Monroe County, Ohio, A Condensed History of the County; Biographical Sketches: General Statistics; Miscellaneous Matters. Chicago/Toledo: H. H. Hardesty & Co, Publishers, 1882.

Horton, Loren N. and Timothy Hyde. Ansel Briggs Project. Iowa City, Iowa: State Historical Society, 1975. http://publications.iowa.gov/12088/1/Ansel_Briggs_Project.pdf.

Jenkins, John Stilwell and George Bancroft. Life and public services of Gen. Andrew Jackson, Seventh President of the United States with the Eulogy Delivered at Washington City, Jun 21, 1845. New York/Auburn: Mill, Orton & Mulligan, 1855.

Kelly, Mary Gilbert. "Irish Catholic Colonies and Colonization Projects in United States, 1795–1860." Studies: An Irish Quarterly Review 29, no. 115 (1940): 447–65. Accessed February 5, 2021. http://www.jstor.org/stable/30097893.

McCullough, David. The Pioneers. New York: Simon & Schuster, 2019.

Meacham, Jon. American Lion: Andrew Jackson in the White House. New York: Random House, 2009.

Moulton, Gary E.. The Papers of Chief John Ross. Norman, OK: University of Oklahoma Press, 1985.

Newhall, John B. Sketches of Iowa or the Emigrants Guide. New York: J. H. Colton, Merchants' Exchange, 1841.

Parker, Nathan H. Iowa as it is in 1857; A Gazetteer for Citizens and a Hand-book for Emmigrants. Chigago, Ill.: Keen & Lee, 1857.

Peavy, Linda and Ursula Smith. Pioneer Women: The Lives of Women on the Frontier. New York, NY: Smithmark Publishers, 1996.

Petersen, Wm. F. Steamboating On the Upper Mississippi: The Water Way to Iowa. Iowa City: The Torch Press for The state Historical Society of Iowa, 1937. https://libsysdigi.library.illinois.edu/oca/Books2008-08/steamboatingonup00pete/steamboatingonup00pete.pdf.

Revised Statutes of the Territory of Iowa. The Authority of the Thirty-Fourth General Assembly. Iowa City: Hughes & Williams, 1843.

Seaman, Gerald LeRoy. "A History of Some Early Iowa Farm Journals (before 1900). MS Thesis, Iowa State College, 1942. https://lib.dr.iastate.edu/cgi/viewcontent.cgi?article=17940&context=rtd.

Tippecanoe and Tyler too! A comic glee. G.E. Blake, Philadephia, monographic, 1840. Notated Music. https://www.loc.gov/item/sm1840.371620/.

Van Atta, John R. "Western Lands and the Political Economy of Henry Clay's American System, 1819–1832." Journal of the Early Republic 21, no. 4 (2001): 633–65. Accessed March 20, 2021. doi:10.2307/3125149. https://www.jstor.org/stable/3125149?seq=1.

Poetry is quoted from the following historical sources:

Sarah Anne Curzon, Laura Second, The Heroine of 1812: a Drama and other Poems, 14, 34, 55, 56, 57, 58, 59, 60.

Sketches and eccentricities of Col. David Crockett of west Tennessee, 164.

Tippecanoe and Tyler too! A comic glee, G.E. Blake (Philadelphia, monographic, 1840), Notated Music, 2. https://www.loc.gov/item/sm1840.371620/.

J. F. Chamberlain, "Away to the Prairie," in Memories of Eighty Years, 80, 81.

Fanny Crosby, "On Their Wedding Day," in Memories of Eighty Years, 213, "Sleep oh Statesman," 85, "What The Old Year Saw," 236.

Martin F. Tupper, "Never Give Up," in Memories of Eighty Years, 99.

James Orchard Halliwell, Esq., The Nursery Rhymes of England, 43.

Andrew Jackson, David Crockett, and Iowa trial quotes are from the following historical sources:

Andrew Jackson as quoted in J.S. Jenkins, Life and public services of Gen. Andrew Jackson, seventh president of the United States with the eulogy delivered at Washington City, June 21, 1845, 171.

Sketches and eccentricities of Col. David Crockett of west Tennessee, 164.

A narrative of the life of David Crockett, 1, 211.

An Account of Col. Crockett's Tour to the North and Down East, 155.

History of Jackson County, Iowa, Vol. I, 231, 232, 254.

About the Author

Kat Christensen is a historical fiction author who is passionate about good reads. Her roots trace back to the Revolutionary War, which has ignited her interest in the countless stories of female forbears that shape our contemporary identity. Christensen is committed to bringing these female figures to life, enabling a broader recognition of women's contributions that have often been overlooked or erased by history. With a foundation in corporate information technology, Christensen has honed her skills and now applies them passionately to the craft of storytelling. As an outdoor enthusiast, she can often be found exploring the trails of the Pacific Northwest.

Thank you for reading *A Profitable Wife*! If you enjoyed reading the story, the author would greatly appreciate your thoughts – please consider leaving a review.

www.historiumpress.com